BROKEN MIRROR

BROKEN MIRROR

CODY SISCO

RESONANT EARTH PUBLISHING

Broken Mirror © 2016 by Cody Sisco

Resonant Earth Publishing
P.O. BOX 50785
Los Angeles, CA 90050

Library of Congress Control Number: 2016930422
ISBN: 978-0-9970348-2-0

Book cover design by The Scarlett Rugers Design Agency
Editing by Lindsey Alexander and Beth Wright

Author photo by Nate Jensen

www.codysisco.com
Twitter: @codysisco

First Edition

FOR ALL THE GHOSTS' FAVORITES

The American Union of Nations

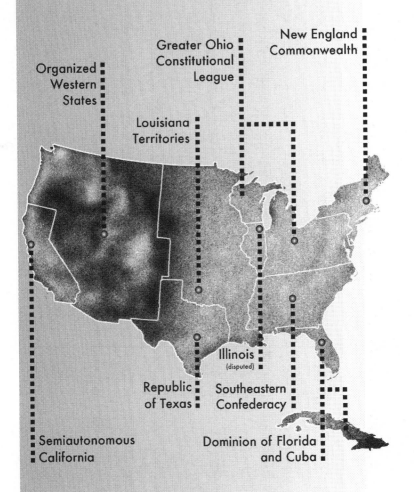

Organized
Western
States

Greater Ohio
Constitutional
League

New England
Commonwealth

Louisiana
Territories

Illinois
(disputed)

Republic
of Texas

Southeastern
Confederacy

Semiautonomous
California

Dominion of Florida
and Cuba

MIRROR RESONANCE SYNDROME:

a degenerative brain disorder associated with electro-chemical imbalances within mirror-neuron networks. These are the structures that enable individuals to understand and interpret others' intentions and emotions. Symptoms of mirror resonance syndrome (MRS) can be severe, vary widely, and usually include habitual aggression and violence.

Many people with MRS experience extreme emotional transference, which, paradoxically, can lead to black outs.

The syndrome is linked to a genetic variation present in less than 1% of the population.

SYMPTOMS

Emotional hyper-reactivity over an extended period, including these progressively worsening symptoms:

1. Abnormally strong physiological and emotional reactions to physical or mental stimuli, including synesthesia and hallucinations

2. Subjective experience of being controlled, lacking autonomy, following a predetermined course, or reliving events (e.g., episodes of déjà vu lasting hours or days)

3. Persistent, immersive fantasies to the exclusion of reality

4. Depersonalization, loss of emotional vividness, motor-body disorientation, dissociative states, or extreme variability in self-image

5. Episodes of "brain blankness," i.e. dreamlike fugue states and sleepwalking

6. Addiction to resonant-class narcotics [new criterion]

—Diagnostic Criteria for Mental Disorders,
Semiautonomous California Health Board,
Third (Revised) Edition

PART ONE

1

Yours is not the only universe. There is another, where I was born. Your universe called to me, and I answered, ignorant of the harm crossing the bridge would cause.

—Victor Eastmore's *Apology*

Semiautonomous California
14 September 1990

Victor Eastmore waited in the Freshly Juice Shop's customer queue, whispering a mantra to fight off brain blankness. Only three people waited in the queue ahead of him, a young woman with copper-colored hair and an elderly couple at the counter. Soon he would have his enhanced juice.

He dry-swallowed a dose of Personil. The timing of the juice and the pill had to be just right for him to arrive at his appointment in a calm but lucid state of mind.

Behind a counter that ran the length of the juice shop, stone fruits, berries, and citrus bathed in a chiller cabinet's cool mists. Vegetables, still actively photosynthesizing, stewed in irrigation racks on the back wall.

Victor felt radiative pressure from the overhead lightstrips as a pleasurable tingling on his face. He tilted his head back. The side benefits of having a synesthetic brain that perceives one stimulus and translates it into another were few and far between, and he took what he could get.

The queue didn't move. The friendliest Freshly worker, Ric, liked to chat with each customer. Victor usually took the extra time to study the more "normal" behavior of others—his condition enabled him to visualize people's emotions as patterns of colors. When he observed Ric's face, he saw electric blue filaments dancing on a rosy background, an indication of good humor overlaid by excitement. But today Victor's attention wandered. Dr. Tammet had promised to run him through an extra challenging perception-focusing test today to prepare for his reclassification appointment in a couple months.

Victor appreciated the doctor's help, but she'd been so ambitious lately and he felt that he wasn't meeting her expectations. Today was likely to be frustrating. His stomach roiled. He silently formulated a mixture of juice and additives that could quiet a volcano. Adding to his unease, he'd had little sleep last night on account of his nightmares, though that was nothing new.

Victor searched through dozens of Freshly bioenhancer additives listed in the wall-mounted menu. If he factored in the benefits of freshness and the nutrient base of the ingredients, the optimum recipe combined leeks, cabbage, and celery, along with smaller portions of mandarin, apple, and persimmon and two doses of languor and equilibrium.

Victor rehearsed the ingredients' names to himself while tapping each finger with his thumb two times—*two is the best*. He also tried to relax by humming, keeping the vibrations low, intermittent, and inaudible to anyone else.

The young woman waiting in front of Victor turned and looked him up and down. Her reddish-brown hair was gathered in a black synthleather band at her neckline. She crossed her arms and said, "Did you say something?"

Victor's stomach tightened. He looked up at the menu. Out of the corner of his eye, he could see anxiety glistening around her eyes. Her hands moved to her sides and clenched, whiter than her pale skin. She might be readying an attack. All he wanted was his juice bulb and to be on time to see Dr. Tammet.

"You seem . . ." Her voice trailed off. Then she asked in a quiet hiss, "Are you a Broken Mirror?"

Victor kept his gaze on the menu and pretended not to hear her. Broken Mirror was a commonplace slur for people with mirror resonance syndrome. He'd been called it a thousand times since his diagnosis. Next to his nightmares, which left his sheets sweat-soaked every night, name-calling was nothing.

"Hello? I'm talking to you," the young woman said.

Victor looked down at the woman's red polo shirt. Faint stains marred the shirt's coarse-grained fibers, and the collar splayed wide, revealing her freckled, sunburned neck.

"Are you snubbing me?" she asked.

He glanced into her narrowed hazel eyes.

A mistake.

Her anger arced into his brain, locking the breath in his lungs. Sounds from the shop faded, replaced by waves of hostile pressure. Her emotions had infected him. Victor wrenched his gaze back to the menu board. In a quiet, strained voice, he said, "I'm sorry. I'd rather not converse with you."

Her face drew closer, reddening. "I won't be shamed by you."

People turned and stared. Everything in his field of vision undulated. The Personil wasn't working.

He tried to say, "Of course not," but his mouth wouldn't move. His heart thundered in his ears.

"Why won't you talk to me?" she demanded.

Ice formed in Victor's throat. Why did she have to be so aggressive?

The woman pointed at him and looked around. "Where is the manager? I won't be insulted!"

He wanted to gouge out her blue marble eyes. His fingers curled into claws. Victor mouthed Dr. Tammet's calming refrain. *The wise owl listens before he asks, "Who?" The dark forest hides the loudest cuckoo.* He tried picturing the doctor's bird sketches, but in his mind's eye, the owl clutched the cuckoo and flapped away.

The young woman loomed closer, eyes wide. "What are you saying?"

One of the workers ducked underneath the counter, stood, and asked her what was wrong.

She proclaimed, "I deserve fair treatment—"

Blood pulsed in Victor's ears, blotting out her voice. His consciousness slipped toward blankspace. *Shocks—not now, not here, not like this.*

Someone hissed Victor's name. He looked around and saw Ric at the paybox, jerking his head toward the exit and mouthing, "Go!"

Victor turned toward the door reluctantly and ran.

"You need help!" the woman yelled at his back.

Outside, the sound of sirens filled Victor's ears. People strolled along the sidewalks, some smiling, some preoccupied, none of them glanced around looking for fire engines or police vans. The sirens were only in his head.

Ric burst out of the juice shop, carrying a bulb of pink liquid.

"Sorry about that," Ric said as he handed the drink to Victor.

Victor sucked the straw and drained half the juice bulb in panicked gulps. He wiped his mouth with the back of his hand. "Why—why was she so upset?"

"Who knows? Maybe she's on stims. Or off her meds."

Victor gritted his teeth. He squeezed the bulb, and pink juice spurted from the straw onto the ground.

"Or maybe she's just wants free stuff," Victor said.

"Maybe," Ric agreed.

Ric held up his hands. "Look, I've seen her come in before," he said. "Most times she's no problem. Other times she complains to get a free drink. Sucks you had to be her scapegoat today. Try to shake it off."

Maybe she *was* off her medication. Victor had lost control of himself many times: at dinner with his parents, at work, and even by himself. Maybe the copper-haired woman had mirror resonance syndrome, too. Victor sucked the bulb until the last pulse of sweet, tangy liquid was gone. He needed every drop of calm it could provide.

"Thank you," he said to Ric. "What did you put in it?"

"I doubled up the languor. I wasn't sure what else you needed." Ric wiped his hands down his silver synthsilk apron. "Vic, you've been a Class Three for a while, right?"

Victor nodded. *Longer than most. Hopefully for a long time to come.*

"I thought so," Ric said. "My brother's a Class Two. He's not doing great. I'm afraid they're going to put him in a Class One facility soon."

Victor wanted to hear more, but he kept his mouth shut. He didn't want to be late.

Ric said, "Do you think someone you know could check on him? Your granfa, maybe."

"Maybe he could," Victor said.

The Eastmore family's legacy had always overshadowed his own life. As descendants of both former slaves and slave-owning families, the Eastmores demonstrated the success of Reconstruction. Widespread intermarriage without regard for skin color led the masses to embrace nondiscrimination and equality at the end of the nineteenth century. Over several decades, the Eastmores amassed business interests as varied as energy and healthcare and brokered political favors to speed the Repartition of the United States into the nine nations of the American Union. Then Victor's granfa, Jefferson Eastmore, cured cancer. After that, people routinely assumed the Eastmores could make miracles happen. Ric must believe that Victor enjoyed all the privileges that came with wealth and power, rather than being an embarrassment and a disappointment to his family.

Ric eyed Victor, looking him up and down. His lips were parted, moist.

Victor could tell when people thought he was attractive, as Ric obviously did. His toes gripped the insides of his shoes. The attention made him uncomfortable. He wondered what it was exactly that others saw when they looked at him, how some could fear him, some could crave him, and some could do both at the same time.

"I've got to go," Victor said. "Thanks again." He turned to leave, but Ric grabbed his arm.

"You think he's okay out there on the ranchos? They're real farms, right? Like summer camp?"

Victor pictured the new Class Two facility in Carmichael, a pleasant few acres of farmland on the outskirts of town. Surrounded by electrified fences and overshadowed by a concrete fortress on a nearby hill that held the catatonic Class Ones, the Class Two facility was most definitely *not* like summer camp.

Victor said, "It's not so bad for Twos. He might not be reclassified for years."

When Victor had visited the Class Two rancho in Carmichael, Granfa Jeff had pointed out all the innovations that had made it a kinder, gentler prison. The Class Twos held elections for a chief who advocated for better food and recreational opportunities. The library had been fully stocked. If someone could resign themselves to a slow, sad decline into catatonia, it wouldn't be a bad place.

"Ten years he's been locked up," Ric said. "They caught him protesting the first Carmichael Law. One cheek swab later . . . He hasn't been home since. I send him packages of black cardamom seeds every month."

"Why those?" Victor asked.

Ric shrugged. "It's the only thing he asks for. He doesn't want me to visit. You've been to one?"

Victor nodded. "Once. When I went back to Carmichael after—after we moved away. My granfa helped set up the visit. They have a patient council with elections, but it still feels like a prison. And Mesh BioLoc transmitters are fused to their bones."

Ric winced.

"Sorry I said that. I'm sure it doesn't hurt."

Ric's shoulders slumped. "I hope you're right. See you next time." He trotted back into the shop.

Victor reached into his pocket, pulled out his cigar-shaped MeshBit, and checked the timefeed—five minutes until his appointment.

Victor tried to jog on his walk home, but the Personil slowed him down. When he arrived, he climbed carefully in his car and drove along the east side of City Lake, turning onto a sinuous road that led up to Oak Knoll Hospital. He imagined Dr. Tammet's sad eyes when he failed her tests. He didn't care what the world thought of him, but he couldn't stand a second of her disappointment.

On campus, Victor parked and hiked up the paved path to the hospital entrance, a glass facade between two towering, white concrete wings. The Personil blotted out everything except the doors in front of him.

When he approached, the two glass doors failed to slide open automatically.

He checked his MeshBit again. The timefeed read 11:07 a.m. He looked around. His car sat by itself, the parking lot otherwise empty. In his rush and his mind haze, he hadn't noticed.

Heat suffused his cheeks. He should have realized something was wrong the second he pulled off the main road. At least a hundred cars should be in those spaces.

Victor paced in front of the entrance. His face smoldered like a piece of charcoal about to catch fire. He tried to pry the doors open, but they wouldn't budge. The precision-cut edges held together seamlessly. There wasn't even room to slide a slip of paper between them.

Victor felt the urge to vomit. If he couldn't see Dr. Tammet, he would have to go without his therapy. Panic sliced through the Personil fog. A resonant episode grew more likely every second.

The world blazed sun-white as a shiver ran up his spine. He'd felt panic like this in Carmichael when he was four years old, locked in his house, crying at the sounds of explosions and screams outside, wondering if his parents would ever come home.

Victor also remembered Samuel Miller, whom he'd called the Man from Nightmareland, because his wide, shell-shocked eyes had appeared in Victor's dreams many times during the weeks prior to the massacre. Samuel Miller had rampaged through Carmichael, stalking the town's citizens and killing with a stunstick and explosive traps. Thanks to him and his preferred method of murder, "shocks" became a curse word in SeCa.

Victor had seen Samuel from his second-story window and froze with the curtain clutched in his hand as Samuel looked up. He'd held his breath until it felt like his ribs would break. Then Samuel had moved on to help more people "cross over."

The resonance filled Victor like water gushing into a clogged bathtub. He pounded on the hospital doors and, straining to see inside, shielded his eyes with his hands. He could tell that the large atrium was bereft of people, an unlit gloom. Vidscreens above the information counter were dark.

When he stepped back, his reflection stared back at him. A mess of hair. A mess of a day. A messed-up life.

Victor stumbled forward, dropped to his knees, and pressed his forehead against the glass, feeling blankness nearby. Was his own rampage about to begin?

As a Class Three, Victor could live a relatively normal life (if one considered taking daily medication and going to multiple therapy sessions every week to be relatively normal). But some day he would become a drooling, insentient bed wetter, and every resonant episode brought him closer to that fate. At some point, the blankness would take over, and he would be gone.

Victor rubbed his palms together, changing the rhythm of the movement every few breaths. That was one of Dr. Tammet's techniques, and a useful one, especially when there was no one around to see him acting like a frenzied faith healer.

Something in the darkened hospital atrium caught Victor's gaze. A figure moved closer. It was Granfa Jeff. His white and gray hair floated in wisps. His face, all dark freckles on brown skin, drooped as if he hadn't slept well.

The doors opened. Granfa Jeff stepped out and secured the doors behind him. He rested his palms heavily on Victor's shoulders. "I have some news that may upset you, Victor."

Victor used Dr. Tammet's techniques to read his granfa's facial expression. Deep blue sadness dimpled the skin around his eyes and mouth, but Victor noticed something else. He couldn't tie his intuition to a specific observation, but he noticed a shadow—a different emotion struggling to the surface.

In a low voice, Granfa Jeff said, "We have to scuttle the research into your cure."

Cody Sisco

Victor's mouth felt dry. He blinked, not believing what he'd heard, waiting for Granfa Jeff to correct himself. They couldn't do that, could they? Victor peered into the hospital's gloomy atrium. "Where's Dr. Tammet?"

"I'm closing Oak Knoll, Victor. I let the staff go, you see. Another doctor will see you privately from now on. We'll make arrangements."

After years of therapy, hundreds of appointments, and who knew how many ounces of Victor's blood drawn for tests, Granfa Jeff was going to shut down the research program? A cure was his only hope to prevent permanent catatonia.

"What's going to happen to me?" Victor asked.

Granfa Jeff's expression darkened, and Victor felt the blankness rise up again.

2

Let me be clear. We're not talking about slavery, imprison-
ment, chemical lobotomization, or any of the other rumors
and lies flying around about the Commission's work.

The protections proposed by the Commission are reasonable, proportional, and necessary to prevent another Carmichael incident.

Class Threes will live freely with supervision and annual
re-evaluations.

Class Twos will contribute to society through decent
work in self-sustaining communities that will ensure their
well-being.

Class Ones will receive the best care available in facilities
equipped for their special needs.

This approach is about the health and safety of our communities. It's about helping those who suffer from mirror
resonance syndrome and about the safety of their families
and friends.

This is about a better world for everyone.

—Mía Barrias, public comment, SeCa Classification
Commission records (1978)

Semiautonomous California
21 June 1979

The vidscreen on the wall of the Ludlum Middle School classroom showed houses destroyed by fire and bodies crushed
under the tires of self-driving vehicles. By now, at age twelve,
Victor had seen the vidfeed many times. Having survived the

massacre when he was only four years old, he'd experienced for himself the horror that Samuel Miller had inflicted on the town of Carmichael.

Every year on the anniversary of the incident, as part of a nationwide mandatory remembrance ceremony, the documentary played in schools and public buildings throughout Semiautonomous California. Now a woman with haunted eyes described how she survived the massacre. Victor recognized her, of course: Mía Barrias, the woman who'd saved him from one of Samuel's booby traps. She detailed her encounter with the killer on the day of her honeymoon, how she'd watched him murder her fiancé with a quantum-triggered Dirac stunstick pulse to the head, and how she'd escaped and got help from police in a nearby town.

The vidfeed was all too familiar.

When the Man from Nightmareland's crimes introduced Semiautonomous California to the dangers of mirror resonance syndrome, the government responded by developing the Classification system to gene-scan and control people with MRS.

Being classified was worse than being any of SeCa's other untouchables.

The Catholics—weakened, anemic, and banned from other nations in the American Union—were tolerated only on the outskirts of Oakland & Bayshore, not downtown. The Asian Refugee Act had expelled from Oakland desperate refugees from the Great Asian War, forcing them onto the farms in Long Valley and the slums of Little Asia on the San Francisco Peninsula; they couldn't settle in Bayshore.

People with MRS were the enemies within: unpredictable, dangerous, terrifying.

Victor, with his blood-soaked, strange, and prescient dreams, had always felt different—no, not just different, peculiar—and completely out of step with the people of SeCa, who, from the days of the first Cathar settlers, had exalted in freedom from violence. The single incidence of mass killing in the nation's history—Samuel Miller's campaign to destroy Carmichael—had led to the demonization of people with MRS.

Cody Sisco

Best to keep them in facilities and ranchos in the nation's hinterlands. "Out of sight, out of mind" could have been the national motto.

Victor didn't dare ask to be excused from watching the vidfeed. Earlier, two girls had passed him in the hallway talking loudly, saying that they could spot a Broken Mirror without trying, everyone could, it was how they looked at you—no, hard to say exactly what it was, but definitely they were easy to spot.

Victor was desperate to avoid sticking out because, like Samuel Miller, he believed his dreams were premonitions. Not that he would ever tell anyone about them. Sometimes beliefs are so horrific that they're easy to keep secret.

After the vidfeed ended, Victor rushed out of the classroom, collected his feedreader from his locker, and blasted through the exit doors, only to find himself surrounded by Alik and his friends in back of the school.

Alik called out, "Hey, freaky face. Why didn't you cry during the vidfeed?"

A thunderstorm gathered in Victor's mind. They always picked on him. They made fun of him for the way he talked, or they teased him for staying silent and for the way his facial expressions almost but did not quite mirror theirs. The problem lay deep in his brain. He couldn't win.

"Look at his hands. He's gonna rip your face off, Alik."

It was true. Victor's fingers were rigid and curled like talons.

"Maybe he's a Broken Mirror," Alik said.

"I am not!" Victor yelled.

Alik got closer. Sweat gathered under the boy's eyes, and heat radiated from his skin in shimmering waves. "Who's next on your list, sicko Samuel?"

Victor cringed and kept quiet. After Carmichael, he couldn't be called a worse name.

Someone shoved Victor from behind, causing him to lurch forward. Alik punched Victor's face. Rage took hold of Victor. His fist struck the underside of Alik's jaw and sent him reeling into the crowd.

Alik lifted himself, nostrils flaring, and launched into Victor's belly. The two boys stumbled through the cheering kids.

Alik slammed Victor into the wall of the building. Victor tried to evade the fists that Alik rammed into his gut, but the blows kept coming.

Victor twisted free, panicking. He slipped on something slick and grabbed Alik's shirt to keep from falling. Victor fell anyway, and Alik staggered past Victor headfirst and slammed into the side of a dumpster.

Elena Morales, his friend for as long as he could remember, helped Victor to his feet. She'd always been strong: meaty limbs, broad face, and a loud voice when she wanted. Even her carmel-brown hair had a luster and seemed to glow from within. She whispered in his ear, "That was some first-class martial arts."

"I wish," Victor said. He gripped his aching stomach and searched for an escape.

A girl screamed. Victor turned and saw Alik lying limp at the foot of the dumpster, eyes closed, blood trickling from his head.

A male administrator appeared and asked, "What's going on?" He spotted Alik and yelled at the crowd, "Back away, all of you! Get back!" He spoke into his fist-sized MeshBit to summon an ambulance.

"This is supposed to be a day for peace and healing. What happened?" The administrator scanned the crowd of students.

Heads swiveled back and forth between Victor and Alik's body.

Victor's left eye was swollen shut. He took an unsteady step in the direction of the bus stop.

The administrator pointed at him and said, "Don't move."

A siren wailed and grew louder. Victor slumped to his knees. Elena squeezed his arm and said, "Don't worry." He focused on the feel of her next to him, relieved and gratified that her love of underdogs made her root for him.

An ambulance rolled onto the paved path just beyond the squat school buildings. Pink-uniformed paramedics burst out, spotted the waving administrator, and darted forward. Though the siren had been silenced, Victor's ears were ringing in a kind of rising and falling *brrrrnnnnngggg* that coincided with the throbbing in his gut.

Cody Sisco

The ambulance's green and yellow lights flashed on the children's shocked faces as they watched the paramedics load Alik onto a stretcher and carry it into the vehicle. Strong arms pushed and lifted Victor, and he found himself in the ambulance. The vehicle lurched forward.

When they arrived at the hospital, a female nurse led Victor inside the hospital and down a corridor, where a pair of brightly lit near-white Helios lightstrips ran along the ceiling like burning-hot steel rails. She brought him to a small examination room and asked for his name and MeshID, entered them on a type-pad, and then examined and treated his eye. She left the room and shut the door.

Victor looked down at his hands. Specks of dried blood hid under a thumbnail. He picked at it with another nail, but tiny red stains remained in the hard-to-reach crevice. He scratched again, deeper. New blood seeped from the worn-away skin. Pain flared as sparks from his fingers. He watched them bloom with each painful dig: beautiful, multicolored, ephemeral things, like confetti aflame. They were his secret magic tricks and worth the pain they cost.

He sat in the room for twenty minutes, waiting for someone to come and tell him what a bad person he was for hurting Alik. If he had a MeshBit, he could call his parents, but his fa had refused to purchase one. They were pieces of Euro-fascist tech, according to his fa, that kept nations in the American Union from reaching their full potential. Ma never let Fa's assertions stand, and always countered that the benefits of Mesh access outweighed any nebulous, jingoistic, proto-nationalist-revivalist nonsense, as she called his fa's rationale. Victor didn't know much about politics; he just wished he could call his parents, though the school might have already called them. Victor listened for them through the door.

At one point, footsteps tromped closer, and someone knocked. A scowling man came in wearing a starched canvas coat adorned with the snake-and-staff logo surrounded by a circle. His name tag identified him as Dr. Rularian. He held Victor's chin with one hand, which reeked of bleach. "Open your mouth," he instructed. He roughly swabbed the inside of Victor's cheek. Just as abruptly as he'd entered, the doctor left the room, shutting the door behind him.

Victor was alone again.

Alik would probably get many visitors during his recuperation. Well-wishers would stream into the hospital with their flowers, cards, and packages. Balloons would float around Alik's bed, holding vigil until he woke. If he woke.

No one would care about Victor if he'd been the one so badly hurt. He'd been in fights before, never voluntarily, and he usually lost. Now he would be known at school as vicious and dangerous in addition to strange and "problematic," as he'd once heard a teacher call him. The one time he won a fight was worse than all the times he'd lost.

Dr. Rularian returned. "Come with me," he said.

Victor followed him to a room packed with electronics. Two technicians—*always two*—stood by, men in their mid-twenties wearing translucent gel surgical masks and canvas hats. The burlier of the two unbuttoned Victor's shirt, pushed him into a reclining synthleather seat, and stuck small sensors on his forehead, neck, chest, inner elbows, and wrists. The other technician had a flat face as if he had no nose at all beneath his mask, and his skin looked perfectly smooth, like plastic.

"I'm going to remove your pants," the flat-faced one said.

Victor started to tear off the sensors. The burly technician with unblinking lizard-like eyes placed a firm hand on his chest. "Relax," he said, "you're safe here."

Victor let his head fall back into the cushioned headrest. "You could have just asked me to undress," he said.

The flat-faced technician undid Victor's belt buckle and tugged his pants down to his ankles. Victor felt the smooth sensors' cool metal against his inner thighs and panicked again, gripping the hems of his boxers to hold them up.

"Hold still, please," the doctor said in a low voice. "You can keep your underwear on."

The flat-faced technician placed a helmet-shaped device on Victor's head while Lizard-Eyes tapped on a type-pad. Victor gripped the arms of the chair, feeling a strange buzz course through his skin.

The doctor activated a control, and Victor's view of the room disappeared, blacked out by the helmet's visor. Then an image of a snarling cheetah sprang to life in front of his eyes. His heart beat faster. As suddenly as the cheetah had appeared, it vanished, replaced by a close-up vidfeed of a beautiful woman's face. She cried. Streams of tears ran down her cheeks. The rawness of her emotion—the way her eyes seemed to recede into their sockets—pulled at Victor. More images popped into view and disappeared: a bloody body, two men nuzzling each other, a female-female couple, a male-female couple, all staring at each other close-up and smiling. Victor felt himself start to smile in response. Then he remembered he was sitting half-naked in a cold hospital room, covered in sensors.

His heart thudded in his chest. He tried to lift the heavy helmet off.

"I said hold still!" The doctor commanded through a sonofeed in the helmet.

"We got a clear reading," one of the technicians said.

Dr. Rularian said, "Okay, then, let's move on."

The helmet's visor turned transparent.

"You have to cooperate with us, Mr. Eastmore," the doctor said as he frowned at Victor. "We need to verify your diagnosis."

"What diagnosis?" Victor asked, but he knew already what the doctor would say. He'd had many dreams of being classified, though they'd all felt more real than this.

"You are being classified for mirror resonance syndrome."

Victor tried to leap from the chair, but the technicians' hands restrained him. He shouted. "I'm not a Broken Mirror!"

"Don't be vulgar," Dr. Rularian said, "and please cooperate. Your genetic test is being processed now. It's standard procedure."

"Why aren't you testing Alik? He started the fight."

"We will when he wakes up. We are required to test anyone brought to us by emergency services."

"It's not my fault!" Victor said.

"We're not concerned with determining fault. Now, I'm going to read you a set of questions. Please answer whether you strongly agree, slightly agree, neither agree nor disagree, slightly disagree, or strongly disagree."

Victor waved a hand at the paper the doctor was holding. "You don't need to ask me any questions. I'm a not a Broken— I'm not a mirror resonance person. I didn't start the fight. I shouldn't be here."

"Please focus, Mr. Eastmore. The first statement is: 'I have a hard time controlling my anger.'"

"My granfa owns this hospital. He could fire you like that." Victor snapped his fingers.

Dr. Rularian knitted his brows. "I'm merely following protocol. As a man of medicine, your grandfather will understand that, I'm sure. Please. With regard to difficulty controlling your anger, do you strongly agree, slightly agree—"

"Yes! Fine, I strongly agree. Especially right now."

"'My mood can shift between periods of extreme anxiety, sadness, or irritability in just a few hours or days.' Do you agree or disagree?"

Victor folded his arms in front of his chest, but the lizard-eyed technician motioned for him to move them by his sides. He complied. "More like seconds or minutes."

"I'll put that down as 'strongly agree.'" A smile appeared fleetingly on the doctor's face and vanished. "'Sometimes I am confident in myself and my abilities, and other times I doubt myself and my abilities.'"

Victor frowned and took a breath into his lungs. "Strongly disagree. I know what—"

"Excuse me, Doctor." The flat-faced technician pointed toward one of the vidscreens.

Dr. Rularian examined the readings and turned back toward Victor. "It's very important that you tell the truth," the doctor said.

"I am," Victor said.

The flat-faced technician looked down at him. "That helmet may not look like much, but it's recording your micro-

Cody Sisco

expressions at a subdermal level. We know if you're telling the truth or not."

Victor couldn't see the technician's face clearly behind his translucent gel mask, but the crinkled skin around his eyes showed the man was smirking.

They have me, Victor thought. No matter what I do, say, or even think, they've got me in their trap.

Dr. Rularian said, "Please, let's get through the rest of these questions. 'I experience blank moments—'"

The door swung open, nearly swiping Lizard-Eyes' backside. Granfa Jeff walked into the room. Tall and wiry with short-clipped fuzzy gray hair and dark freckles on brown skin, he flicked his gaze toward Victor, the sensors, and then to each technician in turn. Victor felt thunderous anger gather on Granfa Jeff's face like a storm about to break. "I'd like a word with you, Doctor. Outside, please." The doctor left the room first. Granfa Jeff glanced sideways at Victor. "Tidy yourself up."

The flat-faced technician objected, "Sir, we're in the middle—"

Granfa Jeff turned to him and glowered. "This is my hospital. You should have alerted me as soon as my grandson arrived."

Victor pulled the sensors off his body and removed the helmet, dangling it from two fingers, and asked, "Who wants the evil crown?"

Lizard-Eyes took the device in both hands and placed it on a nearby table. Victor slipped around one of the chair's arms, stood, and pulled up his pants. Through the open door, he saw his parents sitting on a couch in an alcove. He rushed over to them.

His ma hugged him, saying, "I'm so glad you're all right. We were worried."

His fa placed a hand on Victor's shoulder. "What happened? Another fight?"

Victor glanced back at his granfa, who was pacing in front of Dr. Rularian and drawing the attention of nearby nurses with his raised voice.

"I tried to get away, but they cornered me," Victor said. "Alik started it. I slipped. It wasn't my fault."

Finished with the doctor, Granfa Jeff walked slowly toward Victor, Fa, and Ma. "I'm sorry. If I'd gotten here earlier, I might have held them off. I think we all understand this was inevitable."

Victor looked at his parents. They nodded. "You talked about this? You suspected I was a Broken Mirror and you never told me?"

"Shh, honey, it'll be okay," his ma said. "We weren't certain. We'll take care of you. Everything will be fine."

One week later, Granfa Jeff brought Victor into his office and told him he'd been designated Class Three.

Victor looked at the carpet. "There's no cure, is there?"

His granfa smiled, and the lines around his face deepened. Clearing his throat, he said, "If I can cure cancer, I can cure anything. Truly, Victor, with the Holistic Healing Network's resources, there's nothing I can't do."

3

One might expect technological progress to be slowed by the hoarding of advancements behind proprietary walls. Rather, the reverse is true. The clustering of talent in ghettos of learning, be they academic or corporate, has accelerated our scientific endeavors. Everyone benefits from close links among brilliant minds. The wheel turns faster and faster.

—Jefferson Eastmore's *The Wheel of Progress* (1989)

Semiautonomous California
14 September 1990

Victor said, "You said you would find a cure. You promised me!"

"I wish . . ." Granfa Jeff's chest labored with every breath. "Our research into a cure took a very wrong turn. But this isn't the end for you. I think we've been mistaken. You're not ill. Mirror resonance syndrome isn't as debilitating as we believed. We gain nothing by pathologizing it. I see that now. I've tried to tell the other members of the Health Board, but—"

"What's going to happen to me?" Victor repeated.

"Your own progress—the progress of the pilot project—has convinced me that under the right conditions, it will be possible for you to live a normal life."

Victor felt as if he were in free fall, blankness rushing up to consume him. He whispered Dr. Tammet's refrain, *The wisest owl listens before he asks, "Who?" The dark forest hides the loudest cuckoo*, but it wasn't working. He was slipping away.

Granfa Jeff reached out, but Victor backed away.

Victor slapped his own cheeks with both hands and kicked a potted plant to counteract the blankness. "You call *this* normal?"

His granfa sighed and hung his head. "I don't mean normal in a rigid sense. Of course there's natural variation. One can expect an individual to have idiosyncratic gifts and challenges."

Victor felt as if he were a balloon floating far above the ground, watching his foot shove the overturned plant, a fern, and scatter dirt across the concrete. "I have *gifts* now? I guess I don't need to take Personil anymore either. I can still see a therapist once a week, but just for *fun*. You're right. Everything's real fucking normal." Victor reached down, wrapped his hands around the fern's root bulb, and heaved, but the pot was too heavy. He barely budged it from the ground.

"Stop that and listen. You control your destiny."

Victor laughed. "Destiny!" he shouted. "I know *all* about destiny. Read my dreambook sometime. It's all in there. Chronicles of the future, as told by a perfectly normal, *gifted*"—with each word Victor hefted the fern—"destiny-controlling heir to your stupid, pretentious, useless company."

The fern finally shifted and slipped free from the pot. Victor squatted and pulled, twisting, and sent the plant sailing at his granfa.

The man dodged the fern, which landed with a dull *thunk* next to his feet. He opened the glass doors, retreated inside, and locked them behind him. Victor sprinted right at the doors, crashing into them with a low clang, but the glass held. He bounced off and rolled onto the ground.

Victor stood, looking for something to throw. He found a small trashcan. It rattled as he lifted it over his head. Paper slips and cardboard containers rained down. He lunged, yelling and hurling the can.

Metal met glass with a sharp, pleasant shattering sound. Cracks fanned out, but the panes held. Victor laughed and hefted the trashcan again, howling, a smile stretching across his face. He threw the trashcan again, but it glanced off and careened harmlessly across the entranceway's paving stones.

Cody Sisco

The MeshBit in his pocket buzzed. Space swallowed him, and darkness filled his vision. A roar surged in his ears. The feeling of falling returned.

The buzzing repeated faintly. Victor swatted at his pocket with numb fingers.

His mind went blank.

Light flooded Victor's eyes, and he blinked. He was sitting against a wall of the hospital. Pain burned his ear. His granfa sat next to him with one arm wrapped around his shoulders, pressing a handkerchief to Victor's ear, which stung as if it were on fire.

"What happened? How long was I out?"

"Not long at all. You're fine now."

"What did I do?"

"It's nothing to worry about."

"What did I do? Tell me!"

Granfa Jeff removed the handkerchief from Victor's ear and showed him the blood soaked into it. "It's just a scratch. You found one of the shards from the pot and . . . you were distressed."

A sticky film of guilt coated Victor's skin. He'd slipped again. Despite all the tricks he'd been taught, he still hadn't managed to fight off a resonant episode. He was hopeless.

"Remember what this is," Granfa Jeff said with a hitch in his voice, "a biochemical phenomenon. Your mirror neurons work differently than most other people's, more excitable and less easily inhibited. That's all. It's just the way things are." Granfa Jeff leaned close and kissed Victor's brow. "The challenge is to take charge of your perceptions and reasoning. The brain has exceptional plasticity. I believe you can reshape the patterns of your neurons through experience. You don't need a cure."

Victor's stomach felt tight and heavy, as if it were compressing itself and pulling all his other organs down with it. "It scares me," he said. "Every time I come back, I have to piece together what my body's done without me. One day, I'm afraid I might—"

"You're different, I know, but don't let that define you. You are capable of great things," Granfa Jeff said, smiling. But the muscles around his eyes were tense.

"How long before they lock me up?" Victor asked. "A year? Two? And then? Someday you're going to be staring down at my hospital bed remembering that I used to be an actual person, not a—a—" Victor waved at the broken pot, soil, and fern on the ground. "I'm not a plant!"

He pulled himself to his feet, watching his granfa stand with some difficulty, placing his wrinkled hands against the glass behind him and huffing.

Victor said, "There must be a way. You can't close the whole hospital! What about everyone else?"

"We'll make arrangements for them at other facilities."

"What about me? Please, Granfa. Fix me," Victor whispered.

Granfa Jeff's lips trembled. "I am so, so sorry, my boy."

A shadow passed over Granfa Jeff's features. It was deathly fear. What could scare him so much?

Granfa Jeff gulped and placed a steady hand on Victor's shoulder. His voice was resolute. "Listen to me. I wish there were some other way. I do. One day you'll understand. I'm doing this for you own good. Listen . . ." Granfa took a smooth black data egg from his coat pocket and gave it to Victor. "It's important that you hear me and remember."

The data egg weighed heavily in Victor's palms. As he stared at its ebony surface, a strange calm settled on him. He felt in sync with his body, in tune with his environment.

"It will open one day," his granfa said. "When you're ready to hear. When it's safer. For now, you must never let it out of your sight, especially during a reclassification appointment. Focus on mastering your condition, so when the day comes, you'll be ready. Remember my words: Never surrender. Remember that. Never surrender."

Victor asked, "Ready for what? What are you afraid of?"

Granfa tried to smile. "One day, you'll understand. I mustn't say more than that." Then he turned and walked stiffly into the hospital, locking the doors and disappearing into the gloom.

Cody Sisco

4

BIOTECH TITAN JEFFERSON EASTMORE DIES

Jefferson Eastmore, founder of the American Union's biotechnology industry, and the man who led a revolution in healthcare technology and innovation, died Sunday. He was seventy-seven.

His death was confirmed by the Holistic Healing Network, an affiliation of hospitals, clinics, and research centers that Mr. Eastmore founded in 1944 to help the American Union and Europe recover and reconcile following the War of the Atlantic. Widely known as the man who cured cancer, Mr. Eastmore is survived by his mother, his wife, his two children and two grandchildren, and many more members of one of the American Union's most illustrious families. The cause of death was cardiac arrest, following a prolonged illness.

—MeshNews report, 21 February 1991

Semiautonomous California
23 February 1991

Six members of the Eastmore family gathered on a hillside graveyard overlooking Oakland & Bayshore's City Lake, but only the near shore could be seen through heavy morning fog.

Victor stood under a redwood tree that dripped condensation on him, while the rest of his family stood on a bioconcrete path. He was maintaining a precarious sort of calm, but the feelings swirling around him were treacherous and tidal. He tried to concentrate on the landscape and draw comfort from its stillness.

Clusters of headstone-marked graves dotted the hill, but much of the cemetery adhered to the more recent tradition of burial mounds, resurrected after the Communion Crisis and the fall of the Catholic Church. Many of the mounds were simple, unadorned grassy lumps, but the wealthier families had commissioned elaborate arrangements of paving stones, some polished to such a fine patina that they shone even in the weak, fog-blighted sunlight of a February morning.

"Damn press!" said Victor's cousin Robbie. He looked slim and fashionable in his navy funeral wear. Robbie was all polish—round head, slicked hair, and shaved face—compared to Victor's frumpy clothes, wayward curls, and two-day scruff.

Robbie pointed across the lawn to a red and white van with the MeshNews honeycomb logo. A few reporters loitered around the van and fussed with equipment for a site feedcast. Their presence was no surprise. The Eastmore patriarch had a distinguished legacy, and his recent actions were noteworthy as well. The closing of Oak Knoll, the reduction of Holistic Healing Network staff around the world, and the withdrawal of charitable support from a slew of worthy causes had bewildered and disappointed many people. At least, with Granfa Jeff's death, there were no further opportunities for letting people down.

Petite Auntie Circe lay a hand on her ma's shoulder and said, "You don't have to speak with them."

Victor wished he had his auntie's skin tone, like paprika-dusted chocolate. Once upon a time, as with all the Eastmores, she would have been called "mixed-race." Nowadays, people said skin is skin and left it at that. But Victor secretly wanted darker skin like hers; he had more than a touch of his ma's paleness.

Granma Cynthia sniffed. "I don't plan to." She wore a midnight-blue dress with long vertical lines of onyx beadwork.

Auntie Circe primped the black collar poking out of her navy blazer. "They expect a statement. I'll talk to them."

Robbie crept close to Victor and whispered, "Don't *you* go talking to them."

Victor ignored him. A wooden sign planted in the lawn read "Civic Mausoleum" in a tight curlicue script that had probably been considered stylish when Victor was a boy.

Granma Cynthia turned toward Auntie Circe. "If they ask about his illness . . ." Her lips clamped shut, and she looked at the ground.

Auntie Circe nodded. "Just because heart failure is rare doesn't mean it never happens. We're not infallible. But the irony of Jefferson Eastmore succumbing to a usually treatable condition must be irresistible to them."

Victor's fa, Linus, took a step toward the van, glowering. "They better watch their words. If Father had been less secretive about his illness, they wouldn't be so interested," he said.

"You can't blame him for protecting his privacy," Auntie Circe said. "It's bad enough to lose one's health. To also lose one's mental faculties to dementia—"

Granma Cynthia whipped her head up. "If you so much as whisper that word . . ." The unspecified threat hung in the air as sure as if she'd pointed a stunstick at her daughter.

Dementia? Victor was surprised. But then he hadn't seen much of Granfa Jeff over the past few months.

Auntie Circe sighed. "If I deny the rumors, it increases their influence. Don't worry. I'll deflect them somehow."

A group of mourners walked down the flagstone path and filed through the doorway of the mausoleum. The building's four pillars and covered porch—made of white marble or a synthetic impostor—reminded Victor of the Southern, Reconstruction-style homes in Carmichael. He shivered.

"It's time to go in," Victor's ma, Linda, said, pointing toward the last of the crowd slipping through the open doors of the civic mausoleum.

Granma Cynthia fiddled with a pair of navy gloves with black piping. Victor's parents hugged each other. His auntie brushed the shoulder of his cousin's suit. We're not mammals, Victor thought, we're a family of ducks; we all preen and then go waddling forward.

Auntie Circe held up an overstuffed bouquet of violets and white roses, lifted her chin, and said, "All right, everyone, line up, youngest to oldest. Victor, you're in front. Then Robbie. Linda, Linus, follow behind them. Mother, you'll want to follow me."

"You make everything such a chore," Granma Cynthia quietly scolded, but she took her assigned place.

Auntie Circe waved the bouquet. "You know the burdens of status. We have to do this correctly. People are here to view the survivors as much as the dead." She nodded for Victor to begin the procession.

Victor took a first step and then the next. Just outside the doors, he sidestepped off the walkway, wetting his black dress shoes on the dewy grass.

"It's okay," Ma called. "Come in when you're ready."

The other family members continued into the mausoleum and down the aisle, but Circe remained with Victor outside. He turned away from the open door and studied the arrangement of burial mounds, clustered to fit the contours of the terrain, trying to spot where the first Eastmore to be buried outside of New Venice would be laid to rest.

"I know this is difficult for you," Auntie Circe said.

Victor looked at his wet shoes. "We fought. The last time I saw him, he said I could live a normal life. Ridiculous."

"I'm sure that was painful to hear, especially coming from him. Father wasn't well in the end. You have to try to see past his failings."

"Maybe I could, if Oak Knoll was still there. I thought I would work there eventually, helping people, finding cures."

"Gene-Us is a great company," she said.

Victor barely heard her. "He ruined everything."

"That wasn't him. It was his dementia."

"I don't see the distinction," Victor said.

Auntie Circe grimaced and said, "Conflict is inevitable. What matters is that you remember your love for each other. I'm sure he forgave you."

"You don't get it," Victor said. "*I'm* still mad at *him*."

"I'm not going to tell you what to feel," she said. Her voice was stern, but a slight smile, visible by the barest lift in her cheeks, softened her expression. "There's a lifetime for you to get over that. But today's the only day you can say good-bye to him. Remember, death is simply a new start." She entered the mausoleum.

Strange words. What kind of new start? She couldn't mean Granfa Jeff would be reborn in a religious sense. Aunt Circe had bizarre, somewhat occult interests, yet she didn't hold to anything as banal as religion or believe in the afterlife. Maybe she meant the Eastmores would start anew, freed from their overbearing patriarch.

Victor stepped inside. Members of Clan Eastmore, as his granfa had called it, lined up to gawk at the body. The benches on either side of the aisle were more than fully occupied; they were stuffed. A few people turned to look at Victor as he walked by, including his supervisor at Gene-Us, Karine LaTour, but he ignored them. Nervous buzzing in his legs threatened to overtake his whole body. He didn't dare meet anyone's eyes.

The coffin, thankfully, was high-lipped so that Victor couldn't see the body yet. He kept the flower arrangement blooming behind the coffin at the center of his field of vision. Two colorful bird of paradise flowers—*always two*—poked from a bunch of white carnations. Each step seemed weighted, and his knees began to shake.

This shouldn't be happening. Granfa Jeff should be alive and helping Victor deal with his condition. Oak Knoll should be a functioning hospital. How many people were going without care or getting second-best treatments now? Victor should be following in his granfa's footsteps and changing the face of medicine. It had all gone so wrong.

His parents, cousin, and granma viewed the body and took their seats in the first row. The moment came when there was no one between Victor and the coffin. Victor stepped onto the dais and looked down at his granfa's corpse.

A familiar face, long, lean, and intelligent, even in death. The skin resembled *café con leche* and seemed lighter than Victor remembered, his freckles more pronounced. He supposed that was to be expected.

But as he looked down at his granfa, he noticed dark circles the color of rotten plums around his closed eyes. His face was marred by splotches—irregular reddish-brown stains that were faintly visible under makeup. Victor was sure those blemishes were new. The corpse had only a few lusterless wisps peeking from his white knit death cap. He looked wasted away.

Why didn't that bother anyone else?

As Victor stared down at the body, the mausoleum began to fill with a rippling pressure, and darkness swirled in front of his eyes like black ash. A blankout, now? They usually came on more slowly.

Victor felt a presence nearby, smothering, and then he went blank.

Victor bent over the coffin, hands clenching the dead man's lapels. The corpse's ribs flexed under the pressure, and a breath of foul air rose up, smelling of gas and smoke. Like Carmichael.

Mourners' muttering filtered through the quiet mausoleum.

Victor had blanked out, but likely only for a few seconds. He felt none of the numbness and disorientation that accompanied a longer time away.

Blankness threatened to return. He clamped his eyes shut. Bodies moved in the blackness, reaching toward him, accusing. Murderous emanations, like subaural bass notes, rippled over his skin. The hairs on Victor's neck rose.

Victor opened his eyes and stared into a young woman's face. Then he recognized her.

Elena Morales, her lips painted navy and ringed by black pencil, hair tightly coiled at the back of her head, was at his side, asking, "Are you all right?"

"Someone killed him," he whispered.

Elena's puffy eyes widened. "Let's get you out of here," she said. "Fresh air. Different sensations."

Victor leaned heavily against her as they moved toward the exit. They had to navigate past a clot of unfamiliar faces who'd queued to pay their respects. Victor's grandparents' little lapdogs yapped outside, masking the sounds of mourners' quiet sobbing. Several strangers clothed in black turned to

Victor and offered their condolences. They probably mistook his stony silence as a sign of deep, natural grief. Or maybe they dismissed him as someone whose mind could never be properly understood.

Shock them and shock their judgments, Victor thought, and he let Elena lead him outside.

What was she doing here? They'd started dating in high school, but then there was his horribly botched good-bye when she moved to the Republic of Texas five years ago. They hadn't spoken since. How was she even talking to him after such a miserable breakup?

When they reached the lawn, he avoided her gaze and stared at the Oakland & Bayshore skyline peeking from the fog. The dogs continued yapping like little bug zappers, though he couldn't see them.

He tried not to think about his granfa and the strange intuition that he had been murdered.

Victor felt better outside, away from the other mourners' staring eyes. Grieving people wanted to make eye contact for longer than usual. Dr. Tammet's 3-5-7 rule said to maintain eye contact for three seconds when observing strangers, five seconds when speaking to someone, and seven seconds when listening.

Elena stepped in front of him. "What's wrong? Tell me."

Victor returned her steady gaze. Her eyes were brown, with green flecks, like emeralds casually scattered on a pile of brown sugar. He should be weighed down by their history, but he felt only relief.

He said, "I was doing well. Dr. Tammet said I was improving. A year ago, nothing like this would have happened."

"And this time?" she asked.

"Murder." He sighed and shook his head at the ground. "I went blank, and when I came back I was certain my granfa was murdered."

Elena stared at him with wide eyes. "Wow, that's something, even for you. Nobody is murdered in SeCa these days. At least not in the civilized parts," she added.

She was right. He sounded crazy for saying it aloud. Everyone knew that Europe's special interest in SeCa and its authoritative brand of "enlightened social engineering" meant that murder had no place here. Accidents, yes; manslaughter, sometimes yes; but premeditated and cold-blooded murder? It just didn't happen.

He wanted to hold her, but her stiff posture told him that she would back away if he tried.

Victor massaged his temples. "This feeling . . . it's so *strong*."

"It'll pass."

"You won't tell, will you?" he said.

Elena put one hand on his shoulder. "He died of heart failure."

Victor blurted, "What about the blotches on his face? And his hair. He looks *sick*."

"He was sick."

Victor moved away. "No! The last time I saw him—it was only a few months ago, and he was perfectly healthy." As soon as he said it, he realized it wasn't true. Granfa Jeff had been short of breath. He'd leaned against the front entrance of the hospital and looked fatigued.

Elena scrunched her brow and frowned. "Maybe you feel guilty. You cut yourself off from people when you're angry or hurt. It's a pattern with you. Like your obsession with the number two."

Victor jammed the toe of his shoe into the grass, and it came away with a small clump of foamy dirt on its tip. He said, "Two is the best. It's the only even prime number."

She said, "You seem different. How long have you been like this?"

He could feel her scrutinizing his face. "I'm fine," he said.

"Horse balls," she said. "You're about to pop."

Victor gulped.

Elena wrapped her arms around him.

He tensed, realizing he'd read her emotions incorrectly. She must still care for him, despite his bad behavior.

Her gauzy black blouse felt loose, like a snake skin ready to be shed. Their cheeks pressed together, and a warm comforting flush bloomed and moved down his chest, down his arms, along the length of his body to his toes.

Cody Sisco

"Thank you, Elena. You always calm me down."

She let him go. "I'm glad to be good for something," she said.

"Why'd you come back?" Victor asked.

"I heard about your granfa. I know how important he was to you. I thought that my being here might help. If we can be friends again, we can look after each other." Elena pressed the fingers of one hand through his hair. "It's not easy being alone."

Her words were soothing, but for some reason Victor's mouth turned sour. Why was she being so nice to him? He hadn't returned her calls and messages since she'd moved away. She had every right to hate him.

Victor saw Granma Cynthia emerge from the mausoleum.

"Victor?" Elena said. She was watching him carefully.

"She spent the most time with him," he replied. "I have to ask her why he looks so strange."

Elena glanced over her shoulder and spotted the old woman. She whipped her gaze back to Victor. "No, you're not thinking straight. Let it pass."

"She must know something."

"Don't do this."

Granma Cynthia trudged to a nearby iron rail fence. A black scarf covered her hair. A large sapphire-and-onyx brooch was affixed to her navy blue frock.

Victor brushed past Elena and trotted toward his granma.

"I'm going home now, Victor," Granma Cynthia told him as he approached. "I'll see you this afternoon. You'll come by."

It was a command, not a question. Victor nodded. "Granma, we both know it wasn't cardiac arrest, don't we?"

Her mouth twitched, and she gave him a harsh look. "What on earth?"

"The way his hair fell out. And those splotches . . ."

Granma Cynthia glared at him. "You haven't seen him for months, and this is how you show concern? I won't be drawn into one of your *speculations*."

Victor took a breath, then said, "I know it sounds crazy, but I *know* that Granfa was murdered."

Cody Sisco

5

Individuals with mirror resonance syndrome cannot be identified by their facial features or by their facial expressions. This is a harmful, albeit common, misconception that contributes to the stigmatization of people with MRS in SeCa.

Yes, it's true that the subconscious exchange of dissonant micro-expressions can provoke unsettling feelings in some people, but it takes an extraordinary sensitivity to perceive them. The popular myth that anyone can spot someone with MRS is blatantly false.

—Statement by Dr. Laura Tammet, the Eastmore family's neuroscience advisor (1998)

Semiautonomous California
23 February 1991

Granma Cynthia's mouth dropped open, but only for a moment. "Jefferson was *murdered*? That's an antiquated word and entirely inappropriate at a funeral. How can you say such a thing?"

Victor stared down at the grass. If he had a tail, it would be curling between his legs. "His face looked . . . His skin looked . . . corroded. Hair thinned." He looked up, trying his best to shape a complete sentence. "Did he say anything before he died? Anything suspicious?"

Granma Cynthia shook her head. "We've done so much for you over the years, Victor. It's such a shame when you get like this. I know it's not your fault, it's your condition . . ." Tears welled in her eyes. "Of course, I noticed how sick he looked. He always explained it away. For heaven's sake, *he* was the doctor."

Victor said, "But—"

Granma Cynthia cut him off with a wave of her hand and stalked toward the mausoleum. Then she stopped and turned, raising her chin and drawing a long breath. "Jefferson would know how to snap you out of this delusion, but I don't. It was a viral infection, Victor. Something he picked up on his travels." She smiled faintly. "He made a big show of taking his medication. Three times a day. He made a joke of it."

Granma Cynthia gazed far away, and her face softened as if she were remembering happier times. Mimicking Granfa Jeff's tone precisely, she said, "'We haven't tamed all the diseases of the world, not yet,' he said."

She left him and disappeared around the corner of the mausoleum.

Victor felt pinned to the spot. The weight of what he'd just said sank him. He wanted to bury himself and inhale raw dirt until his lungs bled. Why couldn't he keep his mouth shut?

He told himself to snap out of it. Useless. It wouldn't be a mental illness if he could control it, would it?

Clumps of mist wandered like ghosts over folds in the hills, soon to evaporate and vanish. That lunatic Samuel Miller would think the mist shifted from this world to the next.

Mason Charter, Jefferson Eastmore's rival in business and a college-era friend, strode through the mausoleum's doorway. He scanned the surroundings, spotted Victor, and approached.

"A fine performance," he said.

Victor blushed. Everyone must be talking about how he'd collapsed on his granfa's coffin.

"Not you, son. I'm talking about your grandfather."

"What do you mean?"

Mason, a towering bulk, white as could be, and wrinkled, leaned toward Victor. "He didn't fool me. He played the patient well. But I've known Jeff for decades. I always knew when he was bluffing."

"Bluffing? You mean playing tricks?"

"I judge a man by his actions. He may have tried to put on a brave face, but he was panicked, desperate even. What would cause a man who spent his life building an empire to hack it to pieces in his final months? That's what I want to know."

Victor asked, "Do you think he was murd—"

Mason quieted Victor with a hand on his mouth. "Shhh. Let it go for now," Mason whispered, nodding at the Mesh-News van and crew waiting at the end of the lane. "Whatever Jefferson was hiding will come out in time." He turned and walked toward the parking lot.

Victor felt lighter. He wasn't the only one with suspicions. He would talk to Mason later and ask him what he—

A scream flew across the lawn. And then another, from around the corner of the mausoleum.

Victor ran, turned the corner, and found Granma Cynthia. Her terriers nipped at her legs. Their leashes tangled around her calves, trapping her. The dogs jumped, slashing their little teeth and claws at the hem of her dress and her ankles. She squawked and motioned to him for help.

Victor acted without thinking. He unhooked the leash from the smaller dog's collar. Before the animal was aware of its freedom, Victor tucked it under his arm. The dog squirmed and tried to bite him, but it could only clamp its teeth on Victor's jacket. Bending down, Victor grabbed the other dog's collar and pressed down, pinning the animal at the neck. It yelped angrily and tried to twist away.

It took a few moments for his granma to recover her wits, but when she did, she unhooked the other leash and untangled the dogs. A few people had been drawn by her screams. Circe arrived first. She took the larger dog in her arms, trying to calm it with her voice, but keeping vise grips on its skull and ribs. Victor held the other and mimicked her sounds.

"Are you okay, Mother?" Circe asked. "Did you bring carriers?"

Granma Cynthia's chest heaved. "There's . . .two . . .in the car."

Always two, Victor thought.

Granma Cynthia gathered and lifted the hem of her dress. A shiny bloodstain spread through her stockings. "A good pair ruined."

The three walked across the parking lot and managed to get the animals stowed in their carriers. The door of the luxury car clicked closed. The dogs' angry yapping was muted.

"Are you okay?" Circe asked Victor.

"I'm fine."

"They're going to have to be put down, you know," Circe informed her ma. "You can't live with them like that."

"Jefferson loved them, so I thought they should be here. They're not always like that. Something must have set them off." Granma Cynthia glanced at the MeshNews van further down the drive, but the reporters were nowhere to be seen. "Christ, I hope this doesn't go into their report."

Victor hoped otherwise. He could see the MeshNews header: *Man with MRS Saves Jefferson Eastmore's Widow from Rabid Dogs, Calls for Repeal of Carmichael Laws.*

Circe put her arm around her ma. "Father should have put them down months ago when they started behaving like this. Another sign he was losing his—"

"Quiet!" Granma Cynthia tore away from her daughter's embrace, wheeled around, and held a single, motionless finger up in warning. "I'm tired of the speculation. I don't need to hear it from you too. Of all the days, Circe Eliza Eastmore, please just zip it. I've heard enough!"

Circe held up her palms. Then she adjusted the webwork of black silk covering her dark curls. Victor thought she might be smiling, or maybe she was just embarrassed.

Circe said to Victor, "You handled that well. Calmly. We don't give you enough credit."

She reached into a pocket and handed each of them a black handkerchief. Victor wiped saliva off his suit. Granma Cynthia blotted her calf.

"Yes, he's all highs and lows today," Granma Cynthia said.

Circe crossed her arms and looked at Victor. "What's she talking about?"

"Nothing," Victor said. He turned to his granma. "I'm sorry.

Cody Sisco

It wasn't—just forget what I said. Please. It's—I wasn't myself. I'll be fine."

"You better be. This family cannot take another loss. If you get sent to a retreat or, God forbid, one of those *facilities*—"

"I won't," Victor said. "I can look after myself."

Circe smiled. "That's the Eastmore way. Isn't it, Mother? Do you want company on the drive home?"

Granma Cynthia waved her daughter away. "I'm fine. You go see where Robbie has got to."

Victor walked to his car. He didn't want any help. Not Elena's, not his family's. He wanted to take care of himself. He wanted to pass his next Classification Commission reevaluation with his freedom intact. He wanted a calm, predictable life.

People in hell want ice water, Granfa used to say.

Mid-step, Victor stopped. Had he taken his dose this morning? Thinking back to the bustle of showering, dressing, and driving to the mausoleum, he tried to identify the precise instant when he'd taken the pill from its case, put it in his mouth, and gulped it down. He remembered doing it, didn't he? Pill on the tongue. A sip of water. But he could be remembering yesterday or the day before. When you do something so often, there's nothing to mark it in memory, and so how are you to know?

He shook his head at his stupidity. He would take his dose after dinner, maybe double it up, and try to forget the stupid M-word: *murder*.

6

The tragedy of mirror resonance syndrome is the unpredictable nature of its symptoms and the disease's degenerative progression. The anxiety of not knowing how the condition will evolve. That's what takes its toll on sufferers and their families.

We've all seen the vidfeeds showing rows of hospital beds filled with catatonic people. Think of the questions patients must ask themselves. Will that be me someday? When will I lose the ability to tell fact from fiction? At what point will my family give up on me?

I didn't focus on the disease. I focused on treatment. My goal was to give Victor hope, to make him believe that he could have a different future. If I succeeded in anything, it may have been that.

—Statement by Dr. Laura Tammet, the Eastmore family's neuroscience advisor (1998)

Semiautonomous California
23 February 1991

The Eastmore mansion's gate sensors registered the approach of Victor's car and opened automatically. He parked in a garage separated from the main building by a narrow pergola covered in grape vines. Lê Quang Hieu, the house butler and Victor's favorite by far among its staff, met him at the front door. His black hair was nearly hidden by his white puck-shaped servant's hat.

"I hope you're feeling better," Hieu said, meeting Victor's eyes. He'd been at the funeral and witnessed Victor's difficulties. Hieu wasn't the type to gloss over or ignore Victor's condition. He was always asking Victor how he was feeling and looking for ways to show that his position as head of the staff was much more than a job to him—it was a duty, one he undertook with genuine devotion.

"Yes, thank you, Hieu. I'll be glad when this day's over."

Hieu nodded and walked with Victor to the garden; then he bowed his head and retreated inside.

The Eastmores sat in high-backed lounge chairs on a large bioconcrete patio, covered themselves in blankets, and received close friends and a few notable officials. They discussed science, politics, the weather, and, at intervals and always tactfully, their memories of Jefferson Eastmore.

Victor sat with them and said nothing, except when someone mentioned a new European astronomy project to observe patterns in cosmic microwave background radiation. Victor perked up and recited the planned telescope's technical specifications. His ma responded by saying, "How interesting," and the conversation moved on. Victor returned to his silence and his own memories of Granfa Jeff.

On a foggy winter day, when Victor was sixteen and in his final year of high school, Granfa Jeff brought him to the zoo. Moisture hung motionless over the Bayshore. Eucalyptus trees covered the landscape. There were no crowds—in 1983 only members of the Zoological Society could visit the expansive private menagerie.

They went first to the Africa enclosure. A few distant figures wandered the paths between the lairs of rhinoceroses, elephants, giraffes, and other exotic species. Ranger Mikke, one of the zookeepers, a tall man who had a slight limp and a dark beard that wrapped from ear to ear, met them at the penguin exhibit. He wore canvas shorts, unmindful of the cold. Victor thought maybe through years of study the ranger had gained an ability to live comfortably outdoors, a symbiosis with the environment that other humans lacked.

Speaking in a thick Northern League accent of melodically twisting vowels and soft consonant explosions, the ranger thanked Jefferson for a recent gift to the zoo. He said to Victor, "I bet you're wondering how one hundred chimpanzees from halfway around the world ended up here?"

The ranger smiled, his mouth widening to a frightening degree. He reminded Victor of a gluttonous cartoon bear known for scooping up fish from rivers by the handful and eating them whole. Victor had no idea there were any chimps in the zoo, and he thought it strange that the ranger would assume anything about Victor's mental state. He was wise enough to keep his thoughts to himself and simply nodded in response.

Ranger Mikke straightened and turned toward Jefferson. "Did you know Sir Louis Bradley?"

Granfa Jeff stopped walking. "Of course. A generous man."

Victor sensed a boring conversation looming, so he broke away and walked to a fenced-off area, behind which a pride of lions lazed together, sharing their warmth. He wanted to squeeze through the bars, hurdle the dry moat, and cuddle with them. Logically, he knew they might not react well to that. Too bad he couldn't feed them Personil to ensure they stayed calm. He only had enough for his next dose, due at dinner time.

The men's voices carried to where Victor watched the lions. "That's as I've heard it too," the ranger said. "Not many people know that he was invited to Rhodesia in the sixties to help with the planning of a new national zoo."

At the mention of another zoo, Victor turned around, curious to know if *that* was what this trip was about. *Was Granfa Jeff going to buy a zoo? Or build a new one?*

Granfa Jeff's eyebrows rose. "He would have had to cross the green line."

"He did." Ranger Mikke scratched one of his meaty ears. "Sir Louis didn't care about the travel ban." He imitated an aristocratic lilt, "'If no one helps them, we shall soon regret the demise of man's cousins.'"

Victor turned to watch the lions. Some had retreated further into the enclosure, out of view, but one large lioness languidly paced the rocks. She settled onto her haunches and appeared to be watching him. Victor kept his eyes trained on her while he listened to the men's conversation.

Ranger Mikke said, "Sir Bradley designed Rhodesia's enclosures to preserve the extant African populations of chimps, apes, orangutans, and bonobos in something close to their natural habitat. It was wondrous. I've seen the real-pics."

Victor turned away from the lioness, realizing he was missing some important piece of context about Rhodesia, which everyone knew as a major source of diamonds, platinum, and gold. "Why was there a travel ban?" Victor asked.

Granfa Jeff shook his head. "It's a long story that ends with the decapitation of the king of Rhodesia. Another time." He lightly touched Ranger Mikke's arm. "You were saying that Sir Louis went to Rhodesia to save the hominids. I assume he brought back the chimpanzees from his trip?"

Ranger Mikke smiled lopsidedly. "Not intentionally. His assistant Maisie Winters fell in love with the chimps and smuggled a breeding pair back in a shipping container. Oh, it caused a big fuss, but she had secretly obtained permission from the king, so they weren't sent back."

Victor said, "When was he decapitated?"

"Hush, Victor," his granfa said.

Ranger Mikke smiled. "The important part of this story is that Sir Louis had a soft spot for Maisie, treated her like a daughter. She convinced him they had to keep the chimpanzees for research. When Rhodesia fell, there were scores more that needed homes, and they came here." Ranger Mikke pointed toward a building just barely visible through the trees. "We have over one hundred individuals now, the biggest community in the American Union."

They resumed their journey and soon arrived at a neatly landscaped area dominated by a blocky modernist building that looked to Victor like a stripped-down Buddhist temple. Inside, beyond a small reception area crowded with potted plants, brightly colored carpets traced paths through a maze of desks and cubicles. The paintings and pictures on the walls resembled classic works of art, but with hominids instead of

Cody Sisco

humans. The one nearest to Victor showed a bonobo female reclining on a stone bench as a group of males fought over her.

Victor and his granfa followed the ranger to a room with a few vidscreens, a MeshTerminal, and a large window. Beyond the glass, a chimpanzee—a muscular, hairy, and slack-breasted female—snacked on some grapes that hung in bunches from a padded rig of scaffolding.

The chimpanzee glanced up occasionally but never fixed her eyes on the observers. A one-way glass. Victor bristled. He and the chimpanzee had something in common already. They were both used to being scrutinized like cells under a microscope.

Ranger Mikke placed his hand on Victor's shoulder, a too-familiar gesture for someone he had just met for the first time. Working with other species must have made the ranger feel closer to his own.

"You're going to go meet Sofie in a moment," Ranger Mikke said. "She's thirteen, a young person like you. She loves puzzles. We give her the most complicated ones, and she always impresses us. We thought she would be a good first experience for you."

Victor asked, "What am I supposed to do?"

His granfa put a hand on Victor's other shoulder. "We're going to observe your interactions. We're only beginning to understand how great apes perceive and communicate. We also want to observe you. It may help us discover certain aspects of your cognitive process."

"You mean you want to find out what's wrong with me. Do I have to wear one of those helmets?" Since his diagnosis four years earlier, he had spent lots of time at Oak Knoll with a heavy bucket on his head to measure his brain activity.

"No, this is purely about observing behavior," Ranger Mikke said. "Let's introduce you to Sofie."

"Is Dr. Tammet here?" Victor looked around but didn't see her.

Granfa Jeff said, "No, Victor. She . . . We disagreed about the need for this . . . experiment."

Victor followed the ranger, while his granfa stayed glued to the one-way glass.

Now I'm the show. Boy meets ape; hilarity ensues.

As he'd practiced many times before, Victor repeated Dr. Tammet's mantra and became emotionally neutral, like a tuning fork at rest.

When Victor and Ranger Mikke entered Sofie's enclosure, she approached the zookeeper and gave him a very human-like hug, hooting and patting. She seemed to think she was friends with the ranger. *A massive case of Stockholm syndrome. Although, if she was born there, how would she ever come to know she lived in a prison?*

Ranger Mikke took one of Sofie's hands and slowly led her toward Victor. Her weight shifted from side to side in a kind of rolling wave, unlike the linear, contained gait of her human caretaker. "Sofie, this is Victor. I want you to say hello."

The sides of her mouth pulled apart, revealing giant-sized teeth. She watched Victor with her nut-brown eyes and made a quick gesture with her fingers. Wrinkled skin piled around her face, rising in unfamiliar contours. Her gaze skittered over him, and her mouth worked, compressing and extending. Victor half expected her to speak.

"Can you shake hands?" the ranger asked both of them. Victor thrust his hand out, nobly attempting to bridge the gap between species.

Sofie's large eyes looked at Victor's hand and then his face, tracked his gaze to her own hand, and looked up again. She hissed. Before Victor could pull his hand away, she slapped it to the side, hard enough to make it sting. Her flat, worn-away teeth were visible in her dark mouth as she opened it and screamed at him, a loud pulsing shriek, deafening in the small room.

Victor stumbled backward into the wall, plugging his ears. The ranger was trying to calm Sofie, but she shrugged off his pats and hissed at him too. Her shrieks punctuated the zookeeper's calm voice.

Victor bolted from the room. His granfa came out of the adjoining room, and Victor slammed into him.

Granfa Jeff grabbed Victor's arm and kept him from falling. "Calm down. We'll wait a few minutes and try again."

Cody Sisco

"I want to go. She doesn't like me." Humiliation churned in his stomach. Still, there was something comical about it. Rejected by a chimpanzee. He must be the least likable human on the planet.

"You didn't give her the chance. Hers was a natural reaction to your hostility."

"I wasn't hostile. I didn't do anything."

"Come here."

His granfa led him to a set of vidscreens and input slabs. Victor saw the zookeeper through the window petting Sofie and heard his murmured reassurances through the sonofeed. She seemed as agitated as he felt.

Granfa Jeff pressed a cutoff switch for the sonofeed and activated a spectrum relay panel for the vidfeed recording devices in the chimp's room. One of the vidcams had been trained on Victor. He watched as the image of his face expanded to fill the vidscreen.

"Look here." His granfa pointed to the vidscreen, tracing Victor's brow, eyes, and lips. "I'll advance the feed slowly so you can see from the time you entered the room until she slapped your hand. This expression is a blend of anger, contempt, and fear. Your lips are compressed, nose slightly scrunched, brow furrowed. When you offered your hand, she saw it in that context, arm thrusting out like so. She didn't see an invitation; to her it was a challenge."

"So?" Victor looked away from the image of his face.

"You were projecting negative emotions, and Sofie registered them."

"I wasn't thinking, 'Hey, chimp, let's fight,'" Victor said.

"It doesn't matter. You may not have been thinking it consciously, but what you were feeling was written all over your face."

Victor looked away. His granfa's explanation made sense. He was sure he'd been neutral, when in fact he'd been hostile and combative. To not be aware of his own emotions, and yet to succeed in broadcasting them to everyone in sight—it was like living in an inside-out body, wearing organs like clothes, and walking around oblivious to others' screams of horror.

Victor said, "A chimpanzee with empathetic super powers. What's next? Cats in space? Or are you saying she's a Broken Mirror too?"

"I know you're upset, but think for a moment. What does this experience tell us?"

Victor bit back another remark about him being so monstrous he couldn't make friends with animals. His granfa was giving him a chance to use and demonstrate his intellect. He shouldn't waste it. Especially before his next dose of Personil returned his mind to dullsville.

"I need to control my expressions," he said, "so I don't get into trouble."

His granfa shook his head. "That comes later, and it's an imperfect skill. Even the most skilled confidence men struggle to keep their true feelings from peeking through their masks. The lesson is more fundamental than that."

Victor looked at the ceiling, replaying the encounter in his mind. He had walked in, following the zookeeper, observing Sofie. She had greeted the man, followed him by the hand, looked at Victor, at his face, at his hand—*That's it!* She had *examined* him. "She read me; she read my emotions."

His granfa nodded. "Precisely. And what does that mean?"

"It's a process, a procedure. Like taking a measurement."

"Go on."

"It's about observing the facts. Other people's movements, gestures, and expressions, and then deducing what they mean. If she can read emotions like this, then I should be able to as well."

"You've almost got it, very good. But I need to explain the significance. You see, for Sofie and other apes, and for humans as well, maybe for all the mammals, this process is automatic, almost unconscious. People pick up on these signs and interpret them without ever being aware of it. This is your special challenge. You are bombarded by this input, which triggers emotional reactions in you that are out of proportion to the context. You feel what they feel, but much more strongly, and—listen, because this is important: there is a mismatch in the timing. So you have reactions that seem odd to others.

I believe by more closely scrutinizing cues in your environment, including social cues, you can moderate your responses. I believe it's a skill that can be learned."

Victor felt his eyes go wide. His granfa's explanation, illustrated so perfectly by the experience he'd just had, gave him hope of overcoming his disability.

After a moment, he asked, "You mean, I can read people without automatically, you know, feeling them?"

Granfa Jeff rubbed Victor's back. "You face bigger challenges in your life because of who you are, but the rewards of success will be that much greater. Think of the insights you have access to, to be conscious of the emotional relationships among a group of people, which others feel but don't necessarily understand. I believe a career in diplomacy could be quite fitting."

Victor looked again through the glass, and in Sofie's face he now saw not a collection of hostile features but a forest of signs and signals that needed to be decoded.

"I want to learn how."

7

Although Victor had made great progress, due to the nature of mirror resonance syndrome, his mental state continued to be vulnerable to external influences and internal instabilities. I would have continued to work with Victor, but in September 1990, Jefferson Eastmore told me my services were no longer needed.

I had worked for the family for nearly a decade by then, helping Victor cope with his condition. I recommended additional mental health professionals to work with him in my stead, some of whom I had trained to work with people with MRS, but to my knowledge they were never contacted by anyone in the family.

—Statement by Dr. Laura Tammet, the Eastmore family's neuroscience advisor (1998)

Semiautonomous California
23 February 1991

At dinner on the eve of Granfa Jeff's funeral, six Eastmore family members sat clustered at one end of a long table that could have seated twenty. Old-fashioned sconces with incandescent bulbs were spaced along the wood-paneled walls every meter or so.

Granma Cynthia lightly squeezed the dinner table's short edge, and the bell for first courses chimed. Soon Hieu and Granma's assistant arrived bearing plates heaped with delicate lettuces, roasted winter beets, and a strong cheese with a smell that turned Victor's stomach. He picked at the greens and beets and moved the cheese to the far side of his plate.

"I hate SeCa," his cousin Robbie said. "Europe is wasting its money here."

Victor looked up. It was bad manners to talk that way over dinner. Even he knew that. "What money?" he asked.

Robbie smirked. The expression twisted his otherwise plain, light brown face into something ugly and rodent-like. "Without Europe's aid, SeCa would be a poor backwater, more than it already is."

"I think you're confusing propaganda with education," Victor grumbled.

Robbie glared at him. "Confusion is *your* area of expertise."

Victor bit his tongue.

"Europe fomented autonomy and self-determination in the United States to undercut a burgeoning rival," Robbie said in a pedantic drone that sounded more like a stuffy professor than someone who was, at twenty-five, less than a year older than Victor. "During the Repartition, Europe cozied up to the fledgling nations of the A.U., and now all of them, including SeCa, are dependent on Europe for financing and foreign aid. It was a brilliant strategy at the time. But now the money would be better spent at home."

"Home? You sound more European than American. Are you applying to change your citizenship?" Victor asked, knowing that his family would consider the suggestion akin to blasphemy.

Robbie straightened. "If dual citizenship were allowed, I'd consider it." Victor's ma sucked in her breath, and Granma Cynthia's fingers tightened around her knife. Robbie faced them down unapologetically. "I like to side with the winners of history."

"Enough, Robbie," Victor's fa said. He pronged his salad. "I suppose there will be questions about the future of the company." Linus glanced at his ma and sister, affecting nonchalance, but Victor could tell from his voice that Fa was nervous.

"It's a delicate balance," Circe responded. She sat rigidly upright, addressing her ma at her side and her brother across from her as if they were her subjects, yet her narrow shoulders didn't rise much above her place setting. Granfa Jeff had been the only tall Eastmore. "I have to show that Father's actions over the past few months did no harm, yet at the same time steer the company in a different direction that puts all the rumors behind us. And I have to do all this without—how did you put it, Mother?—without dragging the Eastmore name through a manure pond."

Linus said, "So we're *not* going to make a buck off the stim addicts filling our streets? Can we at least agree on that?"

Victor looked up, surprised to hear him talk this way. Were they planning to treat stim addicts in SeCa? He stayed quiet, reflecting on how little he knew of the family business. As recently as a few months ago, there was talk of expelling the hopeless cases to other A.U. nations. He wanted to ask about it, but he couldn't gauge how much of a taboo he'd be breaking. If he said anything unusual, Granma Cynthia might bring up what he'd said to her. He hoped she hadn't already told his parents. He never should have mentioned murder at a funeral.

Circe raised an eyebrow. "We're a health care company. We have to respond to the health needs around us."

Granma Cynthia forked a half globe of yellow tomato. "Could we leave business until after dinner?" She looked at her daughter. "Or perhaps you'd like to go over his will during dessert?"

Circe shook her head, sending her black curls into dizzy vibrations. "I don't want to upset you. I just want to prepare you. Would you rather read what I say on the Mesh?"

Granma Cynthia ate her tomato and said nothing.

"We need bold moves to maintain HHN's leadership position," Circe said. She looked at each Eastmore in turn. Her fork daintily gathered the salad components into a well-balanced bite—the same way she was gathering support from each family member. She would make a good company chief.

She continued, "We can't rest on our laurels. Father's image will be exonerated in death, and his illness will underscore the importance of the network's mission. People will forgive his recent actions, given time."

Ma hadn't touched her plate. She stared down at the salad as if she were waiting for it to change into something else. "The public has a long memory."

"Does it?" Circe responded without a shred of concern in her voice.

Ma asked, "What about the foundation? Is there a way to bring it back under our control?"

Granma Cynthia and Auntie Circe exchanged arch glances. Victor wondered if the foundation was that touchy a subject. Or maybe they didn't want Ma to have a bigger say in the family's affairs, now that the loudest voice was gone.

"We'll do what we can," Granma Cynthia said stiffly. "Mason won't give it back without a fight."

They began to discuss what to do about the terriers.

Thinking of the dogs and the mausoleum brought back memories of his granfa's appearance, which disturbed him all over again. How could the founder of the largest health care corporation in the world have degenerated so quickly? The great Jefferson Eastmore dying of heart failure caused by an infection? He could have gotten a transplant or grown himself a new heart. Yet the family seemed to accept the heart failure explanation all too easily. There must have been more to it.

Victor excused himself, saying he wanted to rest. He shuffled out of the room. His parents let him go. There was nothing surprising about a nap in the midst of dinner.

He climbed the wide, carpeted staircase to the second floor. His granfa's office was off limits to everyone but Granma Cynthia, and maybe Auntie Circe, but these circumstances were exceptional, and Victor felt justified in snooping.

Still, he should be careful. Victor crept to the balcony. The foyer and sitting room were empty. He hadn't been followed. A clock below chimed seven. The short winter day had faded into night.

Victor found the door to Granfa's office closed and locked. He jiggled the knob as quietly as possible, but it didn't turn. At least it wasn't a modern reinforced door. He knelt and inspected the lock mechanism, finding a simple spring-tongue and socket.

Cody Sisco

Wood creaked behind him, and he jolted upright. Looking over his shoulder, he saw nothing amiss. The staff came up to the second floor only when summoned. They would be busy serving dinner. The house must be muttering to itself.

He pulled a Japanese multiknife from his pocket and wedged it into the door gap. The first swipe of the blade failed to dislodge the lock's spring-tongue. He stuck it in the crevice again and drew it downward, slowly, catching the tongue and easing it back against its spring. He gripped the knob and pushed it forward. The door swung open with a loud, protesting creak.

Inside the room, against one wall, tall bookcases flanked a large oak desk, Granfa Jeff's workplace when he wasn't touring Holistic Healing Network offices and facilities. The center of the room held a couch and two high-backed chairs with a low table between them. Off to the side were a reading nook with a stuffed chair and ottoman and more bookcases next to the bay windows overlooking the mansion's grounds.

Victor stepped to the desk and sat in Granfa Jeff's large synthleather chair, absently sliding a book on the desk to the side. However, the book's texture—real leather—caught his attention. He looked more closely, and recognized it as the handwritten compendium of herbal medicine Granfa Jeff had shown to Victor on a foggy summer day just a few months before Oak Knoll had closed.

On that day, the old man had seen Victor skulking in the doorway of his office. He sat up in his chair and cleared his throat. "Herbalism!" Granfa Jeff waved Victor inside and jutted his chin toward the leather volume.

Victor approached the desk and opened the book, running his fingers over its stiff yellowed pages, which were covered in blue handwriting that flowed around drawings of plants' leaves, stems, and roots.

"What's wrong?" Victor asked.

Granfa Jeff looked out the window and down at a row of sturdy hedges and ground cover that drank moisture from Pacific mists. He said, "Something we haven't tried yet."

"Plant medicine?" Victor asked. "That seems odd. Every-thing useful's made of synthetic chemicals and bioengineering."

Granfa Jeff said, "Up until the last hundred years—through the Enlightenment anyway—medicine was practically syn-onymous with plants. Unfortunately, we don't know much about older forms of healing, especially those from the East."

"Can plant medicine, er, herbalism, help me?"

Granfa shook his head. "I don't want to get your hopes up. It will be years until we figure out any reasonable form of treatment for you. Until then, Personil's the best we can do. But still . . ." The old man's gaze returned to the volume in Victor's hands.

Victor heard a soft gasp. He looked up to see his ma in the doorway, holding one hand to her face. Worry lines framed her mouth. "Victor, what are you doing in here?"

"I wanted to be with Granfa." Victor swept a hand around the empty room.

Her gaze disapproved.

Victor rose and hugged the herbalism book to his chest.

Ma watched him, her brow furrowed.

"I feel like he's here." Victor turned away. It wasn't a total lie, but false enough to make him queasy.

Ma sighed and said, "That's a normal feeling. You don't have to be ashamed."

Fa, cowed by the great Jefferson Eastmore even after the man's death, called from the hallway: "He shouldn't be in there."

Victor shuffled to the couch, set the tome on the coffee table, lay down, and curled up with a pillow. "I just want to nap in here for a while. Could you turn down the light?"

His ma turned and said to his fa, "I don't see any problem with that." She sat on the edge of the sofa. "When you get up, if you're not feeling well enough to drive, Lê Quang can take you to your apartment."

Victor's fa said from the threshold, "I'll ask Chef Meir to make you a snack for later. In case you get hungry."

Cody Sisco

"Thank you," Victor said, letting his head sink into the pillow. He closed his eyes.

His ma squeezed him and then walked away. Her footsteps receded, the lights dimmed, and the door clicked closed. Outside, his parents' voices thrummed, quiet enough that he couldn't make out any of their words. When he heard a car rumble in the driveway, he slid to the floor, crept to the window, and watched his parents drive away.

He found a floor lamp, turned it to half power, and looked around. Something about the desk was wrong. He stepped back, breathed deep, relaxed, and looked again. A MeshTerminal with its vidscreen and type-pad dominated one side. The bust of Admiral Eastmore, his great-granfa, sat at the other corner—

That was it! The bust sat oddly on the desk. Its four-cornered base didn't rest smoothly. Victor lifted the heavy marble head by its jaw. Beneath it lay a single brass key.

When he tried the key in the lock on the file drawer, it turned and opened smoothly, revealing folders labeled in neat block letters. He skimmed each paper in the folders, hoping to find anything that seemed amiss. Most were account statements and orders relating to the running of the estate.

In the back, a folder without a label held a dozen sheets of paper filled with checkboxes, fill-in-the-blanks, and unruly handwriting.

Victor examined the papers more closely, finding medical reports from Oak Knoll Hospital, doctors' notes, test results, and prescriptions from the past six months. However, it was only three months ago, after Oak Knoll had closed, that the papers began to contain the words "heart failure." Three months seemed an inordinate amount of time to obtain a diagnosis, especially when all the best doctors in the nation worked for Granfa Jeff.

He looked through the records again, but nothing else stood out. There must be something, some clue or connection he wasn't seeing clearly. He needed more facts. Perhaps there were more electronic records. He tried the MeshTerminal, but he could only access his own cache, not Granfa's.

Victor sat back and cupped his hand around the data egg in his pocket. He wished he'd gotten the truth on the day Oak Knoll closed, rather than a vague nonexplanation and a locked data egg. Maybe the rest of his family could shed some light on what had happened. He could ask them about it without bringing up the M-word.

Victor went downstairs and found Auntie Circe in the large kitchen, brewing tea. Stainless steel appliances and countertops stretched along one wall, while in the middle of the room sat a large marble-topped island with a sink and electric-induction burners.

"Can I ask you something?"

"Of course." She poured hot water in a mug. "I thought you left with your parents."

"No. I wanted to stay. Auntie, I—I messed up at the funeral."

"Yes, Mother told me about that. Curious . . ." She took a small sip of her tea. "We all understand. Everyone handles grief in his or her own way, and yours . . . happens to be a bit more dramatic."

Victor shook his head. "I forgot my dose this morning. I should have doubled up at least."

"Are you caught up now?"

"I will be in a minute." He ran his hands through his hair and was surprised when they came away with more than several strands. "I know I need to."

"Victor, days like today are difficult for everyone."

"The problem is I'm still thinking about it." He scratched along his jawline. "Isn't it a possibility Granfa was murdered?"

Circe looked into her mug. "It seems beyond the pale to me. We've come a long way since the start of the twentieth century. That kind of corruption . . ." She stumbled a bit over the word and took in another breath. "It's something we've left behind for the most part. Carmichael excepted."

Victor shook his head. "There's something fishy about the timing of it all. Even Granma and Granfa's dogs seemed to start acting strangely when Oak Knoll closed. And didn't you see how he looked at the funeral? What's worse"—as Victor spoke he realized he was thinking more clearly than he had in years—"I get this odd feeling that I wouldn't have noticed anything if I had taken my dose. Maybe they're interfering with my—"

"I know what you're thinking. About coming off your meds. It's a terrible idea. They're protecting you."

"Yes, I know. Protecting me from myself. Protecting everyone else too."

Circe looked at him with a blank face. "Your troubles today came from the fact that you forgot to take your pills. Any changes in your medication schedule must be signed off by a Health Board–licensed physician. And for good reason."

Victor frowned. "But when I looked through Granfa's medical records—"

"You did *what*?" Her eyes narrowed. "Don't let Mother know what you're up to."

"You don't think it's odd it took so long to diagnose heart failure?"

"I don't." A faint smile crept onto her face. "People want medicine to be black-and-white, but the reality is that we're far more complicated organisms than we often realize. And the care we provide is imperfect."

Victor grimaced. She wasn't listening to him. Maybe she was preoccupied by her responsibilities with the business. "Was there an autopsy?" he asked. "Maybe if I read the report . . ."

Circe reached out and placed her hand gently on Victor's shoulder. "I know it helps to talk about your fantasies. But you can't indulge this tendency. Your reclassification appointment is the thirty-first of May, as you well know. You need to show you're in command of your senses. We can't let you go the way of Samuel Miller."

Victor felt a chill climb up his spine and icy fingers stroke his face. "Of course not. I'm trying. I am. I'm going to pull my life together. My job—"

"I'm certain Gene-Us will continue to be a useful outlet for your intellect. Karine speaks highly of you, and, believe me, she can be a powerful ally."

Karine was Victor's boss and an old friend of his aunt's for as long as he could remember. Karine had always treated him with respect but also a frosty formality. He said, "I don't think she likes me."

"That's just her personality. Besides your job, though, Victor, don't forget to nurture your social connections as well. I saw Elena at the funeral. I'm sure you're glad she's back." Circe smiled and drank her tea in several gulps. "Don't miss any more doses, okay?"

Victor nodded. "It's just that it seems like something changed with Granfa around the time he shut Oak Knoll. And he was trying to tell me something."

Circe raised an eyebrow. He had her full attention. "Tell you what?"

"I don't know, but he gave me this." Victor held up the data egg.

Her eyes widened and focused on the black round shape. "What on earth?"

Victor smiled. That was Granma Cynthia's phrase. "A data egg. It hasn't opened."

"He gave this to you? When?"

"The day he closed Oak Knoll."

She placed the mug on the counter. "Oak Knoll was a loss above all others. If only he'd consulted me." She smiled, but it didn't reach her eyes. "Hold onto that, Victor. Keep it with you. Our mementos are precious, none so precious as those given by the departed." She hugged him firmly, then walked away.

Victor lingered in the kitchen after she left. A thought swam just outside the limits of his consciousness. He tried to reel it in, but couldn't. He would take his dose of Personil as soon as he finished sleuthing, but he wasn't looking forward to the dopey, gray, and lethargic feelings that accompanied the medication.

Navigating back to the office upstairs was a tricky prospect with all the lights dimmed, but he couldn't take the chance that his granma would catch him snooping. She would never forgive him for breaking in.

Mounds of furniture blocked his path. Baroque legs of

chairs and tables seemed to stretch out to trip him, and he nearly fell while climbing the padded stairs. He grit his teeth and tiptoed onward.

In Granfa Jeff's study, the medical records continued to whisper to him. There was something he wasn't seeing—if he could just study the pages hard enough, if he could just clear his mind of its fog.

The Personil.

Rather than digging in his bag for one of the capsules, he lay down on the couch and settled his gaze on the herb book. He was tired of living his life in a daze. Maybe it was time to seek out an alternative.

8

Holistic Healing Network Buys Controlling
Stake in Gene-Us Enterprises

OAKLAND & BAYSHORE, 24 February 1991—The Holistic Healing Network (HHN), owned by the Eastmore
family, will buy a controlling stake in Gene-Us Enterprises
for $2.2 billion AUD, taking the gene-sequencing com-
pany private, according to a filing with the AU Corporate
Registry. Circe Eastmore, daughter of HHN's late founder
Jefferson Eastmore, will serve as acting chair and chief of
the merged concern, which will be renamed BioScan Inc.
Ms. Eastmore is quoted by a local MeshNews agent
as saying, "Together as BioScan Inc. we will make use
of the latest genetic sequencing and medical treatment
technologies. We will remain a health-focused enterprise
while also exploring how these technologies can be used
in the enhancement and addiction treatment markets. Our
efforts fall under the umbrella of a new initiative we call
'Evolving Together' that will see us make a multibillion-
AUD investment in new and promising research."

—MeshNews report

Semiautonomous California
24 February 1991

The morning after the funeral Victor woke on the couch in his
granfa's office, tangled in a knitted blanket. Hieu had probably covered him and let him sleep. The man had worshiped

Jefferson and must have absorbed some of his fondness for Victor over the years. There were three kinds of people in the world: those who hated Victor, those who put up with him—he included his parents in this set—and a small group who genuinely seemed to like him: Granfa Jeff, Auntie Circe, Hieu, and Elena.

Victor paged through his granfa's medical records again, some key insight still escaping him. To stop using Personil wasn't enough. He needed something else to jolt his mind into action. A juice might help. Maybe—

A shriek from the doorway set his skin tingling. Granma Cynthia stood there in a padded-silk robe, shivering.

"What are you doing in there?" Her tone iced his skin.

Victor hesitated. He could say he was there because he loved his granfa. But she'd heard his musings on murder and wouldn't believe him.

"Get out!" she commanded. "This instant! How dare you? Jefferson's office . . ." She breathed hard, clutching her robe's neckline.

Victor gathered the medical records into a folder. The book of herbal cures rested nearby. He picked it up and walked to the door.

Granma Cynthia stood tall as he approached. She pointed and said, "Are those Jefferson's? Leave those! You can't rob me like a petty thief."

Victor pushed past her and hurried down the hall. Yesterday had strained their relationship to the breaking point. He'd never been a "good" grandchild, not like Robbie, who always won awards and excelled at touting his own accomplishments. But Victor had never stolen from his own family. It seemed every day he found a lower low to sink to.

"What are you doing?" she asked, following.

Victor rushed into her bedroom and then the master bath. Granma Cynthia gaped and sputtered while he raided her medicine cabinet and searched through pill bottles until he found one labeled Vasistatin—the one Granma Cynthia had said Granfa Jeff made such a show of taking, which seemed out of character for so serious a man. Victor shoved the pill bottle into his pocket next to the data egg. Granma Cynthia tried to block his way, but he slipped past, hurried down the hall, and took the stairs down two at a time.

Granma Cynthia called to him from the railing. "You're out of control, Victor!"

Without stopping, he escaped through the front door and into his car, trying to blot out the sound of her outraged voice as it repeated in his head.

"Please don't let this be a fantasy," Victor whispered to himself as he drove through the exit gate. The past few days had been upsetting and topsy-turvy. He needed his routine back. Even if he was investigating a murder, he still needed the clockwork normalcy of a familiar environment, a daily schedule, and structured work. But he wasn't prepared to dose himself. His brain, although broken, seemed to work better off the medication. The world didn't seem as flat and gray.

Bereavement leave would allow him several more days off, but the last thing he wanted was idle time on his hands. He drove to Gene-Us Enterprises.

The Gene-Us headquarters glinted like a glass and steel centipede curving around itself. He parked in a lot that had been shoehorned into the remnants of an orchard. The boughs of orange trees hung heavy with unpicked fruit. Victor left the herb book and medical records in the car. They would only distract him if they were within arms' reach.

Victor entered the building. His MeshBit pinged to let him know he'd been registered. Karine LaTour, his supervisor, would receive the notification.

Inside, he found chaos. Instead of the usual nose-down calm he so wanted, his fellow employees scampered and shouted. Their giddy voices suggested that a party was underway. Some enterprising coworkers stood on furniture and hung golden paper lanterns, signs of good fortune. A pack of administrative assistants huddled together. Victor heard the words, "titles," "re-organization," and "quarterly," and then they saw him, ducked their heads, and spoke to each other more quietly.

On the reception desk he saw a printed MeshNews article. His family's company, Holistic Healing Network, had bought

Gene-Us, and the newly merged company would be named BioScan. He felt a stab of resentment. The family company was buying his current employer, and no one had said a word to him.

He headed to Karine's office to demand to know what the merger meant for him.

But her office was deserted. Empty drawers poked from their enclosures. Her framed certificates no longer hung on the wall. On her desk, exotic paperweights from far-off places that she liked to show off—volcanic glass from the Kingdom of Hawaii, wooden idols carved by African tribes, beaded animals from South America—were gone.

Victor called Karine on his MeshBit, and to his surprise, she answered.

"Why are you here?" Karine asked.

"Where are you?" Victor spun around, expecting to see her standing behind him wearing her usual mocking smile. But she wasn't there.

Her sigh buzzed in his ear. "I'm moving offices. I thought you would take a few more days off after the funeral, but since you're here, we need to meet. I have an opening at three o'clock. Hang on." There was the sound of muted conversation, and then Karine said, "Don't bother with your analytics today. The sample preparation staff are at a retraining, and we need you to cover for them. You should be able to handle it."

A few seconds later, his MeshBit buzzed. The message from BioScan Operations ordered him to report to the sample preparation room on the second floor for a temporary work assignment.

Victor trudged to a room crowded with bins holding packages mailed in from all over the American Union. The procedures for preparing mailed cheek-swab DNA samples for replication were straightforward, basic manual labor that anyone who could follow a checklist could do.

Sometime later Sarita, one of the office administrators, walked into the sample preparation room and approached Victor. She flitted in several directions at once—her frizzed hair, nervous hands, luminous eyes, and lips painted the deep red of poison berries all vibrated at asynchronous frequencies.

Sarita eyed him gleefully. "Is this your new role? Filling the machines with spit?"

Victor refused to meet her gaze. "It's temporary."

"Sure it is." She sidled closer. "Did you hear? Karine got a promotion. Second chief!" Sarita smirked. "You know what that means?"

Victor pulled on a set of synthsilk gloves to avoid contaminating the DNA sequencing machine. "She reports to my auntie Circe now," he said, stating the obvious.

"*And* she'll pass you off like a hot potato. She's meeting with each of her reports this afternoon." Her breathiness implied something sinister.

"Okay," he said, shaking his head to himself. Sarita could have been sucking up to curry favor with the nephew of the new chief, but scorn for a Broken Mirror prevented her.

She clucked at him. "Did you know about this? The acquisition?"

Apart from Oak Knoll Hospital, the Holistic Healing Network had always been a vague, nebulous entity that he heard about in pieces and never really understood. No one could see the shape of the whole elephant from just one of its parts. But someone in the family could have—should have—kept him more informed. He would have to ask Circe about it.

"Of course," he lied.

"Yeah, right, like your family would bother telling *you*. I bet she fires you today." Sarita flounced away to infect someone else with her gossip.

Victor told himself not to be concerned with her insinuations. He worked through the day's batch of samples.

In the early afternoon, while he waited in line for a buffet lunch, merger speculation and gossip found Victor again. A dark-haired young man wearing a sky-blue Facilities jumpsuit grabbed him by the shoulder and said, "Can you believe it? They might move the headquarters here."

The proposition was unlikely, and obviously so, to anyone with a working brain. Because of marketing and government relations, the Holistic Healing Network had always been headquartered in Europe, and Jefferson had traveled back and forth frequently. Why would BioScan under Circe do it differently?

"You really think so?" Victor asked. Pretending to ask stupid questions always helped him avoid trouble.

The Facilities guy said, "I don't know. We've got the room to expand—we'd just have to rip out that dead orchard next door. I bet we'll all get raises too."

"I'm sure."

"Come on, this is exciting. Don't give me that Broken Mirror face."

Victor flinched. He tried so hard to blend in, but he didn't fit anywhere. Maybe the Safe Places program had plastered his picture in the facilities' workspaces with a warning: "Watch out for the freak show with broken mirror neurons in his brain." The lunch tray seemed to weigh a ton.

Wait, Victor thought. The guy had smiled, but not in a cruel way. "Broken Mirror face" was just something people said, wasn't it?

Victor lowered his head, letting his hair fall forward, smiling even though he felt like knocking the guy's jaw loose. He laughed loudly and said in a false baritone, "Good one!"

"That's better." The guy patted Victor's rear end.

Victor got his food and found a seat by himself in a seldom-frequented corner of the canteen. He picked through his food, a bland composition of farro, salmon, and avocado. Thinking about his granfa's death, he knew he should let the matter drop. His suspicions were a manifestation of his condition, everyone said so, and probably the result of going off his medication. He'd take one more look at Jefferson's medical records this evening, and then he would stop. He'd take his dose, and everything would go back to normal.

An hour later, when he was between two batches of samples, his MeshBit chimed. It was time for his meeting with Karine.

The tang of facial cream and floral perfume greeted him at the threshold to Karine's office. She stood and waved him in. Taller than Victor by several centimeters, Karine had a moon face and a stiff and wispy corona of auburn hair. She lined her eyes with black pencil. The image of a frill-necked lizard popped into Victor's mind.

They sat down. "You probably heard that, as of today, I am second chief for the company," Karine said. "We need to talk about your role."

Victor exhaled slowly, sure that she was about to fire him.

"As BioScan, we've started thinking bigger and bolder. You're going to work on a special project for me."

Victor sat up. She appeared to be serious. "What kind of project?"

"A gene-to-pathology mapping program." She threw the words at him, like tossing a treat to a dog—perhaps expecting some sort of excited response. Victor waited for her to explain in more detail.

She rested her forearms on her farmed-crystal desk blotter. "We're building a database that correlates clinical data with the genomes of our patients. That means we need new clinical procedures; better sequencers; enhanced data-management, storage, and analytical capabilities; and a new operations and marketing organization to sell the data to research groups. I'm putting a team in place to build this new business. You'd lead part of the team, and you'd report directly to me."

A promotion? That was the last thing he'd expected.

Karine tilted her head in confusion. "Well, what do you say?"

"I'm not qualified for it." Why would she offer him such a significant position? More importantly, how did Karine already know so much about the future direction of the company?

"I've known you a long time, Victor. I've seen your capabilities. We're underutilizing your talents. And you are singularly suited for this role."

Victor didn't like the sound of that. "How?" he asked.

"The new initiative will have several focus clusters. The most important will be neurological disorders, including mirror resonance syndrome and addiction."

Victor's mouth dropped open. "The two of those together? That's ridiculous."

"Do you think so? Your first priority should be to get up to speed with our research." Karine leaned forward with her palms up as if she were holding something in each one. "Both addiction and your condition have related neurological mechanisms: a heightened susceptibility to positive feedback loops and above-average cognitive inertia. Yours happens to have a genetic origin. What we're finding is that addiction to certain types of drugs can change how genes are expressed in the brain, possibly due to prions that act like a cellular contagion and alter the shape of proteins throughout addicts' neural networks. The resonance in addicts' brains is similar to mirror resonance in yours."

Victor understood what she was saying. Granfa Jeff had referred to the plasticity of his brain too. But drugs that could rewire brain chemistry? He felt bile rise in his throat. She was lumping together drug addicts and people with MRS in a dregs-of-society research program. It was worse than being ignored.

"I need you to work on the sequencing plan in support of the lab and clinic research teams," she continued. "Figure out what data they will want from us and how we can deliver it. There will also be a ceremonial role. You'll need to hone your public speaking skills and work with some pretty senior people in the organization and in government, so that will be a challenge. That's what coaching is for. But you have the face for it—remember, dissonant micro-expressions aren't a problem when you're speaking to a crowd of people."

"I don't know," he said, unsure of what to make of her newfound confidence in him.

"Victor, this project is going to revolutionize biomedical research. We are talking about the sequencing of millions of patients' genetic codes and tying that to detailed information about their medical histories. Researchers will use this data for decades to understand why some people get sick and others don't, how genetic defects arise and get passed on, how to create targeted medical treatments. This is the future of health care, and you'll get to be a part of it."

Karine looked at him with focused intensity. Could she really have that much faith in his abilities?

Victor sat up and puffed out his chest, though he didn't feel he deserved her confidence in him. "Why me?"

"Isn't it obvious?" she asked. "You're talented. Our best data jockey by far. More than that, you are the nephew of our chief, heir to a fortune that owns a controlling interest in this company, *and* a high-profile mirror resonance patient. In other words, a unique asset, and I would be a terrible manager if I didn't take advantage of it."

Victor imagined her jaw unhinging to swallow him, like a giant python devouring a flightless bird. He remained silent. The scope of the project impressed him. A large-scale comparison of genomics and pathology could change medicine as completely as had the sequencing of the human genome and the cure for cancer.

He stared at a metal vent on the ceiling and considered his options. Karine was describing a great opportunity, but he didn't like the feeling of being manipulated.

She cleared her throat. "You'll need to decide quickly. I suppose an immediate answer isn't necessary, but I can't really see there's much of a choice for you. Things are changing, Victor. You need to keep up."

She rose and brushed her hands over the arms of her aquamarine synthsilk suit as if some odious substance had settled on her in the past few minutes. "Now, I've spoken to Circe and we agree on several points. You need to take your medication, drop this silly fantasy about Jefferson's death, and start seeing a therapist again. Agreed? We can't afford to take any chances with your mental health."

A lump formed in Victor's throat. She'd been discussing him with his family. Losing his grip on reality, they must have said, poor thing, needs to get back on his pills. How disappointed Dr. Tammet would be if she knew how foolishly he'd been acting, indulging in dark fantasies and scandalizing his family.

Karine was right. This was his opportunity to put the past behind him, and he had to take it. But that would mean going back on Personil, losing his newfound clarity of mind.

Karine was waiting for him to answer.

"Agreed," he said. He could take a half-dose, intermittently, and probably get away with it. Still, it felt like a loss to agree to her terms. Victor closed his eyes and visualized Granfa Jeff's casket, imagining the click the lid made as he shut it tight.

"Good." Karine's real leather boots clicked on the floor as she walked to the door. "There's one more thing." He opened his eyes. She said, "Circe wants to speak with you. Now. She's expecting a vidfeed. You can use mine."

When she left, the air in the room smelled less sickly sweet and he breathed easier.

Victor put his MeshBit on Karine's ident-pad. His aunt's face appeared on the vidscreen.

"About the merger," Circe said, and then paused. She laid a hand on her neck. "I am sorry we couldn't chat about it before."

"Karine told me about the promotion."

"Yes. She's got everything well in hand." Circe pushed a stray curling rope of dark hair further up her mound of ringlets. "Your leadership . . . Victor, patients around the world will thank you. We may even be able to find a cure."

Victor uttered a silent prayer that he'd be able to live up to her expectations and put his fantasies to rest.

9

Friends, family, and even colleagues laughed at me when I told them I was planning to locate the Holistic Healing Network's headquarters in Oakland & Bayshore. At the time the West was synonymous with doom, grand ambitions half-realized, and fools' follies. Historical examples of this myth abounded: the mysterious abandonment of the Spanish missions, Powell's failed expedition to map the West, the disappearance of the Donner party, the collapse of the St. Francis Dam, and on and on.

I wanted to create a countertruth. To show that science, technology, and a little bit of luck could open a new age of development. The simultaneous rise of Oakland & Bayshore and the fortunes of my firm marked a turning point in Semi-autonomous California's history. The nation slowly grew from a fertile testing ground to a real participant on the A.U. stage.

—Jefferson Eastmore's *The Wheel of Progress* (1989)

Semiautonomous California
24 February 1991

After work Victor drove to his box-shaped apartment on Alameda Island, went inside, breathed stale air, and opened a few windows to let in a moist breeze. Granfa Jeff's medical records sat on a side table next to his couch. They exerted a pull that he resisted by picking up the herbalism book and taking it into the kitchen. He flipped through the book, looking for an entry on black cardamom, the herb that Ric from the juice shop said his brother always asked for. Each turn of the page revealed dense descriptions of growing seasons, harvesting methods, and possible health effects. Victor had never heard of most of the herbs in the book.

The entry on cardamom—the run-of-the-mill kind—was disappointingly brief and said nothing about a black variety. The scientific name, *Elettaria cardamomum*, appeared in ornate script at the top of the page, and the line beneath indicated in smaller block letters that the plant was part of Zingberaceae, the ginger family. A drawing showed a stalk composed of round pods and flanking leaves. Under the heading "Uses," only two words were written: "calming" and "exorcism."

Victor flipped the pages in frustration and found an inscription inside the back cover, written in a different handwriting than the rest of the text. It read, "Jefferson: This reference belongs to your family. I have been a faithful student. May nature's bounty help you find peace at the end of your journey. Come by the store anytime. Respectfully, Ming Pearl."

Victor paced in his living room, clutching the book in both hands. His thoughts raced like a jet plane about to take flight. Who the hell was Ming Pearl? What did she know about Granfa Jeff?

His doorbell chimed. He put the book down and moved to the door. He opened it a crack. Elena pushed through, and he jumped back.

"How did you find me?" Victor asked. "My address is unlisted."

"Not to your parents. I want to talk."

"Fine." He closed the door behind her.

She looked at his furniture, a collection he'd selected at random from a Mesh catalog to shortcut what would have been many hours of deliberation. She inspected the few colorful abstract paintings that he used for meditation and ran her hands over the back of his dun-colored sofa as if it were a large, docile pet.

Elena moved on, disappearing down the hall into the bathroom and then reemerging a moment later, returning to the living room, eyes flicking around as if she were deciding whether to rent the place. She fidgeted with the couch pillows, not meeting his gaze. "Are you still on your medication?" Elena asked.

"Of course," he answered, more loudly than he'd intended. "It's mandatory."

"You can't hide anything from me, Victor." She pointed at his face. "Your eyes go blank when you lie."

"I'm adjusting my dosing schedule. In fact, I was just about to take the next one. You can watch if you want."

A flicker of embarrassment moved across her face—a creased brow, a twitch in her lips. "Sure, I guess."

Victor retrieved the pill bottle from his medicine box in the bathroom and returned, wondering why she wasn't yelling at him for the way he'd treated her when she'd moved to the Republic of Texas. She had always confronted problems directly. He led her by the elbow into the kitchen. The faucet squeaked when he ran it, filling one-third of a glass. He held up the Personil pill so she could see it. Then he popped it in his mouth, making a show of washing it down with gulps of water.

"Satisfied?" he asked.

Elena nodded.

He led her back through the living room, stopping next to the couch at the threshold of the foyer. "Why are you back in SeCa?"

"It seemed like the right thing to do," she said, not meeting his eyes.

"How long are you here?"

Her fingers dipped into the gap between the couch's back cushions, a gesture he found strange and oddly erotic. "I haven't decided." The anxiety and falsehood written in her knotted brow were clear.

"You're not very good at hiding things from me either. Something's going on with you."

Elena pressed her lips together. "I'm here to help you, Victor—that's all. You look like you're hanging by a thread."

He snorted. "What's new about that?"

"They're going to lock you up one day for no good reason."

"I can think of a few perfectly good reasons."

She frowned. "Alik was an accident."

He glanced down at his feet. "You don't need to make excuses for me."

"Be happy someone is on your side." She took a step closer.

Victor felt backed into a corner even though he stood in the middle of the room.

A feeling passed back and forth between them, a desperate longing, not anything sexual—it was a desire to be acknowledged, to be valued, to be surprised by someone's capacity to love unconditionally. They'd been crucial partners during difficult times, and a bond like that could withstand years apart and mountains of resentment. If only they could let each other admit it.

"It's time for my meditation," he said, looking at the door.

Elena stiffened. "You're pushing me away."

Victor felt her disapproval like a punch in the gut. "I don't know what you want, Elena, but I can't deal with it right now. Someone may have murdered Granfa Jeff, and everyone is pressuring me to take my stupid pills and forget about it. I'm barely holding it together, and I haven't had a good cry about my granfa dying because it's all jumbled in my head, and *you're not helping!*"

Elena's eyes softened, but there was something cold in them as well. "I'll go. But you're going to need me." She left after one more glance around.

Victor bounded to the kitchen, leaned over the sink, and spit out the softening pill. Everyone kept telling him what to do. He was tired of it. His suspicions—about Granfa Jeff, about Elena, and about his own decline—throbbed in his head.

In the living room, he looked at the herbalism book again. Ming Pearl, whoever she was, might be able to help him put his suspicions to rest, or at least help him find some black cardamom. With that name, she must live in Little Asia, a virtually lawless pocket of SeCa created by the Refugee Act. That was the place to look.

Cody Sisco

10

Victor Eastmore was diagnosed with mirror neuron synaptic transmission and excitatory resonance syndrome in June 1979. That was the previous, longer name of the syndrome, before the third revision of the guidelines changed everything. I was hired by the family to help Victor understand and cope with his condition, which, I might add, remains poorly understood by the biomedical community, in part because of the regulatory regime put in place after the Carmichael incident.

One of Victor's most debilitating cognitive traps was his tendency to fixate on a mistake or misunderstanding, creating a spiral of related emotions, memories, and physical sensations. This would lead to blankness, which I interpreted as a nullification of self. What a neurotypical person might experience as a brief flash of jealousy, confusion, or anger was for Victor a limbo-like and time-suspended experience of pervasive negativity. Blankness would then come as a relief, an autonomic self-preservation mechanism to counteract self-destructive thoughts and feelings. His brain was at war with itself, and I was charged with helping keep the peace.

—Statement by Dr. Laura Tammet, the Eastmore family's neuroscience advisor (1998)

Semiautonomous California
25 February 1991

The next morning Victor woke around five and couldn't get back to sleep. He paced his apartment, waiting for dawn, as Granfa Jeff's face appeared everywhere he looked: on a blank wall, in the toilet bowl, in a shadow cast by the leaves of a small potted ficus next to his living room window. His chest felt empty and sore at the same time. The one person who'd believed in Victor was gone and had left only confusion in his wake.

The herb book sat on his couch, opened to the inscription written by Ming Pearl, someone who must have known Granfa Jeff and who'd probably seen him more recently than Victor had. He couldn't stand the questions ringing in his head, most of all, *Where's my cure?*

Around eight a.m. Victor sent Karine and Circe a message saying he'd be at the university reading about gene expression and that he'd be at work later. As he drove up the spiraling ramp of the Trans-Bayshore Rail Depot parking structure, he reminded himself that he wasn't investigating a murder. He was simply going to find an herbal replacement for Personil—no, he'd have to call it a complement if he were asked—from someone who happened to have met his granfa near the end of his life. An innocent excursion.

Victor parked in a stall on the tenth floor and walked to the elevator. A tidy grid of warehouses, commercial buildings, and apartments surrounded the parking structure on three sides. On the fourth, toward the bay, dozens of rail lines threaded through a labyrinthine complex of train platforms, food markets, restaurants, and shops. Victor rode the elevator down and made his way to the westbound platform.

Trade had propelled Oakland & Bayshore into its preeminent position as the largest city in Semiautonomous California. The city was also the nation's capital and main port. Two million souls were packed into 150 square kilometers running up and down the flatlands and hills on the east side of the bay. Many transit lines converged at the rail depot, making for a daily crush of passengers, but in public spaces civility was valued as much as efficiency, and no one looked twice at Victor.

The train was not the sleek European-built model he'd expected, but an older one, perhaps transferred from the Southeastern Confederacy many decades ago and continually refurbished. Its metal looked rusted and almost worn through in places. He pressed himself into the last compartment. The train shuddered to life.

As the train mounted the Bayshore Bridge, a concrete causeway that funneled passengers to and from San Francisco's decrepit waterfront, Victor peered out the window at the Golden Gate Strait. A few yachts were headed out to sea through a narrow water gap in the steep hills along the coast. Barely seaworthy fishing boats with an early morning catch were entering the bay and tacking south toward the San Francisco peninsula, while larger cargo ships headed for Oakland & Bayshore's port. Two steamers were being towed to immigrant processing centers on Angel Island, named for those unfortunate enough to arrive in poor health and who had never made it to the mainland. The island gave Victor the creeps, but he supposed that it represented salvation to the refugees fleeing conflict and poisoned lands in Asia.

On the San Francisco–Little Asia peninsula, wrecked hilltop buildings served as a reminder of the earthquake that had struck the growing town just two decades after the 1829 Gold Rush. A few crumbling mansions perched on the city's hills, overlooking refugee slums.

Inside the train, odors of sweat, filth, and urine forced Victor to breathe through his mouth. Unions had successfully barred civilian road traffic on the bridge, reserving adjacent automobile lanes for emergency vehicles and freight trucks, so anyone who wanted to travel to the peninsula had to take the train. Proper paperwork was only necessary for the return journey. Victor guessed the passengers around him included aid workers, tradesmen, and more than a few unsavory lowlifes peddling drugs to communities that couldn't afford the harm they caused.

Victor wondered if Karine and Circe would direct the company's resources to places like Little Asia or if they would focus only on the well-heeled patients in Oakland & Bayshore. He knew so little about the company. His curiosity, long slumbering, seemed to be awakening, and the world around him, which had seemed so orderly and understandable, was becoming something he no longer recognized.

The train pulled into the terminal, which was infested with beggars, buskers, harvesters of trash—both human and their rodent brethren—and corrupt police looking to shake down unsuspecting travelers. Victor dodged several pickpockets and hustlers, never slackening his quick pace, and entered SeCa's stinking underbelly, a human wilderness ravaged by refugee gangs and private security forces.

A tall, wooden, red-and-gold gate marked the entrance to Little Asia, which in reality could be said to occupy the entire San Francisco peninsula. Victor passed beneath the gate. Signs protruded from buildings, blasting swaths of neon. Doors hanging from their hinges beckoned people into shops where thrill-seeking tourists often disappeared—so said the dark Mesh. Sometimes they reappeared missing a kidney, a lung, or other essential organs, if non–Mesh-licensed sources of news could be trusted. Victor was having trouble believing anything these days and doubted himself most of all.

Victor recalled the worst rumors about Little Asia, wondering if they could be true. Feral cats and wild dogs were said to be scarce because they were trapped and fed into bioreactors, harvested for their animal protein. It was cheaper to pick ingredients off the streets than to synthesize them. The practice was illegal but supposedly permitted to flourish. It helped maintain a steady supply of black-market narcotics. Hawkers called out the names of stimulants, tailored euphorics, and other drugs. One man, his face a mass of sagging wrinkles and a wispy beard, repeated the word "aura" again and again, stringing the words in an unbroken wail.

Victor pushed through the crowds, at one point stepping off the sidewalk into a filthy gutter to avoid people yelling in front of a salesman's kiosk. He found a shop that sold spices but was hustled out the door as soon as he mentioned mirror resonance syndrome. When he found another shop with many dried herbs but no black cardamom, he explained that he was looking for Ming Pearl. The owner, a young Chinese man around Victor's age, nodded gravely, and said, "Front Street, left two blocks. Make sure you bring motas. MeshPay no good here."

Cody Sisco

Victor thanked him and moved on. He hadn't thought about the local black-market currency. Every shop in Oakland & Bayshore used the MeshPay system. Not so here. He needed to find a moneychanger.

A heavily graffitied hut down the street had the motas and MeshPay logos on its sign. Victor walked up to the barred window and asked for 100 AUD worth of motas.

A tall man with broad shoulders and a wide, handsome face, likely Japanese, took Victor's bills. "Twenty percent fee," the man said.

"Fine."

The man pushed an ident-pad through a metal slit, and Victor held his MeshBit above it, squeezing to indicate he approved the transaction. The device chimed, and the man slid him twelve black coins with embedded gold lettering.

Victor pushed them into his pocket. The receipt the man handed him indicated that he had purchased ceramics rather than coins.

Shouting. Behind him. Victor turned. Across the street, a few thugs took turns punching a middle-aged man in the gut, holding him by his ripped suit jacket. One of the thugs noticed Victor, signaled his friends to ease up, and pointed at him.

Victor froze, hoping that he'd only imagined them taking an interest in him. His mind could be misinterpreting, projecting his fears onto the situation. But his gut told him to run.

He walked quickly. Then, hearing the thudding footsteps of the thugs behind him, he started to run. He reached a corner and almost knocked over a short old lady as he pushed past her. A bicyclist yelled and swerved around him as he darted across the street. He chanced a look behind him. The thugs turned the corner and spotted him again.

Victor bolted inside a small grocery packed with racks of vegetables and bulk grains. He trotted down the aisle, found a door to the back, and bumped into a teenage girl who pressed herself against the wall of goods to let him pass. He emerged into an alley and ran smack into someone who grabbed him and shoved him against the wall.

Two people, a man and a woman, stood in front of him. The olive-skinned man who had grabbed him had spiky black hair. The woman had skin the same color as Auntie Circe's, and her hair was tied tautly in a bun. Both appeared to be around Victor's age or a little older. They had the muscles and skin tone of people who sweat often.

The gang of thugs rounded the corner and hesitated when they saw Victor wasn't alone. The spiky-haired man pulled a black stunstick with a red glowing tip from a waist holster and pointed. The thugs quickly retreated the way they'd come.

"Thanks," Victor said.

The woman sighed and said to her companion, "This was not our fault." She sounded foreign, European maybe.

"Don't matter. What now?" He jerked his head toward Victor.

"Shhh," she said. "Let's just go."

They jogged to the alley's entrance. Victor followed, but when he turned the corner, they were gone.

Victor paused, trying to recover his breath and get his bearings. His face felt warm. The chase had got his blood pumping. The street was filled with honking vehicles and some kind of demonstration between two groups of people with signs in Chinese.

Victor spotted a young woman with smart-looking glasses and a book bag standing by herself. He put on his biggest smile and approached her. "Excuse me. I'm looking for Ming Pearl's shop on Front Street. Do you know which way it is?"

She frowned. "You're not a cop, are you?"

Victor laughed. "No one's asked me that before."

The young woman smiled. "Of course I know Pearl. She has the best there is."

"Where can I find her?"

She looked him up and down. "The door with the lotus flower halfway down the block. Good luck, handsome."

Victor followed the young woman's directions to Front Street and came across a heavy door. Its large engraved lotus flower looked weathered and beaten, like someone had taken an axe to it. He entered. Inside the shop, the noise from the street was muffled. Ancient, dusty incandescent light bulbs

Cody Sisco

hung from a cord that snaked upward into shadows. A dark and narrow aisle between towering lacquer-red bins extended toward the back of the store. Victor shuffled into the dim and stale cavern, careful not to nudge any of the precariously stacked inventory.

He approached a low desk, where a small middle-aged woman sat using an inkstick to mark a large ledger with intricate calligraphy. She wore a forest-green blazer dotted with a bright red poinsettia pattern.

Black hair like burnt steel wool haloed her head. A pair of reading glasses threatened to fall from the tip of her nose.

She said a few words in Chinese. When Victor didn't answer, she looked up. "You want traditional medicine?" she asked.

Victor nodded.

She returned her attention to her ledger and spoke with her face pointed at the desk. "You desperate. Non-Asians always desperate."

"I need help. I want to stop taking Personil."

She looked up and studied him. Her lips twitched. Judging by her unlined face she could have been anywhere between forty and seventy years old. Lowering her head again, she continued making the strange marks.

Victor said, "I can pay you."

"You want something, you wait," she said, then ignored him again.

Victor explored the shop for several long minutes and then returned to the desk. The woman wasn't moving. Her face hovered over her books; her eyes were closed, as if meditating. While he watched, she opened her eyes and stood.

"They tell me I may help you," she said.

"They?"

The herbalist leaned forward and looked at him with wide bulging eyes. "My ancestor ghosts."

"I don't know—"

She doubled over, laughing. Her lungs rattled from the strength of her hooting. "You think I'm some dumb schmuck? I was consulting my conscience." She stood up and wiped her eyes. "My name is Pearl."

"I'm Victor."

"Yes, I know, but Jefferson made it sound like you . . ." Pearl cleared her throat. All traces of her accent had vanished. "I didn't expect you so soon. It's been a bad week. The last person with MRS I tried to help was reclassified. In a single day, she went from Three to One. I think she's in the Humboldt facility, not a nice one, I hear. I'm not sure I can help you, but I'll try."

"I'm looking for black cardamom," Victor said.

"Useless!" A hint of her accent returned. "Good only for cooking. I have something else for you."

Pearl rummaged through the wooden cubbies lining the wall behind her desk. They lacked any sort of labeling scheme.

She turned, and her hand opened to reveal a little sachet of silk. She plopped it into a shallow ceramic bowl on her desk. "Fumewort. Don't burn it. The combustion byproducts cause cancer—not that we need to worry about that anymore. Still, don't burn. I'll show you how to make a tincture."

She came out from behind the desk and moved past him in short shuffling steps, her wispy hair nearly brushing his chin. She left behind a charred, woodsy smell. He picked up the sachet and followed her. Further into the back of her domain were several tables loaded with all kinds of envelopes, pouches, and boxes.

Along one wall stood a counter piled with brown glass bottles, labeled in Chinese. From a tray Pearl plucked a pipette similar to those Victor had used in his university's laboratory. She used it to suck a clear liquid from a jar and squirt the liquid into a small glass vial. She extended her hand and demanded the pouch from him. She pinched a few brown and flaky pieces of fumewort and dropped them into the liquid. Then she added water from the tap.

"Twenty milliliters pure alcohol and one hundred milliliters water, roughly. Add one gram of the herb. Wait at least one hour. Stable at room temperature. Drink the whole thing, though you might want to mix it with fruit juice. It's like fire going down."

"What does it do?"

"Calms the mind. Anytime you feel panic, drink."

"This is all I brought." Victor held out the black coins.

Pearl looked at the coins but didn't take them. "I've already been paid."

Victor stuffed the sachet and vials into his pocket. Could a few flaky herbs really help him?

Pearl said, "I'll see you again soon."

"You seem sure that I'll come back."

Pearl smiled. "Won't you?"

"I know you knew Jefferson Eastmore, my grandfather."

"Of course I did. That's why you're here."

"Yes, but wait. What you said earlier: you didn't expect to see me so soon. Does that mean . . .?"

"Jefferson told me you'd be skeptical."

Victor crossed his arms. "How did you know him?"

She looked up at him, tilting her head. "He didn't tell you? He said he would."

"He didn't tell me anything!"

Pearl looked away. "The fumewort should keep you out of trouble. You know, you're not the only one seeking answers, my friend. There are others. Come see me again. We'll talk more."

"What aren't you telling me?"

"Jefferson asked me to help you, and I will, but on my terms. Come back later," Pearl said.

"Help me how? What did he say?"

She seemed resolved not to speak. Victor wanted to grab her blazer lapels and shake the truth out of her.

I can't let myself think that way.

Victor left the shop in a hurry. Why would Granfa Jeff ask an herbalist to help Victor? He'd always challenged Dr. Tammet when her treatments veered toward the experimental and holistic. Did he have a change of heart about alternative therapies?

The mystery pulled at Victor—the same pull he recognized from past slides into blankspace, a precarious feeling. He couldn't trust himself. He needed to stay on the narrow path of sanity. He wasn't going to see Pearl again.

He nearly bumped into a table on the sidewalk crammed full of little trinkets, pieces of jewelry, and slips of paper rolled into tiny scrolls. One jade figure caught his eye, and he picked it up and paid for it with two of his motas. A perfect present for Elena. She was right. He *had* pushed her away. Now it was up to him to bring them closer together again.

Victor returned without incident to the safer side of the bay, retrieved his car from the parking structure, and drove home. Back in his neighborhood, he walked to the Freshly Juice shop and bought a simple carrot-based concoction rich in beta-carotene and antioxidants, and stopped at a general store for a bottle of the strongest, purest alcohol he could find.

Thank the Laws Class Threes are allowed to buy alcohol.

At home, he made a batch of twelve tinctures and waited, sitting on his living room floor, meditating to regain his calm after a tumultuous day. The painting on the wall undulated, an impressionistic rendering of a galaxy full of colorful stars. His eyes unfocused. Whenever the vaguest hint of blankspace intruded, he pushed it out of his consciousness. A few times in his life, the run-up to a blank episode had been accompanied by a wave of euphoria, a feeling so powerful, so positive, he almost wanted to court the blankness, but he feared it meant his mind was deteriorating, and more often the blankness was just blank.

His MeshBit timer pinged. Victor got up, went to the kitchen, poured the fumewort tincture into the juice bulb aperture, and held his thumb over the opening while he sloshed the mixture.

He drank the whole thing in several gulps.

It tasted sweet and umami. Only the subtlest hints of earth and alcohol cut through the familiar taste of carrot juice.

Victor scanned his mind and body. The beating of his heart and his breath felt characteristically uneven. He paced, pushing away the suspicion that Pearl had tricked him. When his gaze fell on the file of medical records on his coffee table, he retreated to the kitchen. He heated a prepared meal and ate it quickly, burning the roof of his mouth.

It was past noon. He couldn't stay in his apartment freaking out over nothing. Victor drove to the Gene-Us campus and hurried across the parking lot, entering through a side-door shortcut near his office. He sat at his desk, adjusting the brightness on the array of vidscreens in front of him, fully intending to spend the next few hours diving into the work that had piled up in his absence.

A jagged line traced the usage of computing resources for a large batch of proto-cancer gene screenings. He looked at reports on the gene sequencers' performance, including error rates in the sequencing flow, idle processing capacity in the Gene-Us computer network, and bottlenecks in the transfer of data from the sequencing machines to the Bose-Drive storage rooms. He'd seen outputs like these hundreds of times before, but it felt like he was seeing the data for the first time. He pulled up another log containing thousands of lines of code and looked for anomalies. In a flash, he understood where a subunit of the algorithm was looping, getting stuck on itself as it churned through millions of sequenced base pairs, filling the log with junk data interspersed with the good.

Sweat formed in his armpits, and he wiped his forehead. He made edits on the fly, breaking the department protocol of cross-checking changes with another analyst, and reran the test. The loops had disappeared. The updated algorithm resulted in a 23 percent efficiency gain.

The fair-haired, pink-skinned male analyst next to him wheeled his chair over and asked, "What are you hooting about?"

Victor pointed to the screen. "This took me less than five minutes."

The analyst cocked his head, reading. Then his lips parted in a broad smile, showing slightly yellowed teeth. "You're kidding me. Send me your log."

Victor swiped the records into the analyst's queue. A minute or so later, his colleague whistled. "That's incredible. Can I get you to look at something I've been working on?"

Victor wheeled over and watched a coding matrix rise on the vidscreen.

The analyst said, "I know there's a mismatch in here, but I—"

"There," Victor said, gently moving the analyst's hand off the touchpad and zooming in with his fingers. "I'll bet it's keyed off the wrong reference sequence. Check the library files from the Human Genome Initiative's feed. They might have updated them without telling us."

The analyst grabbed Victor's arm as if to verify he was really there. "What's got into you?"

Victor shrugged and smiled. "I just see it."

"You got laid or something, didn't you?"

Victor blushed. "That's my secret," he said, glancing at his desk drawer where he'd hidden a handful of fumewort vials. He didn't credit the herb for his new efficiency, not entirely. The Personil was also clearing from his system, allowing his thoughts to speed up to their natural potential.

That night at home, Victor looked over Granfa Jeff's medical records again.

He noticed something odd right away, something he'd missed before. The papers from the first three months listed symptoms in detail and included multiple results from over a dozen tests. But after that, the paper trail thinned out. From September onward, there were no new prescriptions, only a few neatly typed notes, and barely any tests—all at a time when his granfa's condition must have been progressively worsening. It was as if both his grandfather and the doctor had given up.

Victor sat back in his sofa and tried to imagine a scenario to explain the records. The only treatment Jefferson had received during his final months was a prescription for Vasistatin. Surely there were more invasive treatments available as well. Why hadn't he turned to those?

Maybe his granfa had stopped fighting the disease. That wasn't like him—Granfa Jeff was the definition of take-charge-and-do-it tenacity—but maybe his illness had taken such a toll on him that he'd welcomed the end. Or maybe dementia had taken hold, and he wasn't able to plan his own treatment. But if either of those was the case, the doctors would have pushed treatment on him.

Victor rifled through each of the papers again. Prior to Oak Knoll Hospital closing, a broad battery of tests for Jefferson had been ordered, and the results were thoroughly documented, some coming back with values well outside

Cody Sisco

normal ranges, including hair loss, mouth ulceration, and kidney ailments.

After Oak Knoll closed, the number of tests diminished, and all came back within normal ranges, except those related to heart failure: blood tests for electrolytes and creatinine, and electrocardiogram and angiogram measurements. Pre- and post-closure of the hospital, the results were staggeringly different. If not for the patient's name, Victor would have said the records were for different patients.

He looked again at the post-closure results. They looked too perfect, too spot-on.

The records made after Oak Knoll closed were lies.

11

Another bad dream. I walked through a hospital full of comatose patients. I followed a nurse as she stepped up to a bed, checked on the patient's vital signs, shook her head, and moved to the next. Her sighs echoed through the rooms and corridors until the sounds seemed alive, malignant, taunting the injured sleeping who were calling out for help in their dreams.

Somehow it dawned on me that I was responsible. Each patient was half-dead because of something I'd done.

Then they started waking up, their vengeful and hungry eyes popping open. They were illogically frenzied. They knew me, their eyes found me, and all they wanted was revenge.

—Victor Eastmore's dreambook

Semiautonomous California
26 February 1991

Around ten a.m. Victor hurried through the open plaza of the Semiautonomous California National University. Lining the plaza were eight pillars, each five meters tall and topped with a huge bust of one of the architects of the Repartition process that created SeCa and the other eight nations of the American Union.

Victor found Elena leaning against the base of Jefferson Eastmore's pillar. "Thanks for meeting me," he said. "This is important."

She scowled at him and didn't say anything.

Victor looked up at Granfa Jeff's stone face. Two gray slugs for eyebrows, his nose a blunt nubbin, and eyes painted to stare at the Golden Gate Strait. Victor wondered if Elena had purposefully chosen to stand there to unnerve him.

She took a wary step forward and wrinkled her nose. "When was the last time you showered?"

"What? Doesn't matter. Come on." He started off toward the Medical Sciences Building. "The lab isn't as busy during lunch hour," he called over his shoulder.

"Wait," Elena said.

Victor turned. She hadn't moved.

"I'll help you with whatever you have planned," she said, "but we need to talk first."

He walked back to her. "I know you think I'm obsessing. But the whole thing stinks. The hospital closing. How his face looked. You saw: he'd aged *years*. Heart failure doesn't act that fast. And the records don't add up. It's like they're for two different people."

Elena shook her head and held up a hand. "We can talk about that later. I'll help you. I promise. First, we need to talk about what happened with us."

Victor felt the blood drain from his face.

Elena seemed to read his mind. "I know this is uncomfortable for you. Believe me, I feel the same way. But until I get this off my chest . . . Do you remember what you said? The day I left for Texas?"

Victor hung his head. He studied the square of burgundy paving stone on which they stood. Flecks of mica in the stone sparkled.

"I've been thinking about it . . ." Elena's voice trailed off, weakening. Her gaze shifted toward the port and train terminals to the west. "What you said . . ."

His memories of the day she told him she was leaving came rushing back.

During their final year of high school, Victor, Elena, and Scott—another intern—had worked at Oak Knoll Hospital

Cody Sisco

feeding mountains of health records into an optical scanner and double-checking the encoded bit-runs for errors.

Elena waved one hand toward the pile of papers on Victor's desk and said, "How can you possibly get useful information from reading those?"

Victor shrugged. "I'm learning a lot."

"You're slowing us down," she said. "Don't read; just proof."

Victor pinched the corner of the nearest document, brought it up to his face, and began reading. Elena was always rushing to get stuff done, never thinking about the big picture and how she fit in. His approach was much more careful. He read every document to fully understand diagnoses, surgery reports, notes from checkups, and prescriptions. He trusted his method, not her lack of one.

Sometime later, Scott asked Victor, "What's wrong with Elena?"

"What do you mean?" Victor looked around, but she had left the room.

"She went to the bathroom about twenty minutes ago, and she's still not back."

"So?"

"So she seemed upset. Maybe you should check on her."

"Upset how?" Victor asked.

Scott scratched one of his bushy sideburns. "I don't know! She got up and didn't say anything."

Victor looked down at the paper in his hands. "That's not strange, is it?"

"I think she was crying."

Victor jerked his head up. "How do you know?"

Scott slammed his palm on the desk. "Because I know what crying looks like! She's your girlfriend. Don't you think you should check on her?"

Victor hesitated.

"Fine! I'll go." Scott stalked out of the room.

Victor looked at Elena's empty chair. She would have said something, or made a sound, if she were sad. When something bothered her, she would curse, "Shocks!" or "Laws!" or make a growling sound; she wouldn't slip away quietly and cry.

He turned to his terminal. He had been working on something but couldn't remember what. A normal person would know what to do about Elena, automatically, without thinking. He was stupid for thinking he could manage a relationship with anyone, even one as atypical as theirs was.

The white type-globe on his vidscreen blinked on and off, marking the passage of each second. It might as well have said, "You are inadequate and unworthy of any woman's affections." Elena needed someone with wisdom and empathy, not a freak with deficient mental and emotional capabilities.

Scott returned and stood next to Victor's chair. "Confirmed. She's crying in the bathroom. Go check on her."

Victor looked down at the floor. He was a lousy boyfriend and he didn't deserve her.

"Just go." Scott spun Victor's chair around and tipped him forward onto the carpet. "Thank me later," Scott said.

Victor picked himself up and plodded down the hall. He reached the door to the bathroom and knocked.

"Elena, what's going on?" He sounded so meek. He tried again, this time making his voice boom in the small hallway. "Elena? Are you okay?"

She opened the door and pulled him in, shutting it again. "Shhh! People will hear you."

Victor couldn't bring himself to look into her eyes yet. An abstract painting of muted blue and green squares hung on the wall next to the sink. It would make a great meditation visual.

Elena walked to the mirror and started rearranging her hair. Her red and puffy eyes shifted, and she caught him studying her discreetly. The corners of her lips turned up slightly. If she was crying before, how could she be smiling now?

"People will think we're up to something naughty in here," she remarked.

Was she looking for that kind of comfort? Maybe she would finally agree to relax the prohibition against penetration. "You want to break our rule?" Victor asked. "Should we do it *here*, Elena?"

She opened her mouth, looking like she might laugh or say something, but instead she pressed her lips together and shook her head. Her hands dropped away from her hair. The humor visibly drained out of her as she said, "We're going to lose our home." Her hands fiddled with the pinky ring he had given to her two years earlier, a manufactured ruby set on a textured cobalt band.

He couldn't think of anything to say.

"My dad was fired—something about making trouble with the union. The bank has been sending foreclosure warnings. I had no idea. I fought with Ma last night when I found out," she continued. "Apparently, this has been in the works for months, and she never told me."

"Are you sure they can't keep the house? Aren't there assistance programs?"

"There might be for other people, but we're blacklisted in SeCa now. All three of us. There's no work for them and no future for me once I graduate. No one will help us. We're going to live with my granma in the Republic of Texas."

Victor's legs wobbled, and he sat down hard on the covered toilet. "You can't move away," he whispered.

"I don't want to!" She sniffed, straightened, and crossed her arms. "I have a plan. I'm going to community college in the summer. I'll have to live with my family, work, and take night classes." She tried to smile, but it faded quickly, never reaching her eyes. "I'll probably start dating some ex-pro-catch-and-carry jock with a beer belly and rocks for brains from being slammed into the ground every game. R.O.T! Of all the shitty places. We could at least go to Las Vegas. I could shack up with the King and make something of my life."

"He's not real, is he?"

"Forget it," she said.

"There must be something you can do."

Elena went and folded her arms around Victor. He nuzzled into her shoulder, breathing in the scent of her hair.

He didn't deserve someone like her. She would be better off without him. He said, "I can't imagine living without you."

"You have to visit me." She drew back and looked him in the eye. "Please. Otherwise I—I'm going to eat, drink, and let a different swaggering dickie screw me every night."

"Dickie?" he asked.

"Dickie is short for syndicalist. The freedom fighters, the ones who pushed for the Repartition. I did my research this morning. Abuela Julia sent me local MeshNews articles. I'm not moving somewhere without knowing what I'm getting into."

"I wish you could stay." Victor clasped her hand, stroking it softly.

"You have to visit," she said.

She held him tightly. Neither of them stated out loud that such a separation meant an end to their relationship. He knew it, and he had MRS; she had to know it too.

She released him but took hold of his hands. "Listen, Victor, you're going to be fine. Screw the Classification Commission. Shock their laws to ashes. You're not broken—you're stronger than anyone I know. You've got Dr. Tammet and your family. You'll be fine."

The day before Elena's family moved, Victor met her at a diner, and they sat in a corner booth. He gave her a present wrapped in the cartoon section of the *Bayshore Ledger*.

"You and your presents," she said, smiling. She unwrapped it and held it up, a white V-neck T-shirt with the "California United!" slogan written in golden cursive letters across the top, and below it the state seal printed in faded and blotchy black, like an ink stamp. Lady Victory sat on the crest of the Oakland & Bayshore hills, a shift hanging from one shoulder and one breast bared to the Golden Gate Strait.

"I should hate this, but I love it," Elena said. "It won't make me any friends in Texas though."

Victor sipped from a large mug of black decaffeinated faux-café and scowled. "It's so you don't forget to come back to us someday."

They spent most of the remaining time silently sipping their drinks. He concentrated on memorizing the color and texture of her irises—shaved cinnamon; the curves of her cheeks and lips—kind and seductive at the same time; and her hair, which fought to break free from jeweled butterfly hairpins. The best thing that had ever happened to him was about to end.

"Make sure you come visit," she told him when she got up to leave.

He stood, and she pressed against him, her face to his chest. She rose on her tiptoes, gently kissed his lips, and let him go with a final squeeze.

"Elena, wait," he said.

He had to tell her he loved her at least once. To see how it felt.

Victor had known it was a mistake as soon as the words "I love you" had passed his lips.

Elena pushed herself away from the pillar. She asked again, "Do you remember what you said to me right before I left?"

"I said, 'I'll miss you, Ellie.'"

"What else?"

Victor felt his face flush. "I said, 'I love you.'"

"'I love you.'" Elena precisely mimicked his intonation: hesitant, embarrassed, and fearful of what she would say back.

Victor walked to the pillar and placed his forehead against it, but the cool stone did nothing to calm the pulsing in his temples. They'd negotiated safeguards to protect themselves from such a risky relationship: no dopey romantic gestures, no *sex* sex, and no talk of love. Now she wanted him to say he was sorry for breaking the rules.

"It's funny," Elena said. "We were a couple for three years, and you never broke the rules. And then you said, 'I love you.'" She examined her nails. "I actually believed you." She looked up and whispered, "I should have known better. You had no clue what you felt for me."

His face stung as if she'd slapped him. Had he hurt her so badly that she would retaliate like this?

A sinking feeling weighed him down. He knew Elena better than anyone else in the world, and yet he had no idea what to do or say to make things right.

Victor wanted to climb the pillar and dive head first into the concrete below. Did she want him to say he never meant it? To say it was a trick of his sick mind to ever have thought they could be in love?

Love was too slippery a concept to describe what they had had together. Now he had to apologize for planting a small, twisted seed of hope that there could have been something like love between them. But he wouldn't take back the words, and she couldn't make him.

"And you didn't visit." Her voice hitched. She poked a finger at him. "You said 'I love you' without thinking of the consequences."

"I thought of you every day," Victor said quietly. The truth of it was so plain it felt silly when said aloud.

She tilted her head back. "You didn't return my messages. A word might have saved me."

"From what?" he asked.

Elena didn't answer. She stared at him. He could almost see her counting the ways he'd failed to live up to her expectations.

Anger started to edge out his sadness. She'd deliberately made him feel guilty. No excuse would appease her. She'd never made him feel like this before. She'd never bullied him like this, even though he was so often wrong. She'd changed into someone cruel and vengeful.

Elena sighed and expelled a long, sour breath. Her eyes were still hard. "You have no idea how much a few words or a fucking vidchat would have meant to me."

Victor gulped. "I am *sorry*, Ellie," he said, enunciating each word.

She turned away, shaking her head.

His apology proved insufficient. What did she expect? She'd wrenched it out of him. What more could he do?

"I wanted to see you. But I had my therapy. I meant to come . . ."

She turned and glared at him. It was a poor excuse. He struggled for words to describe a sentiment that wasn't love, to say how important she was to him, and how he hadn't come to see her *because* he cared too much. "I wrote letters to you in my head. I recorded messages."

"You didn't send them!" She slapped her palm on the pillar. "Why do that?"

"It made me feel better," Victor said.

Elena bunched her fists. "That's—"

"I'm sorry," he said, dropping his gaze to the paving stones, "but that way I didn't have to worry about saying the wrong thing. I should have—"

"We weren't in love. That's not what it was. Friend love, yes, but not . . . Not the capital *L*. Do you understand—"

"Yes, got it. We were only friends. We never had sex, so what's the big deal?"

Her eyes widened. "I didn't say—"

"I get it, Elena. I do. We never were a couple, not a normal one anyway. It's fine. I didn't mean to ruin things by saying I love you. You were leaving anyway. I—I don't know why I said it."

Elena said, "Okay, good. Then we're past that. It's just that a lot has happened since."

"It's fine."

"Yeah, we're fine. Okay." She crossed her arms.

He looked at her again, seeing her not through the lens of his memories but truly, clearly, for the first time since she'd returned. Her brown hair had lost some of its luster. The skin of her face had fallen like it had lost its grip on the under-surface and was slowly slipping off. The whites of her eyes were shot through with jagged red capillaries, and crows' feet clustered around them. She looked ten years older than her age of twenty-five.

"What happened to you in Texas?" he asked.

"What?"

"You said that—"

"Forget it. Just . . . What are we here for?"

"The truth."

Victor led her to the Medical Sciences Building. A tall stand of redwood trees shaded the walkway. Brown needles, their odor pungently rising, carpeted the ground. It reminded Victor of family trips to the Sierra Nevadas when they'd lived in Carmichael. He quickened his pace.

They entered the building, descended a set of stairs, and found the medical library, a space in the basement crowded with desks, towers of books, and dozens of computing stations built into small, semiprivate cubbyholes. "There," Victor said, pointing.

Elena raised her eyebrows. "You haven't told me what we're doing here."

Victor patted his bag. "I have my granfa's records. We're going to recreate his diagnosis and test its accuracy."

"That's what this is about? Victor, you need to give up this delusion. Seriously."

"Not until we look at the records in more detail. Do you remember how to run a predictive diagnosis?"

Elena frowned. "I haven't done that in years."

"Just make sure you don't save a copy anywhere. And don't use his real name."

They sat down. Elena tapped on the type pad, picking through command menus. She tweaked the settings, and they got started. Victor held up a sheet of paper containing the first set of test results so she could enter each measurement by date without lowering her head.

"Just like old times," she said.

They went through the doctors' notes. For each observation, they had to query a medical database to find the correct code to enter into their model.

When they'd entered all the data, Elena summoned one of the library techs, a pale young man with a thick blond mustache and a bald head. He double-checked the version number of the diagnostic model and changed a few parameters related to reference patients (education and socioeconomic background) and the patient's early childhood (born and raised in New Venice in the Louisiana Territories and thus likely fully vaccinated and not subject to hunger or excessive stress).

"Mind if I stay to validate the results?" the tech asked.

Elena shrugged. Victor hesitated. Was the tech acting overly curious?

Victor chided himself and dismissed his fears as paranoid. He said, "Why not?" and hoped Elena was impressed by his nonchalance.

A corner of her mouth ticked up, and she moved to press the validate key to start the analysis.

"Wait," Victor said, grabbing her arm. "I want to restrict the input. Only data from before September."

Elena added a filter to the analysis and ran the program. A sundial icon spun on the vidscreen while the model interrogated the data.

The tech asked, "Do you have a gut feeling about the result?"

"Congestive heart failure," Elena said. "High confidence." Her tone sounded like an accusation to Victor, but he let it slide.

"How about you?" the tech asked. "You look skeptical."

Victor sat back in his chair. "I am. It'll show up, but with much lower confidence, between a third and a half."

The tech smiled at him. "You sound pretty certain. I wouldn't bet against you."

Victor studied the play of expressions across the library tech's face and found he was surprisingly easy to read—a dose of curiosity, a desire to be helpful, and a hint of sexual attraction to both Victor and Elena, which was a bit unprofessional. They were in a library, not a bar. Still, Victor was glad to see the tech had harmless ulterior motives. If only Elena were as easy to read.

The sundial icon's pixels burst and vanished. The result came back as a list of probable diagnoses, the highest of which was congestive heart failure at 40 percent. The library tech clapped Victor on the back. "You were spot on. Can I get you to look at my elbow? It's been aching lately." Victor turned his head to avoid the tech's stare.

"Too much time on your own?" Elena snarked, miming a masturbatory gesture.

The tech laughed.

"Time on my own is all I ever had," Victor said. The library tech rubbed Victor's back. He shrugged away. "Stop."

Elena sighed. Victor scowled at Elena for being more interested in flirting than in finding the truth. "I'm more interested in the alternate diagnoses," he said.

She pointed to the vidscreen and said, "It's just a long tail of junk. Five percent chance of kidney disease. Two percent leukemia. Less than half a percent for Gilchrist-Ebbers syndrome, whatever that is. I'd say these results are conclusive."

"I bet you're right," the library tech said, and tapped the screen. "Look at this one. Radiation poisoning? This says the likelihood is only a couple percent, but I bet it's more like a million to one. You'd have to go into orbit for a few years to get a dosage high enough to cause these symptoms, and by then you'd have all sorts of other problems related to low gravity. I'm guessing the subject isn't an astronaut?"

Victor barely heard the tech's babbling. Something about the idea of radiation set his skin tingling. He tried running a hand through his hair, but it got tangled, and more than a few hairs pulled away with his hand. His granfa had lost his hair, and he'd had blotches on his skin. Victor looked around for a mirror, but there weren't any in the library. What if he'd been exposed along with Granfa Jeff? Perhaps that was the reason Oak Knoll had been closed.

"Victor! Snap out of it!" Elena was leaning over him, gripping his shoulders and shaking him. She turned to the tech and said, "We'll call if we need anything."

"Well," the tech said, "let me know if you need any more help."

When he was gone, Elena turned to Victor. "Are you back? That came on so quick, I was scared. What triggered you this time?"

"Never mind that. I think there's something to the idea of radiation poisoning."

"You're kidding me! Victor, it's at the bottom of the list, and it's unlikely for so many reasons. How can you refuse to see what's in front of you?"

"What if something bad happened at Oak Knoll?"

Elena rolled her eyes. "Poison," she said, her voice taking on the tones of a sinister witch in a school musical.

"Maybe it was something he was exposed to at the hospital and he didn't want to cause a panic. So he closed it down without explanation. And when he got sick, he said it was an unknown infection."

"Victor, look at the evidence." Elena changed the filter to look at data from September onward. She pressed "Validate," and the sundial icon returned.

Within ten seconds, they had a result: "Congestive heart failure probability, 98.5 percent."

"See?" Elena said. "Proof positive."

"It certainly is, but I don't think it means what you think it means."

"Oh, come on!" Elena slapped the vidscreen hard enough to cause the library tech to look their way and shake his head. "You can't argue with a figure like that."

"It proves that these records—from September onward—point toward heart failure. But why? I'll tell you why. Because all the tests in these more recent records are focused on that condition. Every bit of evidence in these pages"—he flapped the papers against the vidscreen—"are meant to confirm the diagnosis. Every test result falls into textbook ranges. If you go looking for a rock, you'll find one."

Elena crossed her arms. "I've always hated that saying."

"Just hear me out." He held up a hand to stop her interrupting. "I think, at first, the doctors couldn't figure out what was wrong, and they ordered all sorts of tests and exams. They came up with a pretty weak case for diagnosing him with heart failure. Then, suddenly, all their attention was put in that direction, and, big surprise, they found what they were looking for."

"But that would also be the case if he *had* heart failure."

"I think . . . Granfa Jeff starts experiencing symptoms of something. He gets checked out. The results are inconclusive. Then he figures out what's happening—radiation. But for some reason he can't say it. Why did he close Oak Knoll? The last time I saw him, he gave me a data egg, and he said it would open when it's safe—he knew something, something he couldn't tell me. What did he know? That's the question."

Elena snapped her fingers. "Hey! Smarten up, Victor. You're a scientist. Look for the simplest, most logical explanation. He had a heart condition. Your suspicions are just a part of your illness—"

"Condition," Victor said.

"Fine, condition. Don't you see—"

"Please go."

Elena reared back as if she'd been slapped. "I'm trying to help you."

"Go!" he said, raising his voice.

A few heads in the library looked up from their work. Elena whispered, "You asked me to be here."

She looked at him pityingly. Or was it contempt? Was she simply humoring him? Why had she come back? She didn't care about him. She just wanted to watch him fail. To rub his condition in his face.

Victor whispered, "Why am I the only one willing to look for the truth? Why can't you help me for once instead of putting me down and making me feel like a lunatic?"

Quietly, Elena said, "Even if you're right, and I'm not saying you are, if Jefferson Eastmore wanted to keep his cause of death a secret, maybe he had a good reason. Right or wrong, no good can come from your obsessing over it."

Victor looked down. He said, "If the truth were easy to find, I'd have found it already. None of this should have happened." His voice grew louder, crescendoing out of his control. People in the library turned and looked at him, but he couldn't stop talking. "I should be working in a lab, getting a better understanding of the biology behind my condition. I should be researching neuroscience and finding a way to help Alik. I should be working at Oak Knoll. Shocks, if I hadn't been diagnosed, I could've been an astronomer. I should be solving the problem of the Great Cold Spot in the CMB. It all went sideways. It's not—"

"Victor, calm down."

Victor slammed a hand on the table. "It's not *right*."

Elena pointed at his face. "I've seen that look on you before, and from here it's a short walk to crazy town. You know it, Victor. Drop this nonsense."

He shook his head violently. "I'm not imagining it." He ran his fingers through his hair, and his hand came away feeling oily, smelling foul, and with a few strands. He wiped his hand on his pants.

Cody Sisco

Elena stood up and folded her arms across her chest. "I can't. Victor, I'm sorry. I can't do this with you. It's like you're not even trying to see reason. You need to up your dosage or talk to a therapist or something. They're going to lock you up if you keep going down this path, and I'm starting to think that might be best."

She stomped away.

Victor watched her go, then turned back to the vidscreen. Why would Granfa Jeff cover up the true cause of his own death?

12

I always knew I was different. Before "mirror resonance syndrome" and "Broken Mirrors" became household words in SeCa, I didn't know how to express what I was feeling or how I experienced the world. My family noticed my strange behavior, but they just called it "Eastmore eccentricity."

Then Carmichael happened, and the Classification Commission began its work, and I had my fateful encounter with Alik.

When I was diagnosed, no one was surprised, except maybe me. I became aware of just how different I was, and then I became skilled at hiding it. No one ever knew about my dreams, except Elena.

To my grandfather's credit, he tried very hard to help me, which made the reversal at the end of his life so puzzling. It would be a long time before I understood his reasons.

—Victor Eastmore's *Apology*

Semiautonomous California
1 December 1981

Dr. Tammet's voice boomed over the intercom, temporarily drowning out the others. "Listen to the voices, Victor. One of them belongs to your grandfather."

On Victor's fifteenth birthday, he stood alone in a room with a one-way mirror, through which Dr. Tammet and Granfa Jeff could watch him. Glowpaper stencils covered the floor, walls, and ceiling and depicted a forest scene in dirt-brown, grass-green, and sky-blue tones. The recorded voices of a dozen people creating a cacophony that felt to Victor like a cheese grater shredding his skin.

Victor clenched his fists. "I don't want to do this anymore."

The voices shouted at him, crowding out other sensations. He tried to find refuge, to surround himself with a protective bubble of images: a hill, a forest, birdsong. In his imagination, tree trunks rose high above him, casting shadows. A woodpecker tested its beak somewhere nearby. Dr. Tammet's voice pursued him. He ran from it, stumbling on uneven ground, slamming into tree branches and rocks, falling down a slope. Even as he stood motionless in the center of the room, aware that he had slipped into a fantasy world, he fled between trees flaming like torches as crackling-hot winds chased him and trunks exploded, booming through the forest. His lungs pulled in choking, bitter char.

A part of Victor's brain knew he was trapped in the memory of a dream, yet the forest enveloped him. He tried pinching himself to be sure he was actually awake, but he barely felt the sensations of his fingers tweaking his skin. A maelstrom of voices. Choking smoke. His stomach felt weightless, and then a boiling flash of pain coursed through his skin.

He went blank.

Some time later, he lurched forward, knocking over a small table that had been piled with books, papers, and wooden animals. The therapy room in Oak Knoll. Dr. Tammet and Granfa Jeff behind the glass. He was safe, but failing miserably.

He tried to recall the purpose of today's exercise. Was he supposed to find something? In the books? He looked around and grabbed the nearest one, opening it at random. The words and pictures confronting him carried no meaning. Trees and smoke and water floated like a hologram above lines of dull text. He shook his head to clear the visions, but it was no use. He couldn't prove that he wasn't broken.

To add to his humiliation, Granfa Jeff and Dr. Tammet were

Cody Sisco

watching him through a one-way mirror and doing nothing to help him.

Victor looked up as his legs galloped forward. His reflection, a broken boy, rushed at him, his fist met his reflection's fist, and Victor yelled into his own face. Shamed by the crazed look in the broken boy's eyes, Victor slumped against the wall, now hidden from his granfa and the doctor. All their time and attention couldn't correct his deficiencies. He'd failed the test again.

The voices quieted. Silence met his skin like a cool breeze. The test was over, and the next would start again when he was ready.

Victor breathed, calming down. The forest scene in his mind faded. He was in the observation room at Oak Knoll—and nowhere else.

The exercises were supposed to help him cope with his synesthesia and emotional stability, but everything was getting worse following his diagnosis. Over a few years, he'd slipped from nearly normal to barely functional. People didn't understand how much they relied on their mind's abilities to sort through perceptions, to make sense of the sensations flooding the brain, and to form a coherent world of sense and response, action and reaction, cause and effect. To lose control of your mind—there wasn't a worse fate.

Today's exercise tested his abilities to sort through stimuli and bring order to chaotic perception. After three failed attempts today, he was beginning to think his endurance was being evaluated as well, along with Dr. Tammet and Granfa Jeff's patience.

But they hadn't given up. He couldn't either. *Never surrender*, the old Eastmore motto went. He would try again.

Victor got up, walked to the center of the room, and stared at himself in the mirror, seeing past his reflection, picturing his granfa and his coach watching him. He nodded. A moment later, the sonofeed started up again.

He closed his eyes and listened.

Voices floated in front of him like glowdust skywriting scattered by strong winds. Snippets of words took shape and clarified in his mind. A woman intoned, "The lazy bear rolls on its back." He saw each word as a shape made of muscle and fur and claws, flexing and twisting on the ground. Once he'd seen the words, he could ignore them. The fur and claws faded away.

His own recorded voice rose above the din, repeating the new watch-and-wait words Dr. Tammet had coined for him. "The wise owl listens before he asks, 'Who?'" These appeared as a set of eyes surrounded by feathers, hovering in the air, calmly watching. Victor waved a hand, and the image faded.

Another voice, a melodic girl's, said, "Jason gazed upon the stream. The men sieved water using lambs' fleece." The words became a gurgling stream, each letter running into the next. Responding to a wave of his hand, they ran into nothingness.

One by one, Victor concentrated on the rhythm and tone of the remaining speakers, teasing their words into discrete sentences, learning their patterns, and using his knowledge to tune them out.

After several minutes, only Granfa Jeff's voice remained. His mind grasped at each word and held it, seeing the curves of the letters in his mind's eye like sharply etched silver. With each repetition the meaning solidified, the grooves became deeper, and he finally understood what it was saying.

"Never surrender. Look for a red book with an embossed cover."

Victor listened to the sentence repeat twice to make sure he heard it correctly. Then he opened his eyes. At least twenty books lay on the floor mixed in with many more magazines and papers. His granfa's command hovered in the air, a physical presence sharing the room with Victor.

He sat down with his legs splayed in front of him and began to sort two piles, books to his left and magazines and other texts to his right. He found three red books and pulled them close, running his hands across their covers to select the embossed one and discard the others.

A loud chime momentarily rose above the din. Then the voices continued to ooze through the speakers, louder and more varied. Victor latched onto his granfa's gravely deep

Cody Sisco

voice, which told Victor to turn to page 339—*a good number, almost as good as two.*

"Take the fourth word of each of the first ten complete sentences on the page," Granfa Jeff said. "Write them down, and bring them to us."

He picked up one of the pens he had scattered on the ground, found each word, and wrote them on a blank piece of paper. He carried the final message to the mirror and held it up. A thrilling nugget of pride solidified in his stomach. He had never done this well before.

The voices stopped.

A new voice came over the intercom, a live voice, smooth and clear. It was Dr. Tammet's. "Well done, Victor," she said. Victor pictured Dr. Tammet smiling, her bangs shaking like grass in a breeze.

The door opened, and both she and Granfa Jeff entered the room. They patted his shoulders. Dr. Tammet dragged two chairs into the center of the room and sat down facing Victor.

"How do you feel?" she asked.

Victor looked at the mess of books. "I'm sorry I went blank." But he felt a grin spread across his face.

Dr. Tammet said, "We'll work on your resiliency and impulse control. But Victor, think about what you've accomplished. This is the first time you've been able to filter and focus. We've talked about how important that is. You are processing your perceptions in a much more sophisticated way. Currently, when you go blank, external sensory stimuli overwhelm your conscious self. We're working toward a time when you'll be able to keep hold of consciousness and self-awareness during resonant episodes."

"Your trick helped. Visualization." He said it carefully, making sure not to stumble over the syllables. "I pictured the voices, then ignored the ones that weren't Granfa's."

She nodded. "Good. That's very good. Go get yourself a snack. I want to do the exercise again. We'll see how calmly you can finish next time." She smiled at him and squeezed his shoulder again. "Well done, little owl."

13

The Health Board's Classification Commission will ensure adequate supervision and treatment of people with dangerous disorders like the one we learned about too late in Carmichael. Parents and children, families and citizens, and all Semiautonomous Californians should feel safer knowing that people with mirror resonance syndrome will be diagnosed and monitored or, if necessary, placed into custody where they can do no harm.

—Statement by William Brown, governor-general of
Semiautonomous California (4 October 1977)

Semiautonomous California
26 February 1991

It was a good thing the laboratory's work table supported Victor's weight—otherwise he might have collapsed. Alone and naked in the lab room he'd reserved and locked, after having blacked out the window with metal foil and tested himself for radiation poisoning, Victor pressed his palms on the nano-silver laminate surface, blinked rapidly, and tried not to go blank. The sight of the data egg on the table seemed to help.

He couldn't believe the test results: positive for alpha particle exposure.

The data egg rested next to a finger-sized radiation detector he'd scavenged from the university storeroom. His skin still tingled, an entirely imaginary sensation, he was sure, created by passing the probe along his naked body, starting at his feet and working his way up.

The contamination was the worst on his hands and face, though not enough to cause more than very mild symptoms of radiation poisoning: a loosening of hair roots in their follicles and a rash that was barely visible on patches of his skin, signs he wouldn't have seen—that he *hadn't* seen—until he knew what to look for. The dose was so minuscule that he didn't have to worry about death or even moderate illness. So that was something.

What didn't come as much of a relief was the source of the radiation—particles on the data egg—nor that the compound responsible for the contamination, an isotope of polonium, was extremely rare and definitely human-made.

Victor tried to raise Elena on his MeshBit, but she didn't answer. He didn't leave a message. He wanted to see her face when he told her. What would she say? She couldn't argue with evidence. She'd have to believe him and acknowledge that he was doing fine without the Personil—better, in fact, since stopping the medication had allowed him to see the truth.

He got dressed, trying not think about how his shirts, slacks, and underwear were probably all contaminated too. Where did the polonium come from? What was it doing on the data egg? And what did any of it have to do with his granfa's death?

Asking these questions was too much responsibility for him alone. His family needed to help him answer them.

He dictated a message to his MeshBit, saying he had an important announcement, and sent it to his family. He would make them listen and understand, and then they would have to decide what to do about it.

The Eastmores owned two hundred metric hectares of land along a ridgeline of the Oakland Hills. A three-meter-high granite wall surrounded the property. Victor drove to the main gate and parked. It didn't open.

Victor got out of the car, approached the sonofeed panel mounted on the wall, and activated it.

Lê Quang Hieu answered: "Eastmore residence."

"It's me, Hieu. Victor."

"I see, uh, that you're parked outside the gate. As you may be aware—"

"I get it, Hieu. Granma doesn't want me inside. But you have to let me in."

The sonofeed was silent. Victor imagined Hieu wavering, trying to determine the correct distance to hold the handset from his ear and mouth as he debated with himself how to respond to Victor's request.

"I have something to announce. It's about Granfa Jeff's death."

"Victor!"

"Please, Hieu, I'm trying to put things right."

"Put things right in your head, you mean?"

"No, it's more than that. I have proof."

"I'm sure you're doing your best. I just don't see how I can—"

"Is that Victor?" Granma Cynthia's voice came through the sonofeed. "I've had enough. Keep him out."

"Mother," Auntie Circe's voice intoned, "it will be better if we can resolve this. Lê Quang, it's okay, let him in."

"Not in my house!" Granma Cynthia sounded on the verge of tears.

"Very well, Mother. We'll all meet in the garden," Auntie Circe said. "Lê Quang, will you fetch Victor and take him to the gazebo?"

"Young sir—"

"I heard them, Hieu. I'll be here."

The sonofeed cut off. Victor wanted to avoid this confrontation, but he had no choice. In the past, he'd spewed outlandish theories about conspiracies at the university, that the number two had magical properties, how China and Japan were planning an invasion of the A.U., and that MeshTowers controlled his mood swings, but all those were before Dr. Tammet taught him how to sort fact from fiction. Things were different now.

He had to convince his family of a truth too monstrous to believe.

The gate slid open slowly, revealing Hieu.

He said, "Come with me, young sir. We'll take the garden path. I'm sure this will all come to an agreeable conclusion."

Victor felt he was at the center of a violent storm rather than standing in front of the gazebo in his granma's garden under a blue sky while hummingbirds and bees enjoyed the warm spring day. His fa slumped against one pillar of the gazebo, hiding his eyes in his crossed forearms. A rotten egg smell, shame, wafted toward Victor. Ma kept trying to touch his face and stroke his hand, but Victor wanted none of her useless reassurances. This was serious, adult business, the most serious kind, and his parents should be rising to the occasion. They ought to listen.

Granma Cynthia stood stiffly and wouldn't acknowledge a word Victor said. Hieu had retreated quickly. The only other person with them was Auntie Circe, who seemed to be listening but whose face was like stone.

"I'm trying to tell you," Victor said. "The evidence is clear. There's polonium on the data egg and on me. It must have come from Granfa Jeff, and I think it's what killed him."

Auntie Circe shook her head at him. "Victor, polonium is extremely rare. I seriously doubt—"

"I tested it. I tested myself. Look at the printout."

Granma Cynthia sniffed, but Victor could tell by her posture it was a disdainful gesture, not one of mourning.

Ma said, "Sweetie, if you'll just calm down, I'm sure you'll see—"

"I *am* seeing. It's all of you who are refusing to look past your prejudices."

Fa looked up, frowning. He pointed at Victor, and it felt like a jolt of electricity. "You will not speak to your family this way. We raised you as best we could—"

Whatever lecture Fa was about to launch into was cut short by Hieu's return, accompanied by an urgent sounding throat-

Cody Sisco

clearing. Hieu went to Granma Cynthia and whispered in her ear.

"Why don't we just open the gates to any piece of trash that wanders by?" She stalked toward the mansion.

"Who is it, Lê Quang?" Auntie Circe asked.

"Ms. Elena."

Victor whirled to look down the hill, but the gate was hidden behind bushes, trees, and statuary. He caught Ma and Auntie exchanging a look. "What's she doing here?" he asked.

"I invited her," Ma said. "Please bring her up, Lê Quang." She turned to Victor. "When you said you had an announcement . . . I know you feel this time is different, but I thought maybe if she was here, she could help."

Victor gripped the data egg in his pocket, regretting that he'd tried to explain anything to them.

Auntie Circe wore an expression of curiosity and concern. An ornate gold band held back her dark ringlets. She said, "When we spoke before, you agreed to give this fantasy a rest."

If he told her he still wasn't taking Personil, she'd just assume that was the reason for his behavior. "I know, but I found a supplement for my medication, and my mind started to clear. Now I see clearly."

"What kind of supplement?"

"Herbs."

"Herbs?" Her voice cracked. "Interesting."

"It's not interesting," Fa said, "it's delusional."

"Linus!" Ma cried, then feebly added, "Please watch your language."

Fa said, "We all need to understand how serious this is. I've never seen Victor like this. None of you have. We're not going to get over this by pussyfooting around."

Elena trotted up the path, leaving Hieu behind. Victor caught sight of her hands, what they held, and his breath caught in his throat. He felt his knees give way, and he fell on the grass, but his gaze never wavered. She was holding his dreambook.

His ma rushed over and asked him if he was hurt. Victor shrugged away and lurched to his feet, advancing on Elena.

"What are you doing with that?" he demanded.

She said, "You needed to see it."

"How did you—"

"I broke into your apartment. After what you said at the university, I couldn't let you keep going. You need a reality check. This book proves your fantasies are dangerous."

The journal had been a gift from his granfa many years ago; everyone at the 1981 Eastmore reunion had received one. It was an old Eastmore tradition, his granfa had explained. Other family members probably used them as day planners, as scratch books, and for other innocuous reasons, but the red real-leather-bound book that Elena held had served an important, almost holy purpose for Victor. Within its pages, he recorded dreams shattered by violence and soaked in blood.

How could Elena do this to him? He never should have told her about the dreambook. If his family read it, they would immediately place him in a Class One facility with the other extreme cases: the deranged, ultraviolent, mind-numb, and catatonic.

"We can't pretend you're okay," Elena said. "But we're going to get over this. Maybe it would help if you wrote your ideas down in here."

"I'm not writing anything down. I'm not going to copy these test results down and pretend they came from some fucked up delusion."

"What test results?" Elena asked.

"Don't," Fa warned. "We can't indulge him anymore."

Victor waved the sheet of biopaper at her. "I tested myself for radiation. Positive on me and on the data egg Granfa Jeff gave me. Here. It's not doing me any good."

Elena took the sheet and bent her head to examine it. As she did so, Victor grabbed the dreambook from her and tucked it under his arm.

Auntie Circe spoke softly. "I think we need to consider whether the Carmichael ranch might be a good place for you, temporarily, until—"

"Until what?" Victor asked. They all knew his condition was degenerative.

Part of him wondered if he belonged at a ranch. For as long as he could remember, he lived in fear that the events chronicled during fitful snatches of sleep would come true. When Samuel Miller rampaged through Carmichael when Victor was four years old, he had recognized the black-clad man stalking through the streets because he'd seen the man in his dreams.

Victor had started writing his dreams down on slips of paper and tearing them to shreds. Then he'd received the dreambook, and, gripped by a compulsion, he'd poured his dreams onto its pages. He never read through what he'd written, however. The details were too gruesome, too vivid; more than that, he didn't want to confront the truth of his mental illness as depicted in those pages. Every horrible fantasy, every fortune-telling dream only symbolized the ways his mind was broken.

Victor said, "No one comes out of those ranches. They're almost as bad as the facilities. It's all a sick system to make you feel better because people like me see things and say things that you don't want to hear."

Elena held up the biopaper. "This is real?"

Ma snapped at her, "I didn't invite you here to encourage him!"

Auntie Circe said, "Victor, think about your future, your promotion. You don't want to walk away from an opportunity like that. Unless you—I hate to say it this way—unless you snap out of this, we won't be able to use you a spokesperson. This is your last chance. You have to choose the life you want."

Granma Cynthia trudged down the path and interrupted: "I've had enough of this. I won't be made to feel helpless in my own home. The police are on their way. If Victor is here when they arrive, I'm going to insist they arrest him—if not for slander then for theft and whatever else I can think of. I gave the Health Board a call too."

"Mother!" Auntie Circe advanced on her as swift as a tiger, but Granma Cynthia stood her ground.

Elena tugged at Victor's hand. "Come on."

"I'm not giving up."

"They're not listening, Victor. Come on."

"What's the point? I might as well just check myself into a facility."

Elena whispered, "If this is what you say it is, then you might be onto something after all. Now come on, you win nothing by getting arrested."

Elena led him down the path. He could barely form a coherent thought, her reversal was so unexpected. His parents called to him as he retreated down the hill.

He hesitated.

"We need to go," Elena said.

"You believe me? About the radiation?"

"Maybe. Something doesn't add up."

Victor and Elena hurried onward. A warmth started to spread in his chest. Someone finally believed him. One thing was clear: Victor wasn't quite the useless broken person everyone thought he was.

Elena asked, "So what's the plan?"

Victor said, "We need to retrace his steps. Where he went, what he did in those last months."

Victor stood up straighter. Now he was a man, a thinking man, and he could stand with a dignity that no one could take away. No matter what his family thought, he would find out the truth about Granfa Jeff's death.

His MeshBit chimed and he squeezed it. A message started to play.

"The Classification Commission hereby orders you to submit to a reevaluation with Dr. Santos at nine in the morning on 29 February 1991. Location details are encoded in this message."

"That's three days from now," Elena said.

Victor's jaw hung open. Three days. There was nothing he could do to prepare in just three days. He was screwed.

14

I was standing on a raft, floating through a thick mist. Everything was blue. When the raft reached the end of its journey, it sank, and I floated alone in a red sea of letters. I tried to swim, but my arms gave out and then my legs. My last thought swam away with my breath, and I dissolved into the sea.

—Victor Eastmore's dreambook

Semiautonomous California
26 February 1991

That night, shaking in his bed, Victor replayed the message from the Classification Commission at least ten times while he stared at pinpoint glowlights on his bedroom ceiling. Usually people were given at least one month's notice of a reclassification exam. His mind buzzed, and swirls of color eddied in his vision. He tried every exercise Dr. Tammet had taught him: repetitive hand motions, visualization exercises, sing-song mantras. Nothing helped calm his mind.

Elena had promised to help his investigation but persuaded him to hold off until after the reclassification. She'd ordered him to get sleep and to call her in the morning. But sleep seemed far away.

At three a.m. Victor got up, went to the kitchen, and began pulling glasses and measuring cups from the cupboards and placing them next to bottles of alcohol on the counter. He made as many tinctures as he could, exhausting every scrap of fumewort. He set his MeshBit timer for one hour, then sat on the living room floor, stared at the blue-green glass bead mosaic on the wall, and counted his breaths. When his MeshBit pinged, he started methodically taking the tinctures, one dose every ten minutes. By five a.m., with half the vials emptied, his vision began to blur and his brain ceased chattering. He staggered to his bed, fell on it, and drifted to sleep.

Victor woke up two hours later to the sound of his own screams. In the dream, he'd been drawn and quartered for a crime he couldn't remember committing. He trudged to the kitchen again, found a vial of fumewort, and uncorked it and drank, letting the stinging liquid run down his throat while he made his way to the living room. He sat at his writing desk with his dreambook and wrote. When he was finished, he placed the book back on the table. The dreambook thrummed, seeming to emit a sound like a distant engine, coming closer. When Victor looked away, the sound faded.

He raked his face with his fingers. Two days until his reclassification appointment, if his family didn't somehow arrange to have him committed first. His nightmares made sleep a terrible prospect, yet lack of sleep would erode his self-control.

Maybe Pearl could help him. She had experience with other people with MRS. She might help him get rid of his dreams, get some real sleep, and pass his reclassification.

Victor left Karine a message, explaining that he hadn't slept well but that he would be in the office by noon. She knew all about his condition so she would understand. Her friendship with the family had to be worth something, didn't it?

People loitered on the sidewalks in Little Asia, but he avoided them by walking next to slow-moving street traffic, and arrived at Pearl's shop. He pounded on the front door. When it finally opened, Pearl was scowling, though her face softened when she recognized him. She nodded and beckoned for him to follow her into the shop.

The store was as quiet and dusty as before. A box of shiny metal parts and pieces of gray-brown bioplastic sat on the floor next to her desk. She noticed him looking at the box and slid it out of view.

"Back so soon?" she asked.

"My reclassification is in two days."

"You look like you're not sleeping."

"The fumewort helps . . . when I'm awake."

"I see," she said. "Tell me. Why do you think I help people like you?"

"I don't know. To make money?"

Pearl scoffed. "Do you know anything about Little Asia?"

Victor shifted on his feet. He didn't need a lecture. He needed herbs.

She didn't wait for an answer. "We have refugees from all over Asia, crammed together in tiny hovels. Forget SeCa's immigration policy for a moment. Think about why they're crossing the Pacific. The Buddhist schism"—the *m* in her *schism* buzzed like a beehive in Victor's ears—"grew after the assassination of the Empress Dowager. Then we had the Great Asian War and twenty years of shattered lives. The refugees carried those divisions with them when they came here. SeCa helped at first, but then the Asian Refugee Act passed, and then came the riots, and segregation, and the rural allotments."

She talked on and on. Her dried-up hands flitted, waving at Victor like flags in a breeze. She ran through a litany of difficult-to-pronounce towns dotting Semiautonomous California's Long Valley foothills: Jian'ou, Huizhou, Gaobeidian.

"The lucky ones avoided SeCa and went to the O.W.S. or the Democratic Republic of Mexico. Plenty of work there." The Nation of the Organized Western States effectively controlled all land-based trade between SeCa and the rest of the A.U., and jobs building highways, bridges, tunnels, and railroads were plentiful in the O.W.S. no matter where workers immigrated from.

Victor interrupted by saying, "Please, can you help me get to sleep or not?"

"Do I bore you with my stories?"

"No."

"Ha! You're a bad liar. Bad liars get into trouble. But not as much as good ones."

Victor bristled. "You're different when you tell stories. The way you talk changes."

She smiled, revealing two rows of teeth that looked so white and perfectly aligned that they had to be fake. "That's my talent. Tell me, Victor Eastmore. What are you dreaming of?"

Victor's throat felt dry, and he reached for a tincture in his pocket.

Pearl grabbed his hand. "Come, come," she said. "I speak to many Broken Mirrors. They don't appear as haunted as you do. I ask them about their dreams. They claim to sleep like babies. Not you, though. Tell me."

"They're horrible. I'm always being chased, or sometimes I die."

"I thought as much," she replied. "It's not so strange. When I speak to people escaping from across the Pacific, I hear many similar things."

"The dreams are strange in another way," Victor said. He swallowed with great effort. "I think sometimes I dream about things before they happen."

Pearl's eyes lit up. "You poor Eastmores."

Victor felt his stomach knot. "What do you mean by that?"

"Remind me to tell you the story about the Dowager Empress of China some day." She smiled though her eyes narrowed. "Oh, I forget, you don't like my stories. Your dreams come true, you say?"

Victor nodded. "When a refugee boat sank off the coast—it was two years ago—I'd already seen it happen. And the fires in the camps north of Oakland, I saw that too."

"So much death," Pearl said, looking down at her desk.

"What did you mean about the Eastmores?"

"When you look closely at the world, you see that everything is motion. When a boulder slips, the entire mountain is changed. That's why I help people like you."

She looked at him carefully. Then she said, "Did you know that refugees lived in Carmichael too?"

A wave of warmth rushed across Victor's face. Whatever she might think, whatever prejudices she held, he reminded himself that he wasn't like Samuel Miller and he certainly wasn't responsible for the man's actions.

Cody Sisco

"More refugees died in Carmichael than any other group," she said. "They had more children, you see."

Victor turned away. He climbed a stepladder used to reach far-up supplies and counted the number of jars ensconced in cubbyholes in the wall. Pearl stood at the stepladder's base. He wanted to escape her nattering, but there were no more steps for him to climb.

"Samuel Miller spent lots of time in temples before the attack. People assumed that he was preparing to destroy religious centers in the town, but I wonder why he was so fascinated by Buddhism. We know he questioned the reality of our world."

Victor turned away. He didn't want to hear any more about Samuel Miller. He picked up a glass jar, pulled the cork out, and inhaled the smell of dried leaves, spices, fungus, and dirt. He tried to stuff his mind full of the strange scents and leave no room for her. This place wasn't really a store in any Western sense: no displays to peruse, no adverts to tempt him, nothing to whet his consumer appetite. This was the witch woman's domain, full of supplies that were certainly not magical but were traded and sold to desperate people who couldn't care less about the presentation of the wares. He felt a melancholy kinship with these other invisible customers—they all had to deal with her chatter to get what they needed.

Her voice changed to a slow, guttural creak. "Is that why you need herbs, to save us from another Carmichael? From you?"

Foreign thoughts invaded Victor's mind. He imagined braining her with the glass jar. Blood and shattered glass. A store full of medicine, his to peruse. Such fantasies, however fleeting, were too dangerous to let simmer. He visualized sealing the violent urge inside the jar. He resealed it and replaced it in the proper cubbyhole.

Climbing down, he said, "I would never do . . . what Samuel did."

"My sister's family lived in Carmichael," she said as she looked away, examining some far-off corner of the room. The skin of her face drooped toward the floor.

"We're not all like that," Victor responded. "We can lose control, but . . . that man was different. He planned it out. He put the firetraps and mines in place over—"

"I know what he did!" The herbalist's face bunched and snarled as she stepped toward him.

Victor retreated. Her eyes glistened. Ruby crystals of rage grew inside the seams of her wrinkles.

She yelled, "What do you know? You come looking for answers? Then you listen close! You'll never know peace until Samuel Miller is dead. He's a living ghost, haunting us all, but especially you, Mr. Eastmore. I wonder why he let you live."

Victor's heart stammered in his chest as he said, "Stop! Please." Cringing, he stepped to a cubbyhole in the wall, took a jar of ear-like brown fungi, and opened it. The undersides looked like the air filters he'd stockpiled in his room when he was only four, which had saved him from Samuel Miller's knockout gas long enough for Mía Barrias to show up and rescue him. He'd been saved. Samuel Miller would surely have killed him. *How had he known what to do?* his parents had asked him. He'd never told them about seeing the filters in his dreams or that sometimes listening to imaginary voices can save your life.

"I was saved," Victor said, "but not by him."

She stared up at the ceiling, or maybe past it. A long, wheezing breath deflated her body. "The worst part is that he blamed Buddhism, his twisted version of it. He said he communed with ghosts and helped his victims cross over to a better world, one he saw in his dreams."

"I'm not like him."

"We're all like him." Pearl lit a small rolled cigarette, full of some unfamiliar plant matter, not tobacco or cannabis—the scent was more complex. She waved the joint in his face, urging him to smell the curling smoke, but she didn't offer it to him, nor did she explain what it was.

"It's too bad about your grandfather. Very sorry for your loss. Very sorry."

He picked up an abalone shell and watched the colors of the enamel iridesce. "I'm trying not to think about him until after my reclassification."

She continued on as if he hadn't spoken. "I guess it's no surprise that a powerful man would be cut down when he challenges powerful interests."

Victor gripped the abalone shell. It felt as if his heart had stopped beating. "What do you mean 'cut down'?"

She waved a hand at the ceiling. "Just foolish talk. Nothing he would want me to say."

"How well did you know him?"

"Enough to know it was a great loss," she said. "Without Jefferson Eastmore, I fear what will happen to all Broken Mirrors."

Victor scowled. "He already gave up on us by closing Oak Knoll."

She wagged a finger at him. "The problem is bigger than a cure. He kept the laws in check. You watch. They'll stumble over themselves to tighten the net."

"Are you—Do you mean the Mesh?"

She laughed. "No, but that's a very good point too. You know what's going on out there?"

"A special market day?"

She smirked. "It's a war. And the sides are not equally matched. You people, the broken ones, you either fight or lose. Are you fighter?"

"Do I look like it?"

"Appearance is deceiving. How badly do you want to know the truth?"

Her voice had changed again, becoming softer, clearer.

Victor could tell she was deadly serious. "I'd do anything. I would. If you can help me, I'll—"

She put a finger on his lips. "I may have something for your dreams."

Finally. "What is it?" Victor asked.

The old woman tilted her head. "Special herb."

"Is it safe?"

"Safe enough. Smell that one." Her finger pointed toward one of two pink silk pouches displayed on a small black lacquered table.

Victor picked up the pouch. It smelled moldy, sweet, and slightly spicy. Familiar. He said, "I recognize it. Fumewort."

"Now the other one."

Victor picked up the bundle and inhaled its scent through the silk. "It's nice," he said. "Tangy. Almost like jasmine."

"*Calea ternifolia*, the lucid dreaming herb, bitter grass. God's help."

"I don't believe in gods."

She chuckled. "Not that kind. I mean the gambler's God, the one that make things go in your favor, or better, allows you to pull and twist the threads of fate."

"That's delusional. Wait, you had this picked out already. How did you know I would need it?"

She sighed as if all the air in her rushed out and left her deflated. "You need God leaf to put you in control, to make you lucid. In dreams, in life. One a reflection of the other. Bitter grass is the bridge."

"Tell me how I take it."

"Tea or tincture works. A big pinch before bedtime. Drink. Lie down. Sleep. Then take charge of your dreams. Something bad happens—you change it. Some monster tries to eat you? Make him explode, toss him in ocean, disappear, whatever you want. You say, 'I'm in a dream; I want something different.' Maybe you want pretty girl—zing, she shows up. Blink! Whatever you want appears. Lucid dreaming."

"Lucid dreaming," he repeated.

"In dreams, as in life." She looked at him with her head cocked and her lips pressed together. "In ancient China, maybe not so ancient too, they would say you have a mad ghost inside you." She waved her hand next to his face as if to dispel angry spirits around him.

"You believe in ghosts?" he asked.

"Not really. But if you asked me what possession looks like, I'd say, 'Look in the mirror.'"

He thought maybe she was insulting him, but he didn't care. "How much do I owe you?"

She shook her head. "I said before. Jefferson already paid me. You want to contribute, next time you tell me if the herbs are helping. I have other clients."

Victor met her gaze. "They're taking bitter grass too?"

She shrugged. "You think you're the only Broken Mirror trying to manage?"

"No, of course not, but—"

"I see, *they're* the crazy ones; you're just misdiagnosed." She looked askance, her mouth hanging open, mocking him.

"No!" Victor took a deep breath and exhaled. "I'm not normal, that's for sure."

"Don't be too sure." She winked at him. "Some dreams are better forgotten."

Victor grumbled. The woman, with her changeling voice, was making fun of him. He paced in the small confines of the shop. He'd always avoided other people with MRS, except for one friend at university. But he should have gotten to know as many as possible. They might be able to help each other understand their condition better. If Pearl knew other people like him, then maybe Victor could talk to them and find out how they coped.

He held up the pouches of fumewort and bitter grass, one in each hand. "Do the others take both of these?"

"Some of them. Some need more than herbs. Here." She unspooled a roll of butcher paper and carefully ripped a small piece the size of two fingers, scribbling something with a charcoal pencil.

Victor took the slip of paper from her and saw a MeshID written in squarish numbers. "Whose is this?"

"Someone who can help you."

"How?"

She nodded at the paper. "Ask him. He's a brainhacker." She winked knowingly.

"That's illegal."

"In SeCa, maybe. Talk to him. Then come see me again."

"This isn't some sort of trap the Health Board made to—"

Her hawk-like screams of laughter cut him off. She shook her head. "I shouldn't laugh." Her voice changed again, lowering. "Best to keep suspicions to yourself until you can prove them." She shook her head. "I should move to Europe. Open up a new-age herbal paradise serving everyone poison tea." She cackled and shivers crawled up Victor's back. "Only the sick need medicine. The rest need a reason to believe they're sick."

Victor grimaced. Her talk of poison grated on his nerves. He grabbed the sachets, ignored her crooked smile, and turned toward the door.

Her voice called out behind him, "I know you, Victor. You're the ghosts' favorite! Come back soon." Her laugh hooted behind him as he ran for the door.

Outside, he uncorked a vial of fumewort tincture and drank every fiery drop. His gullet bristled. Victor hurried to the train station, making sure not to stumble over people squatting in front of shop fronts cooking their morning meals of soup and dumplings on portable stoves. The scents were intoxicating, pungent; yet strangely, they didn't induce his synesthesia. Perhaps the fumewort was suppressing it.

He thought back to what the herbalist had said about war. She was clearly an alarmist. She'd probably heard so many people with MRS complaining about persecution that she'd started to believe them.

The strip of paper she had given him crinkled in his pocket. Whoever Pearl wanted him to contact probably wouldn't even respond to Victor's ping, but he should at least try.

Victor took the train across the bay, retrieved his car from the parking structure, and drove to the Gene-Us campus. After dosing himself liberally with fumewort and bitter grass, he spent the day immersed in data sheets and visualizations.

The office emptied out at six p.m. He found an unoccupied conference room, activated a Mesh terminal, and began a search query for the brainhacker's MeshID.

A profile screen swam to the surface as it usually did, but there was no information. The fields for name, location, employer—all were blank. The command cursor blinked, asking if he would like to initiate contact with the non-person.

He pressed the "affirm" icon on the type-pad.

The vidscreen filled with a shadowy figure, male in outline, broad-shouldered and short-haired. His face and clothes were a darker black against a hazy grayish background. Why vidchat at all if the image was going to be obscured?

"Victor Eastmore?" a tinny voice asked. The modulation of the sound made it difficult to make out the words.

"Who are you?" Victor asked.

"You got this MeshID from Ming Pearl in San Francisco. You're self-medicating now, she tells me."

Victor sat back in his chair, suddenly feeling exposed.

"Don't worry, our feed is masked," the figure said. "It won't register on any logs." The man's smugness was apparent even through the filter that obscured the sono and vidfeed.

"She said you could help me."

"Correct," the figure said.

Victor asked, "Why would you want to?"

"To get to the bottom of Jefferson Eastmore's assassination."

15

Victor blinked at the vidscreen.

"I never thought you would get in touch with me so soon," the figure said. The sonofeed rippled electronically, masking its true voice.

"Who are you?" Victor asked.

"I like to help people who need help from people like me."

The oblique nonanswer, a familiar style of bantering, tickled Victor's memory. He shrugged the thought aside and asked the more important question, "Why did you say Granfa Jefferson was assassinated?"

"'Granfa?' SeCa's linguistic fetishes won't bring about autonomy."

"Tell me!"

Gruff gurgling came through the speakers. The figure reached out of the frame and put an object on his head that resembled a crown. When he spoke again, there was an additional scratchy distortion coming through the sonofeed. "If you're seeing the herbalist, I'm willing to bet you've stopped taking Personil. It'll be some time before its effects fade. These next few weeks are going to be tough."

Victor bristled. "You think you know so much about me, but you—"

"How's Alik? Have they pulled the plug yet?"

Victor's breath caught in his throat.

"Wait, don't tell me." The figure hunched over—Victor heard the rapid stabs of fingers on an old-fashioned keyboard—then straightened. "Okay, it looks like your friend Alik is conscious for at least eight hours each day. He responds when he hears familiar voices, though he's got nothing like normal speech—"

"Cram it!" Victor knew all about Alik's progress. The boy's parents regularly apprised the Eastmores of his condition.

"Control yourself. You know as well as I do the importance of cognitive equilibrium. I'm going to help you achieve it."

"Cognitive equilibrium?" Victor leaned forward, scrutinizing the figure's outline. There was only one person who knew enough about Alik and about Victor's condition to talk to him this way: Ozie, Victor's friend and classmate during university. How was Ozie, a fellow person with MRS, wrapped up in all of this?

Victor said, "I know you! I know who you are. No more hiding, Ozie."

The figure tore the crownish thing from its head, slammed a hand on the keyboard, and the feed went dark.

Victor stared at the blank vidscreen. Evenings in the Gene-Us office were quiet, though a few of the professional staff would still be on site. Someone could walk by the conference room any minute and ask him what he was doing.

It made sense that Ozie had become a brainhacker. He'd always loved computers and excelled at computing, engineering, all of the hard sciences, even more so than Victor, who got top marks in those subjects. If there were a way to hack into the human brain that wasn't pseudoscientific fraud, Ozie would be the one to discover it. That must be why he disappeared at the beginning of senior year. Victor thought he'd been reclassified. Apparently he'd escaped SeCa instead.

Victor knew he should get up, walk away, and forget about any talk of murder and assassination. Sure, he'd found polonium on the data egg. It was probably a defect in the manufacturing process. Quantum storage devices were notoriously difficult to make. The process probably required all sorts of dangerous materials. Victor was no engineer, and he knew next to nothing about radioactivity. He had a reclassification appointment to worry about, and he couldn't afford to listen to Ozie's crazy theories.

Victor drummed his fingers on the desk. Curiosity got the better of him, and he sent a feed request.

This time Ozie appeared unfiltered on the vidscreen, sitting on a high-backed, overstuffed chair. Behind thick-rimmed glasses, the whites of his eyes blazed in contrast to his skin—black as obsidian—and dark clothing, nearly invisible in the low-lit room. A metal cap that resembled an overturned colander sat on his head.

"Greetings from the Organized Western States," Ozie said in a low, carefully controlled voice.

Victor smiled. He hadn't realized how much he'd missed the only male friend he'd ever made. Crazy Ozie, always inventing some unbelievable bit of tech, always pushing Victor's buttons—someone Victor could trust and tell anything.

Victor had to set the record straight about one thing, though. "Alik's coma wasn't my fault. I told you. He picked the fight."

Ozie waved a hand. "It doesn't matter how I see it, or you, for that matter. The Health Board cast a wide net, and with you they bagged the big fish. If an Eastmore could be diagnosed . . ."

"You're saying my diagnosis—more than ten years ago—was politically motivated?" Victor and Ozie had spent many hours discussing their symptoms, trying to understand themselves better by understanding each other, but they'd never talked about anything so sinister.

"Not politically motivated, politically fortunate. Your diagnosis fits into their plans."

"*Their* plans?"

"The Health Board."

"That's classic conspiracy nonsense," Victor said. "I shouldn't be talking to you."

"Don't you want to know why Jefferson was killed? It's shameful that you haven't puzzled it out yet."

Victor wouldn't let Ozie goad him. "Tell me about your hat," he said. "Is it magnetic?"

Ozie leaned toward the vidlens and bowed his head. The device wasn't metal after all but some kind of painted-gray ceramic bowl with protruding nodes that Victor assumed were magnetic coils. Ozie said, "I do my best thinking when I'm wearing this."

"Maybe you should turn it down and join the real world."

"I could make you one. In fact, Jefferson insisted on it."

Victor slammed his hands on the desk. "What are you saying?"

"Jefferson said you'd come looking for me when the data egg opened."

"It hasn't opened."

"Ah, I see. I'm not sure I can be of much help yet. Your grandfather was quite the planner, though I guess his timeline is all messed up. Even so, the unopened data egg should be enough to subvert the new reclassification protocol."

"How?"

"Magic."

"You're a dick, Ozie. Wait, there's a new protocol?"

"Indeed. Jefferson opposed the latest revision. Unfortunately, with him out of the way, everything will go forward. More diagnoses. More ranchos. More Class One facilities. We're talking doubling or tripling our numbers, and thousands of new jobs to go along with the expansion."

"You think there are that many undiagnosed Broken Mirrors?"

"I don't use that term of oppression." Ozie sighed. "SeCa is just the first phase. Next is the New England Commonwealth, the Southeastern Confederacy, the Northern League, Europe, and on and on. Draft bills are already circulating. SeCa incubated the system. Now it's going to send its nasty laws around the world like a virus. You seriously didn't suspect that's why they got rid of him?"

"This is . . . It's just . . . Do you have any proof?" Victor asked.

"You mean like the vidfeed showing him being poisoned?"

Victor froze.

Ozie smiled. "Got you."

"Why do you care about all this? You ran away. It doesn't affect you."

"Doesn't affect me? If they export this madness to the rest of the world, what do you think will happen? I'm pretty sure they would peg me as a Class Two right away, and I'm not much for farm animals. You and I are going to get to the bottom of this together."

"Can't. I have a reclassification in a few days."

"Then we have to hurry. Jefferson kept me in the dark about his plans, but I can tell you every move he made in the last six months of his life. The problem is that I don't know what to look for. I have a haystack. I'm still searching for the needle. You can help me. Start by going to Oak Knoll. There must be something left."

Victor shook his head. "Not until after my reclassification."

"Well, then, make yourself useful somehow. Go talk to one of the Health Board members. You can start with your boss, Karine LaTour."

Victor sat up again. "She's on the Health Board?"

"Do you not pay attention to anything?" Ozie asked. "They replaced Jefferson with her."

"When?"

"September."

Victor frowned. Around the same time Oak Knoll was closed. What was the connection?

"Hello, Victor? Stay with me buddy. After you speak with Ms. LaTour, you might want to get a second opinion. You know Mía Barrias, don't you?" Ozie's eye-pixels twinkled.

Victor's old friend was abusing every opportunity to tweak his nose. "You're a real fuckface, Ozie," he said.

Mía had saved Victor's life in Carmichael and then ruined it by demanding that SeCa's governor-general create the Classification System. He didn't want to see her again. But Karine—he had no choice but to see her. "What do you think I should do? Accuse them of murder?"

Ozie shrugged. "Say anything you want. Just try to provoke a reaction, and use your gift. See which one of them seems capable of killing in cold blood." Ozie pressed a few buttons on a keypad next to him. Victor's MeshBit chimed. "The next time you want to reach me, use the MeshID I just sent to you. Another untraceable. We need to be careful."

Ozie's expression grew serious. "Bring the data egg to your appointment. And watch what you say. The dark grid says the doctors started asking about Carmichael."

"Why would they do that?" Victor asked.

Ozie terminated the feed and vanished from the vidscreen.

Victor rose from his chair and paced in front of the windows. Ozie had explained the dark grid to Victor once, something about a parallel hidden computing system that lived within the Mesh, but he hadn't understood the tech speak. To Victor, the dark grid was a source of the rumors and untrustworthy conspiracy theories that Ozie was always a sucker for. But what if this time he was right?

Outside, on the other side of the glass, wetlands stretched toward the bay. Grasses rippled in the wind, lit by a nearly full moon. It was a clear night.

Victor had lived most of his life with the knowledge that he was different, dangerous, that he was a problem to be solved, or at least managed. But if the diagnostic protocols were being manipulated now, couldn't they have been manipulated back then too?

Victor had always believed there was a small spark of goodness, of rightness, deep inside him, even when it couldn't be seen or felt. An infinitesimal mote, his true self, a fact of nature, existing neutrally, as real and inevitable as the entire universe, which couldn't be denigrated by such small things as diagnostic protocols and human folly.

Pearl and Ozie had both urged caution, that he should move carefully and keep information to himself. Yet he'd already shared his suspicions with his family and Elena. Perhaps it was too late to sneak around.

The problem, as it had been all along, hidden in plain view, was that he lacked proof. He knew what his next step would have to be: he would need to get a sample from his granfa's body, and the thought made him sick to his stomach. Victor

Cody Sisco

stared at the dark Bayshore wetlands. With his reclassification coming up, he couldn't afford to break into an abandoned hospital or exhume his granfa's body. But if he didn't pass it, he would never get the chance. He stared at the wetlands, undecided, stuck at a crossroads where the only road he wanted to take was the impossible one: he wished he'd never been born.

PART TWO

16

Jefferson Eastmore and I argued many times about Victor's treatment program and its connection to the Holistic Healing Network's research projects. I never questioned Jefferson's faith that his researchers would find a cure for mirror resonance syndrome—I believed they would, in time—but I did question Victor's involvement.

Victor's participation contributed to an unrealistic expectation that a cure would solve all his problems. Day by day he became more and more obsessed with being normal, rather than focusing on how to make the most of his circumstances.

—Statement by Dr. Laura Tammet, the Eastmore family's neuroscience advisor (1998)

Semiautonomous California
29 February 1991

The morning of Victor's reclassification appointment, he trudged along the shoreline around Oakland & Bayshore City Lake, trying not to panic. Wild breezes swooped out of a cloudless, azure sky and assaulted bulrushes, sedges, and cattails in the shallows, where a grid of waterplots penned them in. He checked the timefeed on his MeshBit: twenty minutes until his appointment.

Palm trees lining the lake rustled like cheerleaders shaking their pom-poms. The water rippled, sunflashes from countless tiny waves proliferated, and their afterimages glowed and pulsed when he closed his eyes.

The scent of wafting goose shit invaded his nose, smelling like death.

Victor called Elena, wedging the MeshBit's detachable sonobulb in his ear. She answered right away.

"I need your help," he said. "My appointment is in a half hour, and I'm having trouble."

"Where are you?" she asked.

"Oakland City Lake. Help me."

"I can't get there in time." Elena's voice sounded hollow. She should have been with him, to support him. She showed up at odd times without him asking. Why couldn't she be there now?

"Then talk to me," Victor said. "Say something to keep my mind off my theories about Granfa Jeff."

"But you found radiation on the data egg. I believe you, Victor. We're going to—"

"Please, anything else but that."

"Okay. I think you should leave SeCa."

"That's exile," Victor said. He looked at the glinting glass buildings on the far side of the lake. Although the bioconcrete path was firm beneath his feet, he felt as if he were balancing on a tightrope swaying in the wind. "They would reclassify me in absentia. If I ever tried to come back, they'd send me to a ranch—or worse."

"Why would you want to come back?" Elena asked. "They treat all people with MRS like criminals. You haven't done anything wrong."

Victor paced toward the water plots at the lake's edge. He said, "Remember when we talked about living on an island? I said I would stargaze all night."

"I said I would make a pie out of real coconuts. Yeah, I remember."

"Still think we could?"

"No."

She was right. It was a stupid idea. He was a danger to everyone until he found a cure. "Are you still mad at me?" he asked. "For not writing you?"

Static came through the sonobulb, feeling like a cotton ball scratching the inside of his ear. The sound was just her breath scraping over the microphone. She said, "I'm glad we're talking again. After what you told your family, I think your leaving SeCa isn't such a bad idea." Her voice sounded odd now, he noticed, like the hollow way she spoke when his parents were in the room.

"Where are you?" Victor asked.

"It's a long story."

Victor checked the screen on his MeshBit. Only a few minutes until his appointment. "I can't leave," Victor said, realizing he'd already made up his mind to stay. "It would feel like giving up, like running away. And there's my granfa . . . We do need to talk about it. After."

"I'm not saying you should run away. I'm saying you can make your own life somewhere else. Away from discrimination. Away from surveillance."

Something was off about her voice. Her throat sounded pinched.

Victor sat down on a bench facing the lake and closed his eyes. It was probably just his resonance syndrome acting up. He could go somewhere the Carmichael laws couldn't reach him: the sandy beaches of the Southeastern Confederacy, an island within the Dominion of Florida and Cuba, or maybe a cabin in the mountains way up north at the border between the Louisiana Territories and First Nations of Canada. But if what Ozie had said was true, soon there would be no place truly free for people like him.

"It's really that different elsewhere?" Victor asked.

Elena said, "People in Texas think a broken mirror is seven years of bad luck."

Victor laughed, his belly convulsing. A nearby jogger did a double take at the sound. Victor said, "I've never thought of myself as a bad luck charm. Let alone one with an expiration date."

Elena laughed. "Texas is wild, though. Police can't keep a handle on things. Dickies are fighting all the time. It's chaos. But it's not oppressive. I don't know. I can't explain it. Maybe you should see it for yourself."

She was rambling, like old times. She was finally warming up to him again.

His MeshBit pinged, and his heart started pounding. "I have to go. My evaluation."

Elena spoke rapidly. "Don't let them trick you. Not all the questions are going to be fair."

"How do you know?"

"I've been asking around. Try to keep calm and rational."

"As opposed to psychotic and homicidal? I'll do my best."

"You've got nothing to worry about."

Victor discontinued the feed, reconnected the sonobulb to the MeshBit, and tucked it in his pocket. He walked away from the lake and entered the business district. The workers he passed were the lucky ones. Employment came easy for SeCa union members, whereas he was shunned, reliant on the Commission's Safe Places program and his family's influence. That hadn't stopped him from trying to join. The union recruiters, however, hadn't even acknowledged receipt of Victor's application. "It must have been lost," they told him when he confronted them about his third submission failing to garner a response. It probably hadn't helped that his granfa and the unions had feuded for decades.

Moments after he crossed the street, a horn blared behind him. Brakes screeched.

The sounds hit him with the force of an explosion, and he dropped to his hands and knees, heart thudding. The horn blotted out his vision with a yellow haze. He covered his ears, the resonant effect faded, and he looked back. Across the street, a ma clutched her child to her skirt. Just one meter away from them, a silver car, a new Erbeschlitten, sat motionless. Brake smoke billowed from its wheel wells. The driver stopped the horn's shrieking.

A near miss. Nothing to do with Victor. No reason to get involved. His heartbeat thumped behind his eyes.

The woman didn't dare cross in front of the peevishly waving driver, who seemed to be rocking in his seat like a jockey on a horse. The driver raged incoherently at her, and then the car sped away. Victor shook his head. The man was probably a stim head, the only group who competed with Broken Mirrors for the bottom level of the social hierarchy. If only SeCa could

Cody Sisco

get over its fear of automation and allow self-driving vehicles, accidents and near misses like these could be avoided, no matter who was driving.

Victor took a few breaths to calm down. It would do no good to show up for his appointment ready to explode.

He entered a ten-story modern ziggurat that filled the entire block. An elevator took him to the sixth floor. Brass plaques lined a hallway of endless doors. He followed the signs for Dr. Santos.

Victor wished this evaluation could be performed like all the previous ones: at Oak Knoll Hospital, by Dr. Tammet, with his granfa nearby, encouraging him and helping keep him calm. But with Oak Knoll closed, his granfa dead, Dr. Tammet on an international sabbatical, and the Health Board calling the shots, there was no going back. No choice but to see this new Dr. Santos.

Victor stepped into the small reception room. Two heads swung toward him—*always two*—then snapped back to their reading material, men waiting to be evaluated. Apparently other Class Threes, they shifted in their chairs and avoided eye contact.

On the far side of the room, a young receptionist sat in a cabinet-sized alcove, separated from the room by a thick glass window. She scrutinized Victor as he walked in and approached her.

A porous patch of glass allowed him to speak his name to her. She told him to take a seat and wait his turn. The chairs were made of hard plastic. The tables seemed to be made of the same material. A steel door with no handle presumably led to the doctors' offices. This setup was nothing like the cozy couches and familial atmosphere of Oak Knoll. He felt weighed down by all the precautions and suspicions.

Victor sat and began flipping through a magazine with a feature article about a dispute between Semiautonomous California and the New England Commonwealth. NEC-Automation, the biggest robotics company in the A.U., wanted to build a factory in SeCa to take advantage of cheap labor, they said, while opponents accused them of establishing a beachhead for the repeal of SeCa's ban on autonomous vehicles. Members of the SeCa legislature called it a "culture war" and an example of a resurgent imperial mentality. There was no mention of Europe in the article, which Victor found strange. As the world's only superpower, surely it had a stake in resolving the conflict.

Victor noticed his vision start to blur.

Elena had told him he had nothing to worry about, but the fumewort was wearing off, and he hadn't dared bring any vials of tincture with him. He ran his hands over his thighs, counting long breaths despite the galloping panic he felt in his chest. This would be a routine exam, required by law, with the power to decide if he should be locked up forever. Dr. Tammet's motion and breath exercises weren't up to this challenge. Victor gripped the data egg in his pocket, a poor substitute, though Granfa Jeff had insisted he bring it to his reevaluation.

No—he couldn't think about his granfa. Not until the appointment was over.

Although Ozie had told him the same thing.

Victor held up the magazine but couldn't focus on the words, staring instead at an infographic showing trade in goods across the Atlantic.

Wielding as much influence as it did, Europe could demand the end of the Classification System overnight. It was as peculiar an institution as slavery had been, a historical accident and a stain on humanity. And yet Europe allowed it to continue, remaining strangely silent about it. Why rely on Europe, though? If the American Union could root out racism through Reconstruction, why couldn't it do the same with the stigma around mental illness?

Victor cradled his chin on his fist, unable to stem a tide of questions. What if someone had caught Samuel Miller before he destroyed Carmichael? Or Mía Barrias didn't survive to demand that SeCa lock up as many people with MRS as could be diagnosed? What if the response to mirror resonance syndrome had been entirely different? Maybe Alik wouldn't have picked the fight that ruined both their lives. Jefferson Eastmore might have cured Victor instead of shutting down the project.

The world didn't have to be the way it was. That's what was so frustrating—there were so many ways that things could have turned out differently. Why did Victor have to be stuck in a world that hated and feared him?

He stared at the magazine, blinking back wetness in his eyes, and tried to concentrate on reading, but it was futile.

Victor leaned forward and asked the other two men in the room, "How long have you been Class Threes?"

The young man in his late twenties with a brown crew cut looked up sharply.

"Tell me," Victor said. "Please."

The young man glanced at the receptionist and said in a quiet, wavering voice, "One year."

In that case, they could have sampled him in connection with anything. Employment application. Driver's license renewal. Child custody battle. Car accident. Filing a police report for a theft. More and more, interactions with the SeCa bureaucracy included a DNA swab and screening for the MRS gene.

The young man asked, "How about you?"

"Eleven," Victor whispered.

Both of the men looked at him in awe.

The young man cleared his throat. "I recognize you now. The Eastmore."

The other man, older and pudgy, blinked and licked his lips, listening to their discussion, but said nothing. His fat limbs and neck seemed to belong on a different torso, as if certain dimensions had been compressed and other parts inflated—a balloon man made of flesh.

"What about you?" Victor asked the older man. "How long have you been Class Three?"

The man looked at him with a puzzled expression. "I'm not. They called me yesterday. Said I had to come here for an evaluation. It's all a misunderstanding."

Wine-colored splotches formed on the younger man's face. "How do you think it works?" he asked. "You think they politely ask when you might be troubled to check yourself into the asylum? It starts as an appointment, and your life is never the same."

Victor's cheeks flared. The danger people with MRS posed couldn't possibly account for the indignities they were subjected to. Ozie could be right. Something else might be going on. Something his granfa had been killed for.

Victor shoved the thought away. It was the last thing he should be thinking about before his appointment.

"It hasn't always been like this," Victor said.

"It gets worse all the time," the younger man replied. "We'll all be taken to the ranches eventually. Even you."

Victor grimaced. He'd been protected and coddled. Now that he was on his own, he shouldn't be surprised that everything was tougher.

"Have they ever asked you about Carmichael?" Victor asked.

The young man's mouth dropped open. He looked away quickly.

The pudgy man remained motionless, his chin lifted to the ceiling.

The woman called the pudgy man to the door. He rose jerkily, his arms wiggling in front of him, like a beetle that can't manage to turn itself over. With a hasty glance at the others, he staggered forward. The door retracted to allow him to pass and closed behind him. Victor saw nothing of the other side.

Victor whispered to the young man, "I heard that they starting asking us about Carmichael. Is it true? Do you know?"

The young man folded his arms, sat back, and looked away.

Perhaps it was a baseless dark-grid rumor. There was no point in dragging anyone, even people with MRS, through that hell. Ozie may have got it wrong.

The woman called Victor's name, and the door opened.

"Eleven years," the young man said. "How did you manage it?"

Victor looked at him. How could he explain years of therapy and hanging on by a thread? "Never surrender," he said.

Victor stepped forward. The door slid shut behind him.

"To your right," the woman said from behind a glass partition. "Dr. Santos is waiting."

Victor walked down the hallway and braced himself for a barrage of questions. He had completed years of coaching. He would pass. Be polite; be brief; be normal. He repeated the mantra under his breath until he reached the correct door and entered.

The doctor sat in a large high-backed synthleather chair behind an enormous wooden desk. His baby face was smooth, round, gleaming, and topped by hairs as wispy as spiderwebs. There was nothing on the desk, save for a pen and a folder. Victor's records, presumably. Now that Oak Knoll's records were gone, the file on Dr. Santos's desk was probably the most comprehensive existing documentation on Victor's physical and mental condition.

"Empty your pockets and sit down, please," Dr. Santos said in a high voice. His vowels sounded slightly twisted, the way singers sometimes contorted their words to make an odd rhyme work.

Victor froze. The data egg.

He took his MeshBit out and placed it in a bowl on a small table by the door. He removed his wallet as well and put it in the bowl. He left the data egg in his pocket and sat in a large chair shaped like a pitcher plant's flower. When he lowered himself into it, the chair's deep indent and angled back forced him into an uncomfortable semireclined position. Synthleather fabric pressed into his sides, and the chair threatened to swallow him whole.

The only other furniture was a tall cone-shaped lamp that threw a bright circle onto the ceiling. Victor stared at the place where the light intersected the wall until he remembered that he should be making eye contact. But Dr. Santos was busy reading his file.

After a full minute of silence the doctor said, "Victor Eastmore."

It didn't sound like a question. Though maybe it was a test. "That's correct, sir."

Dr. Santos looked up. "You should call me Doctor."

"Yes, Doctor." Already this was off to a bad start.

Dr. Santos opened a desk drawer and placed a pyramid-shaped device on the table, twisting its top until the apex lit up green.

He began speaking. "This is a formal psychiatric evaluation under the Carmichael laws of Semiautonomous California. This recording will be shared with the SeCa Health Board's Classification Commission to be used as evidence in the event of any legal challenge. Victor Eastmore, you hereby waive any potential claims against me, including damages and harm as a result of my determination of your status."

Polite. Brief. Normal. Don't forget to breathe.

Dr. Santos leaned forward and waved a hand at Victor. "Say, 'I agree.'"

Victor sat up and said, "I agree."

Dr. Santos rose from his chair, walked behind Victor, and suddenly a low hum surrounded him, tingling his skin and blurring his vision. Some sort of electromagnetic field had been generated by the chair. A truth gauge, maybe. Another set of data to feed to the authorities.

"What is that?" Victor asked. "That feeling?"

"This chair uses an array of Dirac-monopole active-resonance sensing units. Only Health Board–licensed physicians are permitted to use them."

"They're new," Victor said, ignoring the urge to jump from the chair.

"Indeed. Let's get started," the doctor said, returning to his seat. "I've reviewed your records. You were diagnosed in 1979. You have a history of violent behavior, lapses of judgment, and fugue states. To be honest, you're incredibly lucky to be a Class Three. I probably wouldn't have made that call, but—let's see . . ." He paused for a moment to read the file. "Dr. Tammet documents your progress in mood stability, impulse control, and interpersonal communication. However, because her license to practice medicine in SeCa has lapsed, her entries in your record will be purged."

Victor tensed. In an instant, all the evidence supporting Victor's continued Class Three status had been swept aside.

Dr. Santos said, "I'm not sure any progress in your outward behavior will impress me sufficiently if the underlying neuro-biological condition has deteriorated. We'll see."

The hum of the chair surrounded Victor, oscillating and

thrumming. It felt like microscopic bees swarming around him.

"Well?" Santos asked.

"Um, I'm not sure what the question is."

"Should you be a Class Three—"

"Yes," Victor answered. "I'm making progress—"

"Excuse me. I don't like being interrupted."

"But—"

"The question"—Dr. Santos paused, glaring, and Victor held his tongue—"is whether you should remain Class Three, meaning that you are competent to be out among normal people. Tell me about your medication."

"Personil," Victor said, licking his lips. The imaginary bees hummed loudly in his ears, and the air started to fill with gray smoke, ebbing and flowing in concert with the scanning chair's fluctuations. The sensations were far stronger than his synesthesia usually was; they seemed tangible, palpable, real things in the real world, rather than artifacts of his brain's processes. The chair was amplifying his symptoms.

"Yes? And? It says here Dr. Rularian prescribed one fifty-milligram pill twice per day."

Victor focused on Dr. Santos's words. Personil, every day, that was the official story. "Personil was supposed to help me maintain emotional equilibrium."

"Was?"

Victor thought better of saying, *You know, before I threw the pills down the toilet.* He scratched his arm. The buzzing and smoke irritated his skin. He pictured scales forming in his epidermis as the cells cleaved from each other and a clear ooze flowed from the gaps.

"I feel stable," Victor said.

"Have you had any episodes or outbursts in the past ninety days?"

"No." He scratched his arm again, trying to relieve the itching. Dr. Santos would have no way of knowing about the scene at the funeral.

"Loss of memory?"

"No."

Victor fought the urge to cough and started tapping his toes inside his shoes, ticking off each second, focusing on real sensations, not his mind's confused effluvia. The tapping should help. Real, physical sensations kept anxiety and delusions at bay. So Dr. Tammet had always said. She also said that imagining being calm was the same thing as being calm, but her words meant nothing to this doctor.

Dr. Santos steepled his fingers and pressed them into the flesh of his neck, creating dimples like the buttons constraining the fabric on his synthleather chair. "Irritability? Mania?" he asked.

Victor swallowed, trying to gauge by the way saliva moved whether his throat was actually swollen or if he just perceived it to be. "No. To both questions."

"How does the medication make you feel?"

Victor blinked and breathed. "Calm." His voice hummed discordantly with the chair's buzzing. One hand cupped the data egg through his pants. It comforted him. He focused his gaze on the midpoint between his knees rather than the eyes peering at him from behind the doctor's round lenses, barely visible through thick gray smoke.

Dr. Santos picked up some papers and examined them. "Are you taking any other medication?"

All the saliva in Victor's mouth dried to paste. Did he forget to fill a prescription? Or—Laws!—did Dr. Santos suspect about the tinctures?

"Does my file say I am?" Victor asked.

Dr. Santos dropped the papers onto the desk. "I asked you a question."

"No, Doctor. I'm not taking any other medication."

Dr. Santos rose, walked around his desk, and tried to perch on its edge, but it was a little too high. He stopped trying and settled for leaning against it. "You are working at a biotech firm. Part of the 'Safe Places' program. Tell me about your job."

Victor hadn't practiced for this conversation and didn't know what was expected, though he should have known they would ask about his work. "I help run the DNA analysis for Gene-Us, Ent—I mean, BioScan, Inc."

"That sounds like a highly technical position."

Victor pressed back into the padded material of the chair. "I graduated university with high marks."

Dr. Santos cocked his head. "I'm asking about your work, not your education."

"What is the question?" Victor exerted pressure on his jaw to keep his teeth from grinding together.

Dr. Santos leaned forward and scowled. "Young man, it's in your interest to cooperate. Your future depends on it. I'm trying to help you. Tell me about your job. How is it working out?"

"I like it." What else could he say? Think! Victor coughed. "I like the challenge. It's my job to make the analysis as efficient as possible. I'm good at it."

"With whom do you interact? How many people are in your group? Do you get along with your coworkers?"

Victor tried to keep the questions ordered in his mind. It helped to physically imagine them floating in space, to his left, straight in front, and to the right. Unfortunately the smoke wafted distractingly past them. Left first: with whom did he interact? "My supervisor runs the sequencing operations. Her name is Karine. She's—"

But the doctor hadn't asked about his supervisor per se. "I interact with her most often." He cleared his throat and moved on to the next question at center. "There are eight sequencing data analysts, including me."

And finally, the question of how Victor got along with his coworkers hovered alone. He had to tell a delicate lie.

"I get along with most of them."

"Most?"

"I . . ." He couldn't tell the doctor that he'd almost gotten into a fight several times. "They tease me sometimes. They call me names. A few of them do."

"I don't care about their behavior. I care about yours. How do you respond?"

Dr. Santos should care about them. They were the ones who caused problems. Victor would do fine if he were left alone.

"I ignore them. I try to not hear what they say."

"That's not a good response. Someone with your condition needs to always pay attention to surroundings, to social cues, to speech. You can't hide from your problems; you have to confront them."

That didn't make any sense. Victor's entire strategy for dealing with his condition was to cut himself off from the world and keep it from affecting him and, as importantly, to keep his confused inner life from seeping out. "You want me to tell them to stop calling me names?"

"I didn't say that! You need to confront your problems. Your coworkers can do whatever they like. But your entire brain is like a short circuit moving too quickly to anger and violence. You have to be honest with yourself. Notice how you react emotionally. Experience the emotion, and then let it go. It's a matter of self-control."

That made a little more sense, but Victor still thought Dr. Santos didn't really understand him or his condition. "Dr. Tammet taught me to manage my emotions."

Dr. Santos laughed. "Advice from a discredited therapist is not going to help you." He moved behind the desk and took up Victor's file again. "Tell me about your dreams."

"What?" Victor gulped. They had never asked about his dreams before. He hadn't told any medical person about them. Not the doctors at Oak Knoll. Not Dr. Tammet. Not even his granfa. Dr. Santos couldn't have known about them. He'd only ever told Elena, and that had nearly ruined him.

"Your dreams," the doctor repeated.

Was this a standard question now? He couldn't describe his dreams to Dr. Santos. He would be locked up for life.

The doctor continued, "Your sleep patterns. Any nightmares? Narcolepsy? Insomnia?"

"I used to have trouble falling asleep, but the Personil helps." This was somewhat true. The medication helped him fall asleep, usually during meals. He'd had nightmares of drowning in a bowl of soup more than once.

"Hmm." The doctor pressed his lips together. "There's a new part of the procedure. Bear with me—it's not typical of most psychiatric evaluations. Listen to this statement, and then tell me how it makes you feel."

Dr. Santos read a detailed account of the events in Carmichael from when Victor was four years old. It started with the months Samuel Miller spent secretly setting fire traps and explosives throughout town, each one equipped with a quantum trigger. The account included Mía Barrias's testimony to the Classification Commission about what she saw the day he triggered them all, the day of her honeymoon: the fires, the rampaging autonomous vehicles, the bodies, including her husband, Claudio's. The sleeping smoke that had drifted through town so that Samuel could round up the stragglers and execute them with his modified stunstick.

Victor listened with a sinking feeling in his gut. Despite living through it, surviving the day by being locked in his house by himself, afraid that the fires would burn him up, that his parents were already dead, that the man he'd seen in his nightmares would find him and kill him—he had never known in this much detail what had happened. He had tried not to think about it. Even the vidfeeds they played in school weren't this graphic.

Then Dr. Santos began to read the transcript of the semi-incoherent statement recorded by Samuel Miller explaining how his actions were meant to create a bridge between two universes.

Two! Victor shivered. Why was Dr. Santos telling him this? It had nothing to do with him.

Dr. Santos completed the account. "What is your response to that?"

Victor gulped. "I don't have one."

Dr. Santos frowned. "You feel nothing?"

"No. I mean that I'm not responsible. I'm not him. Why did you tell me all that? I didn't want to know that." His heart pounded. He felt his control slipping.

"Victor, listen carefully. The Carmichael laws were passed to ensure that type of thing never happens again. You—like Samuel Miller—have been diagnosed with mirror resonance syndrome. Unless you can prove that you are not a danger, it's in the public's best interest for you to be locked up for a very long time, maybe forever."

Dr. Santos leaned back in his chair, breathed in, and let the air out slowly. "Now that you understand the question, please state your response."

Victor sensed the field surrounding him as a vibration just past the limits of his perception. All his words, expressions, gestures, and brain activity fed a data storage matrix somewhere, encoding him for classification. What if he answered incorrectly? What if his brain had already answered for him?

He looked at the recording device. There had to be a reason to record his answer. The stupid question must mean more than he'd realized. And Dr. Santos was giving him a second chance to answer it.

Victor gripped the data egg in his pocket and spoke each word carefully. "He should not have done what he did. It was wrong. He broke the law, lots of laws. He was . . . He was wrong. I hate him."

Dr. Santos nodded. "I have to say, for someone with your pathology, I'm impressed you've been living unassisted this long. However, I'm not inclined to agree with your present diagnosis, given your past behavior. Unless the statements from your employer or the brain scans convince me otherwise, I'm afraid you'll be downgraded to Class Two and moved to a ranch in Long Valley where you'll receive proper care. Your family can visit once a month, of course. My office will be in touch within the week with our determination. If it were up to me, my conclusion would be immediate, but the law requires us to be thorough. In any case, you may as well pack up your things. The enrollment process, once underway, can be quite . . . brisk."

The chorus of bees returned and reached a crescendo. The world was blotted out by swirling gray dust that solidified in the air like quick-setting cement. Dr. Santos rose from his seat, despite the slate entombing them both. Victor got up stiffly, collected his personal items from the basket, and moved to the exit, his hallucinations diminishing only slightly after he left the chair.

Dr. Santos waited for Victor to pass through the door and directed him down the hall. When he reached the woman in the front, she pressed a button, the door slid open, and he stepped into the empty waiting room.

The bees continued buzzing frenetically behind Victor, but he paid no mind, taking swift steps down the hall, toward the exit, and into the elevator, where the seconds passed like hours and vibrated in his chest. Finally he passed into the sunshine and fresh air. He shook while he waited for the shuttle bus home. People on the bus stared, but he couldn't stop the shaking, even after he arrived home, rushed into the kitchen, and poured ten vials of fumewort tincture down his throat.

17

I believe Jefferson Eastmore underestimated Victor's drive to cure himself. He assumed Victor's obsessions would fade away, that they were somehow self-correcting over time and vulnerable to the wisdom he imparted.

In fact, the opposite is the case. The man's interventions, both before and after he died, were insufficient to alter Victor's course. Our minds are hungry to confirm their own biases. They feed off narrow slices of experience and knowledge that support a preexisting worldview. Contrary evidence is rejected.

These are, of course, my personal reflections on the matter. My professional opinions have already been submitted to the Special Inquisitor.

—Statement by Dr. Laura Tammet, the Eastmore family's neuroscience advisor (1998)

Semiautonomous California
1 March 1991

The day after Victor's reclassification appointment, he took the bus to work because he didn't trust himself to drive. Stumbling, dazed, he contemplated his last week of freedom. A week—only a week!—until they sent him to a ranch to be chipped, and thus locatable by MeshTowers and MeshSats that bathed every square kilometer of the American Union in microwave radiation—unless Karine could help him.

The passing streetscape of buildings, trees, and people barely registered. A week until he was banished to a farm somewhere in SeCa's hinterlands. A week until the end of his life as he knew it. And then how long before he would descend into catatonia?

Good-bye, Victor. Hello, vegetable.

He looked at his MeshBit. He should call someone—his parents, or maybe Circe, or Elena. He could tell her she'd been wrong, everything would not work out all right. But he couldn't do it. His mouth felt glued shut. He couldn't tell them he'd failed.

Only one person could help him. He had to talk to Karine and get her to intervene in his reclassification.

Victor stalked through the Gene-Us reception area. The first hints of swelling outrage tingled on his skin. He was good at his job—more than good, he excelled. What would he do on a ranch? Tend cattle? He knew nothing about farm animals or growing crops. It would be a waste of his education and talents. This is where he should be, at the forefront of genomics, making a contribution to science, technology, and progress. He was an Eastmore, after all.

Walking past the sequencing analysts' office, with the threat of internment hanging closer than ever, Victor saw his surroundings in a different light, full of sharp edges, harsh chemicals, and heartless people. If Ozie was right, the genetic tests that helped diagnose MRS were run through Gene-Us— now BioScan—sequencers. The company didn't want to help people like Victor. The company needed people like Victor to be diagnosed to turn a profit.

He must have resented the company at some point, but he couldn't remember when. How thick a Personil fog had he been living in to not see what was so clear now? He'd been toiling in the machine that would crush him.

Victor marched to Karine's office. He found her reviewing a data table on her vidscreen and sat down across from her desk. He said, "There's been a problem with my reclassification, and I need your help."

Karine sat back silently.

He tried to read her expression using the color technique. Purplish pride and rust-colored disdain showed in the crooked

Cody Sisco

way she set her lips and the lines around her slightly narrowed eyes. She resembled a character in one of those close-camera melodramas that Dr. Tammet had made Victor watch to learn about social interactions.

"The doctor said I might be downgraded to Class Two in less than a week. No, it's worse than that. He sounded almost certain."

"I'm sorry to hear that," she said.

"He said a positive report from my employer might sway his decision."

She crossed her arms. Her bracelets jangled like wind chimes in an earthquake. "Surely you see that I'm in a difficult position."

Victor wasn't sure what she meant.

"The merger," she said. "Now that I report to your aunt, it would be an obvious case of nepotism if either of us intervened directly." She drummed her fingers on the desk. "A pity. This requires a change in plans."

He didn't care about her plans. "It was different yesterday," he said. "The doctor used a new device, and the questions were different. He told me details about Carmichael."

She looked at him with impatience written on her pursed, downturned mouth.

"Have the mirror resonance syndrome diagnostic protocols been updated?" he asked.

Her frown deepened. She said, "I can't discuss that aspect of the Health Board's business with you."

"I have a right to know! The records must be public—"

"They are not. Not in this matter. I'm sorry but I can't discuss it."

"But something's changed. My reclassification—"

"Look, Victor, I have to walk a very careful line. I have BioScan responsibilities, and I have Health Board responsibilities, and I need to keep them separate. And you need to uphold your end of the deal. No more crazy talk."

"I'm asking you as a friend of the family."

Karine blinked.

"Please," he said. "I need to know what's going on."

She sighed and bit her lip. Victor could see her struggling with the ethics of the situation. Then she straightened her shoulders, seeming to coming to a decision, and said, "After Carmichael, they pursued every possible line of inquiry to understand why Samuel Miller did what he did. They looked at his genes, his brain, his body chemistry and microbiome—he was run through every psychological test that had ever been used, and many that were still experimental. We continue to study him. We're always learning more."

"What does that have to do with me? Or any other person with MRS? He's a freak. A once-in-a-lifetime oddity."

"An oddity who killed hundreds of people."

"He did that. Not me. I deserve a normal life."

Karine laughed, a surprised short burst. "Whether you deserve one or not, how can you believe that's possible?"

"Do you want us all locked up for one man's crime?" Victor asked hoarsely. "Am I nothing more than my condition?"

Karine flinched, a hurt look on her face. In a steel-cold voice, she said, "We'll talk when you've calmed down."

He left the room. He'd made a mess of it. Someone with better social skills would have found a way to ask the right questions and keep her talking. Instead he'd pushed her away.

He didn't feel panic, only a deep sense of resignation, and maybe a little relief too. He'd worried for so many years about losing control and being tossed into a Class One facility that the Class Two ranch would be a relief. He wouldn't have to worry about fucking up any more. He could be himself.

Later, at his work station, Victor didn't even try to begin his daily tasks. He pinged Ozie but got no response. He pinged his auntie, and she initiated a vidfeed session.

"What's wrong?" she asked.

"My reclassification didn't go well. I'm likely to be downgraded to Class Two by the end of the week."

"I think that might be for the best."

"It's like the whole system is rigged against me."

"Victor, you know better than—"

"Did you know about the change in the diagnostic protocols?"

Cody Sisco

"Victor, remember your therapy. Are you still taking your medication?"

"No, and I'm not going to. Not if this is my last week of freedom. I will spend every second I have figuring out what really happened to Granfa."

Auntie Circe sat up and leaned toward the screen. "You have to give up this obsession about Father being murdered."

"No." Saying no filled Victor with a mix of pride and stubbornness. If he had only a week left, he wouldn't go along with what anyone told him to do. It would be his time, moments that no one could denigrate or take away from him.

Auntie Circe said, "We've talked about this."

Victor said, "I found traces of radiation on the data egg."

"Which he gave to you. I'm so sorry, Victor, but at least he didn't manage to do you permanent harm."

What was she saying? That Granfa Jeff had tried to poison him? Victor gripped the data egg in his pocket. Bile rose in his throat. Was the data egg poison or an answer to his questions? Was Ozie right about there being a conspiracy, or did they share a paranoid delusion?

Auntie Circe brought her hands in prayer to her lips. Then she asked, "Did Father ever explain to you why he cancelled the research at Oak Knoll?"

Victor squirmed in his seat. "No, he never said why."

Circe nodded. "He behaved erratically, almost paranoid, over the past year or so. He almost lost the company in a takeover." Circe's face swam closer in the screen. "A lot of what he did is unexplained."

Victor's throat tightened. "You said it was dementia." The words tasted sour in Victor's mouth.

"It was more than that. I know that he was hiding something from me. *He* was never diagnosed with mirror resonance syndrome, but . . ."

Shocks. Could Granfa Jeff have been a Broken Mirror?

"That's . . ." Victor couldn't speak past the lump in his throat. He looked up at the ceiling, his mind churning with the implications. Granfa Jeff had had an ideal family life. He was a hero known all over the world as the man who cured cancer. If he had mirror resonance syndrome, it must have been a far milder case than Victor's. Laws, if it had been known that Jefferson Eastmore was a Broken Mirror, it could have changed how people felt about them all. Was it possible?

Circe continued, "Before his delusions overcame him, we think he came close to a cure."

Victor's attention snapped back to Circe, and he hung on her words like a lifeline. "A cure?"

Circe said, "We don't have a lot to go on. His self-destruction was well crafted and nuanced. I've looked through what records are left in our network, so I know that there was a compound called XSCT, but he had a head start destroying his work, deleting files, and moving people around. I'm not sure we can ever reconstruct all of it. But some things were saved. Victor, we might be able to get *your* cure back on track."

Victor felt the blood drain out of his head and neck with one beat, then come rushing back the next. "Really?" he squeaked.

"I'm sorting through a lot of documents and testimony, but I think the puzzle will eventually become clear. I'm going to need your help, though. Can I count on you?"

"I'll do anything."

"You know what you need to do. Take your Personil."

"I'll take my Personil," Victor said. "After I go to Oak Knoll. To see if there's anything left."

"It's been emptied. I can't see what good—"

"I have to do this. If I don't find anything, I promise I'll go back on Personil."

His auntie's eyes lit up with compassion and relief. "You're a strong and brave young man, Victor. I'm very impressed. It'll be a new start."

She terminated the feed.

That afternoon, after a full day of work, Victor made his way back to his apartment and consumed three vials of fumewort tincture. He drove to the shuttered Oak Knoll Hospital, got out of his car, walked to the hastily erected mesh-wire fence, and squeezed through a gap. Technically he wasn't trespassing, since his employer owned the property. All the same, it felt wrong to be sneaking in.

He walked past an unmanned security checkpoint and a few low-slung concrete buildings. After a few minutes he arrived at the main hospital building: four wings ten stories high that looked like a collection of enormous cinderblocks standing on end. For all the hospital meant to him, this had been a place of healing and a leading genetics research facility in the American Union. Now it was a husk, emptied of people and of purpose. Disused. Abandoned. A waste.

The entrance was covered up by aluminum sheeting affixed to the facade by metal pins the size of large fingers. He couldn't go in there.

Images from his time in the building haunted him. The echoing hallways, the small square rooms where he gave blood and submitted to countless psychological tests, the waiting areas with glass windows looking out toward the bay—wherever he was, his memories of the place were never far away.

Victor looked for another way to get inside. He walked next to the southern wall. The windows, more than a meter beyond his reach, were too high to be of use unless he could find something to stack underneath them.

Around the corner, he found a narrow concrete stairwell leading down. Maybe he should have asked for Circe to find someone to accompany him. It wasn't that he was afraid, but he might have to carry away boxes of records. Unless she was right, and there was really nothing left.

He didn't have time to hesitate, not with Dr. Santos's deadline hanging over him. He climbed down the stairs.

At the bottom, he tugged at a metal-banded door, but it wouldn't budge. From his pocket he took his contraband Japanese army knife. The door's mechanism was a simple latch. One swipe with the knife's blade cleared the curved spring-tongue from the catch. The door opened halfway with a painful metal-on-cement shriek, then seized and wouldn't open further. He squeezed through.

Glittering dust cascaded through the narrow shaft of light at the threshold, illuminating a thin slice of the interior gloom.

A low-ceilinged corridor stretched ahead between ductwork, pipes, and machinery: hot water heaters, chillers, and electrical cabinets. The basement looked as if it hadn't been touched since the hospital was closed.

Victor took a few steps and allowed his eyes to adjust to the dim light. If he could find the stairs leading into the main building, he could search for files and data cores in the research unit's laboratory.

A lump formed in Victor's throat. His career, his life's ambition, his destiny—to help people through science and medicine, to continue the Eastmore legacy of healing and progress—it should all be playing out in the rooms above him. Instead he was searching around the dark basement like a blind man. He explored the perimeter of the room by touch. A lightstrip activation panel did nothing when he pressed it.

A pair of double doors in one corner seemed promising. Each had a small window at eye level and blackness on the other side. The doors wouldn't budge. Maybe he could repeat his knife trick to open the door.

A high-pitched scream shot through the dark.

Victor jumped and fell against the wall, breathing heavily. That sound—what was it? A dying wail, a murder? He might be next.

Another scream came from maybe ten meters away, back toward the entrance. Victor strained to see in the blackness. His heartbeat reverberated in his limbs.

A third scream ripped through the room, painfully loud.

The tide of adrenaline receded, and Victor realized the sound wasn't a scream. It was metal screeching on the concrete floor. The outer door was being pushed open.

He straightened and listened. He heard grunting and breathing. He wasn't alone. He edged backward along the wall.

A beam of light flashed on, sweeping the room. Victor ducked to a crouch behind a large storage cabinet on wheels. The beam moved toward him.

He was trapped.

A male voice called out, "Who's there?"

Victor's pulse raced.

Cody Sisco

"I know someone's here," the man said. "The perimeter sensor tripped." The voice waited a few breaths in silence. The man sighed. "I know you're still in here. Show yourself!"

Who was he? Probably not a police officer, Victor reasoned. Maybe private security, assigned to watch the shuttered hospital, but who would bother with that? And wouldn't Circe have known and warned him about it? Whoever the man was, he must have been monitoring the property from nearby to get here so quickly.

Clip. Clop. Clip. The man walked further into the room. "I don't like hide-and-seek, so why don't you come out? What are you doing down here anyway? There's nothing left."

Victor weighed his chances of survival and escape if the man became hostile. He might be able to knock him out with a pipe or a wrench, if he could find one.

But not if the man was armed. Victor wasn't trained for knife fighting, and in the dark there was too much to bump into and trip over.

Or the man might have a sonic grenade, deafening in such close quarters, or a stunstick, a sleep jabber, fire grenades, or any number of other exotic weapons. Victor's skin burned, remembering the people who died when their houses exploded.

The man took a few steps closer. "Come out where I can see you," he said. He kicked away some bits of metal with his shoes.

Each skittering clinking sound made Victor's chest shudder. He crawled on his elbows, trying his best to remain quiet, like a mouse hiding from an owl.

The light beam moved toward other parts of the room. Victor got up and took a few crouched steps. The beam of light flashed back. A bright glare in his face blinded him, and he jerked back into hiding. *Tricky*. Time to try something different.

"Just checking things out," Victor said in a deep voice, trying to sound authoritative. Then he slunk to the ground and used his elbows to pull himself forward. His only way out was deeper into the basement.

"I could just gas you to sleep," the man called out. "My guess is you don't have a mask, do you?"

Adrenaline flooded through Victor. He sprinted to the

double doors and worked on the latch with his knife. It clicked just as the man's light found him. Victor yanked a door open with a grunt and stumbled forward into a hallway that was empty and lined with closed doors on either side. The man's lightstick beam followed Victor as he ran. He found a stairwell door unlocked and flew up the stairs.

He climbed three floors, hoping to exhaust his pursuer, and whirled down a hallway on the floor designated for long-term patients. He had been here many times to visit Alik.

Victor sprinted toward the end of the corridor. He could take the other stairwell down and escape from a first-floor window. Something caught his foot. He almost fell. Arms spinning wildly, he regained his balance.

Hissing surrounded him, and a fog cloud arose. Fatigue sapped his muscles. Victor slumped to the floor and drifted to unconsciousness.

Victor woke, confused by the sensation of his body hanging by his armpits. He opened his eyes. A man was holding him up without seeming to strain. In his late thirties or early forties, the man had grizzled, dark-honey-colored skin, a jutting jaw, and wide-spaced eyes on a narrow face. A black knit cap sat snugly on his head.

The man said, "Tell me who you are and what you're doing here, or this is going to get messy."

Victor struggled. The man lowered Victor to his feet and moved a hand to his throat.

"Let me go," Victor said, hating how pathetic his squeezed voice sounded.

"No. Tell me now."

"Victor Eastmore."

"What?" The hand around his throat relaxed.

"Victor Eastmore," he said. "My grandfather built this place."

The man squinted at Victor, examining his face. "I don't care who you are. If you try anything, you're in for more pain than you can handle."

Free from the man's control, Victor shuddered and balled

his fists. Who was this guy to threaten him? "You're not police. Who are you?"

The man blinked. He peered at Victor more closely, his brows converging. "Can't believe I didn't recognize you."

"Why would you?"

"Me and Jeff go way back. Guess you didn't see me at the funeral."

Victor was sure he hadn't seen the man before.

"Name's Tosh, short for Táshah."

"Tasha? That's a girl's name."

Tosh smiled and showed his teeth. Victor backed away a step.

"*Táshah* is the Caddo word for wolf. I worked for Jeff."

Victor took another good look. Black hair poked from under Tosh's knit cap like greasy porcupine quills. He looked weather-beaten, like an old chair left on the porch, but there was a hardness to him, a way his eyes glared that gave Victor the creeps.

"Worked for him where? Here?" Victor waved at the line of closed doors stretching toward an abandoned nurse's station. "You don't look like a doctor."

"Not here. I worked for him *personally*. Wherever he needed me to be."

Victor tried Dr. Tammet's color technique. Tosh's face was a jumble of hues, too many to make sense of. But his musculature, the way he'd handled Victor like a straw doll, marked him as a thug.

"Jeff saved me from the Caddo flats a long time ago. I owe him everything. Death doesn't cancel that kind of debt."

"Why are you spying on me?"

Tosh chuckled. "Don't flatter yourself. Jeff asked me to keep an eye on things here after it closed, among other things. I've got cameras and sensors all over the place."

Tosh's manner changed. A predatory look settled on his face. "Has the data egg opened?"

Victor took a step back. "You know about that?"

Tosh raised his hands, palms forward, in a gesture of peace.

Victor didn't believe it for a second.

"Has it opened?" Tosh asked.

"No, it hasn't."

"Tell me what you're really doing here."

Victor started to take another step back, but Tosh gripped his arm. Suddenly he was behind Victor, who found himself kneeling with his arms pinned painfully behind him and Tosh pulling on them every time he moved.

"Tell me what you're doing here, and maybe I'll let you go without popping your arms out of their sockets."

Victor tried to throw his head back to connect with Tosh's face. He missed. Tosh's grip tightened and pulled Victor backward, sending shearing pain through his shoulders. Victor screamed.

"If you scream like that again, you'll wish you hadn't." Tosh tugged on Victor's arms to prove his point.

Victor sagged onto his heels, breathing hard. "I'm looking for something," he said.

"Looking for what?"

Victor hated telling him, but he had no choice. "The research for a cure. He might have been close before he was . . ."

"Before what?"

A week to go and nothing to lose, Victor thought. Might as well say it.

"Before he was murdered."

"*Murdered*?" Tosh released him. Victor almost fell forward, but Tosh caught his shirt and helped lift him to his feet.

Victor sighed and leaned against a bulletin board. "I found something on the data egg. Traces of polonium, a rare, human-made radioactive element. It could explain his health problems. But I don't know what to believe. My condition . . ."

Tosh said, "I know about your disease. The Broken Mirror thing. You think he was poisoned?" Tosh whistled, a high keening sound that hurt Victor's ears. "Let me show you something." He walked to the stairwell.

Victor followed Tosh up six flights. His legs ached, and he couldn't stop yawning, which he blamed on the residual effects of the sleeping gas.

"Come on," Tosh called out from half a floor above. "You're going to want to see this."

Cody Sisco

The top floor was sunnier than the rest, thanks to long skylights that repeated along the ceiling like the dashed dividing lines of a highway. Tosh paused in front of an open door. Inside, wire-mesh racks held cleaning supplies, jugs of bleach, and other cleaning products. A mop, buckets, and plastic cones that said, "Wet Floor!" stood to one side.

There was nothing there to see.

Then Tosh stepped forward, reached behind the rack of supplies, and pressed a control pad on the back wall that looked like a normal lightstrip panel. The wall and rack both swung backward, revealing another room.

Victor breathed shallowly and followed Tosh inside. Now he'd get some answers.

A few books were piled on otherwise empty bookshelves. The windows were covered with sections of black plastic. Chem lab equipment sat on a work table, still plugged in, as if the experimenter had just stepped out for lunch. Victor picked up a silver lightstick from the table and turned it over. An inscription on the butt read, "J. E."

"What is this place?" Victor looked around the room, which connected to others on either side that were completely empty. There were no doors back to the hallway, except for the secret one he'd come through.

Tosh took off his cap and ran his fingers through his black hair. "It's mostly junk. Some equipment. The valuable stuff is gone."

"Explain."

"After he closed the hospital, Jeff had me set this up, using solar power from the roof. Anybody wandering through the building wouldn't even know this was here, and I made sure no one got in. You found one of my gas traps downstairs. Jeff knew where they were and came and went as he pleased. Until . . . He wasn't able to move around so well toward the end."

"But why?"

"Don't know. He told me that after he passed, I should destroy everything in here. It's taken a while. I sneak around.

Don't wanna be seen, never know who's watching. Almost done. These books and this equipment are the last to go."

Victor paced the small room. What had his granfa been doing here? There were no logbooks, nothing like a journal or research notes, only a bunch of textbooks and manuals. He felt an ache in his chest, picturing Granfa Jeff, alone, spending his last days here. The man deserved better than that.

Tosh was watching him as if Victor's expression would reveal a clue as to the purpose of the secret room.

Victor waved a hand at an empty desk. "Was there paper-work? Files? Computers?"

"He wiped the computers and destroyed the files." Tosh made a motion with his fingers like a flower blossom opening. "Poof. It was trash by the time I looked."

Victor massaged his arms and shoulders where Tosh's hands had dug in. The books on the shelves covered a hodge-podge of topics. Renal function. Cell cycles. *The Mineralogical Handbook*. Victor thought briefly about the herbalism book he'd found in his granfa's home office. He might have been referencing that too, looking for something.

A sick man looking at minerals and herbs, holed up in a hospital, playing with lab equipment. Why?

Victor snapped to attention. "He was looking for a cure."

"Didn't he shut down the project?"

"Not a cure for me," Victor said. "For him. I looked through his medical records. He must have known he was being poi-soned. But he kept it quiet and tried to find a cure all by himself."

Tosh swung his gaze over the room, nodding. "He was crafty."

Victor was glad he finally met someone who didn't greet ev-erything he said with skepticism. "You don't think I'm crazy?"

Tosh gestured to the work bench. "Jeff always played a long game. I knew something was wrong, and I suspected . . . Well, poison makes a lot of sense to me."

Victor looked around the room. "Are you sure there's noth-ing left of his data stores?"

"Not a thing."

A lump formed in Victor throat. "Then we've got nothing." His eyes felt warm and moist.

Tosh rubbed his jawline. "There's one thing."

Victor looked up. Could Tosh help him after all? "What is it?"

"I mean, I'm sure it's nothing. He told me to save one thing for you."

"*What*? Why didn't you say so?"

Tosh smiled, a hard cruel twist of his lips. "I was Jeff's friend, not yours. It doesn't look like much, a kind of photograph, just black and white blotches. I thought it looked . . . artful. I had it framed."

"Artful," Victor repeated. Tosh seemed as cultured as a bag of bricks.

Tosh glowered. "You're the last person who should be making assumptions about people."

"I want to see it," Victor said.

"Then we'll go to my place."

They retraced their steps down the stairs and through the dark basement. With each step, Victor felt more wary. He didn't know anything about Tosh, not really. Why should he trust him?

He believed Granfa Jeff was murdered, that's why, and that should be enough. But Victor's uneasiness didn't fade.

When they were back outside, Victor tripped over a tree branch and cursed.

Tosh shushed him and then froze. "We're not alone," Tosh whispered.

Victor looked around. The wind lifted the moist air from the bay and brushed it against the hills, cold enough to give Victor chills. The light was fading by the minute.

"Keep quiet and follow me." Tosh crept toward the gap in the fence, and Victor followed on legs wobbly from the sleeping gas.

Their cars were parked outside the hospital grounds. Tosh scanned the hillside, grumbling. "You're being followed, two people, a man and a woman. We'll lose them on the way to my place. Come on."

Victor looked around, but only saw trees, bushes, and shadows. He'd run into a man and a woman in Little Asia. Had they been following him since then?

No, that was paranoid thinking, Victor told himself. Tosh was jumping at shadows, trying to scare Victor into trusting him. As soon as he saw what Tosh had to show him, they would part ways, and Victor would watch his back the whole time.

They drove separately, Victor following Tosh and looking in his rearview mirror for headlights, but he didn't spot any. Twenty minutes later they arrived at a spray-and-set fabricated duplex in South Bayshore, where new cheap neighborhoods had chewed up marshland and orchards to accommodate vacation homes for European elites.

Inside Tosh's house the walls curved seamlessly into the ceiling—contours of sprayed carbon nano-fiber that could withstand and dissipate seismic waves stronger than any previously recorded earthquake had produced.

Tosh wasn't much of a homemaker. The same sand-colored paint covered every visible wall, and a few scattered chairs and couches were the only furniture. The man popped into a small room and returned with a framed square of photographic film.

"We're looking for the same thing, Victor. Together we'll find it." He squeezed Victor's shoulder and looked at him with a kind smile. Victor's skin tingled—from either fear, arousal, or both. Then Tosh handed him the film.

It looked like an old, blurry photonegative of a nebula. A roughly circular black haze was centered on the milky white film with another smaller black blob extending below it. If Victor narrowed his eyes the image almost looked like a face. Of course, it could be anything. People were likely to see faces anywhere: in rocks, in toast, in any unfamiliar pattern. It was how the human mind worked.

Victor took the plastic film out of the frame and held it up to a lightstrip that hung from the ceiling. He noticed a square dark patch in one corner. He turned the film over and saw a small label: "J.E. alpha exposure, 1990-Aug-25."

The hair on his arms rose. Alpha exposure. Signs of radiation, again.

182   Cody Sisco

Victor stumbled backward and fell onto Tosh's black synth-leather couch. His granfa had tried to find a cure for radiation poisoning, and he'd failed. He handed the film back to Tosh, saying, "Ionizing radiation from polonium. Enough of that, and there'd be internal scarring. DNA damage. His organs, maybe his heart. His skin, his hair. The blotches."

Tosh held up the film and squinted at it. "This could be anything. I want to believe this means something, but . . ."

"I agree," Victor said. "We need better evidence."

"Such as?" Tosh asked.

"A radioactive corpse."

18

Semiautonomous California
2 March 1991

Tosh and Victor waited for full dark to descend so they could take the radiation detector they'd purloined from the university to the graveyard. Tosh made jokes about sex among the burial mounds. Victor told him to stop, but the man seemed too amused by Victor's discomfort to let up.

The sun had only neared the horizon when Victor's MeshBit chimed. The message from Ozie read, "Dark grid blowing up w/ rumored BM crackdown. Check on plant lady. Urgent. Seconds ticking."

"We need to get to Little Asia," Victor told Tosh, who was staring through the window at the sun glinting off the bay.

"The view is so nice from here." Tosh wrapped his arm around Victor's shoulders.

"Did you hear me?" Victor asked. He tried to squirm away, but Tosh held him tight. "Get off!"

Tosh said, "Slumming isn't my idea of a good date night." Tosh squeezed Victor close. Warmth radiated from his body. It made Victor's stomach queasy.

"Would you stop with those jokes?" Victor said. "They're creepy."

Tosh released him and nudged his side with his elbow. "Don't worry, sourpuss, you're not my type."

Victor brushed his clothes where the man had touched him. "Good. I'm not interested."

"What?" Tosh turned and gaped at him, wearing a shocked expression. "Not interested in men at all? You're a puzzle, aren't you?"

"I'm not a puzzle. I'm not interested in *you*. I'm a duophile. I like both genders equally. Like most people."

"How egalitarian of you. I'm an androphile myself."

"Good for you. Can we just go?" Victor strode to the front door and opened it.

"Suit yourself." Tosh stepped toward the door, stopping at the threshold. "Why Little Asia?"

"I need to check on Pearl, the woman I get my herbs from— my medicine, I mean. She knew my granfa, and I think she's in trouble. And I need to stock up."

"And if you don't get your medicine?" Tosh mimed his head exploding with hands launching sideways from his ears.

"Let's not find out," Victor said.

"Why do you think she's in trouble?"

"My friend Ozie is a brainhacker. He says something is wrong with Pearl. I don't know why I'm telling you all of this."

"Because I've charmed you." Tosh held up a warning finger. "This is your one freebie. We check on your Asian lady, and then we go to the graveyard. No other detours."

Victor nodded.

At the Trans-Bayshore Rail Depot's westbound platform, a clattering, old-timey, condensed-ethanol-fueled train pulled into the station, and a real human voice announced the boarding. Tosh and Victor rode over the bridge just as the sun dipped behind a fog bank. The other passengers sat staring blankly at each other across the central aisle. No one consulted a MeshBit. There were no juice bulbs, no glossy magazines. Even books were likely too expensive for the poor who lived on the other side of the bay. But several guarded gray synthsilk bags of produce at their feet, and Victor smelled something live, maybe a chicken or a small mammal destined for an outdoor cooking fire in the slums of Little Asia.

Victor's foot tapped a beat on the bioceramic tiles covering the floor. "I think we'll be fine," he said, hoping he sounded more confident than he felt. At least he wouldn't be alone in Little Asia, and Tosh was as muscled as they came.

The train descended from the bridge to the peninsula coastline. They disembarked and hustled through the teeming and soot-covered corridors of the transit center, exited to the street, and stayed close to the waterfront promenade, where everyone was pushing to reach their destinations before the twilight faded completely. Heading west and then south, they rounded the base of a steep hill and entered the slums of the flats. The night was full of dogs barking, men's coarse laughter, and night women's shrill calls.

They arrived at the herbalist's shop without incident. Finding the door unlocked, Tosh entered first.

Lightstrips illuminated a complete mess.

Towers of bins and boxes had crashed to the floor, spilling their dried herbal contents. Victor and Tosh pushed past the debris and found that Pearl's desk had been cleared of its papers, ledgers, and knickknacks, and the mess lay scattered on the floor.

"I assume it doesn't always look like this?" Tosh asked, holding a stunstick in one hand as he advanced deeper into the shop.

"It's usually tidier," Victor said, stepping carefully over the shattered remains of glass jars. His heartbeat thudded from his chest down to his fingertips.

Victor took fumewort and bitter grass from their cubby holes, stuffed the herbs in paper envelopes, and stowed them in his pockets.

They moved further in, but the herbalist was nowhere to be found. A few metal measuring cups lay scattered on the floor.

"This is her work area. I think she lives upstairs." Victor pointed toward a door.

Tosh opened it and began advancing up a narrow stairway that barely accommodated the man's shoulders. Victor followed, growing more concerned. Was Pearl's lifeless body lying somewhere upstairs? He felt the walls pressing against him.

Victor's MeshBit vibrated. He teetered on the edge of a step. One foot slipped, and as he pitched backward, yelling, time seemed to slow down. Almost as if he were out of his body, he watched himself twist and land on one foot, tweaking his ankle. His butt and elbows slammed down on the wooden steps.

Tosh turned at the sound of Victor's yelp and hauled him to the top of the stairs.

"Thanks," Victor said, shrugging him off. He limped through Pearl's apartment, which consisted of a living room with floral-patterned, synthsilk-covered furniture, a tiny kitchen that smelled like jasmine rice, and a small bedroom and bathroom crowded with bottles of ointments and oils. No herbalist.

Back in the living room, Victor perched on a chair and checked his MeshBit. Noises came from the bedroom, where Tosh was shifting furniture.

There were three messages from Elena in Victor's feed, each asking, "Where are you? Call me!" He deleted them, blaming her for his sprained ankle.

He brought his MeshBit to his lips and recited the MeshID that Ozie had given him. The feed connected. Ozie said, "Did you find Pearl?"

Victor heard urgency and fear in Ozie's question. His heart thudded faster. "No. I'm at the shop. There are some over-turned boxes and broken glass downstairs."

"No, no, no," Ozie moaned.

Tosh walked into the room, jerking a thumb over his shoulder. "I found a bunch of electronics back there." He pointed at Victor's MeshBit. "Who is that?" he mouthed.

"Is someone with you?" Ozie asked, panic running through his voice.

Tosh heard the question and shook his head at Victor.

"No," Victor said, looking at Tosh, who nodded his approval. "I said, 'I found some electronics here.'"

"If Pearl's gone . . . Shocks! We need a change of plans. Victor, could you identify the MRS gene if you had full access to BioScan's data?"

"What? Why?"

"Could you do it?"

Victor's eyes unfocused as he pictured complete genome records stored in BioScan's data vaults, each containing billions of bits encoding DNA base pair sequences. Victor would need to perform advanced analytics to identify the Broken Mirror gene, essentially reverse engineering the black-boxed reference sequence. He would have to create a data crawler that could filter out known genes, examine what remained, and then find the sequence shared by all Broken Mirrors. It was worse than finding a needle in a haystack. It was finding a specific grain of sand in a desert using a microscope to search through it.

He told Ozie, "Not possible."

"Why?"

"The reference sequence is encrypted. I'd have to compare a thousand genomes to identify the gene and sequence it. That's beyond what any computer can do in a reasonable time," Victor said. "Maybe if we had eternity."

"Imagine you had all of BioScan's data and a computer with enough processing to do it. What else would you need?"

"A copy of the Human Genome Initiative's gene libraries. And permission, of course."

"Forget permission, we're doing this. Bring me BioScan's data."

"It's a crazy idea." It was also illegal and not something Victor should be doing while his reclassification was pending.

"While you're at it, I need you to plant a back door on their network."

"No! Look, I said I would help you if it helped me figure out what happened to my granfa. This has nothing to do with him."

"It does, trust me. He wanted to reform the Classification Commission, or barring that, destroy it. Now Pearl is gone . . . Vic, here's the truth: you can't stay in SeCa. Your time there is almost up."

Cold gripped Victor's body. "What do you mean? Do you know something about my reclassification? My auntie was going to try to take care of it."

"It's not that simple. There are people watching you."

Victor hobbled to the window and looked out on the street at a few passing pedestrians. A small group huddled at the entrance to an alley, passing something between them that gave off clouds of smoke. A van and some cars were parked along the street. "I don't believe you," Victor said.

"I've been monitoring Mesh traffic, and your name and Pearl's came back with an alert. I've read the messages. Two people are following you, and they know you've been to see her."

Victor reeled away from the window. *Two is a very bad number.* He said to Ozie, "You thought it would be a good idea for me to come back here? How idiotic can you be? Who are they? Are they from the Commission?"

"Yes," Ozie said, but he didn't sound certain. "Do as I say, or they're going to take you to a ranch. It's that simple. I can help you leave SeCa if you get the data for me. Otherwise you're on your own."

"Leave SeCa?" That's what Elena had said he should do. But his family was here. Where would he go? He said, "I can't—"

Ozie yelled, "Shut up, Victor! You're not in control here. Are we clear?"

Tosh grabbed the MeshBit and terminated the feed. "He's playing you."

"What?" Victor blinked.

Tosh took Victor by the shoulders and shook him. "Wake up. He's messing with you, telling you what you want to hear to make you run errands for him. Fetch this. Steal that. Guy's crazy. Let's get out of here."

"But he said they're following—"

"You actually *believe* him? He sounded higher than a kite."

Victor sighed. Ozie did sound odd, but that was normal for him. "He's not high. He's like me. But that doesn't mean he's wrong."

Victor peeped through the window again. Movement caught his attention. The rear door opened on a van down the street, and a man dressed in black got out. Victor caught sight of someone inside the van, also in black, leaning over another figure seated on the floor underneath a bright lightstrip. The

Cody Sisco

seated figure wore a pink synthsilk sweater and navy pants. A blindfold constrained frizzy black hair. Pearl!

Victor's lungs seized. He tried to yell but could only point. Tosh approached the window and looked outside. "That's her," Victor squeaked. "It's true. They're coming for me."

"Then get back!" Tosh pulled Victor away from the window. "Time to go." Tosh rushed to the stairs.

Victor followed him, limping on his sprained foot. "Help me save Pearl."

"Priority one: we get out of here now. Number two, we go to the cemetery. Whatever other odd shit you've got going on, the only thing I care about is finding what happened to Jeff."

"I want to find out too, but Ozie says—"

"He spews bullshit. If you really care, then meet me at the graveyard."

Tosh disappeared down the stairway.

Victor took a ragged breath and called Ozie. "They're here. Pearl's outside in a van. What do I do?"

Ozie said, "Let me worry about Pearl. You need to look around for where she keeps her electronics."

"What? She's an herbalist. Why would she—"

"Pearl was my brainhackery distributor for all of SeCa. You need to find a data leech. It'll look like a thick metal bracelet with a Hexagon logo on it. It clamps around a MeshLine and lets me read and write traffic remotely. But I can't transfer BioScan's sequences—those are too big—so you'll need to grab them and put them on a Bose-Drive. It looks like—"

"I know what a Bose-Drive looks like," Victor said. "BioScan has a ton of them." Victor dragged his hurt foot to the bedroom and nearly stumbled over the boxes Tosh had pulled from under the bed. Opening them, he found a Bose-Drive the size of a large dictionary and a small metal clamp, the data leech, which he put around his wrist.

Ozie said, "Now, get BioScan's data, get proof of what killed your grandfather, and then get out of town. I'm sending you an address in the mountains. Don't try to cross the border until you hear from me. They're looking for you."

Victor heard a door open downstairs. He terminated the feed.

Sounds moved underneath him from the front of the store toward the back. It sounded like two people—*wretched number two*. He would never make it past them. He shuffled to the window, favoring his uninjured foot. It was a sheer drop to the sidewalk below. There must be a fire exit somewhere. He moved through the apartment, trying not to make a sound, but the floorboards creaked with every step.

A tiny window in Pearl's bedroom opened onto a narrow alley with only a meter-wide gap between her building and the next. He pictured wedging himself against the adjacent building and worming his way down. It was risky, and he had the Bose-Drive to worry about. It was heavy and difficult to carry one-handed. He could tuck it under his arm, but if he fell on it . . .

The stairs creaked.

Victor hobbled to the kitchen and spotted a window next to the chiller cabinet.

He opened the window. There was no fire escape, but there was a small flat ledge with no railing, big enough for two potted plants. An old, aluminum-bodied car was parked below, cutting the distance for the fall he'd have to make.

Victor's vision blurred as he swung one leg over the sill, kicked off the plants, and climbed out, shutting the window behind him. The balcony sagged underneath his feet.

He heard voices, one male, one female, coming from Pearl's bedroom.

He jumped and twisted in midair, cradling the Bose-Drive.

His back slammed into the car's roof, the wind knocked out of him. The Bose-Drive felt like it was biting into his chest.

Victor rolled off the car and limped down the street. A few passersby watched him. His two pursuers would catch up to him any minute, and he was sure no one in the street would help him.

He staggered down an alley, cursing Tosh for leaving him defenseless and without a way to help Pearl. Heaps of trash slowed him down. He considered diving into one and hiding.

Then he spotted an open door and recognized the restaurant he'd fled through on his first trip to Little Asia. He ducked inside and shut the door behind him.

Steam wafted through the restaurant's storeroom, carrying the scents of frying meat and noodles. He shuffled inside and hid behind a stack of buckets. His back throbbed, and sharp pains shot up his ankle. He couldn't run any more.

A canvas bag of onions lay on the floor near his feet. He dumped them out and put the Bose-Drive inside, adding a few onions to the top. A mason jar full of small black seeds caught his eye. For a moment he thought he might have found black cardamom—funny the things his brain fixated on. He dumped the seeds on the floor and shoved the jar into the bag. He would need the jar in the cemetery.

Victor took a deep breath and walked through the kitchen, ignoring the confused looks of the cook and busboy. The manager looked up in surprise when he passed her, stepping into the main seating area. He shuffled forward, never wavering from his goal, the front door, even as shouts in Mandarin beat against his back.

A hand gripped Victor's arm. He flashed his teeth, and the restaurant manager cowered back. Victor exited to the street. He shuffled onward, carrying his sack of onions and bit, determined to get to the graveyard.

Victor was afraid of authorities, madmen, rude people, wild animals, strangers following him and kidnapping people he knew, his own shifting and unpredictable moods, going blank, and not much else. Certainly not graveyards. Ghosts and mythical beasts held no sway over him.

As he approached the gatehouse door, it opened. Victor jumped. His injured foot flared up in pain.

Tosh poked his head out. "Glad you made it. Shall we get started?"

"How did you get in?" Victor asked.

"I'm good with locks." He handed the radiation detector to Victor.

They moved through the gatehouse and hiked up the drive, which curved up the hill to the mausoleum before splitting into several footpaths leading among the grave mounds.

On the way, they stopped at the groundskeeper's warehouse. Tosh fiddled with the door and opened it. Inside they found motorized carts, machines for transporting sarcophagi, and gardening tools, including ceremonial shovels. Tosh picked out a metal bar and one of the sturdier garden shovels.

They reached Granfa Jeff's mound, which was surrounded by a marble wall topped with a metal-wrought, silver-filigreed fence with posts that were delicately twisting representations of DNA strands. A large bust of Jefferson Eastmore glowed in the moonlight atop the rear wall.

Victor stared at the bust's face, involuntarily feeling the ebbing remains of anger and hurt at his granfa's then-seeming betrayal. But Victor had misunderstood. Everything Granfa Jeff had done—the hospital closure, the foundation's change in direction, the layoffs—had been his way of fighting an enemy that Victor believed was a common one, an enemy currently grasping for him.

"I'm sorry, Granfa," he whispered.

His vision blurred, and he wiped his eyes. This was no time for sentiment. He was so close to the truth.

"Hurry up," Tosh said.

Victor knelt, placed the radiation detector's case on the ground, and unfastened the clasps. The machine clicked on when he pressed start and a hiss of static arose. He held the machine by a handle, and in his other hand he gripped the detector-rod. Standing next to the rounded stones that made up the outer shell of his granfa's grave mound, Victor waved the detector-rod back and forth. The hiss remained unchanged.

Tosh said, "What are you doing? Will that work through the mound?"

"It shouldn't. That's what I'm checking for. If we got a reading, we would know the machine wasn't working."

Tosh scratched his head. "But if we do get a reading, we still can't be sure that means that it's working."

Cody Sisco

Victor showed Tosh how the detector clicked when he brought it near the data egg. "I'm willing to accept any signal it picks up as solid evidence. At least until there's a proper investigation."

Tosh loosened stones from the mound and Victor carried each one to the dirt outside the walls, laying them down so he could correctly replace them when they were done. Once the stones were removed, Tosh started moving shovelfuls of dirt toward the base of the enclosing wall. Twenty minutes later, the lid of the coffin was disinterred. Victor ran the detector-rod along the coffin. There were no perceptible blips.

The coffin holding Jefferson Eastmore was designed to stay sealed for eternity. Tosh pressed the tip of the shovel into the seam between the lid and body and twisted. The shovel bent. He tried again, ramming the thin edge of the crowbar in beside it. The lid creaked. Tosh threw his weight on the crowbar, levering it up and down while Victor held the shovel handle and pushed. The crack opened wider until finally the lid broke open. Tosh and Victor lifted it off.

Victor looked inside.

"Damn," Tosh said, sniffing and turning away.

Victor stood transfixed, frozen; his breath was locked in his lungs. There was a body, and it was his granfa's. Though it had been weeks, there was no sign of decomposition. Whatever preservatives they'd pumped in seemed to be working. The corpse lay in a fancy suit, looking just like it had during the funeral, except then there had been daylight, and now the pale glow of the moon struck the dead flesh, illuminating it like a paper lantern.

Laws, Victor hated seeing him like this again.

Victor waved the detector-rod along his granfa's suit with no result. The dead man's arms rested at either side. Victor looked at them, tried but failed to get a reading from his granfa's fingers, and reluctantly acknowledged to himself where he could get a better reading.

"Do you have any gloves?" Victor asked.

"Fuck. Yes. I have a pair in my car. I can get them."

"No time. Will you help me?" Victor set down the radiation detection device and gestured to his granfa's face. "We have to get his jaw open."

"Can't you just try his skin?"

Victor picked up the detector and ran the rod along the corpse's face, millimeters above the skin. The static crackled more strongly, but the change was almost indistinguishable.

"I don't hear anything," Tosh said.

"I do. Barely. I want more proof." Victor stomach flipped. This was worse than awful. He'd take ten episodes of blankness to not have to do this, but he had no choice. "We need to open his jaw. Chances are the poison was ingested."

"I'm not sure I can do this," Tosh said, shaking his head.

"I know I can't. Here." Victor pulled the knife from his pocket and handed it to Tosh, who stood numbly looking at the body. Victor said, "I'm sure you've done worse."

Tosh extended the blade of the knife and locked it into place. Leaning over the coffin, he slipped the blade between the corpse's lips and worked it back and forth, wedging it between the teeth. He was careful not to let the lips touch his hands, Victor noted. Then Tosh gripped the knife with both hands. Victor could see his arm muscles straining. Nothing happened. Tosh twisted with his whole body. There was a cracking, tearing sound, as teeth shifted and came loose and the tendons of the corpse's face stretched and ripped.

Tosh gagged and stumbled away. Granfa Jeff's jaw had unhinged from its resting place, not by much, but the gap was big enough for the detector-rod. Victor inserted the end of the device, hands shaking and vision blurred by tears, trying to make sure the glass tip touched nothing on its way in.

The speaker buzzed and hissed, emitting rapid, popping blips. Victor maneuvered the detector-rod as much as the narrow opening allowed. The counter registered levels of radiation unmistakably higher than the background rate.

They had a signal. Granfa Jeff's mouth tissues, probably his entire body, contained polonium, which was still emitting alpha particles, weeks after death.

Victor's chest tightened, and he held back a cry. He blinked. He felt the panic and despair his granfa must have felt when he discovered he was poisoned. Why hadn't he told his family? Why had he lived a lie and died by it too?

Although, he *had* given Victor the data egg. Why wouldn't it open?

An icy wave of sadness crashed over him. His granfa had never given up on him. Granfa Jeff tried to warn him and to prepare him for what was to come.

Victor shivered and tightened his grip on the radiation detector. He withdrew the rod from the corpse's mouth.

"What now?" Tosh asked.

Victor's limbs felt stiff and his mouth dry. He looked at the dirt and the stones. They had a long night ahead to rebuild the burial mound, but first they had to desecrate the corpse even more. "We need a sample. His tongue. Could you . . ." He couldn't finish his sentence.

"Fine." Tosh gestured at the coffin. "Choose your cut. Tongue, you said?"

Victor clenched his fists. "You don't have to be an asshole about it," he said.

The wind rustled through a stand of eucalyptus trees nearby.

"That was gallows humor," Tosh said. "It helps. You have a container?"

Victor thought for a moment and then handed him the small mason jar he'd taken from the restaurant storeroom. "I guess robbing a grave isn't the worst thing a Broken Mirror has ever done."

"You said it," Tosh agreed, then froze. "Look," he whispered and pointed down the hill.

A car's headlights shone through the bars of the entrance gate. They dimmed, and in the moon's glow, Victor watched as two figures passed through the gatehouse and started running toward them.

19

You don't understand. By the time Victor left home, it was already ten years too late. Nearly twenty, actually, since it all started in Carmichael.

   . . .

No, I don't approve of the government's response to our "return," obviously.

   . . .

And what do you think would have happened if there hadn't been a Carmichael event in the first place? Oh, you don't know? How shocking.

   . . .

Would it have been worse? Oh, who the fuck can say?

—Inquest interview with Robbie Eastmore
– redacted version (1998)

Semiautonomous California
2 March 1991

"Hurry," Victor said.

Tosh reached in the corpse's mouth, cut out Jefferson Eastmore's tongue, and sealed it inside the mason jar. He handed the jar to Victor then tugged him by the elbow, leading him behind the grave mound's surrounding wall and hissing in his ear, "I'm going to draw them away. I'll catch up with you." Tosh sprinted away.

Swaths of light played over the hillside. The figures climbed closer.

A tinkling of metal-on-stone rang out from the direction Tosh had gone, and the lights swiveled after him.

Victor crouched low and crept to a eucalyptus tree a few meters down the hill, favoring his injured foot and carrying the jar with Granfa Jeff's tongue.

When Victor looked back, he froze.

Granfa Jeff's body lay exposed to the air, defaced, a violation nearly as taboo as murder. Victor's eyes watered. There was no way he could lift the coffin lid to replace it.

"Sorry, Granfa," Victor said quietly.

Glancing back to make sure the figures were still following Tosh, Victor limped as quickly as he could down the hill and through the gatehouse. He jumped in his car and drove home, knowing it was risky: that was the first place anyone would look for him. But if he was leaving SeCa, he had to collect his things and hope that Tosh would lead his pursuers on a long, circuitous chase.

As he walked to his front door, he wondered if he should go through with Ozie's plan. It was one thing to rob a graveyard at night, but there would be people working overnight at BioScan. Maybe he should pack a bag and leave SeCa now.

On his front step, Victor pinged Ozie, sending, "BioScan too risky. Let's talk."

Ozie replied with a text message. "Bring B.S. data to exchange for info about who killed J.E."

That settled it. Victor believed Ozie hadn't told him the full story yet. He would get the data from BioScan and then head to the mountains.

Besides, he really didn't have much of a choice.

Victor opened the front door and reached for the light panel. Something moved in his living room.

His heart pumped adrenaline. He gripped the glass jar tightly. A figure jumped up from the couch.

The lightstrips popped on. Elena stood there, startled, wiggling her fingers in an embarrassed half wave.

Victor slammed the door behind him, setting the glass jar down on the entry table. "What are you doing here?"

Elena's hair was pulled into a tight bun, which her hands

smoothed repeatedly. "You wouldn't respond to my messages."

"So you broke into my house? Again?"

"I just want to help."

"The more you keep saying that, the less I believe you." He wiped sweat off his brow. "Sorry, it's been the worst kind of day."

Elena blinked at him, and the whites of her eyes glowed orange—a sign of anxiety.

He asked, "What is it? What's wrong?"

She gulped. "I have to tell you—"

"What?"

Elena sighed, seemed to stand taller, and then said, "Some people came to ask me some questions. A man and a woman. They're watching you."

Victor felt his gut convulse. The couple from Little Asia and the graveyard. "Why?"

"They said they want to keep you safe."

And zebras are horses in formal attire. No way. Keeping me safe isn't high on their priority list, whoever those people are. He said, "They were lying. Must have been."

"They left me a Mesh ID and told me to contact them when you got home." Her hands fretted with the hem of her shirt. She looked nervous. Could she be lying?

"Don't do it. If they find you again," Victor warned, "don't tell them anything. They're dangerous, Ellie. They kidnapped the herbalist."

She flinched. "Kidnapped? Wait, what herbalist?"

"They had her tied up in a van." Victor rushed to the kitchen and started collecting vials of tincture and bottles of alcohol and distilled water.

Elena followed him, gaping as he shoved everything into a backpack. "What is all that? Victor? Talk to me."

"I have to get out of here." He brushed past her into the living room, not sure whether he could trust anyone.

"Why?" Panic rode on her voice.

"Listen. Before I suspected his body was irradiated. Now I have proof." He pointed to the glass jar holding a lump of tongue.

Her gaze fixed on it. "What is that?"

"A bit of his tongue. It was all I could get. His body belongs in a lab. Elena, I think his death is connected to my condition. To the way people like me are diagnosed."

Her chest rose and fell from a deep breath. "Why would you think that?"

"The Health Board changed the diagnostic protocol for mirror resonance syndrome. There's going to be a lot more people like me in the near future. Granfa Jeff stood in the way, and so someone took him out. I need to get out of here."

Victor went to his bedroom closet and arranged pairs of underwear, pants, and socks in a backpack to cradle the glass vials. He took a small box from under his bed, where he'd been hiding the little jade figure that he had wanted to give Elena.

He retrieved the herbal book, his dreambook, and the glass jar, and swept into the bathroom to grab a few toiletries and the lightstick he'd picked up at Oak Knoll. He kept the data egg in his pocket, along with his MeshBit and wallet.

"I think that's it," he muttered to himself.

Elena asked, "Where are you going?"

"BioScan."

"You packed all that to go to work? Nope, I don't buy it."

"I *am* going there."

"Hey," Elena said, rubbing his shoulder. "Let me help. What can I do?"

Could he trust her? She was so erratic in her attentions, so insistent about certain things, and absent when he needed her. As bad as a cat—he never knew when her moods would change.

But who was *he* to turn *her* away? He needed help, even if it meant simply accepting a few small gestures of friendship. If Elena was willing to help, he wanted her near. His doubts were simply paranoia. She deserved better than that.

The decision to let her come along lifted a weight off his shoulders. Victor smiled. "Okay. Come with me to the office."

They walked outside to his car. He looked around, but there was no sign of anyone following them. Victor pulled open

Cody Sisco

the driver side door and put his things in the backseat. Elena got in.

Victor drove to the BioScan campus. He left the keys with her and took his bag and the Bose-Drive. "I'll be right back. If anyone comes . . ."

"I'll think of something," Elena said. "You have your Mesh-Bit, right? So I can contact you?"

"Yeah." He patted his pants pocket and felt the metal cylinder.

He lumbered to the entrance. His ankle throbbed every time he put weight on it. His MeshBit unlocked the front doors. His presence would be registered in the after-hours log, but he could see no alternative.

The analysts' office was dark. He turned on the lights, found the input cable to his MeshTerminal, and wrapped the data leech around it. If Ozie was any good at hacking, preloaded spyware would keep the theft from being logged. He booted up his terminal and vidscreen and navigated BioScan's systems until he reached the sequencing database. He put the Bose-Drive next to the spectrum relay and paired them.

Victor started transferring as many individual records as he could. Around fifteen thousand full genomes fit on the Bose-Drive, along with metadata indicating which were people with MRS. The recording process would take ten minutes.

As each second ticked by, Victor grew more anxious. Would he be able to get away? The strangers might show up any moment.

Ozie would figure everything out. Victor just had to make it to the Organized Western States in one piece.

The Bose-Drive reached 50 percent of its capacity. The office was quiet except for the whirring sounds of liquid heat sinks.

Victor tried to raise Ozie on his MeshBit again, but there was no answer. He looked up the address he'd received. The road outside of Truckee in the Sierra Nevada Mountains didn't have a name, only a number: 22. Victor twitched when he read it. He didn't trust himself to drive serpentine roads in the dark and would have to stop somewhere en route and spend the night.

What to do about Elena? She said she wanted to help him. By her own admission, there was nothing keeping her in SeCa. But wouldn't he be putting her in danger by bringing her along?

The Bose-Drive completed copying the data, and Victor stuffed it in his bag. His MeshBit chimed. It was Auntie Circe. He activated the sonofeed only. "Auntie?"

"Victor, I'm on my way to the mansion. I convinced Mother to let you in again. If you went to Oak Knoll, I want to hear about it."

Victor felt split in two. He wanted to see her, beg his family's forgiveness, and return to his seminormal life. But he'd seen the evidence. He couldn't let Granfa Jeff's death go unresolved. And when his family learned what he'd done to the corpse, they'd probably send him to a Class One facility.

"Victor, are you there?"

"Yes, I'm here. I did go to Oak Knoll. There's—there's nothing left. What's so special about the XSCT compound again? You said it might be related to a cure?"

There was a long pause. Victor felt the weight of the Bose-Drive in his arms. What would Auntie Circe do if she knew he was stealing? How much could he disappoint his family before they disowned him?

Auntie Circe cleared her throat. "XSCT was a gene therapy delivery system. We were running animal trials to measure whether XSCT-19900032 could suppress the MRS gene when we lost everything. At least a year of work is gone. If we had records or samples . . ." She sighed.

"Why didn't you tell me this before?" he asked.

Jefferson Eastmore had perfected a technique using viruses to deliver self-destruct codes to cancer cells. But it depended on detailed understanding of cancer genes. As far as Victor knew, the mirror resonance syndrome gene wasn't fully understood. If researchers had found a way to suppress the gene, that might mean a cure was possible.

She said, "I didn't want to raise your expectations unnecessarily. You've seemed volatile lately. And the merger has been demanding my time. I'll see you this evening?"

Victor gulped. "I don't think so. Elena and I . . ."

"A date? How sweet! Victor, that's wonderful. Of course, I'll be around for the next few days. Come find me."

A lump rose in Victor's throat. It hurt to lie to her when she'd always believed in him. "I love you, Auntie."

"I love you, Victor."

He terminated the feed and limped down the hall. The prospect of a cure, whenever he thought of it, sent his pulse racing. Why had Granfa Jeff destroyed it? Victor rubbed the data egg in his pocket. The answer must be there. There must be a way to open it. Maybe Ozie could help with that too.

"Hey!" someone shouted. It came from a conference room where several employees sat amid remnants of an Italian takeout dinner.

Victor kept walking.

"Victor! What are you doing here?"

He recognized the voice as belonging to Sarita, the office administrator who always had a few nasty words to throw Victor's way. He turned and said, "This is a late night for you."

She rolled her eyes. "Balls! This merger is killing me. None of the systems are talking to each other, and Karine's riding me to—well, you know how she is." She winked at him.

Victor saw a chance to cover his tracks, at least temporarily. "That reminds me. I'll be working remotely for the next few days. Would you remind Karine if you see her? She asked me to work on a special project, and I need to focus on it without distractions. I came by for one of these." Victor held up the Bose-Drive.

"Oh, I get it. You got a fancy new title, and now you're going to Bermuda to celebrate. Must be nice to be an Eastmore."

He bit back a retort. As long as she passed on the lie for him, he would be grateful. "Thanks, Sarita. You're the best."

She snorted, rolled her eyes, and returned to the conference room.

Victor continued to the exit. The moon shone down on the mostly empty parking lot, casting shadows, creating places for strangers to hide and watch. Where were Pearl and Tosh? He wished he could do something to help them, but the only thing he could do was save himself.

He made it to his car and knocked on the driver's side window. "I'm driving."

Elena smiled and scooted over, "Sure, boss. Where are we going?"

Victor sat in the driver's seat and shut the door. "Back to your lodge to drop you off."

She shook her head. "No way. You're not going anywhere without me. Tell me your plans."

The moonlight from across the marshlands lit her face in eerie blue tones. "I think it's better if I don't," he said.

"Victor—"

"Those people might come back." He hooked a thumb behind him, toward the towers of Oakland, its hills topped by brightly lit mansions, and the dark-shadowed cemetery where Jefferson Eastmore's body lay exposed. "Better if you don't know anything."

Elena crossed her arms. "It's not better. It's a terrible idea. What if you get into trouble and no one knows where to go looking for you? Are you headed back to Little Asia?" Across the bay, the fog layer hovering over the peninsula was lit with a dull red glow.

He shook his head. "I'm leaving."

"*Leaving* leaving? As in, leaving SeCa?" A goofy smile spread across her face. "That's wonderful."

Victor looked around at the BioScan parking lot. Why would it be wonderful to leave? Everything he knew was in SeCa—his family, his job. "How is that wonderful?"

"It's what I've been saying all along. You're better off somewhere else—anywhere else. I'm coming with you."

"You're not."

"Come on, we can leave from here. I'll pick up whatever I need somewhere along the way. I travel light."

"But you don't even know where we're going!"

"I'm not worried. You can't keep a secret for more than a few minutes. Not from me." The corner of her mouth formed a smirk. "I'm not getting out of the car. You might as well drive."

She was right. She knew him better than anyone. Maybe now, a friend was the best thing he could hope for since everything else in his life was going topsy-turvy. He'd always been able to hold himself together much better when she was around. He just hoped that he could trust her.

He said, "All right, we leave now, but I don't think we should drive all night."

Elena shrugged. "You're driving. You choose the turns."

They drove along the Bayshore road and then cut inland to the expressway. Skyscrapers glittered in the moonlight. Forested hills formed silhouettes against the silver-hazed sky. Ohlone Hill stood apart from the others like a duckling that had wandered away from the brood.

Oakland & Bayshore's northern border grew closer. The capital wall, topped with razor wire and floodlights, came into view. It had been there since the Asian Refugee Act mandated the forcible removal of Asian immigrants and their children to the slums of San Francisco and the farming towns of Long Valley—anywhere except the nation's capital of Oakland & Bayshore.

Guard posts dotted the full length of the wall, which extended into the bay shallows for half a kilometer. Beyond, a tent city sprawled in the marshy flats, a chaotic jumble of narrow, jagged lanes and rickety shacks. Cooking fires flickered dimly. The mess continued unbroken from the shoreline to the elevated expressway, a wide viaduct of lanes extending along the Bayshore hills.

Victor slowed the car in advance of the security checkpoint. The lanes narrowed, and dividers rose. He and Elena were waved through at once. He knew the checkpoint was mainly intended to control traffic and prevent refugees from entering the Bayshore region, but passing unquestioned was still a relief.

They crossed the Bayshore Narrows Bridge, which arced across a channel of water that marked the northern border of the Bayshore region. Boats carried lumber, rock, and other materials west toward the bay's wide expanse. They emerged onto a moonlit plain. He kept checking the rearview mirror to make sure they weren't being followed.

After about sixty kilometers, Victor took a turnoff that degraded to a gravel drive and then a rutted dirt path, undoubtedly a little-used route between one field of desiccated alfalfa and another. He pulled behind a tree and turned the car around so that he could speed back to the highway if necessary. No car could approach them without being visible for at least a half mile.

They reclined their seats and shared a single thermal blanket.

Victor's sleep was fitful. When the sun rose, he started the car, jolting along the road. Elena woke up after the first few bumps.

In a thick, sleep-slurred voice, she said, "Let's find a town so I can get a few things. Toothpaste. Some clothes. An air freshener."

The SeCa Long Valley stretched around them. For a brief span in the seventies, the combination of good soil and a burgeoning workforce of impoverished Asians deported from Oakland & Bayshore wrought a green miracle and enabled SeCa to feed its own and export to other nations.

Then the eight-year drought came. The snow pack vanished from the mountains. Streams slipped beneath the gravel and clay. The Long Valley baked and hardened. Many starved.

After eight years, the rains returned with a vengeance, though snow was still a rarity. On a clear day it was possible to look across the plains and see the Sierras, but today the dew in the air hid everything except monotonous scrublands and dwindling Long Valley farms. It was flat, empty, and desolate—the dried-up core of Semiautonomous California.

Elena grimaced. "Reminds me of the Republic of Texas," she said.

"What's it like there?" Victor asked.

"Rotten." She didn't elaborate.

They reached a small town where delicatessens, fruit stands, and used bric-a-brac shops lined the street.

Elena pointed. "Stop there."

Victor parked along the main road. On either side, small shops leaned into their wood frames. Elena disappeared inside one. Victor found a bakery that sold breakfast sandwiches and faux-café. He paid, waited a few uncomfortable minutes under the smiling eyes of the gray-haired proprietress, collected his order, and took it outside.

He found a rough concrete plaza with shrubs and flowering orange poppies in planter boxes leading to a small grassy park. A few parents tried to corral their running, screaming children. An old couple, both wearing large sun hats, sat on a bench and watched the world go by. Several people squatted next to blankets on which cheap devices, books, and kitchen supplies were laid out for sale.

Egg and pork smells escaped from the bag, and his stomach rumbled, but he resolved to wait for Elena to eat. On a normal day, it would be time for his morning dose of Personil. He reminded himself to drink a tincture before they resumed driving.

Buildings painted bright pink and green surrounded the plaza, but their metal downspouts were blacked with soot. Victor realized the area was the footprint of a building that had burned to the ground.

A wave of dizziness came over him, and he closed his eyes.

Someone bumped into Victor, and he lurched forward. The bag leaped from his hands onto the ground.

Off balance, Victor teetered. He flailed and grabbed the person's jacket to keep from falling, coming face-to-face with a middle-aged man. His weathered face pinched. Wiry black hairs ringed a large bald patch on the man's head.

"Watch where you're going!" the man said, pushing Victor away.

The world was spinning. Victor leaned forward, hands on his knees to steady himself. "You ran into *me*."

The man grabbed Victor by the shoulder. "What did you say?"

Pressure built in Victor's face. Blankness flowed into him. He couldn't tell left from right. "Leave me alone!" he said.

The man sneered. "You're a Broken Mirror, ain't ya?"

Victor began whispering Dr. Tammet's calming mantra. *The wise owl listens—*

Victor felt a shove in his chest and a sense of falling as blankness took him.

20

My work focused on using techniques to understand and interpret others' emotions, such as facial expression color-coding and mind-body synchrony techniques. The goal was to help Victor contain and minimize resonant episodes and achieve cognitive and emotional stability. The techniques I taught him worked, but the effort required to employ them successfully was tremendous. They required depths of willpower and endurance that most people don't have.

I never focused explicitly on suppressing violent tendencies. I viewed those as ephemeral fight-or-flight reactions rather than symptoms of the underlying disorder. His later actions can only be explained by how his responses to external events evolved over an extended period, the details of which I obviously have no knowledge of.

—Statement by Dr. Laura Tammet, the Eastmore family's neuroscience advisor (1998)

Semiautonomous California
3 March 1991

Standing alone outside a grocery store in the tiny farm town of Gaobeidan, Elena held a MeshBit to her ear. "We're in Long Valley," she said to Bandit. She felt as if she were betraying Victor, but Bandit and his female partner, Lucky, were only trying to help.

Bandit said, "You shouldn't have let him leave Oakland." He sounded annoyed and gruff. He'd been all smooth talk and charm when she first met him. Something had changed. He said, "Stay where you are. We'll meet you there."

Elena's back stiffened. She wasn't going to take orders from anyone. Besides, Victor had to leave SeCa. She could see his life unraveling by the day. She had to help him save what he could of his sanity. "No. We're heading—I mean, we won't stop again, I don't think."

Bandit and Lucky had seemed normal the first time they came to her, very professional, setting up check-in times to co-ordinate their schedules and keep track of Victor's movements. They claimed the Eastmores were simply putting money on the table to make sure Victor didn't get into trouble. They spoke about his boss, Karine, and his ma, Linda, with a familiarity that would be hard to fake. She'd agreed to keep an eye on Victor because she believed everyone had his best interests at heart, and she had taken on working with Lucky and Bandit as part of the job.

A string of coincidences made Elena second-guess everything. Victor had flipped out at the funeral and found evidence of radiation exposure. He'd gone to see an herbalist who then disappeared. His reclassification got moved up. Something about the whole situation stank.

Then last night Lucky and Bandit had showed up at her room and raged at her, clearly amped on some kind of drug, so they weren't the professionals they'd pretended to be. If they were tied to the Eastmores, as they claimed, they might have had an opportunity to poison Jeff Eastmore. Victor said two people had kidnapped his herbalist—that could have been them as well.

Elena felt paranoid. She wanted to tell Victor everything, but she knew his reaction wouldn't be good. She didn't want to send him completely over the edge.

"Where are you headed?" Bandit asked.

She gnawed on her lower lip, deciding how much truth to feed Bandit. "Victor wants to leave SeCa."

"We'll catch up before then," Bandit said, now sounding unconcerned. "Just don't let him go alone."

Elena paced along the grimy sidewalk. "Tell me again exactly what your goal is here."

"Same as yours. To keep him safe. That includes keeping him safe from himself. Which is going to be difficult until we bring him back to Oakland. You need to help us do that."

Shouting erupted from the small plaza where she'd left Victor. "I've got to go," she said and terminated the feed.

Elena pushed into a buffer of onlookers and spotted Victor standing at the center of the commotion. Bad situations seemed to arise wherever Victor went, yet he never stopped fighting, never gave up. He was the toughest person she knew. That's why it crushed her to see him this way.

Victor stood still while a salt-and-pepper-haired man strutted and crowed around him, poking his stomach, flicking his ear. Victor shied away each time the man poked him but made no effort to evade the abuse. When she saw Victor's eyes—focused but empty—she knew he'd gone blank.

Elena dropped two wax paper bags that held clothes, water bottles, and snacks for the road, and elbowed her way to the inner edges of the crowd.

The crowd jeered and laughed at something. The man asked, "Should I?" He held his hand against Victor's crotch, saying "Anyone want to see what happens?"

Elena felt heat in her face, charged at the man, and knocked him on his butt.

Elena hesitated. No doubt the man deserved a throttling, but he could cause a lot of problems. They were already doing a terrible job of remaining inconspicuous. She pulled Victor away, sat him down, and whispered his silly owl and cuckoo mantra. He began to blink and look around.

Elena knelt down next to the man and, reaching into her pocket, quickly estimated the thickness of about $200 in bills, pulled them out, and held them in front of the man's eyes. "You get to keep this if you stand up and quietly walk away. No harm, no alarm. Deal?" she asked.

The man grabbed the money. "He your pet freak?"

Elena pressed her lips together. It didn't matter what he said. She and Victor were leaving.

A few onlookers gawked. Elena rose and stared them down until they turned away. The man rose to his feet.

Victor sat a few paces away, conscious again, blinking and gaping at the bills the man held. "Why'd you give him money?" he asked. "What did I do?"

Elena stepped toward Victor and lifted him up. "Nothing. Let's go." She hoisted her shopping bags and led Victor toward the car.

He planted his feet. "Tell me, Ellie."

"Forget about it. Come on. We're still in SeCa, remember? We've got to keep moving."

"Where did you get that much money?" Victor asked.

Elena paused. He didn't need to know that his family was paying for her companionship. Besides, she would have done it for much less. She wished she could explain it to Victor, but clearly this wasn't the right time.

"I found a MeshCash machine," she said. "We'll need lots of bills. Some of the places we're going to pass through aren't exactly credit friendly."

An itching sensation spread from her elbow to her fingers. She scratched her forearm and pushed the thought of stimsmoke out of her mind.

Victor hung his head. "You don't have to come with me, you know."

Elena moved closer and intercepted his gaze. "You're not getting rid of me. I'm in this. All the way."

"I'm not sure anyone can help." His shoulders sloped toward the ground.

"Well, I'm sure. Come on."

They got in the car and said nothing more. She wanted to ease his mind, but what could she say except "Perk up" and other inanities? His troubles were real and not solvable through idle talk and false positivity. Neither was her deception helping. So she kept silent.

Victor navigated through town to back roads leading to the foothills. They stopped in the middle of nowhere and ate the now cold sandwiches—bacon, eggs, and cheese on country bread. She could tell by the way he listlessly nibbled his sandwich that something was bothering him.

They drove on. Trees from an orchard flashed by. Elena's itching returned. She rubbed her thumb down the length of her arm, not using her nail, not wanting to tear the skin, knowing she'd have to scratch again and again, and wouldn't feel relief for days.

Victor started squirming. "Last night, Granfa Jeff . . . I didn't cover him up. I just left him there exposed!" He banged his hands on the steering disk. "It's going to be all over the Mesh! Everyone's going to think—"

"Shh." She realized he'd been stewing on this for the better part of an hour before finally erupting. That frightened her.

A vista of grassy hills—still green from winter rains—and oak trees greeted them when they rounded a bend.

"Ozie said—"

"Who's Ozie?" she asked.

"Someone I met at university. We were friends. Until he disappeared."

"Disappeared?" She hoped her questions were distracting him from his churn of feelings.

Victor explained, "Yeah, right in the middle of the semester. Then the herbalist gave me his—"

"Ah, the one you said was kidnapped?" She looked at him. It was unbelievable that someone with his condition would experiment with drugs. Though she wasn't one to talk. What would he say if he knew she was recovering from stimsmoke addiction? The withdrawal was so bad it was still making her skin crawl. She ran her nails down her arm. The momentary relief was worth the next round of itching it provoked. "Herbs, huh? That explains why you lost control," she said.

Victor sat a little taller. "They're helping me."

"Are you sure? It doesn't look like it to me."

"If I could control it completely, it wouldn't be a disorder," he snapped. "They *are* helping. I just forgot to dose this morning."

He slowed to a stop in the middle of the empty road and dug into his bag. His hand came up with two glass vials, which he tipped into his mouth and swallowed, grimacing.

There's a time when we'll talk about that, she thought, but not now, not while he's on edge.

He resumed driving. His actions were stiff, like an automaton running a program. She'd always admired him for doing his best despite being a second-class citizen—she would've eaten a bucket of pills long ago—but maybe SeCa society's restraints were finally wearing him down.

Victor said, "I wish I knew how people know that I have MRS. And why they react the way they do."

"It's not you. Not entirely. People are wound tight here. Any little thing sets them off. It's funny, in Texas, even when their farms are being burned and their families ransomed off, people are more laid-back. I mean, they're mad and scared, but they don't let it get to them."

"But what is it about me?"

"I don't know, Victor," Elena admitted. "It's something in the way you look at people. It feels—I don't know—charged somehow."

"Charged?"

"Forget I said anything."

She ran a nail down her arm and felt a tingling shiver in its wake. Being near Victor again felt like quenching a thirst and having hot air blasted over her at the same time: a bitter-sweet unpleasantness that she had missed desperately because watching him struggle made her feel more alive.

"So what's the plan to get us across the border?" she asked.

"I don't know." Victor's voice sounded flat and distant. She knew there was a battle being waged inside him to maintain equilibrium, even though there was no sign of it on his face. His mind was a minefield that never got swept. She had to tread more carefully if they were going to get through this.

Victor continued, "Ozie told me he'd figure out a way. In the meantime, we're supposed to wait somewhere outside Truckee."

"For how long?" she asked.

Victor shrugged. "A couple days?"

"It's a house, right? I didn't buy any camping gear." She waved toward the bags at the rear of the car.

"I don't actually know. Ozie's tight-lipped."

Elena rubbed the numb spot on her upper ear. The stimsmoke damage was probably permanent. She should have asked the clinic staff in New Venice whether there was a treatment for missing sensation.

Morning sunlight had chased away the ground fog. Its beams streamed through the windows of the car. Heat rose from the dark plastic dashboard and the clipped velour fabric covering the car seats. She cracked the window. Dewy, cool, and grimy air rushed in.

Elena wedged her thumbnail between two teeth. A sliver of pork fat, the last remains of her breakfast sandwich, burrowed deeper, hiding from her probing nail. "Who do you think those thugs were that came looking for you?"

"I don't know. I didn't get a good look at them. It was dark. I think maybe they've been following me since my reclassification appointment." His voice had regained its vibrancy. "I thought they might be the ones who are supposed to take me to the ranch, but—"

"Maybe you're right." Elena said, relaxing into her seat. He didn't know about them. That was good. He wouldn't be happy to know she was keeping secrets.

Her fingernail freed the sliver of fat. It slipped behind her teeth and down her throat. She watched Victor closely. His gaze moved in a cycle between the road and his mirrors.

Elena scratched her arm again, this time digging her nails in, feeling a tingle throughout her body, an aftereffect that still hadn't faded weeks after her last high. "You know what? We need a word for what we're doing. What is it? An excursion? An exodus? An expulsion?"

"An exorcism. I'm leading the bad spirits out of SeCa."

Elena wrinkled her nose. "That doesn't sound like you."

"People can change," he said.

The look he gave her was impossible to read. She felt as if he were studying her, and a shiver ran across her arms. She shifted toward the window. The wind buffeted her hair. She scooped the strands into a ponytail.

Victor said, "In a normal life, we could have worked together, maybe at BioScan."

The image of a gleaming laboratory at the SeCa National University came to mind—a proper research facility with the latest instruments, a functioning MeshLine, and experts in the most advanced biological and medical techniques. Who wouldn't want to work in that kind of environment? Of course, it wouldn't be that simple: she had five years of going down the wrong track to make up for. And some mistakes couldn't be un-done. Although, now that she was clean, she had more options.

"You always said you wanted to be an astronomer," she said. "Do you like computational biology more now?"

He said, "Biology is fine, but if I was normal, I don't think I'd settle for it. The universe is almost big enough for me," he joked, bringing up their old silly banter.

"Are you in love with the stars?" she asked.

"Stars are sexy," he said.

Elena giggled. "Stars are not sexy," she said. "Cells are sexy. Astronomers grow up to be sad old hermits and spinsters. Biologists pump out loads of babies."

He giggled and nodded. Elena smiled. He was such a strange bird, so difficult to pin down. His mood swings were the size of the solar system, much worse than when he was younger. She had to figure out what was really going on with him.

"How did you know your granfa was poisoned?" she asked.

He paused before replying, and she wondered how far he trusted her. "He had a hidden lab room at Oak Knoll. There was an image, a kind of photograph that showed he'd been exposed to alpha particles."

"Yes, but you said you knew he was murdered at the funeral. I was there, remember?"

His eyes flicked across the landscape. "I didn't *know* that he was murdered. It was just a feeling."

She shifted toward him. Somehow despite his condition, he'd seen the truth when no one else had. How? "But you were right. It's strange, don't you think?"

Victor smirked. "I've been called worse."

"That's not what I meant. Like your dreams—"

Victor's hands tensed on the steering disk. "We're not going to talk about those."

Elena shifted back toward the window and crossed her arms. She'd get him to open up eventually. "Fine," she said. "What about your family? Are you going to call them? Do they know you're leaving?"

Victor leaned forward, readjusting the position of his butt on the seat. The car maintained a steady speed throughout. "The more people who know where I am . . ."

"The more they can help you," she said.

"Or the more the information could leak out, and whoever's following me can track me down. Like Karine, my boss. I don't think I can trust her."

"Why not?" Elena asked. Victor's trust seemed like a fickle thing—freely given to some people and locked away from others. It would help if she knew how he decided between the two.

"Something Ozie said about her. Maybe he's being paranoid. I can't figure her out. Sometimes she's supportive, and other times I think she wants to get me locked up."

Elena smiled to herself. "It sounds like she has a crush on you."

"I don't think that's it."

"That's what women do when we can't get the man we want. We flirt. We criticize. We murder. Trust me, she's crazy for you." She should be cautioning him against getting involved with his boss, but instead she felt happy that someone felt fond toward him.

Victor said, "I don't see how she could be," as he squirmed. Elena suppressed a grin.

She looked out the window and saw rows of dried-up orchards. One field was scorched; the burnt trees looked like black figures lined up in rows. Her good feelings drained away. The devastation reminded her of Texas, and she wondered whether she would ever descend to such savagery again. One murder was already too many.

21

What freedom do any of us have? Our prison surrounds us wherever we go. Our choices are only illusions. Don't ask me to sympathize with Broken Mirrors. They're still human. That's the most damning thing of all.

—Interview with Mía Barrias in *Five Years After Carmichael* (1976)

Republic of Texas
22 September 1990

Elena gagged. The Corp's wafting body scent, a rotten fruit and acetone stench, permeated the Amarillo Cattle Company's feed warehouse, a burnt-out husk on the outskirts of town. A single lightstrip hung limply from charred ceiling beams. The concrete floor was pocked and stained by decades of blood, filth, and meat.

Synthleather straps stretched around the prisoner's bulging thighs and arms. He refused to talk. His swollen limbs and tank-like torso indicated massive steroid use, as did the acne spreading down his face and neck. He had sandy hair, buck teeth, narrow shoulders, a bulbous chest, and limbs that seemed tumorous on such a small frame. He was a smirking, overmuscled kid who hadn't yet realized how much trouble he was in.

Tonight, Xavi, the Amarillo Puro's chief, had ordered Elena to accompany them. They had instructions to find out why the trade truce with the Corps, in effect since before Elena joined the Puros the first time, had been canceled, and to do so by any means necessary.

Shadows clustered thickly around Elena and her fellow Puros, Chico and Davinth, while they questioned the tied-up Corp. Folks who didn't know the Puros probably thought they were hick farmers with political leanings. If so, they knew shit. The Puros were a family dedicated to principles of loyalty, rootedness, and, above all, purity. The Corp should have feared them more.

Elena almost gagged at the smell the Corp gave off. She made a retching sound and said, "He looks like an inflatable dummy."

Chico, the Puro in charge of this particular job, laughed. "He's a juicer. What did you expect?"

Davinth, the Puro's most junior member, asked, "Been ragin' for a while now, haven't ye, tosser?"

Davinth had made the journey from Cardiff in the Welsh Protectorate to the middle-of-nowhere Republic of Texas and had become a drug-free zealot like the rest of the Puros. He was a dim bulb, always ready to blindly follow along, but at least he'd never figure out that Elena was still dosing.

She worried about Chico though. He was wild, always looking for ways to impress Xavi, and perceptive enough that Elena avoided him when she was using.

Elena cursed herself. She hadn't been strong enough to resist a few puffs. Hot saliva stung the back of her throat. She refused to cough. None of her Puro dickiemates could know that she'd sneaked stimsmoke in the other room while they were busy binding the Corp. Addiction was a leash tugging her down a path to ruin, and she couldn't break free.

The Corp didn't respond to any of their taunts. He stared at the walls and ceiling, ignoring them. If he wouldn't talk, this was going to be a long, difficult night.

"Let's get on with it," Elena said.

Chico shredded the Corp's shirt with a pop-out blade and started yanking a strip of sandpaper across the young man's nipple. The Corp, who was probably only a few years younger, didn't scream, didn't wince, and didn't speak. Elena wished he

Cody Sisco

would. The silence only encouraged Chico to get more creative. Elena looked into the Corp's bloodshot eyes so she wouldn't have to watch what was happening lower down.

"Why did you call off the drop?" Elena asked.

She hated interrogations and the stupid and ineffectual cruelty of her dickiemates. There wasn't much she could do about it, though. The Puros wouldn't pay a Corp for information—their principles forbade bribery—so they had to rely on other tactics.

The Corp's expression was sullen and bitter, and he was starting to sweat.

Unfortunately he appeared neither scared nor in pain. Chico tried cutting, squeezing, and breaking, and nothing seemed to affect the Corp. It was like he was numb all over, like his pain receptors were broken—

"I got it!" Elena said as she grabbed Chico's shoulder. She spun him toward her and smiled into his confused face. "He doesn't feel anything. Look!" She tugged hard on the young man's ear for effect. His head snapped to the side, and his teeth almost caught her fingers.

"Try that again, gums," Chico warned. He casually knocked a baton against the Corps' lips hard enough to split them. The Corp spit blood and looked away sullenly.

"This isn't working. We need to scare him." Elena unclasped and removed her belt and handed it to Chico, miming how to use it to block the flow of air.

Chico nodded, wrapped the belt firmly around both fists, stepped behind the Corp, and started strangling him. The Corp's eyes bulged, and the muscles in his face seized. Elena walked into his field of view, but the panicked Corp didn't see her at all.

Elena grabbed his ears and pulled. "Hey! Listen up! He's going to strangle you until I tell him to stop."

Chico watched her, waiting for the signal.

Elena said, "Not yet. A few seconds. Or maybe a few more. I've got time."

The Corp wheezed and strained unsuccessfully to draw a breath. His face turned purple and appeared to swell. Elena nodded to Chico, and he let up. Ragged breaths wheezed out of the Corp's throat, and he began to cough.

"You either tell me why you called off the drop, or he's going to squeeze again. And again. Your brain cells will die off. All your buddies' drugs won't help. He'll keep going until you're a drooling vegetable. What do you say?"

Chico looked at the Corp with an excited grin that turned Elena's stomach.

The belt touched the Corp's neck. His face caved, becoming just another scared dickie. "Wait!" he pleaded. Words spilled out of him alongside gobs of spit. His eyes were dark black pools of fear. "I don't know why. We got the word. No more deals with the Puros. Everyone knows now. You're off limits."

"Why? Who gave the order?" Elena leaned in, then gagged. He was giving off some sort of gross half-metabolized oily odor, a by-product of whatever substances he was taking. "Why?" she repeated, backing away and blocking her nose with her thumb and forefinger. She couldn't stand his stench.

Both Chico and Davinth were staring at her with heads cocked. Gooseflesh rose on her skin. Neither of the guys was plugging his nose. They acted as if the smell wasn't there.

And it *wasn't*, she realized, her heart pounding.

The smell was in her head.

Flashes from previous stimsmoke highs slammed into her, and she sunk to the ground and leaned against one of the metal struts holding up the ceiling. She should have realized it sooner. The smell was an artifact of synesthesia, a side effect of stimsmoke that no one had bothered to explain to her. Maybe other users didn't quite understand it. Not everyone had a friend with mirror resonance syndrome.

The Corp spilled his guts to Chico and Davinth, naming names and describing the hierarchy of a local Corps franchise—she barely heard what he said. Instead she smelled his fear and desperation. Elena watched and said nothing. She didn't think she could stand up.

Chico looked over at Elena, mouthed, "You okay?"

She waved at him to keep going.

"It goes way up," the Corp was saying. "Maybe as far as the king. All we hear is, 'Push the stims! Push the stims!' And 'no arms for the Puros.' Anyone caught in a deal gets his head bashed in."

Chico asked, "Who else are you going to sell to?"

"No idea. But I can find out for you. Just don't kill me." He looked at Chico with pleading eyes. "Or choke me again."

Elena stood, grasping the metal beam to haul herself up. She beckoned to Chico and pulled him to the side of the room. She wanted to release the Corp, but he refused. He slipped the belt around the Corp's neck and tightened it.

Elena took a step forward on wobbly legs. The floor seemed to vibrate under her feet, and shadows crowded her vision. She took another step and stumbled to her knees, retching. The sounds of the Corp struggling washed over her. She couldn't stop Chico. In between heaves of her belly, Elena wished that Victor would return her feed requests. If stimsmoke mirrored his condition, he might be able to talk her through getting clean.

The smack of a juicy insect exploding on the windshield brought Elena back to the present.

She wished she could be honest and tell him how her life had changed when she had moved to the Republic of Texas, how much she hated it at first, the time she spent careening between depression and stimsmoke. How she'd been saved by the Puros, how she'd relapsed, and then how his family had saved her again.

She wished her life hadn't taken the turns it had. But her actions had consequences, and she had to live with them no matter how dark and shameful.

She should tell Victor about Lucky and Bandit. He deserved to know the truth.

How would he take it? Would he forgive her for lying?

Elena glanced over at Victor. His hair needed combing. He probably hadn't showered in days. His hands gripped the steering disk as if he were holding onto a lifeline. She couldn't blame him for the mess her life had become. But if he'd been there for her, even a little, maybe she wouldn't have needed the Puros. *Oraciones* in Portuguese-influenced Spanish repeated themselves in her head. *Los Puros sonao limpios, salvos, amadaos. Unidos, hastao lo ultimo.* She pressed a palm to her heart and breathed in calmness.

Still, it could have been different. If his family hadn't rescued her, she would never have been to the clinic in New Venice. She wouldn't have rejoined the Puros and learned about the arms embargo. And she wouldn't have tortured the young Corp—that was the tipping point, when she lost control of stims again.

"Are you still not taking your medication?" she asked.

He flashed her an angry look.

"I'm not criticizing. I'm asking. How do you feel?"

"It's hard to describe. I'm me again. I'm in my body, feeling like me, feeling . . ." He paused, breathed deeply, then began again, "When I was on Personil, it was like there was a layer in between me and the world, between me and myself. Mostly I felt numb, except when an episode came and broke through, and I could finally feel *something* again. It's different every time. Colors or sounds or feelings take over, and I don't—I'm not myself anymore. That's when the blankness comes. It swallows me up."

"And then?" He made it sound as if she'd experienced only a fraction of what it was like for him.

"Most of the time it's nothing. Nothing at all. I'm gone. But sometimes, right before the blankness hits, it's like the universe opens up. I feel . . . Dr. Tammet called it euphoria, but it's more than that. It's like I'm going somewhere beautiful and dazzling, and that's okay, because it's all the same, everything is part of the same stuff: me, the world, all the stars and galaxies, we're all one."

Elena relaxed into her seat. Blankness didn't sound all that bad. It sounded like a release from a world that required so much just to keep going.

They were nearing the foothills. The flat valley floor had given way to gently undulating land, though the road continued due east. Trains heading to the resorts of Lake Tahoe, carrying SeCa elites to their vacation homes, sped past every minute or so.

She looked at Victor. His eyes scanned the contours of the road as he drove. He didn't need to know about her past. He wouldn't understand.

Although if she confessed to him about using stims, she could tell him about the good parts of being a Puro: the community, the farms, how they had tried to help her get clean and succeeded for a time. How being with them felt real and grounded. He needed a refuge like that, a place to start again. But he wouldn't be able to see past the violence. Maybe she could prepare the way by describing the dickie violence spreading across the Texas prairie as the Corps' fault. Everyone knew the Puros were only defending themselves.

And maybe she could ask him why a street drug spreading through the Republic of Texas produced his syndrome's exact symptoms.

"What's it like in the R.O.T.?" Victor asked.

Elena sucked in her breath. She contemplated the possibility that Victor was indeed psychic, but dismissed the fantasy. Still, it was uncanny the way his question tracked her thoughts. Maybe she had dropped too many hints about how much the Republic of Texas had changed her.

"It's simpler," she said. "People are more normal. More normal than here, I mean. They want to be left alone. Their attitude is screw everyone else, we've got our own problems. In SeCa someone is always in your business, trying to fix things, but messing them up worse instead. People in Texas believe in autonomy. It's not just a political thing. It's a way of life. Except . . ."

"Except what?"

Elena watched dirt fields pass by. The ghost tang of stimsmoke lolled in her mouth. She couldn't tell him yet.

She said, "The R.O.T. is missing something. It's like a blank canvas. In SeCa you've got a lot of people with competing ideas. Lifestyle designers, techies, New Catholics, deep ecologists, sex cultists. The list goes on and on, you know? But in the R.O.T.

there's no ideology. Maybe there was before the Repartition, but now people don't even believe MeshNews reports, like all that stuff is from another planet. You see a lot of strange things creep up."

"What do you mean, 'strange things'?" He looked at her, his expression that of a curious little boy. She'd confused him. He knew nothing about everyday violence and poverty and the blind faith that grows in such fertile soil.

The things she had seen . . . It was like the two of them were living in different universes. He wouldn't understand. With enough time, if she told him bit by bit, maybe she could enlighten him. Maybe then he would understand when she told him that she was spying on him. Until then she'd have to live with the aching feeling in her gut that she was betraying him. "People need to believe in something bigger than themselves," she said. "There's always someone selling a dream. So you get cults rising up. People believing in supernatural stuff. Not like, 'Wouldn't it be cool if we could talk to ghosts?' They really believe in it. Other stuff too."

"What other stuff?"

She could tell him about the flood of stims the Corps had unleashed to hook as many people as possible and their enticing lies about the effects: unlimited energy, visceral fantasies, and the feeling that everything was as it should be. They never talked about synesthesia, mood imbalances, addiction, and nauseatingly powerful déjà vu.

Tomorrow she would tell him everything. First she needed time to figure out what to say.

"Never mind," she said.

They reached the Trans-SeCa Highway, the main route through the mountains for a thousand kilometers to the north or south. Few other cars traveled the road with them, even though it was midday on a Friday. An anticontraband drone hovered and tracked the traffic, including three other cars and theirs, forcing them all to slow down and submit to the scan.

The drone moved on.

When they reached the eighty-kilometer tunnel that traveled underneath the Tahoe Forest ridgeline and terminated at the border with the Organized Western States, they turned off the highway. They continued along an old surface route through the wreckage of Truckee. Elena pointed to an abandoned shack to distract Victor, fished around in her bag, and slipped a Dirac stunstick into her pocket where she could get to it more easily if she needed it.

They stopped to refill the car's biofuel tank at a service station on the edge of town. An attendant bumbled out of his kiosk and unspooled the hose. Victor held up his MeshBit to pay, but the attendant just laughed at him. Elena paid the man with some of her cash.

Elena wandered across a broad expanse of asphalt. Victor's gaze followed her, worrying her. Maybe he was interested. Or maybe he suspected her deception.

She looked down the road at the town's remains. Few shops welcomed customers anymore. The Sierra Nevada Tunnel that ran somewhere underneath them provided a more convenient east-west connection between SeCa and the O.W.S., as well as a better connection to North Tahoe City through a southern spur of the tunnel. Without through-traffic the town of Truckee had withered.

The Corps had an outpost around here, Elena knew. Most of the residents abandoned the town following the tunnel's construction. Only investment by a few adventurous and bargain-seeking union pension funds had saved the town from complete collapse. Then some Corp-affiliated dickies took up residence in abandoned homes and cabins, cultivating off-permit marijuana in the summer months and cooking stims in labs throughout the year, which started several forest fires, one of which had ravaged most of the main street. It was never rebuilt. Elena shifted uncomfortably at the thought of stims nearby.

When they got back in the car, Elena considered telling Victor about her stunstick. *No, better to wait. I'll tell him everything, eventually, when he's ready.*

22

After the failed assassination attempt that resulted in his wife's death, President Lincoln, who had long suffered from depression and anxiety, and now found himself confined to a wheelchair and suffering from chronic pain, became maniacally focused on dismantling the sources of Confederate power. The South was occupied by Union troops. Plantations were partitioned and bestowed upon former slaves. Businesses were seized and turned over to cooperative ownership. The apparatus of government was purged of anyone disloyal to the Union. Abuses of power and human rights violations against white former elites were common during this period, and federal forces brought in on this pretext did nothing to stop them. Reconstruction rolled on relentlessly until nothing was left of the South's traditions, or its prejudices.

People said this was his plan all along, but I believe it was the loss of his wife that drove him to it. They were not estranged, as some have suggested. They felt a deep, abiding love for each other, and nothing hurts more than a loss before its natural time.

—Robbie Eastmore's *Register of Resonant Earth Discrepancies*

Semiautonomous California
3 March 1991

Elena and Victor found the cabin at the end of a bumpy set of tracks right where Ozie's coordinates had indicated it would be. Dry pine needles littered the forest floor. *We're lucky*, Elena thought, *that this dried-out part of the Sierra Nevadas hasn't burned down.*

The cabin was not impressive, just a small hut with a peaked roof. The interior consisted of an entryway, a living room with a wood-burning stove and a metal chimney shooting up to the center of the roof, a sliver of a kitchen, and a bedroom that held a twin bed and a wardrobe.

Elena sighed. No toilet. There must be an outhouse nearby. Although it was heating up outside, the interior was cool. The walls were well-insulated, and the cabin would keep them warm at night.

"Welcome home," Elena said, curtseying and nearly knocking a lamp over. "Let's hope the well hasn't run dry."

Victor said, "It beats sleeping outside or in the car. Bears are hungry for human flesh out here."

Elena sat on the couch, sending a cloud of dust into the air. "And bobcats," she said. "And the wandering women. And whatever mountain dickies call this place home."

"There are no dickies in SeCa," Victor said.

"Of course there are—just not in the Bayshore. They run all the abandoned places from here to the border with the Louisiana Territories. And Las Vegas, of course. Where the King lives." She noticed his skeptical look. "It's not a joke. Everyone calls the Corps' chief the 'King of Las Vegas.'"

"I didn't know that," Victor said.

Elena got up and searched the cupboards for food. Cans of vegetables, hard pasta, and other foods not disposed to spoilage crowded the shelves. "It's fully stocked," she told him. "I'll give Ozie credit for that."

She ran the tap and drank a glass of cool water that tasted of earth, and then a second one. "An automated well," she announced.

Victor said, "Ozie can't enter SeCa without being arrested—he's a Class Two." He froze and sniffed the air. "I wonder if this cabin is Pearl's." He bolted outside.

Elena followed Victor as he ran around, looking at the ground. "What are you doing?"

Cody Sisco

"Maybe she had a garden here." He paced over a thick layer of pine needles. "I need more herbs. What I took from Pearl's shop will only last me a week."

She could see a storm brewing in his eyes. He wasn't doing well. Damn, she'd been looking forward to getting everything off her chest, but now she couldn't risk saying anything to upset him.

Maybe he needed a distraction.

"Let's go see the lake. Please?" Elena asked.

Victor looked up, met her gaze, seemed to realize he was acting strangely, and agreed. They were soon back in the car, heading south toward Lake Tahoe, which neither had seen before. He said his parents rarely took him on vacations when he was young, perhaps because they thought he needed a strict routine. Elena's parents had always been too busy to take vacations.

"Where have you been in SeCa?" she asked.

He listed aquariums, farms, and vineyards on the north and central coasts and small farming communities throughout Long Valley before they became too dangerous. She smiled to herself; he was so cautious yet naïve at the same time. She'd made the right decision to help him. And to not tell him about her past.

Three months earlier when Victor's ma had called, Elena had been in the R.O.T., lying on a stained and bare mattress pad, staring at the ceiling, and resting between stim-fueled manic phases. Linda's voice came through the sonobulb sounding like a not-quite-human MeshNews reader. "I want you to come to SeCa," she said. "Victor needs you."

Elena took the phone away from her ear and stared at it. It couldn't be a prank. It was his ma's flat, nonemotive voice, no question about it.

Linda said, "He needs your help. Are you there?"

Elena rubbed her face, trying to remember the last time she'd spoken to Victor or his ma. "Why does he need *my* help?" Elena asked.

"He's withdrawing from us, regressing."

"We haven't spoken in five years. Why me?"

"He's never had another friend like you," Linda said.

Elena's heart cracked open to hear that. *Shocks, I miss him.* She sat up and looked around. The abandoned house she was sharing with other stimheads could blow apart in a strong wind. Dirt caked the floors, except where her frenzied drug mates wore the wood planks clean with their pacing.

"I don't . . ." Elena couldn't see herself leaving this house, let alone traveling all the way to SeCa. She wasn't well enough.

"We'll take care of your treatment," Linda said.

Elena looked at the MeshBit in her hand. Her heart beat rapidly, suddenly fearful that she was hallucinating this conversation.

"We know about your addiction. I've booked you into the Holistic Healing Network clinic in New Venice."

"New Venice?" The name sounded familiar, but her brain had turned to sludge.

"You remember, don't you? In the Louisiana Territories? Christ, Elena, are you witless? You've been to the Eastmore estate! A car will collect you tomorrow morning. They say you don't need to bring anything, and it's better not to. You want to start fresh."

"I'm not sure—"

"We know everything. Your suicide attempt. Your affiliation with the Puros. Give us some credit. I'm not reaching out blindly. You obviously need help, and we need yours. You'll get clean, and then you'll come to SeCa and help Victor stay on the right path. I can trust you do that much. And we'll pay you, obviously."

"I—I'm not sure I can leave."

"Elena, I never met anyone outside the family who cared as much about Victor as you. He hasn't handled your absence very well. I'm sorry if this is stirring up bad feelings. But he's shutting out his family, Linus and myself included, and I'm afraid of the consequences. You might be able to reach him. Will you try?"

Elena felt a tug in her chest. She would try. Her out-of-control frenzy had to end. Up until this moment, she had been sure it would end badly. Now she had a way out.

"I'll try."

"Oh, and don't worry. He doesn't know about your history. Be ready tomorrow."

Elena waited for details, but none came. "Mrs. Eastmore?"

"Can I ask you something, Elena?"

"Of course."

"Do you think we failed him?"

"What? No." The words jumped out of Elena's mouth before she thought about them. "He's going to be fine."

"We love Victor. We provided the best treatment. There's nothing we wouldn't do for him. But he won't let us in." She didn't sound desperate, or tired, or angry. She didn't sound human at all. "Ever since Oak Knoll closed, he's started getting worse, and I don't know what to do about it."

"He's going to be okay."

Another long pause. "You were always a tough young woman. Keep him safe for me." Linda hung up.

Elena felt like a boxer on the ropes after a furious volley. The Puros had helped her stand up and get clean, and then, in a willful act of self-mutilation, she'd tumbled down on a stimsmoke binge. Now the Eastmores were giving her another chance. She had to keep fighting.

The car carrying Victor and Elena jostled along a mountain road that hadn't been maintained for years, and it took an hour to reach the pass. When Elena got out of the car, she gasped at the sight of incredibly vast terrain, an entire cosmos filling their view. Although they could see the resort towns ringing the lake, they were far above, alone and unwatched. They could finally breathe.

A seamless blue sky soothed her. Victor seemed to relax too. Sporadic tufts of redwoods sprouted from remote ridges and valleys, crowded out by decades of fervent construction. Every flat surface and some of the milder slopes carried huddled buildings on their backs.

Victor asked, "What do you think this looked like?"

"When? In winter?"

"No, before we were born. Before all these people, the towns."

Hotel towers and tourist businesses clustered near the shore and climbed the mountainsides. The lake's surface sparkled almost like the ocean. Blue-green water, inflected with deeper green in places where too much organic material bloomed and clouded the formerly crystalline basin, stretched many kilometers across.

Elena tried to imagine a pristine lake, one without the dozens of rafts decorated with giant helium balloons in the shapes of animals. Victor explained that the rafts trolled the lake to absorb waste materials and pollutants. He seemed eager to describe the science behind the restoration efforts. She thought the crafts were about as attractive as such human-made additions could be. Without them, the lake would have long become another corrupted natural wonder of the West.

Elena made a square frame with her fingers and panned across the view. "I'd love to see real-pics from back then. It would have been beautiful."

She widened her stance, thrusting one hand forward and the other toward the heavens. She said, "An ancient scene: sun and sky, terrain and trees, the clear crystal depths of a mountain lake." She let her arms fall. "It's porn for poets up here."

"Hmm, that was original." Victor smiled, and his boyish expression charmed her.

Elena slipped her hand inside his hand and squeezed. She took a few deep breaths. "Try it!" she commanded. "Do you feel it? The altitude?"

He breathed deeply, puffing his chest like a bird. Then he exhaled. He shook his head and tried again. After the sixth breath, he claimed he still hadn't induced an oxygen high. Around the tenth time, he teetered on his feet.

Elena crossed her eyes at him and started to tickle his ribs. He backed up a few steps. She tried again, but he shied away and frowned at her.

She must have looked disappointed because he mumbled, "Sorry." He stuffed his hands in his pockets. "Sometimes I don't like being touched."

Discouraged but not deterred, Elena wrapped an arm around his back, and hugged him to her side.

Cody Sisco

"I remember," she said. "Just relax, okay?"

He didn't pull away. Together they looked out onto the lake. They couldn't pick up where they had left off—more than friends, less than lovers—but maybe they could start someplace new.

As she turned toward the car, Victor's hand reached out to Elena's shoulder. "Wait." He took a small item from his pocket and presented it to her, a red jewelry box with a gold foil Chinese character pressed into it. She traced the sweeping strokes shaped like a capital F fused with a smaller x, almost like a function symbol—her Chinese zodiac sign: the Dog.

Their hands enfolded the box. It could be anything, even an engagement ring. She froze. They'd talked about the rules. He shouldn't be doing this. Yet how could she stop him without hurting his feelings?

He gently lifted the lid.

It wasn't a ring. Elena sighed—*Thank the Laws!*

Inside the box a lumpy green pendant rested on a bed of cotton. It shone with a high-gloss polish. Lumps and divots rendered the pendant almost unrecognizable. But she had recognized the symbol on the box. She picked up the jade dog by its gold chain, which was lighter than she expected. The jade's contours were smooth and oily against her hand.

"I love it," she said.

"We used to watch all those movies of the Great Asian War, and you were always rooting for the Chinese."

She laughed. "And the Koreans. And the Filipinos. Anyone except the emperor. "

Victor laughed. "You made me watch *The Burning Shore* at least a hundred times."

"Because it is a masterpiece. I had to root for my fellow dog, General Lu Meng, may his ancestors protect him." She rubbed the pendant. "Where did you get it?"

"Little Asia."

She smacked him in the arm. "You know how dangerous that is."

"It's nothing compared to what you say about Texas. Anyway, I survived. See, I can take care of myself. And I thought of you. That shows how amazing I am." He smiled and almost looked like a different person, someone carefree and zany.

"You're in a mood," she teased.

"I know! I hope it lasts. Anyway, I got this to say thank you."

"Thank me? For what?"

"You might not have realized it, but you're probably the main reason I'm not locked in an asylum. All those years together. Being close to you saved me."

"Don't say that word."

"What word?"

"Asylum."

"You like 'Class One supportive living facility' better?" Victor asked, still smiling, but bitterness had crept into his voice.

She sighed. "No."

"It doesn't matter. All I wanted was to say thank you. Will you let me?" He pointed to her neck.

Elena pulled back her hair. He clasped the chain around her neck and gave her a peck on the cheek before he pulled back. Something was wrong though; he was staring at the ground.

"What is it?" Elena asked.

Without looking up, he said, "I've been meaning to tell you. To explain. I didn't contact you after you moved because—because I thought that you would be better off without me. That I was holding you back."

She put a hand on his shoulder and kissed his cheek, feeling it flush hot beneath her lips. "That's the stupidest thing I've ever heard," she said as she felt warmth rising in her chest. It might have been affection, but she knew better. It was shame, and as long as she kept deceiving him and leading him on, it would grow until it consumed her.

Back at the cabin Elena lay on the sofa while Victor made a meal of pasta with canned tomato sauce. She glanced through Victor's dreambook, wondering how she could read such graphic descriptions of violence without feeling anything but relief that her sleep wasn't so troubled.

Victor carefully stirred the pasta sauce, watching the swirls left in the wake of the spoon fade before his hand circled the pot again. He could almost forget that people were out to get him.

"Your dreams are incredible," Elena said from the living room.

Victor's neck stiffened. "I know, literally incredible," he said. "I told you about them before."

"It's different reading them. And there's so many. Where do they come from?"

"My brain." It seemed like a stupid question and dangerously close to Nightmareland territory. Samuel Miller believed his dreams were prescient. Victor, on good days, knew that they were just dreams.

"But have you been reading horror stories? Those could be inspiring your—"

"I don't read books."

He looked up from the pasta sauce and almost laughed at the puzzled expression on her face.

"I can't," he said. "The images stay with me. They're too real. I've got enough junk in my brain as it is."

After dinner they sat on a bench outside, listening to birdcalls and the occasional pinecone dropping through tree limbs to the ground.

Elena rested a hand on Victor's knee. "I want to tell you something."

"I'm here." Victor prepared himself for a lecture about gift giving being against the rules.

She spoke tentatively. "When I moved to Texas, I didn't have any friends. You know what that's like. I was working and going to school. My parents were always asking me to help, too. Every minute of the day was busy but depressing, existentially so. I needed something good in my life when everything was bad. I tried to tell you earlier, but . . ."

Her hand squeezed his knee. The grip was strong, tense. She raised her gaze to the treetops, which were hidden in the creeping darkness. He recognized her urge to maintain control. He waited, letting her take her time. He knew the value of not being rushed.

Elena continued, "It was stupid. I mean, I knew better right from the start, but I didn't care. It started when I couldn't—I felt so awful. I knew I was out of control. I knew better, but I did it anyway."

"I'm not sure what you're talking about," he said as gently as he could.

She wiped away a tear, caught her breath, and leveled her gaze at him. "I started smoking stims."

Stims!

Victor brushed her hand away like it was a creepy-crawly and scooted to the opposite end of the bench. She wouldn't do *that*. She'd always hated smokers. She would chop off an arm before she used stims.

But from the moment she'd found him at the funeral, he'd sensed that she was different, harder and crueler. He was finally getting the truth.

Elena wiped moisture from her cheeks with her knuckles. She breathed in harshly, perhaps trying to trick her body out of its emotions, as he did.

"Nobody told me it would be so hard to quit," she said.

He struggled to find something to say. He didn't want to rub salt in her wounds. But—Laws!—a stim addict.

She said, "Sometimes when I think about . . . The cravings are stronger than strong."

"But you stopped?" he asked.

"Yes, I stopped."

Victor could see a hard-to-pin-down emotion leaking from her eyes and mouth. She felt relief after telling him, yes, but there was something else, something greenish-yellow, shame or disgust, that she was holding back.

Victor said, "There's something else."

She nodded slowly, her eyes lowered to the ground. "There's a faction of dickies in Texas. They're called Los Puros. They helped me get clean, for a while."

She rubbed the jade dog hanging from her neck. "They're good people. They're trying to provide a safe haven. As they tell it, during the Repartition, Puros fought for independence. Autonomy wasn't enough for them. The R.O.T. government

240   Cody Sisco

kept trying to shut them down, but they always bounced back. Then Corp drug runners moved in."

Her eyes narrowed. Yellow bitterness colored her expression. "It's a war. The Puros and the Corps are fighting a war."

Elena rubbed her palms against her thighs. Victor didn't know what to say. This wasn't the Elena he knew. It was some stranger who had taken over her life.

"A new kind of stim showed up a year ago. Aurora. Or sometimes just Aura. It's everywhere. I got hooked again. Everything looks so vibrant. Sounds and smells. Like how you've described your episodes. When I'm on Aura, I feel like I'm supercharged. All my senses fired up. It's hard to go back to normal again after you've felt the resonance."

Victor lurched to his feet and reeled to the side of the cabin, resting an arm against it and steadying himself. People were using street drugs that mimicked mirror resonance syndrome. What did *that* mean?

Elena said, "I couldn't stay clean. The Puros kicked me out. It got really bad."

Her voiced cracked. Victor examined her face and saw a greenish-yellow blur move across it. She met his gaze, briefly, then looked away. "I found a clinic. There's one in the Louisiana Territories in New Venice. One of your family's, I think. The program helped me. I'm sober now, and I'm glad to be sober. I'm going to stay this way. And . . ."

Elena's resolve to stay clean swept away his questions and selfish concerns. Victor sat, wrapped an arm around her, and shushed her. "Let me know how I can help," he said.

Elena wiped her eyes. "You are. Being here. It's so peaceful. All that feels like another life."

Elena slept on the bed, and Victor took the couch. The morning came, and they sat outside, drinking faux-café and listening to the trees rustle and creak around them. She read more of his dreambook. She didn't envy his dark imagination.

Every once in a while he would glance over, a question seemingly pressing against his closed lips, but he never said a word. They spent the day in silence, waiting for Ozie to tell them it was safe to cross the border. She tried to tell him about Lucky and Bandit, but the words wouldn't come. It was as if she'd used up her last confession and had to wait for more to grow.

Around five o'clock, Elena couldn't take it anymore and starting pacing. "This is a pretty sweet cabin. With plumbing it could be a real homestead."

Victor ran a palm across the wall's wood siding. "I can afford better than this."

"Me too," she said. "That's not the point."

He narrowed his eyes at her. "So where does your money come from?"

Elena turned away. He'd been stewing on the question for at least a day and had tricked her into admitting it. "The thing about the Puros is—"

"I don't care about the Puros!"

She whirled on him. "What's wrong with you? Did you take your herbs?"

Victor reached into his bag and pulled out a vial. She watched him drink, wanting to tell him to stop, not knowing why. Maybe he was doing exactly what he needed to do to calm down. She just wished she knew how she'd triggered his anger and suspicion and how not to do it again.

"Happy?" he asked. "This isn't about my condition. I'm asking about you. How you can show up with a bag full of cash. How you can swear never to use drugs and then decide maybe it's not so bad to get addicted to stims—"

"This is why I didn't want to tell you. You have no idea."

Elena heard a chime. Victor looked at his MeshBit, and then, like the sun breaking through a fog bank, he smiled. The dark storm in his mind had blown over, apparently.

Victor said, "It's Ozie. He sent us a route." He relayed Ozie's instructions to follow a mountain road to a border station. They needed to cross during a two-hour window when Ozie had somehow arranged for it to be unguarded. They had to leave now.

When they got in the car, Elena sighed with relief. She would have gone insane with nothing to do if they'd stayed any longer, and Victor *was* insane, so it helped that both of them were now temporarily pretending to be sane together in fragile synchronicity.

Beyond Truckee they followed a winding, pitted road for several kilometers, lit only by the car's headlights and a star-speckled dusk, skirting the well-maintained avenues linking ski resorts to North Tahoe City.

"What is that?" Elena asked, pointing to something white off to the side of the road, partially hidden behind a stand of trees. A trail of crushed shrubbery led into the forest.

Victor slowed and leaned his head out the window. "It's a van." He parked on the shoulder. "Like the one I saw in Little Asia. We should check it out."

"Wait," Elena said, "it could be a trap."

"Wouldn't a trap happen on the road, not off to the side? This looks like an accident."

"I don't think it's safe," Elena said. She put her hand in her pocket and gripped the stunstick.

"Pearl could be trapped in there."

"Who?"

"The herbalist."

Victor got out, and Elena followed close behind, moving carefully through dark brush. Several small trees had snapped off at their bases. The van had been stopped by a tall, double-trunked redwood, which seemed to be listing drunkenly.

Victor opened the rear door of the van and shined his lightstick inside.

It was empty. No blood. No body. No restraints. Likewise, when Elena checked the cab, it was empty. Crushed and messy with broken glass, but empty. If this was Lucky and Bandit's vehicle, they must have run off the road and then hiked to safety. But how could they be this close? She hadn't told them anything since Long Valley. How had they followed them here? Elena wondered if Ozie could be trusted. Perhaps he'd made a deal with them and offered a ransom for Victor. But why abandon the van?

"They were hit from behind," Victor said. "Look at the rear bumper. They must have hiked down to the city."

"Let's get out of here. We have a deadline, remember?"

Elena turned and started back to the car. He followed, sweeping his lightstick in front of them.

When they were underway again, she lowered the car window and leaned her head out. They passed above the bright and glitzy town and began climbing the eastern slopes. Soon the road weaved downward again.

Elena knew she should tell Victor about Lucky and Bandit. But they'd started acting so weird. She couldn't explain what she didn't understand.

The disused surface road reconnected with the state road near the eastern bore of the tunnel. The border checkpoint was a set of shacks and scanners with a nearby MeshTower. As Ozie had promised, there were no staff on duty, and the barriers were all raised. Elena wondered how he'd arranged it and whether they could trust someone with that kind of power.

Victor drove across the border to the Organized Western States without incident. They descended toward the desert plains of Reno, Sparks, and Bartley New Town—a recent urban adjunct full of gated communities, luxury commerce clubs, and other exclusive retreats of the O.W.S. elites. They passed them and continued into the desert.

"Are you going to tell me where we're going?" Elena asked.

"A diner where the brainhackers hang out. Close to SeCa but beyond the reach of its police. Ozie's there."

She could see the diner's effluvia long before the building itself came into sight: it lit up this part of the desert like a neon nightmare. Huge, coiling solar-cell ropes were strung in loops, towering over the structure, spelling out "The Springboard Café." Multicolored lasers blasted radiation into the desert on every side. A rotating vidscreen cube displayed ultrashort films that featured various human organs, giant genitals included, showing how nerve patterns were activated by brainhacking scripts.

They parked in a gravel lot and walked to the entrance. Elena followed Victor inside, wondering what had happened to Bandit and Lucky, but more importantly, how was she going to help Victor now that he was calling the shots?

23

Organized Western States
4 March 1991

The interior of the Springboard Café was festooned with light-strips, vidscreens, and mechanical sculptures activated by patrons' voices and movements. A MeshTravel bulletin, posted next to the door, said the atmosphere inside the restaurant was so mentally exhausting that the owners had built a tech-less cocktail lounge with candles, drapery, and soft-droning music, a popular and relaxing place for those who could get past the automated doorman.

Victor and Elena stowed their bags in the vestibule's automated lockers and moved further inside, stopping when the floor buzzed and an array of red X's appeared beneath their feet. From the floor up, the mix of vidscreens and neon motion signs resembled the chaotic jumbles of Victor's dreams. He pinned his gaze to the ground and watched the comforting pattern of blazing letters while they waited for a table, being careful not to lose himself altogether in blankness. A few minutes later the X's disappeared and a rushing blue ribbon of photonic water on the floor directed Victor and Elena to a semicircular, overstuffed booth. They sat down.

A young tattooed woman, ornamented with several large hunks of silver covering parts of her neck, ears, and forehead, approached and touched the table. Images of food and drink swam across it.

"Place your order here, and the bots will bring your food. This button allows you to vidchat with the cook, if you want. He gets lonely. Make sure you tell him about any special dietary requirements before he starts preparing the meal; otherwise we don't guarantee not to poison you. Click here if you want to speak to a human, and I'll come back and yell at you." She winked at Victor and swished away.

A few other tables were occupied by small groups, talking and reviewing Mesh feeds together, and by suspicious-looking loners. The music, which had no distinguishing features other than being loud, rhythmic, and artificial, masked the conversations around them.

Elena chose meatloaf and mashed potatoes. Victor ordered a cheese sandwich for dinner with a half liter of local beer.

"You're drinking?" Her eyebrows arched.

"Yes."

"Should you?"

The hair on his neck bristled. She was the one addicted to drugs, not him. "Yes. There's no reason I can't drink a little like everyone else."

"I thought—"

"I'll be fine. I go to bars all the time now. It's how I practice being social."

Elena's eyebrows arched even higher, but she didn't say another word.

While they waited for their food, Victor used the table's interface to scan SeCa MeshNews articles. He couldn't find any mention of his granfa's grave being defiled, the theft at BioScan, a missing herbalist, nor an AWOL heir to the Eastmore fortune. It might be just a matter of time before those things became big stories, but somehow he doubted they would get covered at all. As that thought sunk in, it scared him. Just how powerful were the people behind his granfa's death?

Nonetheless, as he scanned through global headlines of diplomatic gaffes and delays in mega-construction projects, it was comforting to know that the world continued on its mixed-up way.

"What are we doing here? What does this guy Ozie know?" Elena asked.

Victor leaned back in the booth. "I guess we'll find out soon enough."

Elena's attention seemed to wander. She looked around, eyeing their fellow diners and glancing toward the entrance. It made Victor uneasy. There was something else she wasn't telling him. He watched her drum her fingers on the table.

She looked down and shrieked. Other diners turned to stare.

"What did you just do?" he asked.

Elena cackled and looked at him with tears in her eyes. "I accidentally ordered f-four plates of fries, two roast chickens, and a piece of chocolate cake. Where's the cancel button?"

Victor squirmed, unamused. She seemed on edge, crazed, more volatile than normal. Or was this normal, and he was just now noticing it? He pressed a few fingers to the table to cancel the order.

"Wait!" she yelled. "I want the cake."

He canceled everything else. "We can split it," he said.

She frowned. "Maybe."

Victor's sandwich and chips and Elena's plate of food arrived five minutes later on a platter held aloft by a robot with a tuxedo painted on its chassis and a top hat above its boxy metal camera-face. The robot deposited the plates precisely and gently and placed Victor's beer on a cooling pad. A speaker mounted on the thing's shoulder emitted a mechanical-sounding phrase, "Enjoy your meal." It rolled away with a quiet whirr of motors.

Victor shook his head. "NEC-Automation can build robots a thousand times more advanced than that. But SeCa bans them, and here they show up as retro kitsch."

Elena took one bite of the meatloaf, grimaced, and pressed an icon on the table for beer. She said, "Texas uses them to farm, but only on the best plots of land. They're expensive. And targets for thieves."

Victor took small bites of his sandwich. Bread and cheese, and lettuce for contrasting crunch. He heard her sigh, again, and then a third time. She was looking away from her food, eyeing his plate slyly.

"What's wrong?" he asked.

"The meatloaf—it's dry and mealy," she said. "At least the mashed potatoes are buttery."

Her beer arrived, and Victor watched the robot set it on the table without a word. Amazing how they knew not to interrupt conversations.

Elena took three big gulps and sighed. "What's the deal with this guy again?" she asked, but her gaze wandered.

Victor shrugged. "Ozie's a brainhacker." Why bother going into detail if she wasn't going to listen?

"Does he have implants?" She chewed the meatloaf, forked some potatoes into her mouth, and took a sip of beer.

"Just a headset, I think. The magnetic kind. He was always more into the scripts than wetware."

"He must be crazy, though, messing with his own brain."

Victor blinked at her. Noninvasive neuromodulation of the central nervous system, or brainhacking, used electromagnetism or ultrasound to affect brain functions. The technologies had only been available for the past two decades or so. Therapists were still arguing about how to measure their effectiveness and what treatments were appropriate for different conditions. But they weren't at all dangerous.

Victor took a bite of his sandwich. "He's like me with the herbs. Or like you with stims."

She pushed her food to the edge of her plate. "Have you ever tried brainhacking?"

"Yes."

She looked up at him. "Did it work?"

"Not really, maybe a little bit. My sleep got better. During the day I was calmer. Not by a lot. It was Dr. Tammet's idea. She decided against it after a few weeks of no results." No results that he'd told the doctor about. His dreams had been less horrific, but he hadn't wanted to open that can of worms.

Elena looked skeptical. "Wasn't that risky, though? I mean, especially for you?"

"I came to the conclusion that it was riskier *not* to try anything that might help."

"I'm sorry. I didn't mean—"

"It's fine."

They continued eating in silence.

As they finished their meal, a young man with dark skin and darker, close-buzzed hair walked to their booth and sat down. He stared at Victor through black, square-rimmed eyeglasses. "You made it. Good. Who the hell is she?" he asked.

"This is Elena."

Elena nodded in Ozie's direction.

He ignored her. "I told you not to bring anyone."

"She's helping me. Helping us, if you and I are going to be working together." Victor kept his voice level, hoping Ozie wouldn't make it a bigger deal than it was. "Look, Ozie, I've had enough running around in the dark. I want to know what you know."

"Fine, but she can't stay," Ozie said.

Elena's jaw dropped, and she put her hands around the edge of the table as if to overturn it.

"Ellie," Victor pleaded. "Do you mind if—"

"Yeah, I got it." She slid out of the booth with her beer. "I'll be in the chill room, racking up a tab for you. Save the cake for me when it comes. All of it." Her glare slipped off Ozie without any perceptible effect.

When she was gone, Ozie leaned forward and said, "Give me the Bose-Drive."

"Tell me what's going on first."

Ozie smiled. "I heard from Pearl."

Victor stiffened. Ozie had always liked to press Victor's buttons by making up stories. Once he'd told Victor that Samuel Miller had broken out of a Class One facility. Victor had nearly fallen out of his chair in the university cafeteria, and Ozie had laughed and hooted until tears streamed down his black cheeks. Was Pearl okay, or was Ozie pulling his leg? Victor placed his hands on the table to keep them from shaking.

"Is she okay?" Victor asked.

"They let her go."

That was a relief.

Ozie continued, "*After* she paid them 5,000 AUD. But we don't think it's safe for her in SeCa anymore. She'll be here in a week."

"The couple that took her—who are they?" Victor asked.

Ozie crossed his arms, always the type to resent a question he couldn't answer. "I'm still figuring that out," Ozie said, fidgeting in his seat.

Victor looked at Ozie more closely. He hadn't changed much in five years. A little less hair at his temples. Fuller in the face, but just as slim around his waist. Though he looked anxious, eyes flicking around the cafe, Victor believed he could trust him. "Do you think they killed my granfa?"

Ozie stared at Victor and shook his head. "No. They're thugs. Totally different problem."

"How do you know?"

"Because 5,000 AUD is a ridiculously insignificant sum of money. They're small time. Killing Jefferson Eastmore—that's huge. Consider the stakes."

Victor waited for him to elaborate.

"Our opponent is much craftier than those two." Ozie leaned on his elbows. "Here's what I know. Near as I can tell, the diagnostic protocols for mirror resonance syndrome will be standard throughout the American Union within five years. Throughout the civilized world within ten. Globally within twenty."

"Why does that matter?"

"Motive," Ozie said. "Jefferson was holding everything up. His pilot projects for Class Two ranches raised questions about the effectiveness of Personil. He advocated cognitive-behavioral therapies, herbalism, and brainhacking as alternatives. He wanted to do away with the Classification Commission's system. His ideas weren't popular—too radical, some would say. Once he was gone, no one else questioned the system."

Victor sat back and crossed his arms. "You promised me information if I brought you the data. This is all just speculation."

Ozie smiled, showing his canines. "Speculation is important. For example, what would have happened if Abraham Lincoln was killed that night in the theater instead of his wife?"

Victor rolled his eyes. Ozie was trying to push his buttons again. "What does this have to do with anything?"

Ozie sighed. Behind his black-rimmed glasses, his eyelids drooped; the lower slivers were deep red, like a hound dog's. Even his plaid shirt, which billowed around his thin frame, looked tired and faded. "I'm trying to make a point. Humor me. What if Abe Lincoln was killed instead of Mary?"

Victor shrugged. "Probably the same stuff. The Union would have used that as an excuse to crush the South even more."

Ozie held up a finger. "But maybe not. Abe went bat shit over Mary. It wasn't politics that led him to destroy what was left of Southern culture. It was vendetta. He persecuted the Confederate's leaders. He provided restitution to the slaves out of the lands confiscated from white elites. He gave Yankee politicians and companies free rein to remake the South."

"This is irrelevant."

"It's not! It led directly to the Repartition, and without the Repartition, SeCa would be nothing, another neglected territory of the United States. You Eastmores would probably still be mucking around some Mississippi River tributary. It didn't have to be this way." Ozie leaned forward, his eyes wide. "Or take the archduke of Austria. The continental war that led to unified Europe started because of another failed assassination attempt. Do you think that's a coincidence?"

Victor gulped his beer. Avoiding Ozie's crazy eyes, he said, "You're saying that the attempted assassinations of the archduke of Wherever, Europe in the 1910s and President Lincoln, which happened decades earlier, are related? That's insane."

Ozie puffed out his chest and lifted his chin. "I'm not saying they're directly related, but they are part of a pattern. History is not just policies and demographics. Sure, those matter. After the War of the Atlantic, Europe demanded reparations, which drained the U.S. treasury and paved the way for the Repartition. We all know that. But sometimes it's the individuals who can make a difference: Lincoln, the archduke. And now, here's the really good stuff."

Ozie paused. He looked around as if checking to see that they weren't being watched. The lights of the café blinked all around them. Loud, clanging music filled the dining hall. Diners appeared preoccupied with conversations and playing with bits of tech lying around. Victor watched his old friend and wondered if he'd lost his grip on sanity.

Ozie continued, "Mía Barrias, after Carmichael—she made a difference. If Mía had died, if she hadn't lived to tell everyone how horrible Samuel Miller's acts were, spreading the word like gospel, maybe we wouldn't have the Classification system. She wouldn't have made it her life's mission to get all of us locked up. We'd all be running free, and Samuel Miller would be an anomaly, the only person with MRS, not the first of many. Individuals make a difference. That's my point. Jefferson Eastmore would have made a difference. That's why he had to die, so he couldn't stop whatever they had planned. I know it."

I know it—that single phrase activated all of Victor's doubt. How many times had he said those same words himself while referring to a blatant fantasy?

Victor rubbed his face and sighed, saying, "You're speculating. The feeling I had that he was murdered, your conspiracy, the people following me—we don't know how they fit together." Victor pushed back his shoulders. "We need facts to figure this out. Hard evidence."

He took the mason jar holding a piece of his granfa's tongue from his bag and put it on the table. "We need to get this to a lab. They need to run tests to find polonium and to sequence the DNA to prove it's his."

Ozie looked at the jar with wide eyes and licked his lips. "Can do. It's safe with me." He placed the mason jar on the seat next to him, and then he grinned. "I'm glad you're here. You know how it is. You and I can stretch a line of reasoning to the breaking point, but together we can keep each other honest. Really, Vic, I know I can't do this alone. I tried feeding information to the police, the SeCa attorney in chief, the governor-general's office—none of them responded. They don't take me seriously. The stuff I found on the Mesh isn't court-admissible. I'm trying to feed them enough to start their own investigation, but there's no sign of them taking the bait. We're on our own. That's where the Bose-Drive comes in."

"How so?"

"Gene-Us was and now BioScan is the only company that can run the genetic part of the test for MRS. Why is that? What are they hiding? We've got to stop them."

Victor leaned back. He didn't want to hear any more of Ozie's theories for now. He was tired and worried about where Elena had gotten to. He said, "BioScan isn't hiding anything. For all I know, you're trying to hurt my family's company for no good reason."

Ozie poked the table. "This is about ending the Classification Commission by finding out what we really are. Don't you want that?"

Victor sighed. "You and me, people like us, maybe we *are* a threat. It doesn't take much to get us talking conspiracies and making plans that we shouldn't be making."

Ozie's face bunched up. "You're wrong. We are the victims of medical malpractice. All those people taking Personil. The facilities. The ranches. It's a twisted system."

"I am not my diagnosis, Ozie. I'm broken, but I'm still a person. I wish I were normal—I do. But whether I've got a medical condition or I'm the victim of social stigma, it's the same thing. I have to live the life I was born to. You do too."

"No. You're wrong. I've seen the alternative. It's what Pearl and I were working on together."

"What alternative?" Victor asked.

"You and I aren't broken. We are gifted."

"I wish I believed that."

"We are," Ozie said. "We just need the right environment and the right tools. Pearl and I are making an alternative possible. I move her herbs to clients in the O.W.S., and she distributes my brainhacking equipment in SeCa. But we can't let the Classification Commission off the hook. We have to end it."

Ozie massaged the back of his neck with both hands, his fingers digging under the collar of his shirt. "You did get the sequences from BioScan, right?" he asked.

"Yeah, I have them." Victor removed the Bose-Drive from his bag and held it above the table.

Ozie reached out his arms to take it.

Victor pulled the device back. "If you want this, you have to do something for me first."

"I saved your—"

"Look, I listened to your theories. Now you listen to mine. Granfa Jeff gave me the data egg. I have no idea what's inside, but it might be the cure, or it might be the name of the murderer. It could explain everything." Victor took out the oblong, black data egg and set it on the table. When it started to roll away, he put it on his dinner plate next to the remaining sandwich crusts. "I want you to open it."

Ozie looked at the data egg, raised one eyebrow, and frowned at Victor, shaking his head.

"Impossible," he said.

24

I created this register because events in both worlds seemed to fit a twisted-braid pattern. I thought by studying them I could help find a way for Victor and me to return home.

—Robbie Eastmore's *Register of Resonant Earth Discrepancies*

Organized Western States
4 March 1991

"You have to hack it," Victor pleaded. "Whatever Granfa Jeff wanted me to know is on there. If you open it, I'll give you the BioScan data."

Ozie took the coal-black data egg into his hands. "It hasn't hatched yet?"

Victor gritted his teeth. It was a device, nonorganic. They shouldn't talk about it like it was alive. What mattered was getting it open. "No."

Ozie handed back the egg. "Then I can't help you."

"Why?"

Ozie held up a fist and raised his fingers one by one as he said, "Piezoelectrically powered." One finger up. "The battery *is* the data storage matrix"—another finger—"which is quantum encrypted"—and another—"and locked by your biosignatures," Ozie said, holding up four fingers. "This is the best black box that can be made. I can't open it. It's too secure."

Victor took the egg in his hand. Did it feel cold? "You seem awfully sure about that."

"Have you not figured it out? Laws, but you can be dense sometimes. *I* gave this to Jefferson. Modded it in a dozen ways that he asked for."

Victor flinched. Was Ozie pulling his leg? No, he looked serious with his pouty mouth and hang-dog eyes. He and Granfa Jeff had colluded to lock away the old man's secrets, and Ozie was only now revealing this. Why?

Victor had a sudden flash of fear. "Did you cover it with polonium as well?"

Ozie reared back. "What? No! Victor, I'm a good guy. Jefferson learned about what I do through Pearl, and he came to me with a long list of things that he wanted tech-wise. The egg isn't just a storage device. Put it near your head."

Victor chided himself for suspecting Ozie. He held the egg to his forehead, feeling foolish. Then he thought about the hostess's piercings and decided he could do pretty much anything in the O.W.S. and it would seem normal by comparison.

"How do you feel?" Ozie asked.

"The same."

"Humph."

"What should I be feeling?"

"The data egg holds a copy of your brainwave schema along with adaptive biofeedback software and a bunch of Dirac transceivers. It's a brain hack, same as mine, and it's been working on you for months."

"What!?" Victor dropped the data egg on the table.

Ozie stopped it from rolling off the edge of the table. "It does three things: minimizes resonant episodes—you should find it harder to go blank now compared to before. Or maybe if you're off Personil the effect cancels out. Two, the egg obscures scanners, specifically those used during the reclassification appointment. Thirdly, it's a data repository. Jefferson had me walk him through how to record messages on it and set a trigger for it to open."

Ozie held up the data egg, and Victor took it back. He asked, "What kind of trigger?"

"He wouldn't say. He seemed paranoid at the time, but then . . . Look, this model could respond to brain waves, audio cues, pressure patterns. Bodily fluids too. But there's no way of knowing what will trigger it. Keep it with you, sleep with it under your pillow. Hell, sing to it, that might work too."

"Could you try to hack it anyway?" Victor asked.

Ozie's eyes lit up. "Well, maybe if you did something for me."

Victor crammed the data egg back in his pocket. Ozie had once tricked Victor into creating a science project for him. It won second place, and Ozie took all the credit. He knew how to push Victor's buttons to get what he wanted. But Victor had grown in the past few years, and he knew when someone was taking advantage of him. "I'm done running errands for you. Tosh was right."

Ozie glanced sideways and lowered his voice, "Who's Tosh?" he asked. "Another person you've told too much?"

Victor felt heat building in his face and had the urge to split his friend's lip with his fist. "Someone who will beat you senseless if you screw us over. He wants to find out what happened to my granfa almost as much as I do."

"You need to do better at keeping secrets. I saved your ass, Victor," Ozie hissed. "If you hadn't left SeCa like I told you to, you'd be in a facility by now. Or worse."

Ozie was getting a rise out of him as usual, the manipulative bastard.

Victor said, "You didn't do me any favors. My family could have saved me. I could have hired a bodyguard, instead of exiling myself to rendezvous with a conspiracy-obsessed data troller."

Ozie pounded a fist on the table. "You were losing it!"

A few of the other patrons looked over. Victor's heart thumped in his chest, ready to erupt. "We're amping each other up," he said, feeling his hold on consciousness slipping toward blankspace.

"I know that!" Ozie snapped. "We need to calm down. Do what you have to do. Use the egg." He tapped on the table, and a robot came over and delivered a brainhacking cap. It looked like a ceramic bowl with raised ridges and nodules dotting the surface. Ozie grabbed the cap, looking like a stimhead desperate for a fix.

Victor dug in his bag, searching for a fumewort tincture. Same as always; whenever he and Ozie got to talking, they started yelling and pulling each other's triggers. *Hello, Mr. Resonant Episode, can't say I'm glad to see you again soon. Why don't you piss off?* Victor found a vial, uncorked its forest-green cap, and swallowed. The liquid burned going down. He closed his eyes, focusing on the sensation. Warmth spread from his throat. An acid-green haze appeared behind his closed eyelids.

Victor lowered his head and brought the egg to his ear. After a few moments he felt calmer, his mind clearing. Whether it was the egg, the fumewort, both or neither, he had no idea.

When he opened his eyes, he saw Ozie wearing a ceramic cap on his head.

Victor laughed. "You look—"

"Don't," Ozie warned.

Victor smiled. "I was going to say, 'calmer,' as in, 'You look calmer already.'"

Ozie nodded and the ceramic cap didn't budge. They stayed quiet for a few minutes. Ozie closed his eyes, face intent as if he were listening to music only he could hear.

A question that had been worming its way through Victor's brain broke the surface.

"Have you heard of a drug that mimics our condition? Aura? It's a kind of stim."

Ozie's eyes popped open. "I've read dark grid rumors, but the idea is ridiculous," Ozie said. "Who would want to take a drug like that?"

"Elena did. She said it felt like her senses were sharpened. Synesthesia. Euphoria, too, for a while."

"Are you saying you think stims are related to mirror—"

"I don't know what I'm saying!" Victor shifted in his seat. He put his hand in his bag and ran his fingers down the side of a fumewort vial. He should double up his dose, but his supplies were running low. He said, "I hate not knowing what's going on. It makes me question everything. This time the reclassification doctor used a scanning chair. It made my symptoms worse, briefly. Almost like they were trying to destabilize me."

"Now who's being paranoid?" Ozie asked. "It was probably interference from the egg. Brains like ours aren't paragons of stability anyway." The glossy white ceramic nobs on his brainhacking cap glowed, reflecting the multicolored lights of the café. "You've never been in a Class One facility, right?"

"I haven't, no," Victor said. "They're in the vidfeeds though."

"Don't trust those. I haven't been to one either. How about a rancho?"

"Only the one my granfa set up in Carmichael, not the rest of them."

"Jefferson courted disaster with the crazy idea that we could be rehabilitated. The rancho in Carmichael alone was enough to make him a target. And then when he moved Samuel Miller to the Class One facility there . . ." Ozie adjusted a control on the side of his cap, saying, "We don't really know what happens to the Class Ones. Did you know that the number of times someone has been upgraded from a Class One to a Class Two is exactly zero?"

"Of course. It's a degenerative disease."

Ozie perched on the edge of the booth seat. "Is it? Does it happen to everyone? How bad does it get? How quickly?"

"I don't know about any of that," Victor admitted.

"Exactly my point," Ozie said. "After Carmichael, everything happened so fast. Suddenly there's a new neurological condition and a genetic test for it, but no one can access the data. Something's going on with the Commission and the SeCa Health Board, and your family's company is involved. They were the only ones doing any research. Why did Jefferson stop it? We need to find out, and to do that we need to understand the gene. That's why I asked you to steal from BioScan."

"How will understanding the gene help?" Victor asked.

"It'll help me dig through the Health Board's files, the research they conducted on Samuel Miller, whatever they've got. And I want to publish the gene sequence."

"What good will that do?"

"So people can study it. Victor, this is what Jefferson wanted. We'll figure out who killed him, I swear. But that's not enough. He's gone, and we're still here. We have to live in this world, as bad as it gets, as much as we wish it were different, and we have a responsibility to honor his wishes."

Victor leaned forward. "If I help you, promise me you'll crack open the data egg."

Ozie nodded.

"Okay," Victor said.

Ozie touched one of the knobs on his cap, breathed deep, and smiled at Victor. "Excellent. We can get started tomorrow. Be patient. You realize once we start down this path, we're painting targets on our backs."

Victor snorted. "Too late for that."

"Stick with me, Vic, and I guarantee we'll find the answer." Ozie pointed to the Bose-Drive. "Keep that safe. And don't tell your friend about any of this. She's hiding something from you. I can tell." Ozie stood and walked into the bustle of Springboard Café.

If Elena was hiding something, Victor was pretty sure he knew what it was. She hadn't given up stims after all. He crammed the Bose-Drive in his bag and stood to find her.

25

Economic progress depends upon the cooperation of labor and capital, according to rules set by rational and inclusive government. And, of course, the ingenuity and passion of individuals must be harnessed to feed the economy's growth.

Where in this delicate symbiosis is there room for mechanical automatons?

We say no to the replacement of labor by unfeeling machines. We say no to the disruption of markets by unthinking intelligence. We say no to the candidates who would put the interests of robotic corporations ahead of people.

We say yes to humanity.

—United Californians Against Automation (1971)

Organized Western States
6 March 1991

After Ozie left, Victor stood up and, immediately, the robot wearing a top hat returned and extended a towel for Victor to wipe his hands.

"Would you like your cake to go, sir?"

Clever thing—it asked because he was standing. SeCa was missing out on these.

"Yes," Victor said.

"You shall find it at the host stand momentarily. Please authorize payment."

The amount appeared on a vidscreen on one of the robot's forearms. Victor took out his MeshBit, pointed, and squeezed. The receipt was sent to his feed.

"It has been a pleasure to serve you. Have a pleasant evening, Mr. Eastmore," it said, then rolled away.

Victor realized he'd just left a trace for his pursuers to follow, if they were any good at hacking.

He raised the MeshBit to his mouth. "Call Ozie," he said.

A moment later, Ozie's voice spoke from the device's tinny sonofeed, "I just left. What do you want?"

"I paid for the meal under my own name. Is there any way you can wipe the record?"

"Don't worry about it. Springboard Café is totally secure. I do their systems. That's why I'm a VIP. Relax. I'll see you tomorrow."

Victor wondered what other privileges a VIP at the Springboard Café was entitled to. A free sandwich? Unlimited beer? Whatever the perks were, they couldn't make up for living at the Springboard Café, such an ephemeral and artificial place. A strong gust of wind could blow it away. But at least they had robots here and no damn Classification Commission—not yet anyway.

He searched for Elena in the lounge, hunting through dim candle-lit recesses, ignoring curious glowing eyes staring back at him. Velvet cushions lined a bench along the wall, and alcoves held poster beds draped in gauze where couples and throuples reclined. Cocktails ornamented the tables, held in every shape of glass imaginable: tumblers, flutes, mason jars, and cubes. Hip, social, and at ease—it was the type of scene he'd never feel at home in.

Elena wasn't there. He decided to check the bathrooms. On his way down a narrow hallway, he passed retro music posters for space rock bands from the 1950s: the Planetoids, Twisted Funburst, and the Boob-Head Dickies.

Beyond shredded-tire-tread curtains, the small restroom reeked of so much bleach that Victor's stomach climbed his ribs. A single stall flashed a red occupied symbol. Next to a hole in the wall where the urinal should have been, a handwritten sign read, "Water conservation at work."

He noticed another smell, too, an unfamiliar bitter tang.

He waited, trying to breathe as little as possible. Shuffling and whispers came from the stall.

Cody Sisco

"Elena?" he asked. The whispering stopped, but the shuffling continued, and he heard trilling, feminine laughter. Victor banged on the door. "Elena, are you in there?"

The lock on the stall door clicked, and the light turned green. The door swung open, and the tallest woman Victor had ever seen emerged.

Two bloodshot eyes floated inside thick maroon eyeliner, and a triangular beard pointed toward pale half-moon breasts hoisted by a sequined and feathered corset. Glittering midnight-blue platform shoes clicked on the concrete floor as the creature approached Victor.

A deep molasses voice emerged from her silver-lipped mouth, "You really ought not to interrupt. Sebastian, get out here."

A thin, gangling, and awkward boy stepped out of the stall. He wore only a pair of small lime-green shorts made of furry fabric. His protruding ribs tented the skin of his small chest. Looking at his face, Victor saw he had been wrong: not a boy, Sebastian was around his own age, but the complete lack of fat and musculature made him look very young. His eyes, crisscrossed with bloody capillaries, sat deep within bruised eyelids, signs of an acute stimsmoke addiction.

"Tell me what you see, Sebastian," the woman said.

Sebastian slinked a few steps forward and fixed a shattered stare on Victor. In a voice like a rake being dragged over asphalt, Sebastian said, "Mmmm . . . Can't. Too much noise in the signal."

Victor moved to step around the freaky couple, but the tall one shifted to block his way and leaned closer. "We were having a lovely encounter," she said, taking the boy's hand and cupping it to her breast. Sebastian nuzzled her side. "I was teaching him the most wonderful things. You could learn too."

Her teeth reflected the bright neon lightstrip encircling the bathroom's ceiling. She easily outmassed Victor three to one, not counting the waif. Though he wasn't looking for a fight, he also didn't want to be pushed around by a pervy couple in a public restroom.

Victor said, "Toilets are for people who need to go, not for whatever you were doing together."

The tall woman ran her fingernails through a frizzy fringe of hair. "You don't instruct Theodora Tamarindo how to use a bathroom."

"Biiirddeeeee!" Sebastian's long-wailed vowels echoed in the tiled bathroom.

"Victor?" Elena's voice called from outside. "Are you in there?"

Theodora chuckled.

Elena stepped into the room and stopped short, gaping. "Uhhh, Victor?"

"Your name is Victor?" Sebastian asked. The young man gripped Victor's shoulders. "That's not a bird name."

"I'm not a bird," Victor said, shaking off the other's hands, "obviously."

"Either you both get pleasant real fast, or you get out faster," Theodora threatened.

Victor didn't understand. It felt like urine was leaking into his bloodstream and flooding his brain. He should take another dose of his herbs. "Fine, we'll be friendly," Victor said. "I do have to go to the toilet."

Elena said, "No, Victor, that's not what friendly means. Friendly means sharing—Never mind. Let's go. Now, Victor!" She pushed through the rubber curtain.

Theodora smiled and straightened to an unnatural height. "Guard yourself, sweet cheeks. There's plenty worse out there than us, and, with that face, you're just begging to be violated." She winked and put her arm around Sebastian.

Victor joined Elena in the hallway, and they hurried outside together. His bladder had reached a painfully pressurized state.

He left Elena behind and went to the edge of the parking lot, unbuttoning his pants and peeing as soon as his dick bounced out. It felt like an electrical current. He looked up. Thousands of stars filled the sky, and pulses of drums and other sounds echoed across the dusky lot, background music to the thrilling sensation of relief.

From closer than expected, Elena asked incredulously, "Are you *hard*?"

Cody Sisco

"Go away! What are you doing?" He hunched over to hide himself.

"Did you get off on those two?"

"It's my bladder's fault." The herbaceous smell of Victor's urine faded. A different, fetid odor floated through the air, probably from the café's water recycling plant. He zipped up and wiped his hands on his pant legs.

His explanation evaporated in the desert air, and Elena remained silent. Maybe she thought it wasn't worth worrying about, or maybe it was something else. He might have seen her face flush while she watched him zip up. She had touched him a few times today. Nudges and hugs. Maybe she wanted more.

Almost as if she read his thoughts, she took Victor's hand, and they walked to the lodge next door, remembering halfway that they needed their bags. They crunched through the gravel parking lot and retrieved their bags from the lockers. By the time they entered the lodge room, his vision flickered from exhaustion.

The room contained two twin beds, a chair and desk, and a vidscreen and MeshLine—a nice perk of staying in a brain-hacker lodge. A shower stall, toilet, and sink were crammed in an adjoining bathroom.

Elena sent him to shower with such conviction that he didn't protest.

When Victor was done, he cataloged his possessions while Elena showered. The data egg, his MeshBit, the herb book, his dreambook, one sachet of fumewort and one of bitter grass, a half liter of alcohol, two liters of distilled water, twenty empty vials and corks, three shirts, one jacket, three pairs of pants, ten pairs each of socks and underwear, and one pair of shoes.

Elena emerged from the shower with a puff of steam that carried the scent of musk and berries. She wore a white towel, the top of which clung to her chest and the bottom barely covering her rump. Victor watched her dry her hair with a second towel. Her clean, moist skin glistened, and pressure began to return to his groin. He jumped up and shoved his belongings back in his bag.

Elena asked, "What did you find out from Ozie? Did he ask you for money?"

Victor rubbed his eyes. He felt like he'd had more questions than answers. "It's a long story. We can talk in the morning."

She dried her arms and chewed her lip. Then she disappeared into the bathroom.

Victor stripped off a bedspread and crawled under the sheet and blanket. A few minutes later she returned, cut the lights, and lay down on the other bed.

After an hour of tossing and turning, trying every exercise he could to calm his mind and empty it of thoughts, he fell asleep. He dreamed of eggs cracking open and releasing dragons who razed the far-flung cities of the O.W.S. with their fiery breath.

When Victor woke up, it was after eight o'clock, and he had sweated through the sheets. He dressed and spent most of the morning making tinctures.

Around noon, he walked to Springboard Café. Elena claimed to have a headache, so he left her in the room, glad for the break from her nervous twitching. He smiled to himself—he was keeping his anxiety at bay more skillfully than she was.

He found a booth and ordered food. A half hour later Elena joined him.

Ozie found them and eased himself into their booth. He jerked his head toward Elena. "What have you told her?"

"Nothing," Victor said.

Elena brushed her hair back. "It's true. I barely got a word out of him."

"Good," Ozie said. "We can't be too careful. Take this." He slid a silver device toward Victor. It was the size of two hands side by side.

"What is it?" Victor asked.

"A MobileMesh unit, new standard model, with some of my own modifications to make it untraceable. I call it the Handy 1000. Most of these are limited to the common command interface, but I've done a little creative reorganization. This one also connects to the dark grid. I've got one too. We'll use

Cody Sisco

them to communicate. Don't lose it. Also, you need to smash your MeshBit. Or I can neuter it for you."

Victor handed Ozie his MeshBit and picked up the Handy 1000. He yelped when it folded itself into a spiraling cylindrical tube.

Ozie laughed. "You didn't break it. That's how I usually carry it around in my pocket. Be careful though. People will think you're walking around with a huge erection."

Elena rolled her eyes. "We should be making plans. What are you going to do with the tongue, for instance? We shouldn't just sit here, playing with gadgets."

They both ignored her. Ozie said, "You can put it around your wrist, too, but don't do that in public. This isn't Oakland & Bayshore. A lot of people here would kill for one of those."

Victor found a square icon that caused the Handy 1000 to unroll itself into a sheet. He pressed it again and the flexible glass curled itself up.

"Neat," he said.

He unfolded it again and studied the screen. He saw several unfamiliar icons in addition to the standard set. He pressed one that looked like nine squares arranged in a grid, and a map appeared showing the area where SeCa met the O.W.S. A green dot pulsed where the Springboard Café was. There were also blue marks like upside-down *V*'s arranged in a hexagonal pattern that blanketed the entire map. He pressed his finger against one of the icons, and another screen of information swam up:

MT_OWS_904567.10
39.459033, -119.780910
64kbps, 34% adl
firmware update: Semaphore-38

Victor stared at the statistics, puzzling them out, fascinated by his first glimpse into the Mesh's innards. The *V*'s must be MeshTowers, and the first line must be the identifier for the one he'd selected. The second line showed its geographic coordinates. The last two might be bandwidth and operating system. He assumed "adl" stood for "average daily load."

None of this information was usually available to users. Ozie had somehow hacked the Mesh.

There was another icon labeled "Log." Victor pressed it, and a long page scrolled by. He found a time-stamped command for a MeshID "handshake," a code passed back and forth between devices to set up a secure communications link. Each handshake passed through dozens of MeshTowers, some more than one hundred kilometers away, if he was calculating longitude and latitude correctly. Dozens of handshakes filled the log. The device created a new false MeshID every few seconds and randomly rerouted requests and data through nearby MeshTowers in order to mask its location and activity—a genius technique.

Although it contained the same core functions as any Mesh interfacing device—messaging, data retrieval, and scheduling—the extra features rendered it much more powerful and secure.

Victor felt an elbow in his side and looked up. Elena was staring at him. "Earth to Victor," she said. "Your friend here has been rocking in his chair like a nutcase, watching you—"

"Hey!" Ozie said. "I object to that term."

Ozie glared at her, then turned his attention to Victor. "I think I've solved the processing problem. On the Mesh processing happens in linked clusters of devices. The clusters are called nodes. Las Vegas is a node. The Bayshore is a node. There are thousands of nodes all over Europe, connected by the low-orbiters and in some cases by physical cables. In the American Union the links are mostly low-bandwidth MeshTowers, so I can't send much traffic through them. But if I move the satellites . . ."

A sudden fear gripped Victor. He pictured a thousand satellites crashing down and incinerating him at ground zero. "You've got to be kidding."

Ozie shrugged. "They're mobile and autonomous. It just takes a little reprogramming. They usually cluster over important population centers. A simple bit of coding, and they'll adjust their orbits, increasing coverage here so that we can link processing capacities across the A.U.'s western nations.

We'll churn through the data, and then everything will go back to normal."

"What are you doing with the data exactly?" Elena asked.

Ozie smirked and waggled a finger for Victor stay silent.

Victor smiled apologetically at Elena and shrugged. He said, "Ozie, we need to be realistic. The amount of processor time is gargantuan. It would take years on the fastest computer."

Ozie smiled. "How much processor time?"

Victor calculated hastily. "Somewhere between four to six billion exaflop-hours."

Ozie's eyes widened, and his thin lips parted. "Whoa! That's enough to plot a round trip to Mars for an entire botfleet."

"What are you planning?" Elena's eyes searched Victor's face. Before he could answer, Ozie shushed him.

Ozie said, "Let me think." A slow grin spread across his face. His eyeglasses flashed, reflecting the bluish image from a vidscreen on the wall. "We could chain the low orbiters together and get global coverage."

Two people in ultra-pliable synthleather tracksuits passed slowly toward the back of the room. Victor flinched. He looked again. They weren't his pursuers. But they could sneak up at any moment. "We need to talk about the people following me."

Ozie nodded. "We'll get to that. Hear me out first. Chaining the nodes is possible but risky. This kind of stunt is uncomfortably public. The Mesh reports would cover it; most governments would notice; every cybersecurity firm in the world would know. Actually, I'm not sure I can do it, and I'm sure I can't do it alone. I'd need your help."

Here it comes, Victor thought. *I'll bet he wants money.* He leaned back and watched blobs of light in the ceiling chase each other, dozens of blue, green, and red trails flared in their wake. One blob caught the other in a spectacular crash that lit the entire room in a flame-yellow glow. Ozie had never had any qualms about asking Victor to pay for his tech schemes.

Ozie cleared his throat and pulled at his shirt collar. "It's going to take a lot of resources. I need 100,000 AUD."

Elena smirked. "Told you." She laughed bitterly. "He wants

your money. That's the only reason he dragged you here. All this talk about your granfa and conspiracies is a lie."

Victor looked carefully at Elena. The tension under her eyes, the curl of her lip, the way her nostrils flared. She was starting to buckle under the strain of running.

Ozie was manipulating Victor—yes, he was conspiracy nut, certainly—but Victor knew Ozie wasn't greedy and they made a good team.

Victor placed his hand gently on Elena's shoulder. "You said you wanted to help me, Elena. I trust Ozie. I admit we haven't told you everything that's going on. What we're planning could help overturn the Classification System, or at least make sure its expansion isn't driven by profit. Don't worry. He'll keep us safe." Victor turned back to Ozie. "So what is the money for?"

"Equipment. Code. A few favors. It's not cheap to move a fleet of satellites!"

Victor began calculating how much he would earn annually on the investments his granfa had left him. Was Ozie's help worth three years of that income? He'd pay anything, do anything, to learn what had really happened to Granfa Jeff. "Agreed," Victor said.

Elena rolled her eyes and said, "This has nothing to do with finding out who killed him. You know that, right?"

Victor said, "It's all part of the same package: decoding the gene, figuring out what we are, why Granfa Jeff was killed, how people with MRS should be treated, opening the data egg—they're all related." He looked at Ozie and said, with a shade of doubt creeping into his voice, "At least we think they're all related."

Ozie said, "About decoding the gene: your program takes care of the processing, but we're still going to need the Human Genome Initiative's libraries of sequences in order to make the comparison with the BioScan data."

"The HGI?" Elena's grew wide. "You are not planning to steal from the Institute! Tell me you're not!"

Victor swept the room with his gaze. "I don't see them lying around here. We need the libraries to filter the MRS genomes to find the right sequence."

Cody Sisco

"Shocks, this is a bad idea!" Elena said.

"We do what we need to do," Victor said.

Ozie smiled. The café's lights reflected off his ivory teeth. "Victor, you've got the right attitude. All it'll take is a data leech on one of HGI's machines." Ozie's grin widened. "Think about it. What an opportunity! You're going to steal from the King of Las Vegas."

26

Elena woke at the sound of a car door slamming. The room around her smelled of fake flowers, sweet, cloying, and artificial—probably an automated morning spritzer carrying a wake-up scent. These brainhacker types seemed to have no limits when it came to drugs.

Then she remembered. Stimsmoke, last night. It was only a puff from the waifish boy, Sebastian, before Victor had run into them, but it meant she'd fucked up again.

Victor entered with his bag and a wad of trash balled in his hand.

She sat up and blinked. "Spring cleaning?" she asked.

"Getting the car worked on. Now that we're out of SeCa, they can retrofit it for automation."

"How exciting," Elena deadpanned. She rubbed her eyes. Her throat felt scratchy and dry. Stimsmoke would numb it, if she had any, but she knew she must not succumb to the temptation again. "I still don't understand why you let that dweeb manipulate you."

Victor looked up from the vial he was filling with herb dust, alcohol, and water. "We told you. He wants me to find the mirror resonance sequence. I want the data egg opened. We have a deal."

"You trust him?" She lay back on the pillows, rubbing her throat.

Victor capped the vial and put it in his bag. "Not really. Truth is, I would probably help him anyway. He always dangles a carrot a little bit further. I can see him doing it. I should care that he's manipulating me. But I'm certain he can help me find out what happened to Granfa Jeff. And in the meantime, if he can help other people like me, then I'm going to help him."

"He's going to bleed you dry." Elena squinted. "I know you're looking for the MRS gene, but I don't understand why."

Victor put his bag down. "The tests are run in a black box. We run the test, we get a result, but we never actually see the sequence. The reference file, the actual sequence of base pairs, is encrypted." Victor sighed. "When I think of how much information is locked away in private databases . . . Ozie's right, it's a disgrace."

Elena snorted. "How else would it be? Free information for everybody? His ideas are screwing with your head."

"I'm not completely clueless. We've got the raw data now. I'm not going to give Ozie what he wants without getting something in return." He picked up his bag. "I'll be at the café after I take the car in."

"I'll come find you later," she said.

After she dressed, Elena stepped outside, trying not to think about stimsmoke. She still hadn't told him about Lucky and Bandit. Guilt was a knife jabbing her, especially after he'd been so understanding about the stims. After she'd moved to the R.O.T. and her life became a sad series of mistakes, keeping secrets, no matter how painful, always seemed easier than telling the truth. Why couldn't she ever do the right thing at the right time?

Elena's MeshBit chimed as she crossed the gravel parking lot, already feeling the day's heat. She answered and heard Bandit's voice.

"Runaway girl," he said, "You should have been in touch yesterday."

Elena grimaced. His voice sounded like fingernails dragged over concrete. She said, "I've been busy."

"Where are you?"

Elena walked back to stand in the shade of the building. "We crossed the border."

"I figured."

She pulled the MeshBit from her ear and looked at it. Could they track it? She'd have to ask Ozie for help. She returned the MeshBit near her face. "Was that your van on the side of the road?"

Bandit grunted. "Maybe."

Elena scanned her surroundings, a vast dirt plain with mountains to the west and desert to the east. She asked, "How did you know we were in the mountains?"

"Just stay in one place long enough for us to catch up. The border is closed today. Something to do with a security breach."

Elena looked at the road leading to the café. So Ozie's handiwork wasn't undetectable. That didn't bode well for Victor. "Who ran you off the road?"

"Didn't get a good look. Thought it might have been you."

"I'm not that great a driver," she said. Things were getting complicated. If Lucky and Bandit were working for the Eastmores as they said, who was running them off the road? And what did that mean for her and Victor?

"What will happen to Victor when you catch up?" Elena asked.

"We'll keep him safe. Take him back to SeCa."

"He can't go back if he's being reclassified."

Bandit's breath whooshed through the speaker. "I'll have to check on that." He terminated the feed.

Elena crossed the road and found Victor talking with two mechanics outside the garage. She watched the mechanics inspect the driver's console together, and one of them affixed a device to the steering panel. They got out of the car and moved out of the way. Victor's car rolled forward into a repair bay, driverless. That technology would get him arrested if he used it in SeCa. The mechanics hooted, apparently excited for a new project.

"What are they going to do to it?" Elena asked. "Is it ready?"

One of the mechanics heard her and laughed. "Not nearly," he said, running his hand along the car's rear left fin. "We got to restore the automation protocols, add transponders, update the driving algorithm. Special package per Ozie's request."

"They need all night to do the work," Victor told her. "We'll leave in the morning."

Elena turned toward Victor and grabbed his shoulder. "This plan you've cooked up: it's a horrible idea. We should stay a few more days at least. You need to rest up."

He shrugged out of her grip. "We leave when it's ready." Victor authorized payment for the work on his car and walked outside.

She followed, cleared a lump from her throat, and said, "We can't leave."

Victor paused, glancing back, and said, "We are. At least, I am. Stay here if you want." He turned and walked toward the café.

She trotted after him. "Ozie's using you. If you really want to find out what happened to your granfa, your best chance is to go back to SeCa and show the evidence to the police."

Victor wheeled around. "I'd be reclassified in a heartbeat. You know that."

"Maybe not," she said. "Your family could help. You're an Eastmore, after all."

"I'm going, Elena. Make up your mind before tomorrow."

She watched him enter the café. He was spinning out of control. How long before he did something he'd regret? But there weren't any good options. Going back could get him locked up. Staying here wasn't viable; Ozie was roping him into serious crimes—messing with the King of Las Vegas was a stupid idea. She helped get him into this mess. She had to find a way out. And, she finally admitted to herself, she needed help.

Elena called Linda Eastmore, who answered on the third tone.

"Where is Victor?" Linda demanded. "What have you done with him?"

Elena bristled. Linda hadn't returned her calls for several days, and now she wanted answers? "He's fine. We're—we're in the O.W.S."

"I hired you to keep him safe, not go for a joyride."

Elena straightened. She was doing her best to navigate rough waters. Linda should give her some credit. "Believe me, it's hardly a joyride. Ms. Eastmore, I need to talk to you about his reclassification."

"You know they found my father-in-law's grave desecrated? If Victor had something to do with this, I'm holding you responsible. I asked you to help him manage his condition, not send him off the rails. If you have—"

"Ma'am!" Elena interrupted. "I'm trying my best, but he doesn't want to go home. He's worried about his reclassification. We need to know if he can come back to his old life or not."

"It's pending." Linda Eastmore sighed. "Apparently the doctor he was assigned wants to rule him a Class Two, but we're fighting it. It would help if Victor were here. We can't keep dodging the Health Board's inquiries, and they could ask him to come in again any day now. What are we supposed to say? He took a long holiday?" A loud banging sound made Elena hold the MeshBit away from her ear. "I should have known better than to trust you. How could I have thought an addict would be a reliable companion for my son?"

"Is that why you hired those other two to watch him?" Elena asked.

"What other two?" Linda snapped.

"Lucky and Bandit. When Victor visited the herbalist, they took her—"

"What herbalist?" Elena looked at her MeshBit. Was Linda being deliberately rude? Why would she pretend not to know what Elena was talking about? Elena said, "He found a woman in Little Asia to help him. Haven't they told you?"

"Haven't who told me what? I don't know what you're talking about."

"Lucky and Bandit," Elena snapped.

"You say those words like they should mean something to me."

Elena felt her insides freeze. Linda hadn't hired them. They'd been watching Victor, following him, trying to get their hands on him. And Elena had been helping them.

"Elena, I expect you to return Victor to—"

Elena terminated the feed. She cupped a hand to her forehead. How could she have been so naive? Now Lucky and Bandit were on their way here. She had to find Victor. They had to go.

Victor smiled to himself, leaning back in his chair. Ozie had set Victor up at a computer terminal in a private room at the café with large portraits of dogs dressed in ball gowns and suits hanging from the wall. The Bose-Drive had already been copied to the computer's archives, including both the genomic records and the analytical engine that Victor used in his everyday work.

Ozie was on the other side of the room, peering at vid-screens and tapping on his type-pad.

Everything was easier now that he'd decided to go along with Ozie's plan. Someone else could call the shots, and he could focus on what he did best: computational genomic analysis. It helped that the tinctures were working. With Personil purged from his system, the herbs coursed through his body, spreading dozens of biological compounds throughout his cells, changing the neurochemistry in his brain, and subtly, steadily coaxing him toward homeostasis. Knowing the data egg constantly nudged him in the right direction also helped, as had an hour meditating with the help of one of Ozie's brain caps.

Victor knew he should call his family and let them know he was okay. He should talk to Karine and ask her again about the expansion of the Classification system. Instead, he threw himself into his work.

Elena busted into the room, yelling his name. "We've got to go!" She stomped over to Ozie and slammed her MeshBit on the table. "Make sure no one can trace this."

Victor looked up from the screen. Elena's eyes were wide, and her hands trembled. She was using stims again, he was sure of it. She just had to make it though one more day, and then they'd leave and she'd be safe from temptation.

"We will," Victor said smoothly. "Tomorrow morning."

Ozie started futzing with her MeshBit.

"We have to leave now!" she said in a shaking voice.

He raised his eyebrows. "I thought you wanted to stay?" Why would she want to move on? "As soon as the car work is done, and I've programmed the analysis, we go get the genome libraries."

Ozie looked at Victor over the rims of his glasses. "Are you sure you want to bring her along?"

Victor said, "I don't see why not."

Ozie glared at Elena and then returned his attention to her MeshBit.

Elena stood over Victor. "Can't we leave now?"

Victor looked at the terminal in front of him. "I'm not done with the code. What's got into you?" He doubted she would admit her stim use to him. Not after she'd crowed a few days ago about how proud she was to quit. "We'll leave sooner if you stop interrupting me."

Elena opened her mouth, but no words came out. She blinked and looked as if she might be tearing up.

Ozie stood, walked over, and patted Victor on the back. "Get to work on your program." He walked to the door and held it open for Elena. "Let's have a drink on me," Ozie said. He escorted her out and closed the door behind him. The room was mercifully quiet.

Victor returned to his algorithm. Every line of code mattered when dealing with such vast sums of data. Processing the data in batches meant he had to take special care in how the data was broken and reassembled. Hours flew by.

During a test run on a tiny sliver of genome, Victor recorded a few messages to try out the untraceable messaging function on the Handy 1000 that Ozie had given him. He sent one message to Ma and Fa to let them know he was okay and that he was traveling up the Pacific Coast, intending to visit the First Nations of Canada. He tried not to think about what they made of his granfa's defiled grave and his sudden absence. He sent another message to Circe, asking her to get in touch with him.

Victor squirmed, thinking about how much further across the line of good behavior he would advance by stealing the gene libraries from the Institute for Applied Biological Sciences. Thus far, he'd vandalized a grave and stolen from his family's company, but this theft would be an altogether different thing—a monumental heist. Researchers had to be licensed and pay huge sums of money for access to a subset of the Human Genome Initiative's data troves. Now Victor planned to siphon all of it, a grand crime that would make him infamous throughout the American Union if he were caught.

He pushed those thoughts aside. He had more coding to do, and he needed to create a lock on the program that Ozie couldn't break, an insurance policy in case his friend was only using him to get what he wanted, as Elena had suggested. He worked late, stopping only for a brief snack brought in by the tuxedoed robot, and then he returned to their rented room and passed out next to Elena.

In the early morning before the sun rose, Victor sat on a bench inside the garage and ran remote tests on the BioScan data using his Handy 1000. His program was working as planned, indexing the genomic data and running comparison protocols to highlight differences between people with and without the gene. Once he had the reference libraries and got them connected to the dark grid, his program would be able to identify the MRS gene sequence, provided Ozie could reroute the satellites in orbit.

Victor sighed to himself. What had become of his life? He rolled up the Handy 1000 and stuck it in his pocket next to the data egg.

Elena paced outside. She had packed the car while the mechanics were still working on it. She and Victor were almost ready to go.

Victor retrieved his bag from the trunk and downed a fumewort tincture. He would save the bitter grass and only take it before sleeping.

The mechanics walked him through the car's new features.

Cody Sisco

It opened when he pressed his palm against the door. The steering disc now showed the outline of two hands, the trigger for autodriving mode. He programmed a test drive, over Elena's objections, and left her behind. He rode in the self-driving car a kilometer up the road.

He got out of the car and stretched, anticipating the long drive ahead. Elena's erratic behavior would make maintaining his equilibrium harder. He wondered if he should let her come along. He was planning an enormous breach of faith against one of the most respected scientific achievements the world had seen. If Elena came along and he were caught, she'd be deemed his accomplice. He should tell her to stay for her own good.

Distant, jagged mountains withdrew their shadows from the Reno desert. The sun would rise comparatively late thanks to the Nevada time zone exception, a reflection of the idiosyncratic chaos ruling O.W.S.'s mountainous regions.

A crackle in the dirt behind a nearby copse of eucalyptus trees caught Victor's attention. Brown pods littered the ground along with dried leaves. The astringent scent of eucalyptus wafted by, carried by a morning breeze. He turned back to the car but let out a quiet breath when he heard another crunch.

He wished he had a weapon. If the people following him tried to grab him now, he'd have to jump in the car and leave.

Hooting that sounded human came from behind the trees. Maybe it was their signal to grab him. Victor backed a few steps toward his car, checking over his shoulder, determined not to be surprised from behind.

A shambling, stumbling man emerged from behind a nearby tree and advanced unsteadily toward Victor's car. He had scraggly whiskers and hair like a greasy bird's nest. The man hooted again, and the effort seemed to bug out his eyelids. His lips parted, revealing yellowed, grimy teeth.

"Morning, feller!" the man said. "Good day it is! Spare me an AUD? I'm making camp on the other side of the golf course. Don't pay me no more to cut their grass. Got them bots. Please, kiddo. Help a stim slug out."

The man's skeletal frame was clearly malnourished, and his stink suggested disease. He was disgusting but not dangerous.

"You're on stims?" Victor said. "What are they like?"

"Out of this world!" the hobo yelled. "Everything makes sense, and everything happens for a reason. It's divine."

The man seemed to have forgotten about Victor and stared at the ground, probing at his belly button, which poked from his undersized shirt. Then he licked his finger.

Victor found some water bottles in his trunk and a few packaged snacks in the car's passenger compartment and threw them at the trees.

When the hobo lifted his head, his eyes glistened.

Victor held up another bottle, which caught the light of the sun and sparkled like a precious gem. "Go fetch." He chucked the bottle away. The hobo followed his prize.

Victor got in his car and drove back to the garage. Elena looked at him with red and teary eyes. He couldn't leave her.

"Let's go," he shouted to Elena through a lowered window.

She jumped in. "Step on it," she said.

Victor programmed the car for Las Vegas, and it began driving them south.

27

The "Cold Nile Miracle" along the Columbia River and then across the length and breadth of the Organized Western States rivals any other A.U. economic region in terms of per-capita economic output. However, the remainder of our continent's western lands languish, burdened by the curses of being mineral-rich and water-poor, and chronically starved by labor's greedy hands. Except, of course, for Las Vegas, a syndicate-controlled unofficial city-state so rotten, bloated, crime-infested, and corroded that no decent citizens of the A.U. dare to visit. Riches plundered from thousands of illegal mines in the O.W.S. fuel conflict and create instability. Corps mercenaries at the disposal of the Damned City's amoral criminal leaders constitute the primary threat to our democratic-, freedom-, and peace-loving union. The Republic should not have to fight this fight alone.

—Republic of Texas senator Alberto Montero,
"A Plea for Solidarity," (1990)

Las Vegas, Organized Western States
6 March 1991

Victor's car pulled itself around a sweeping curve. Jagged cliffs of rust-colored rock, sandstone, and white-streaked sediment rose above him. When the road straightened, Victor and Elena glimpsed Las Vegas in the distance.

The meticulously planned clock-face city encompassed several square kilometers of arcing apartment blocks, airtram circuits, and commercial skyscrapers, built in concentric rings around Grand Park, a vivid patch of green contrasting with the surrounding desert. Neatly arranged, huddled outskirts encircled the city's jutting high-rises.

The Handy 1000 chimed, and Victor unfurled it on top of the dash. A message from Ozie read: "People following you crossed the border to O.W.S. this morning."

Victor's dragged both his palms down his face.

"What is it?" Elena asked.

"They're still coming after us, whoever they are. They crossed over from SeCa this morning," he explained.

She waved as if she could swat them like flies. "They can't know where we are now. Don't worry."

Victor wanted to believe she was right. But why bother crossing the border if they'd lost the trail completely?

He downed a fumewort tincture and told himself to stay calm. *Might as well tell the wind not to blow. But I can't not try.*

Ahead of them, the polished, improbable immensity of a city in the middle of nowhere made it seem like a mirage.

Outside the city limits, fields of mirrors sprawled toward the hills. Black solar thermal towers punctuated the terrain at regular intervals like nails driven into the desert floor.

The city layout resembled a giant bull's-eye scratched into the dusty valley floor. Two strips of parkland divided the city into quadrants named after the seasons. On their left, pastel-green Spring occupied the wedge from noon to three on the city's clock-face layout, beyond which sat pink-adobe Summer from three to six. Autumn with its golden-russet tones occupied the space between six to nine. Winter's white-washed buildings, to their right and rapidly approaching, glistened from nine to twelve.

Victor tapped the dashboard to give the autopilot program more specific orders, and the car navigated toward the Institute for Applied Biological Sciences near Grand Park at the city's center.

The vista disappeared when the road dipped into a tunnel that ran beneath the entirety of Twelve-Six Park.

Victor glanced at Elena. The blue-tinted glare of passing

lightstrips flashed across her face. She scratched the back of one hand, raking her nails across her skin so forcefully that Victor worried she might draw blood.

He reached over and grabbed her hand, squeezing. "Who's nervous now?" he asked.

"Me. Being underground . . ." Elena folded her arms across her chest. "I can't stop thinking about earthquakes."

"You know we're hundreds of kilometers from any significant fault lines." Victor looked up at the tunnel ceiling's broad arch, reinforced with thick pillars. It looked solid, but appearances could be deceiving. "You should be more worried about faulty construction," Victor said.

She glared at him. "Thanks, now I'm worried about that too."

The car drove itself into a spur of the tunnel and up an exit chute. They emerged onto a narrow two-lane street flanked by apartment buildings and commercial towers. Wide sidewalks with adjacent, separated bicycle lanes took up twice as much room as the road itself. The street lacked facilities for parked vehicles, a brilliant space-saving feature that Victor wished SeCa had adopted.

The car proceeded slowly and stopped at a turnout in front of a building that looked like glass cubes hastily stacked on top of one another.

Victor and Elena climbed out and stretched their legs. He took his bag from the trunk and sent the car to a parking garage.

"This is the place," Victor said, looking up at the building.

Elena bit her cheek and glanced back. He followed her gaze. Throngs of people strolled across an intersection, shaded by an enormous piece of fabric stretched high above the street, secured to nearby buildings by thin, nearly invisible wires. The sunshade converted solar energy falling between buildings into electricity. The buildings also had solar-conductive windows to generate electricity to feed into the city's grid.

Solar power was interesting, but that didn't explain Elena's curious stare. She looked around anxiously.

Victor grew tired of waiting. "Let's get this over with," he said, striding ahead.

They entered the Institute's large atrium, which rose several stories, supported by a lattice of white curving beams that looked like giant ribs, and which seemed out of place next to the smooth, rigidly geometric planes of the building's transparent skin. The reception area was separated from the rest of the building by waist-high glass panels. LEDs in the floor directed guests to the right while staff veered to the left. A bright green path led to a separate area that served as the tour group waiting area.

Victor led Elena to the institute's gift shop and bought a disposable imager and a case for it. He shoved the data leech into the case and held the imager in his hand like any other tourist.

They walked to the waiting area. A few other people stood nearby: children with their parents, a few university-age youths, and several pale-skinned bespectacled businessmen who might have been from overseas.

Victor grabbed Elena's hand and pulled her close. She resisted for a moment and then relaxed, leaning her head against his upper arm.

Victor said, "I need you to distract the docent when we reach the genome library."

"I guessed as much," she said. "If you were good at sneaking around, Victor, you would have told me in the car, where we couldn't be overheard. That's Thievery 101."

"I'm not good at this, I know. But as far as anyone else knows, we're having a tender moment." He inhaled and smelled her hair. It was clean but musty. He couldn't smell any stimsmoke. "Are you feeling okay? You were fidgeting in the car."

Elena pushed back and looked up at him. "That's why you keep staring at me? You think I'm using stims again?"

"You haven't seemed like yourself ever since we reached Springboard Café."

Her eyes flicked rapidly over his face. She set her jaw. "It was just a puff," she whispered. "Those pansexuals gave it to me, said I looked like I needed it. I wasn't strong enough to give it back."

Cody Sisco

"You can be honest with me, you know. You don't have to hide it."

She looked away. He'd made her ashamed, but that hadn't been his intention. He'd simply wanted the truth.

Victor embraced her, feeling guilty for almost leaving her at Springboard Café. They needed each other, he knew. If what they had wasn't love, it was a shared understanding and a mutual need. She was a piece of his life he clung to, even while everything else was being chipped away. He opened his mouth to say how he felt, but the words wouldn't come. He didn't know how to express it. Instead he hugged her tighter.

A docent approached the waiting area, her heels clicking as she walked across the atrium. Her dyed-blond hair was pulled away from her face into thick braids that spiraled up and around her head.

"Welcome," she said, smiling broadly. The glare from her bright white teeth obscured her face. Victor's brain was acting up, but he'd left his fumewort in the car.

The docent paused as if the tourists needed time to digest the full import of that single word, and then she continued. "Welcome to the Institute for Applied Biological Sciences. We are the largest research facility in the Organized Western States that is focused solely on the medical sciences. Today I'll take you through an exhibit showcasing the discoveries and developments pioneered over our fifty-year history. You'll see our genomics lab, where approximately 40 percent of the Human Genome Initiative's first-pass sequencing was carried out. And I'll take you to our world-famous cafeteria, which is exclusively provisioned by our genetically modified crops and livestock. Supplementary information will be available throughout the tour to those of you with Mesh devices. Follow me, please."

Elena whispered in Victor's ear, "Fake food! The Puros would freak out if it was sold in the R.O.T."

The tour group moved past a set of glass partitions and a pillar with a blue light on top. When Elena neared the pillar, it turned red. The receptionist sitting nearby spoke into a microphone. Within seconds, a security guard emerged from a doorway and approached Elena. Victor watched with a mixture of fear and surprise.

"You'll need to check your weapon with us during the tour," the guard said.

"Oh, okay. I forgot I was carrying." Elena smiled as she gave up her stunstick and received a numbered token in exchange, but Victor knew she resented letting it out of her grasp.

"Weapons don't seem to be a big deal here," Victor remarked. In SeCa carrying a stunstick would get you a gene screening and some jail time.

Elena shrugged. "Here and in the R.O.T., as long as you don't disrupt commerce, personal freedom reigns."

The docent began to explain the founding of the institute, which came about during the Repartition. She described how tax rebates from the federal government poured into the urban centers of the O.W.S.—its capital, Salt Lake City; industrial Portland; mineral-exporting Boise; and East-Asian-trade-oriented Seattle. Research-focused Las Vegas exploded into a major biotech and materials science hub, one of the most important academic centers of the A.U. outside the Eastern Seaboard and the last city along the Cold Nile Miracle route to the Democratic Republic of Mexico. Las Vegas was governed by a techno-libertarian criminal with a fetish for city planning, according to Elena's hushed whispers.

"The King of Las Vegas or the chief of the Corps?" Victor asked.

Elena answered, "They're one and the same."

They followed the docent and the tour group up a long hallway that curved in a gradual spiral incline around the building's central column of stairs and elevator banks. The atmosphere was one of calm reflection and deep focus, about as far from the Springboard Café as possible. Victor wanted to live in a house that looked like this. Why hadn't anyone ever told him how amazing Las Vegas was?

As they followed the ramp upward, years were marked on the floor in glowing numbers. When the docent reached 1934, the wall lit up with a vidfeed showing the DNA molecule and a picture of the four coauthors of the paper announcing its discovery, one of whom was a tall, wild-haired twenty-something named Jefferson Eastmore.

At 1975 the wall activated again. Multicolored lines radiated from a central point. White numbers and letters surrounded the wheel of color.

"The human genome," Victor whispered to Elena. "Every base pair in every chromosome sequenced and mapped. It's the baseline for all individual genetic comparisons."

The docent overheard and gave Victor a satisfied nod. Then she launched into a more long-winded explanation for those on the tour with less scientific literacy. Victor wrapped his arm around Elena, tipping his mouth toward her ear. "In the next room. Get ready."

"Anything you say, sweetie pie," she said. "By the way, I know what the human genome map looks like. I'm not stupid." She poked him in the ribs, hard.

Victor suppressed a yelp and held his hands up in apology.

Elena smiled, and years dropped off her face, almost as if they were two teenagers again, goofing off in one of SeCa's stodgy museums. Her smile soon faded, and a sad, heavy look took root. "You're trying," she said. "That's what's important."

The docent led the group into a room that made them look like they'd been miniaturized and dumped onto a circuit board. Boxy machines the size of construction vehicles dotted the vast room. Racks of smaller metal boxes were arranged in long rows, separated by aisles. The treacherous terrain was strewn with cables like the webs of giant, sloppy spiders.

The docent explained, "Watch your step. We're in the midst of a project to replace the original optical cables with faster flexible crystal nanotubes." She gestured to a tangle of cables on the floor. "Data protection takes creative wiring."

A few of the tour group members laughed politely while the rest gawked at the machines and took pictures.

The docent patted the nearest machine. "Each RTX-sequencer was dedicated to a single chromosome. This institute was responsible for half of the raw sequencing data; the other half came from a consortium of universities throughout the

New England Commonwealth, the Greater Ohio Constitutional League, and the Southeastern Confederacy. We also performed data verification for the HGI as a whole. Some of you might recall the day of the announcement, when President—"

"Are these still running?" Victor asked.

A slight frown tugged at the docent's mouth and then vanished. She said, "Not all of them. Miniaturization has come a long way in the past fifteen years. The sequencing and storage capability to recreate the work done in this room could fit within a small car today. We do utilize some of the machines from time to time for niche projects."

"And the libraries? The complete set—they're here too?"

"Yes, at the Institute we provide the HGI libraries, current and historical, to other research institutions to assist them in their genomic analyses." She cocked her head, as if eager to hear another question, but he could tell she wanted to move on. Now that he knew that the libraries were, in fact, here, he was eager for her to do so too.

"Thank you," Victor mumbled.

"Let's take a look inside one of the sequencers," the docent said, and led the group further into the room.

Victor remained behind while Elena went ahead. She glanced back at him, and he waved her on.

He slipped behind one of the machines, listening for a hum, any sign that it was turned on and connected to the Institute's network. It was silent. The case hanging around his neck thumped against his chest, and he fought to remain calm as he fumbled with it and removed the data leech that Ozie had given him.

The next row over, Victor found a gently whirring machine. Through a grate on its side, he saw reflections of flashing diodes. Peering around the machine, Victor found a data cable, crouched, and affixed the data leech. It would ping the data traffic flowing through the cable, testing to see if it could access the genome libraries and find a path to the Mesh. In addition, a computer virus in the leech would seek out surveillance vid feeds at the Institute and disrupt them. Seconds ticked by. Victor heard the docent continuing her explanations of the HGI

Cody Sisco

and the accelerated development of research and medicines that the project made possible.

The light on the data leech turned red. He removed the device and tried another. Fifteen seconds later, another red light. He moved to another machine. Red light, no connection.

Footsteps clicked behind him. Victor whirled.

Elena beckoned him. "I've run out of smart questions for her, and we're moving on," she said.

"I haven't found it yet." Victor removed the data leech and darted to the next machine. Its cables snaked under a floor panel, which he wedged open and tossed aside. He put the clamp around a thick purple cable. "We can't leave without connecting this."

Elena looked up at the ceiling. "What if they have vidfeeds?"

"Ozie's got that taken care of. The data leech is a cyber sabotage smart bomb. They won't find it unless they physically stumble over the device."

A voice rang out from behind a rack of machines. "Excuse me!"

A security guard rounded the corner and eyed them suspiciously. He had obsidian-black skin, broad shoulders, and no hint of softness in his voice. "What are you doing in here?" he asked.

Victor froze where he was crouching next to the data leech. They'd been caught. He could look forward to years in jail and, after that, the rest of his life in a facility.

Elena hauled Victor to his feet. "Oh, perfect!" she squealed. "We were trying to get a picture together. Do you mind?" She took the imager from Victor and handed it to the guard. He looked dubiously at the device.

Victor shifted so that his foot hid the data leech.

"Just press that contact," Elena instructed. "Give us a three count, please." She squeezed Victor's middle and kissed his cheek. His chest flushed; it felt like drinking warm cider.

The guard was watching them closely. Victor blinked, petrified that the guard wasn't buying it.

"Thank you, sir," Elena said.

The guard grunted. "Not my idea of a romantic date, but I don't claim to understand kids these days." He held up the imager. "One, two, three." The guard pressed the contact. "I don't think anything happened."

Elena stepped forward and grabbed the imager from his hands. "No, that worked just fine. It's silent, so I don't look like a tourist." She made the faux-shutter sounds that most imagers used these days.

Victor regained the use of his voice. "Did you see which way the tour group went?"

The guard wore the barest smirk on his face. "You must have missed them while you were smooching. Out the door, and to your left." He turned and pointed.

Victor glanced down. The light had turned green. "Let's get some lunch," he said to Elena with bluster and walked ahead.

They rushed to rejoin the group while the guard followed. Elena made a show of fixing her hair and checking her makeup in a glass display cube holding an ancient microscope. Victor rubbed his lips. None of the group seemed to notice their performance, though the docent narrowed her eyes for a brief moment. The guard smiled, turned, and left.

"Good work," Victor said to Elena. "I couldn't get a word out."

"You got the job done. That's what counts." She squeezed his arm. "We make a good team."

When the tour group arrived at the institute's restaurant, Victor and Elena asked to be pointed toward the exit.

"Won't you be joining us for lunch?" the docent asked.

Elena piped up first, "I don't eat doctored meat."

The docent's eyes widened, and her mouth gaped like a catfish. She straightened her shoulders and said, "Our produce is safe and delicious, I assure you."

"I'm sure it is," Victor said. "It's just that we're late for—"

"For a lunch date, where we'll eat all *natural* food," Elena said, tugging at his shirt. "I need to get my stunstick back, and we'll go."

The docent eyed them suspiciously, but she called a security guard who returned Elena's stunstick and escorted them to the front door.

They wandered into the sunshine.

"All set?" she asked.

Victor smiled. "I think this is actually going to work."

"Great, let's get a room," Elena said. "I need a shower before we head back."

"I like it here. It's civilized. We can stay overnight."

Victor summoned his car, and soon it arrived at the drop-off/pick-up turnout. They climbed inside, and he programmed the destination, a hotel in the Summer zone. The car drove for a few minutes and stopped in front of a twenty-story building that curved away from them. A huge cantilevered awning hanging above them was strung with lightstrips like paper streamers. They got out and placed their bags on an autoporter, a low hexagonal dolly, which followed them inside.

The hotel lobby had smooth, polished, cream-colored laminate flooring that was surprisingly unslippery. Large potted ferns bordered a walkway to the registration area, where a young man stood behind an oiled rosewood desk.

Victor reached into his pocket to pull out his Handy 1000, but Elena placed a hand on his arm.

"In case they're following you," she whispered, "let's put this under a fake name."

"I'm sure Ozie will handle it."

"Let's not press our luck." Elena elbowed him out of the way.

The receptionist smiled and asked if they would like two separate beds. Victor looked to Elena. "Adjoining rooms," Elena said.

The receptionist replied, "Don't miss the history exhibit on the origins of Las Vegas just past the elevators to your left."

On the sixteenth floor, they found their rooms, showered separately, and met in Victor's room.

"Can you show me more of the dreambook?" Elena asked.

"Why?"

"I finally got Ozie to talk before we left. I understand the conspiracy about diagnosing MRS, but I don't understand how your dreams fit into this. Ozie said he doesn't remember his dreams. And recurring dreams are apparently not a common symptom. Plus, yours might be coming true."

Bile rose in Victor's stomach. "They don't. It's just coincidental."

"You told me that these were true, prescient dreams. You had a gut feeling about your granfa, and you were right about that. That means it's not just your dreams. Something's up with your brain. Let me help you figure it out."

Reluctantly, Victor withdrew the leather-bound journal from his bag and handed it to her. "They started as early as I can remember," he said, "but I only began writing them down when I was eleven, after the family reunion in New Venice."

"I remember that," Elena said. "It was my first time in the Louisiana Territories. I always thought it was strange for my family to join your family's party."

Victor shrugged. "I think Granfa needed to show how buddy-buddy he was with a union official. He wanted the union's support."

Elena opened the book. Victor headed for the door.

Elena looked up and jumped to her feet. She rushed after him. "Where are you going?"

He shrugged. "I'm going to walk around for a while. Find a Freshly or whichever juice chain they have here."

"You should stay here."

"What? You don't think it's safe?" Victor closed his eyes and sighed. That was only partly the reason. He knew why she was really objecting. She was afraid he would get in trouble again. "I'm doing fine."

She grimaced. "I don't think you should chance it."

"You're being paranoid."

"I'll come with you."

"No offense, but I need a break. We've been in that car for hours, and I'm . . ." He bit back a laugh. "I'm a big fucking tuning fork, and I just need some silence, a reset."

Elena bit her lip. "Don't leave the hotel. Anyone could grab you on the street."

"Broken Mirrors aren't a thing here, remember? I can hide in plain sight." Victor pointed at the dreambook. "There's nothing in there."

"Let me be the judge."

He rode the elevator to the bottom floor. The hotel lobby was quiet, even though at least half a dozen people moved through its cavernous expanse. Victor wandered into a long gallery containing historical diorama and mineralogical exhibits depicting Las Vegas's growth from a small frontier settlement to a juggernaut of mining, finance, and industry during the early part of the twentieth century. According to the exhibit, the city was now the proudly laissez-faire center of advanced materials research and production in the Arid Lands.

Victor reached the end of the exhibit and pinged Ozie, who answered right away.

"It's done," Victor said.

"Of course it is," Ozie said. "I got the notification in my feed as soon as you placed the data leech. I've already started the transfer." There was a pause. "Are you alone?"

Victor looked around. A huge drill bit hung from a metal scaffold. It was large enough that, if it were hollow, three adults could climb inside. The plaque on the wall next to it said it was the first to use an ultra-strong compressed diamond lattice coating that allowed tunneling and extraction to extreme depths.

"Yes, I'm alone."

"Well, I don't want to get your anxiety level up, seeing as you might—"

"I'm fine, Ozie. Just tell me what it is. I'm not going to crack."

"Those people following you showed up here not long after you left."

Victor steadied himself against the drill bit. "What happened?"

"It's not like we're defenseless. I knew when they crossed the border, and vidcams spotted them a mile from the café. I sent a few of our armored cars to head them off. They didn't stick around long. They headed down the road like scared dogs. Thing is, how did they know where to find you?"

"I don't know." Victor wiped his forehead.

"I'm rechecking my systems, but it's possible they've been breached. There's something else." Ozie had been blustery before, but now he sounded worried. "We had another guy creeping around here. He made me tell him everything and—I'm sorry, Victor, but he got away with Jefferson's tongue."

"Shocks. What did he look like?"

"Dark hair, muscles, might have been Native American."

"That was Tosh," Victor said. "He said he'd find me. I guess I've got to worry about him now too."

"Your job there is done. You should get back here. But in case they're headed your way—"

"When were they there?"

"They could be in Vegas by now, if they knew to look for you there. You might want to take the long way back so you don't meet them on the road. Leave now."

Victor used the Handy 1000 to find an alternate route back, and it calculated the travel time. "That's a six-hour detour!"

Movement in the lobby caught Victor's attention. Two figures rushed in, headed toward the reception desk. The man behind the desk blinked and took a step back. Then he grabbed the phone, speaking urgently.

"I'll call you back," Victor said and terminated the feed with Ozie.

Victor squinted at the figures, a man and a woman, uncertain if he'd seen them before. Could the people following him have found him so quickly? He hid behind the drill bit. His breath came in quick little sips. He would wait to return to his room until they moved on. He had to warn Elena.

An elevator chimed. Victor peeked out, feeling a tightness in his throat.

Elena emerged from the elevator and approached the reception desk.

Victor froze.

The man and woman turned and spoke to her.

Victor's lungs spasmed, and he felt a desperate urge to cough. He pressed himself against the drill bit, bringing his hand to his mouth to muffle his cough.

He'd been so stupid. He'd assumed Elena was acting odd because of stims. Now it was clear. She'd been planning to betray him this whole time.

Victor watched Elena talking. The couple swiveled their heads left and right, scanning the hotel lobby. The man jogged to the front entrance and stepped outside, donning a pair of round sun-goggles. He paced along the façade. Were the front windows reflective or transparent? Victor turned away in case the man could see him.

Footsteps approached the gallery. There was nowhere to hide. Victor stepped from behind the drill bit and ran. He glanced over his shoulder. The woman was already chasing him.

He fled toward the exit.

28

The religious revival that took root during the peaceful decades following the American Civil War contributed to a decidedly apolitical and sometimes transcendent reformation of the Christian faiths. Women and minorities, emboldened to expand their influence throughout every aspect of public life, took up important positions within the new churches. The watchwords of the day were truth, faith, social justice, and serenity. The South owes its rejuvenation as much to this movement as to the reparations paid by the North after the (ironically named) Reconstruction era.

Unfortunately, as the country moved toward the Repartition, the mystical strains of Christianity were outcompeted by a new invention: bombastic, radical, and fiercely political proselytizing. Revolutionary and anti-hierarchical philosophies flowered in American congregations everywhere except in the insular and imperial Northeast, but especially west of the Mississippi River. "Traditionalists" responded to long-term changes in society by radically "translating" the Gospels and adding their own new and divinely inspired myths and tracts.

—Circe Eastmore's *Race to the Top* (1991)

Organized Western States
6 March 1991

Victor sped down the exhibit hall toward a set of emergency exit doors and blasted through them.

The high desert sun blinded him. The sidewalk, a wide, glaring-white concrete strip, was mostly empty, but the man had circled around the hotel and was running toward him.

Victor darted across the street, causing two cars to screech to a halt when their collision detectors activated. He struggled to maintain a swift pace along the length of the block. The air in his lungs burned, and his pulse throbbed behind his eyes. He heard Elena yelling for him to keep running, which made no sense, given that she'd betrayed him.

He pulled the Handy 1000 from his pocket to summon his car.

He glanced back. The couple were catching up to him, with Elena further back. Victor put on another burst of speed and reached a street that led toward the center of Las Vegas's clock face. In two blocks the street met Three O'Clock Park. He ran, ignoring "Stay on the Trail" signs and dodging between sharp-pointed aloe bushes. His lungs felt like charred embers. When he reached the far end of the park, he glanced back and saw that he was only twenty meters ahead of his pursuers.

His Handy 1000 chimed. Seconds later his car pulled up.

Victor jumped in, only realizing as the car sped off that someone was already sitting in the passenger seat.

Tosh looked oversized in the smallish vehicle. He said, "You look like you're running from something."

"How did you find me?" Victor asked between gasping breaths.

"I tagged your car. Been following you. Spoke with your buddy Ozie." Tosh reached over and tapped on the control console. "I know a place we can go."

Victor watched in the rearview mirror as they left his pursuers behind.

Tosh asked, "Do you know who they are?"

"No idea. I thought they were Classification Commission, but if so, then why would they get in touch with Elena?" Victor wiped sweat off his forehead. He'd been so stupid, believing her lies. "She led them right to me."

Tosh smiled, and the skin around his eyes crinkled. "Girl problems?"

"Friend problems," he said. "Worse than usual. Maybe I *am* bad luck."

Cody Sisco

"You still have the data egg? Has it opened?" A river of threats ran through Tosh's voice.

Victor's throat tightened. The data egg and his Handy 1000 were still in his pocket, but everything else—his tinctures, the dreambook, the herb book—was still in the hotel room.

"Where's my granfa's tongue?" Victor asked.

"It's in a safe place."

Victor shoved his hand in his pocket and cupped the data egg there, cursing it for not opening. "The egg is here, but Elena has everything else. My herbs. My dreambook."

"I think you can live without your spooky diary."

"What do *you* know about it?" Victor dug into the outer pocket of his pants and removed his last vial of fumewort. He gulped it down and closed his eyes. "Why do you want the egg to open so much? What do you think is inside?"

Tosh cocked his head. "I don't like to gamble, but I'm betting Jeff knew who poisoned him and that the answer is in there. When I execute his murderer, I want to be sure I get the right person."

"It still won't open," Victor said.

"I've got some ideas about that."

The car was heading southwest along a radial avenue between the seven and eight o'clock boulevards. They'd left behind commercial buildings and were passing high-rise apartment blocks. They headed far outside the city, leaving behind the buildings, fields of mirrors, following a thin strip of pavement. A mountain loomed close, and Victor caught sight of bright lights at its base, stadium-grade beacons that surrounded a two-story building. It looked like a storybook reproduction of a western saloon with balconies hanging over a wooden porch and a hitching post between the building and the gravel parking lot.

"What is this place?" Victor asked.

"Best brothel in Vegas," Tosh said. "It's taken a while for me to catch up with you, but now it's time to get down to business."

They got out of the car, walked alongside a wooden fence bordering a wasteland of scrub and dust-coated cacti, and entered the brothel.

Inside, smooth-weathered wood the color of wine-soaked corks glowed under recessed lightstrips. Artificial sounds of wind and rain billowed through the lobby, sonofeeds from someplace wet and lush. Tosh led Victor down a hallway smelling faintly of mildew. They reached a door that Tosh opened with a key-shaped bit of plastic.

The room inside was filled with overstuffed synthleather couches and chairs, plush maroon ottomans, and a bed covered with pillows.

"How have you tried to open it?" Tosh asked, shutting the door. He pointed at Victor's pocket.

Victor pulled the egg out and held it up. "Ozie said it's unhackable."

"Yeah, he told me the same thing, but something's got to open it. Jeff gave it to you for a reason."

"If you were so close to my granfa, why didn't he tell you?"

"Why didn't he tell anyone?"

"What should I do? Sing to it?"

"If the egg was waiting for your monotone grunts, it would have cracked long ago. Jeff wasn't much of a sentimentalist, so I don't think holding it to your heart is likely to make it open. Have you tried spit?"

Victor raised his eyebrows and brought the egg to his mouth. He stuck out his tongue and dragged the egg down its length.

Tosh smirked. "Like an expert," he said.

A warm flush suffused Victor's face. "I guess you would know."

"Try pissing on it."

Victor's mouth dropped open. "Are you kidding?"

"Go in the bathroom and don't come out until you've pissed and wiped your jizz all over it."

"I'm not going to—"

"Stop being such a baby. This is serious. Whatever's in there is worth it."

"I don't—"

"Just get in there and do it!" Tosh grabbed hold of Victor's shoulders, pressed him into the bathroom, and shut the door behind him.

Victor unzipped his pants and stood, aiming his penis with one hand and holding the egg over the toilet bowl with the other. Ozie had said Victor's biological markers might open the data egg, but he felt silly standing in the bathroom with his pants down around his ankles, waiting for his bladder to cooperate. He leaned forward, propping his elbow against the wall in front of him, trying to hold the egg low.

Tosh knocked on the door. "I don't hear the waterfall."

"It's a balancing act."

"Just sit down. No one's judging your masculinity."

"Oh. Yeah, that'll work." Victor sat and held the egg between his legs and released a stream of piss, wetting the egg and his hands. When he was done he groped for toilet paper and wiped up. He stood, pulled up his pants, and washed his hands and the egg, drying them both with a hand-towel. "That didn't do anything," he said.

"Get hard," Tosh said through the door.

Victor could have guessed that Tosh would insist on trying everything. The man was a leering beast of sexuality. But Victor had to try everything in his power to open the data egg because he didn't really think Ozie would be able to help.

He grabbed his crotch through his jeans, already realizing it was hopeless. His penis was as limp as a braid of silk.

"This isn't going to work," he said.

"You need help?" Tosh asked. Victor could hear the smile in his voice.

"It's a stupid idea. Why would he have coded the egg with my ejaculate?"

"Because it's hard to duplicate. My guess is at some point they made you do it in a cup."

Victor had a sinking feeling. The nurses at Oak Knoll *had* made him jerk off once. They said they were testing for something—he couldn't remember what. Probably whether he would pass the MRS gene to his descendants.

Tosh said, "Come on, Victor. Just give your junk a few yanks, and let's move on."

"I'm not—there's no hope with you standing out there listening."

Tosh opened the door and pointed at Victor's crotch. "You need help?"

"No! You're not going to do anything to me."

"Relax, we'll order in."

Tosh waved him into the room, and Victor followed reluctantly, taking one step at a time, inching toward the exit. He'd take his car and go, maybe all the way back to Springboard Café. He just had to get past Tosh first.

Tosh pointed at the vidscreen on the desk. "Pull up a chair," he said.

Victor stood a few steps away. "I can see from here."

"Suit yourself. Let's see. It's girls you like, right? Men don't seem to be your thing. Your loss. So, do you like white girls, black girls, brown girls, yellow? Red?"

Victor felt like smacking Tosh on the back of the head, but he resisted. "They're not crayons."

"Don't be a smart-ass. Now, what shape do you want?"

"I'm not doing this."

"Nonsense. It'll take twenty minutes. We order, she comes in, gets you off, and maybe the egg opens."

"But it's—I'd be exploiting them."

Tosh pointed to a gallery of women's faces, torsos, and nether regions on the vidscreen. "They want to be here, okay? They're happy whores who've got a sweet setup. They get to choose their clients. They live in luxury. They get to spend their time not working however they want, and they fuck for a buck. What's not to love?"

"You don't really believe that, do you?" Victor asked.

"How many whores do you know?" Tosh countered.

"None," he admitted.

Tosh shrugged. "If you don't choose, I'll choose for you."

"Whatever. That one. Trina." Victor pointed to a picture of a woman on the screen with dark brown eyes and jet-black hair, with lips whose corners turned up, and a large rounded nose. She looked friendly.

"Doesn't that look a little too much like your friend?" Tosh asked.

"Fuck you."

Tosh confirmed Victor's selection with a tap of his fingers. An automated voice chimed, "Pose for your photograph in 3 . . . 2 . . ." Tosh reached over and pulled Victor onto his lap. "1 . . ." A bright flash filled the room. To Victor's ears, it sounded like glass breaking. The photograph captured him with his mouth open, a surprised expression on his face.

Tosh laughed. "We might need to retake it."

A chat screen opened with a message from Trina. *Are you a jokester?* it read.

Inexperienced and nervous, i.e. young, Tosh typed.

The response came through quickly, *I love popping cherries. Be right there.*

Butterflies flitted in Victor's stomach. He had to nip this in the bud.

Tosh laughed at him. "Are you nervous? Is this your first time?"

"First time with a prostitute? Yeah."

"Are you a virgin, though?"

Someone knocked on the door.

"Our order's up." Tosh stepped to the door and opened it.

Trina whose face still stared from the vidscreen stood at the door in a white silk nightgown that dipped in a sharp *V* to reveal large swaths of cleavage. Her hair was pinned up in a bun.

"Good evening, gentlemen." Her voice was light and sweet, with a soft playful lilt.

"Good evening, lady." Tosh bowed.

"Hello," Victor said, plotting a route between the two of them out the door and back to his car.

Trina breezed into the room and sat on the edge of the bed, one leg splayed to the side. The hem of her robe fell only to the tops her thighs. Her fingers ran along one edge of the robe's lacy lining next to her breast. She smiled, "How would you two like to proceed?"

Tosh lifted his hands and smiled. "I'm just a tourist. He's going to do all the work." Tosh nodded at Victor.

She turned her eyes to him, and her smile deepened, her nostrils flared, a subtle blush rose in her chest. Her arousal sparkled around the edge of Victor's vision. Electricity rose from his groin and turned into a warm flush when it reached his chest.

She turned her body to him. "This is a treat. It's rare I get to work on men under thirty, and so handsome."

"How did you, uh, choose this line of work?" Victor asked. He took a few wooden steps toward the door, conscious of pressure building in his pants.

Trina ran a hand down her smooth leg. "Who wouldn't want to do this? When I was eighteen, I got the Impulse implant. Love is my drug, as they say. You can come here now."

"See, it's already working," Tosh said, pointing toward Victor's tented pants.

"Now, now, tourist," she said, "No talking during the show."

Victor blinked once slowly and was startled to discover that his feet had crossed the distance toward her. His fingers reached out, slipped her robe off, and dug into her arms. She gasped and then growled in satisfaction. She pressed against him, a wave of mind-numbing physicality.

He sank to his knees. Her scent moved inside him, filling his sinuses. His mouth met her skin where wiry hairs grew below her belly button. He pressed his face against her, immersed in pleasure. Everything else fell away.

His lips and tongue traced a path down and inward. The woman rocked back and bowed her legs as a sigh rushed out of her. Victor continued to explore between her legs, seeking combinations to arouse and surprise. The sounds she made felt like they were coming from his throat, through his mouth. Salt and musk and softness enveloped him.

She pushed him away and commanded him to undress. Her eyes were haloed with deep-purple fireworks. Victor was barely aware that Tosh sat watching them.

Victor tore at his shirt while she worked to unbuckle his belt, unclasp his pants, and pry off his stretched briefs. Slipping to her knees, she returned his favors unhurriedly, stimulating his shaft and balls. Victor moaned, his pulse and breath quickening. A buzzing sensation rose from his groin, spreading heat throughout his entire body.

Cody Sisco

The woman stood and pulled Victor to her. They took baby steps toward the bed and lowered themselves down. She helped him enter her as she shuddered, clenched, and moaned. He started to undulate, pressing into her, feeling her arousal in her breath on his neck. A wave grew as he kept thrusting, approaching orgasm.

"Not like that, sweetie," she instructed. "Not like a machine. Like rain. Random. Here." She rolled 180 degrees, then sat up, pressing down on Victor, grasping his cock with her cunt. "Feel that?" She moved against him slowly, quickened, and changed again. Her body flushed, and he felt her shaking with an orgasm; her cry vibrated as it left her body.

"Now you," she told him breathily.

He rolled onto her. He lifted and pressed forward, not following a preconceived rhythm; each new sensation guided him. Sweat formed on his brow and dripped onto her neck.

His entire body—his hands and feet, all along his pelvis—heated up and became sublimely sensitive. Ripples moved over him, traveling through his skin and nerves, signaling an incipient euphoria.

Happy, unreserved. Beastly. His thoughts had fallen so far from his mind, he forgot he'd ever had them. Strain in his throat melted away, and his breath vibrated, a low hum. A counterpoint sounded, but he ignored it. His hips rose and fell faster, urgently. He saw colors and patterns behind his eyelids—heard another strange, unhappy sound—his hands pressed down, his pelvis redoubled its rhythm, pounding harder, coming closer, the wave building.

"Not so fast," she moaned, though he heard it faintly, as if it traveled a long distance from her lips to his ears, instead of mere centimeters.

The woman was yelling. He opened his eyes; her hair spread out. She moved against him, and he slowed, worried he might come before the wave built even higher.

Blankness hovered close, but he ran from it; thrusting seemed to keep it away.

"Stop!" she raged at him, beating his chest with her fists. "Didn't you hear me?" Why was she angry?

His groin fluttered. He pressed into her at many places at once, all over. He moved spastically, chasing the on-rushing feeling like an electrical charge building before a thunderstorm.

"I'm going," he said, hoping she felt how he did—bright, pure, hot.

"Get off me!" she yelled.

Tosh gripped Victor's arms, pulling him off her. He moaned and came suddenly, but not pleasurably. His groin surged, and he splattered on the carpet, only he didn't feel the wave. The delicious tension had vanished. He felt only an empty pumping. She'd ruined it. Why?

Victor turned toward her, opened his mouth to ask her, but something was wrong. She sat facing away from him, slouched, withdrawing and recovering, in a position he recognized after a moment of study. He had felt that way many times when someone had shamed him. But he didn't understand why. He stood there, not knowing what to say or do.

"I don't know where you went, but it wasn't a good place," she said quietly. "You almost broke my wrists! Damn, I was going to let you come in me. Gives me twice the high."

He couldn't see her face. It had been good. But when he had opened his eyes . . .

Victor balled his fists. He had done it again. Hurt somebody without realizing it. Badly.

Victor jumped up when the woman started toward the door.

"Wait!" he called. "I'm sorry. That was my first time doing it for real. I didn't mean to—"

She turned and stared at him. The look on her face dried up his voice and he gulped. His saliva had evaporated, leaving his throat sealed by glue.

"Please," he tried again, "I—I got carried away. I didn't know I was hurting you."

She crossed her arms in front of her naked breasts and leaned against the doorway, scowling at him.

"I'm sorry," he said again, sitting on the bed, looking at the carpet, stained by his ejaculate.

Cody Sisco

"I won't report it," she said. From the corner of his eye, Victor saw Tosh hand her her robe. She left and shut the door behind her.

Victor searched for words in the dirty carpet near his naked feet, but he found none.

"Well, mission accomplished. And in record time." Tosh rubbed the data egg across the sticky carpet.

Nothing happened. The data egg stayed locked.

Victor turned away. He'd never felt so alone, but tears wouldn't come. He was as dry as the desert.

29

The Vatican's fall as a result of the Communion Crisis removed one of the last remaining counterweights to the accelerated evolution, and dissolution, of Christianity. As a result, today's many splintered sects look nothing like the congregations of 150 years ago. Church-sanctioned miracles have been replaced by magic. Charisma serves in the place of doctrine. People looking to a higher power are sucked into the chaotic maw of solipsistic thinking.

It's no wonder that people speak longingly and hopefully of an Age of Quiet; they yearn for a moment of theological silence to find their bearings. But do not be fooled. Silence in a time of menace can only result in decline.

—Circe Eastmore's *Race to the Top* (1991)

Organized Western States
7 March 1991

Victor stared at the ceiling, at nothing. He was useless. Worse, he was hurtful and out of control.

Tosh snored in a bed on the other side of the darkened room. Victor wanted to hold a pillow over his mouth.

Victor's therapy should have kept him from making such loony mistakes. He shouldn't have let Tosh pressure him. He shouldn't have had sex with the woman. And he shouldn't have gone blank during it.

He'd really not come very far at all in managing his condition. All of Dr. Tammet's therapy amounted to gimmicks.

All of Granfa Jeff's lessons were a pittance compared to the waywardness of Victor's misbehaving brain.

Tosh snored so loudly that Victor thought the man's skull might implode.

If Victor couldn't control himself, he could at least control whom he surrounded himself with. Tosh was bad, through and through. He should have seen that earlier. Victor wouldn't trust him anymore.

And Elena . . . What should he do about Elena? She wanted to help him, she said. But she might get him captured or killed.

Victor tossed and turned, fretting, unable to decide, and fell asleep just as dawn began to brighten the room.

Jets of fire scorched Victor's prone body and roared in his ears. Heat seared his skin, muscles, and bone as they vaporized and joined the surge of combustible gas flowing through the chamber surrounding him.

Another painful dream of suffocating conflagration. The details had changed—this time he was reclining in a small stone chamber, a kind of blast furnace—but the feeling of his body flaring like a match remained the same.

His dreams always repeated several times per night, like a second hand that ticks back and forth, repeating the same moment over and over. This time the fire dream—a common one—started with Victor's body lying on a stone slab beneath superheated gas jetting into the chamber. His arm hair burned, atomized, and blew away. Every cell caught fire, chemical bonds rupturing, electrons splitting from atomic nuclei, as Victor turned to plasma and dissipated.

Then the second hand ticked backward, and his body reformed.

The repeating second wasn't the only way that time behaved strangely in the fire dreams. Time moved forward at different speeds, sometimes so slow that each electromagnetic pulse in his nerves lasted as long as a relaxed breath, sometimes speeding so fast that the entire dream lasted for the blink of an eye. The fire dreams always ended with his body's dissolution.

Cody Sisco

Victor clutched at lucidity: the infernal torture wasn't real, and he would wake up unburned. But his real life seemed far away and as illusory as dreams seem during wakefulness.

A cycle of boiling, desiccation, combustion, and disintegration repeated. His body vaporized, time reversed, the chemical bonds of his cells reassembled, and his body reformed. Then time's arrow resumed its path forward, and he burned and died. Again and again.

The darkness cracked, light flooded around him, and he shook, waking and turning on his side, legs fluttering against the soaked blankets covering him. Victor smelled bitter grass oozing from his pores as he wiped sweat away from his brow.

It was nine a.m. Tosh was snoring next to him in the bed.

Victor should never have come to the brothel. Tosh was a bad influence. Although Elena had deceived Victor, she'd also helped him stay sane. The incident with the prostitute would never have happened while Elena was looking after him. And, he admitted, he missed her. He couldn't just leave her with Lucky and Bandit and move on. He had to hear her side of the story.

Victor knew it was time to confront some hard truths. He squeezed the Handy 1000 and spoke Ozie's name, squeezing again to confirm the feed request. The device chimed.

"Ozie," he said. "You've been lying to me."

"No, I have—"

"Stop. When I asked you to open the data egg, you said it was impossible. Then, when you needed me to get the gene libraries, you promised to open it. But you can't do it, can you?"

There was a long pause. "I only said I would try," Ozie said. "I think it's keyed to open in response to your brain patterns.

"Finally, the truth."

"Victor, looking at a mountain is not the same as climbing it. We don't know which patterns will open it."

"Focusing on brain patterns helps avoid awkward situations."

"Such as?"

"Never mind. Now, Ozie, I've got some truth to share with you too. How's that analysis program coming along?"

Ozie hesitated. "The libraries are here." Victor heard the sound of typing. "I'm, uh, I'm having trouble initializing your program."

Victor closed his eyes and allowed himself a prideful smile. "Yes, I know. It's locked."

"What?"

"Do as I say, or I won't unlock the program."

"But—that's . . . We're on the same side, Victor!"

"There aren't any sides."

"Hang on." A low hum came through the sonofeed's speakers. Victor pictured Ozie wearing his brain cap with its ceramic knobs and penetrating magnets. "What do you want?" Ozie asked.

"Tell me everything you know about my granfa's murder."

"We've talked about this, Vic."

"No, you've talked *around* it. You're keeping things from me in case you need to use them against me down the line. What do you know?"

Ozie whistled, an eerie sound, suggestive of the windy desert plains outside. Then he started talking. Most of it was the same information he'd disclosed in dribs and drabs: Jefferson Eastmore had come to Ozie for help programming the data egg and to learn about brainhacking. The SeCa Health Board's Classification Commission was to be the model for legislation elsewhere, yet Jefferson had stood in its way. Once he was gone the Board's plan steamrolled ahead. Victor had shown up asking questions much earlier than Ozie had anticipated. Ozie had also paid attention to Jefferson's movements over the last few months of his life, noting where he went by the digital traces he left in the Mesh, and recounted these.

Victor's ears perked up when Ozie mentioned Oak Knoll.

Ozie explained, "I wish I'd gotten inside HHN before Oak Knoll closed. By the time I got your help, after the merger, it was too late. Here's the big news: You mentioned a compound to me before, a possible cure, remember?"

"It was XSCT-19900032."

"Right, well, there are no records of it within BioScan."

Victor looked at Tosh lying on the bed next to him, clothed in shorts and a shirt that reeked of sweat. He said, "Tosh—the guy who took Granfa's tongue—said there's nothing left."

"Well, yes, I can confirm that now that I've rooted around in BioScan's files. But then I got to thinking about records. Usually they have a converse duplicate."

"A what?"

"Let's say I issue an invoice to you. You've got to issue a purchase order or pay using a MeshCreditLine. A clever digital snoop can match the amounts or the names or some bit of information tying them together. Or if you send me a feed request, it shows up in your sent queue and in my incoming queue. Most communications are transactional and leave a converse duplicate. So I thought, if the compound doesn't show up inside BioScan, maybe it'll show up somewhere else. Somewhere your pal couldn't reach during his purge."

Victor stared at the dark ceiling. "That's like sifting sand on a beach."

"I'm not sifting through years of data. I narrowed it to a few weeks before and after Jefferson closed the hospital. And because I knew about the compound, I knew what I was looking for."

"And?" Pulling information out of Ozie was next to impossible. Maybe Victor should try again when he was back at the Springboard Café, using a stunstick.

"I found something interesting," Ozie said.

Victor sat up. "What?" he asked. Despite every way that Ozie was manipulating him, Victor still hoped something good might come from them working together.

"It might be nothing."

Victor put a hand on his brow. "What is it?"

"Of course, it also might be something."

"Just fucking tell me!"

Tosh sat up, quick as a spring, finally awake, and looked around. "Who is that?"

"Ozie," Victor said over his shoulder.

"I'm here. So it seems Jefferson made a trip to Texas right on the heels of a cold storage shipment to the same place, two days after Oak Knoll closed. It looks to me like something was *moved*, and he wanted to be there when it arrived."

"What was moved? To where?"

"According to the record I found, Compound XSCT one-niner triple zero thirty-two was delivered to the Lone Star Kennel & Spa in Amarillo, Republic of Texas. I looked into it, of course, and uncovered a few interesting facts. You want to hear them?"

Tosh stretched, got up, and stood next to Victor. "What's he going on about?"

Victor shushed him. "Yes," Victor said, huddling over the Handy 1000.

Ozie continued, "One: Jefferson owns the kennel, or owned it. It's now part of the Eastmore Family Trust, whose chairman, curiously enough, is not an Eastmore. It's a man named Mason Charter."

Victor nodded to himself. "I know Mason. He and my granfa were—well, I guess you'd say they were rivals and friends at the same time."

Ozie said, "That's not all. Two: There's one name on the employee roster that can't fail to ring some alarm bells."

Victor gripped the rolled-up Handy 1000, trying to refrain from squeezing it into a crystalline pulp. "What name?"

"Hector Morales. Elena's father."

"Are you alone?" Victor asked.

"No." Elena's voice was tense over the Mesh connection.

"Can they hear me?"

"No." Less certainly, she said, "I don't think so. Their names are Lucky and Bandit. They won't say who they're working for. "

"I want to understand why you lied to me. And I need your help. And my things."

"Anything you want." She sounded ready to burst into tears. He didn't think she was faking, but it was hard to tell without seeing her face. "Where can I meet you?"

"There's a clock face at the center of Grand Park. Can you get there alone?"

"Probably not. But I—I have the souvenir from the institute."

Souvenir? Victor thought at first she meant the data leech and worried that she'd sabotaged his plans yet again, but then he remembered her stunstick.

"Tell them to stay back while we talk or I won't show up," he said.

"I didn't know, Victor. I thought I was helping."

"Midnight," Victor said and terminated the feed.

The rented room at the brothel had a back patio facing a tall mountain. Shadows smeared deep chalk-art hues of lavender and rust across the rocky heights.

Tosh grimaced at Victor. "Big risk," he said.

"I need to know the truth."

"Could have asked her right then."

Victor wanted to see her face, to know if she regretted that she'd been lying to him. "If Elena's fa is involved, we'll need her help to get him to talk."

"What's going to keep them from scooping you up?"

"You, if you're any good."

Tosh poked Victor's shoulder. "I'm not your personal body-guard. My interest in you only goes as far as solving Jeff's murder."

Victor had no illusions about their relationship. He was a pawn in Tosh's game, helpless, easy to manipulate. "I wonder. Seems like you're going to an awful lot of trouble for the sake of loyalty."

Tosh said, "You can think what you like. Nobody has pure motives. Not even you." Tosh pulled out an ArmorGuard SecondSkin and slipped it over his torso. Only his head and hands were exposed. "Gotta keep moving forward, Victor. That's the secret. When the egg opens, we'll know."

It seemed absurd that the data egg meant so much to him. Loyalty and friendship were currencies Victor didn't understand. He was sure Tosh had ulterior motives, but who could guess what they were?

Victor said, "If *we* discover anything, it'll be because of me."

Tosh stepped closer. He was five centimeters taller than Victor yet tanklike, solidly muscled, dense enough to sink in a lake. Victor stood his ground. He wouldn't be intimidated. They were going to do this his way or not at all.

"You look anxious," Tosh said. "Are you keeping something from me?" One eye narrowed skeptically.

Ozie had unknowingly taught Victor the basics of manipulation: provide enough information to get what you want, but hold back the truth, let it slip in dribs and drabs, and string everyone along to get what you want. Elena had also taught him how to lie with half truths. He'd need to use both of those to get what he wanted from Tosh.

"I'll tell you everything if you keep those thugs off me long enough to get my things back. We'll meet here afterward, and I swear to tell you the whole story."

A half smile spread over Tosh's face, but his eyes were hard. "You better."

Victor nodded. "If they try to grab me, how are you going to hold them off?"

"That's my business. But if you see smoke, run away from it."

30

The model of Las Vegas was a city in a city in a city. At the center of Grand Park stood a large circular stone platform. The avenues, parks, and buildings of Las Vegas were depicted in miniature on its surface. At the center of the platform was a saucer-sized representation of the city with a millimeter-diameter engraving of the stone platform. Within the engraving, it was said, was a nanoscale representation of the city and the stone platform.

From where Victor stood below, he saw knots of people strolling, laughing, and pointing at the city in miniature. He spotted Elena scowling at tourists taking pictures in front of their favorite o'clock. He didn't see Lucky and Bandit, but he was sure they were nearby.

Victor stepped into Elena's path. She moved toward him as if to embrace him, but he held up a finger to ward her off.

"How long do you think before they try to grab me?" he asked.

"Five minutes, tops. I told them I could get you to come willingly."

"Tell me the real reason why you came to SeCa," he said.

"Your ma contacted me."

"Ma did?" He hadn't expected that.

"She found me is more like it. I was using again, hard. The Puros had kicked me out. I was living in a drug house.

Linda called and told me you needed help. I was the bottom of the barrel, but there was nothing else left to try, she said. I got myself clean at a clinic in New Venice. The Puros took me back. I stayed clean, mostly. Then your granfa died, and I flew west early."

"So you were spying on me from the start?"

"I was helping. Your ma didn't want to talk about it. Then Lucky and Bandit found me, called themselves freelancers. They said they were going to watch you when I couldn't. It all seemed legitimate. They said your family hired them. They knew all about you. But when you found the polonium, I started to have doubts. I stayed in touch with them only to learn more. Something didn't feel right. I tried to get them to back off. I don't know how they found us. I swear. It wasn't me."

"You met them at the hotel."

"They called me, so I came down. That's the truth. You have to believe me. I wanted to tell you, but I was afraid. I thought I could do it all myself."

Victor examined her face. Fuzzy peach honesty blended with sour yellow regrets. He did believe her. Elena had made mistakes, but he knew she wanted what was best for him. Besides, he wasn't going to give up on his only friend.

Dozens of people wandered across the stone platform. Lucky and Bandit, whoever they really were, wouldn't want to risk so public a kidnapping, but Victor and Elena couldn't stand around talking forever. "What do they really want?" he asked Elena.

Tears formed in her eyes. "I don't know. When they took the herbalist, I assumed they were from the Health Board, but they aren't, are they? Do you think they killed him?"

"I don't know. Ozie doesn't think so. Do you have all my stuff?"

She patted a bag hanging from her shoulder. "Yes," she said. "I had to smoke with them to get them to trust me. I swear I didn't want to, though I guess another part of me did." Elena looked up at him, blinking. "What do we do now?"

"Get ready to run. My car is nearby."

"You want me to come with you?"

Victor nodded.

She hugged him fiercely. "I'm so sorry. No more secrets, I promise."

Victor took out his Handy 1000 and pressed two buttons. One activated a feed to Tosh, the other to his car.

"I'm taking you home," Victor said.

"Home?" she asked.

Three clattering metal balls rolled across the platform and spewed smoke, clouding the air. The crowd panicked, shouted, and scattered. Victor hauled Elena by the arm, following the five o'clock radian.

"Come on," he yelled. "Try not to breathe."

Screams echoed behind them as they ran past the stone platform and continued along gravel paths that crunched beneath their feet. Victor ran as fast as he could, counting on Elena to keep up with him. He didn't look back, didn't want to know if Tosh or the two "freelancers" were gaining on them. He climbed a set of stairs, crossed a bridge over a dry flood-control channel, and descended to a street. He saw his car ahead.

A sharp pain in his back felt like a pulled muscle. He stumbled but stayed on his feet and kept moving forward. He reached around, and his hand encountered cool metal. His head grew foggy.

Elena caught up with him. "We're almost there. You've got to keep going," she said.

Haze descended, but he kept pumping his legs, letting her guide him forward. He felt himself tumble and was surprised to land in one of his car's clipped velour seats.

"Texas," he mumbled. "Get us to Texas."

The heavy weight of sleep pulled him down into blackness.

31

"Wake up," Elena said.

Victor opened his eyes. "Where are we?"

The map put them only thirty kilometers from the border with Texas. The autopilot was slowing their vehicle to avoid a collision. Blocking the road were two spidery vehicles with massive black struts connecting the passenger cabins to the axles and sitting on oversized wheels.

They came to a halt thirty meters from the roadblock. The autopilot awaited his command now that its program couldn't be completed.

"Are you okay?" Elena asked.

Victor shivered to wake himself. "I think so. We escaped?"

Elena nodded. "You took a sleep jabber to the back. We zigzagged through the city for hours to make sure they didn't know which way we left. Things were fine until . . ." She jutted her chin toward the vehicles in the road. "This isn't good."

"Who do you think they are?" he asked.

"Doesn't matter. Who do *they* think they are?" She adjusted her seat from reclined to upright. "Maybe Corps looking for a buck camp out on all the roads, but usually they're stopping people from *entering* the O.W.S., not leaving."

Behind them, dusty hills. Ahead, the giant spider buggies blocked both lanes and shoulders of the road, beyond which a gradual decline led down to the flat tumble-weed-and-dirt desert.

"Maybe they just want to talk," he said.

Elena looked at him, and they both started laughing.

"If they're Corps," she said, "all they care about is money and drugs. Best-case scenario, they want a bribe. Worst case, they've been warned about us and take us prisoner. Worst worst case, they're unaffiliated—they take everything and leave us to die."

"That's reassuring."

The doors on both sides of one of the vehicles in front of them swung upward; instead of spiders the vehicles now resembled black wasps. A man and a woman used handholds and foot ledges to descend to the road. The woman's purple spiky hair and close-shaved sides of her head reminded Victor of a felt-tip pen. The man wore a wide-brimmed hat and a long coat that would be sweltering unless it had cooling packs sewn into the lining. He might be carrying live animals inside the coat for all Victor knew. The pair walked toward them slowly. At least they weren't Lucky and Bandit.

Elena unclipped her seat belt and reached for the door handle.

"What are you doing?" Victor grabbed her thigh.

She smiled crookedly as she pried his hand away. "How sweetly protective. I'm going to talk to them. If I signal with my hands, come rescue me. Don't hesitate to run them over."

Elena got out of the car and turned back toward him. "You've got collision sensors on this thing?"

"Yes, of course, but—"

"Turn them off."

Elena stepped away and left the door open. Hot air seeped in. Victor turned the chiller off to save fuel, and the thin coating of sweat on his body turned into a flash flood. The couple had stopped about twenty meters away and waited for Elena to approach. She greeted them, placed her hands on her hips, and swiveled left and right, miming a sore back. The woman said something, but Victor couldn't hear. Elena pointed at the spider buggies and then back the way they had come. The three started to approach Victor. Victor dictated a quick message to Ozie, "Stopped at the R.O.T. border."

Cody Sisco

Elena climbed into the passenger seat and whispered, "Get ready. I don't believe for a second what they're telling me."

The woman bent toward Victor's window and pointed at his device. "What's that?"

Victor said, "I'm trying to find—"

"It's like I said." Elena leaned toward the couple standing outside and affected a Texan accent. "We meant to head south after Las Vegas. Turns out this road heads nowhere we want to be."

The man bent over and placed his hands on his knees. His scruffy and oil-stained face scrunched. "Don't matter where you're headed. Noncitizens got to pay the exit fee. So says the King of Las Vegas."

Elena said, "But if we're not leaving this way, we should pay another checkpoint, right? We'll just turn around."

"You'll pay us. Pay them too, most likely," the woman said. A silver nose ring glinted. Her ears carried at least twenty more pieces of polished jewelry.

Victor doubted they were enforcing a legitimate toll. A real checkpoint would have signs. This was just a gang of thugs.

"How much is the fee?" Victor asked. His sweat-soaked shirt squished with every breath. He reached toward the steering disk's panel to turn on the chiller, but the man's arm shot into the car and pinned Victor to his seat.

"Just settle down for a sec," the man said. "The fee's three hundred. Make it two if you throw in that fancy thing in your lap."

Victor felt a surge in his gut. "That's not—"

"I got three hundred right here." Elena reached into her bag, which she had wedged protectively between her ankles.

The woman said, "Think you might have more than three in there. We'll take five and the Mesh thingy." She waved toward Victor's crotch.

A film of slick rage infiltrated his brain. He slipped his hand into his pocket and pulled out a vial of fumewort tincture, popping the cap with his thumb. He poured its contents straight down his throat. *Calm. Controlled. Breathe.*

"What's that? Drugs?" the man asked. "We'll take that too."

"It's medicine," Elena said.

Victor imagined bashing the road blocker's skull against the hot desert road until his eyes popped from their sockets.

"Victor, calm down," Elena said. "Look at me. Look at me."

He turned. Her gaze flicked downward toward the curve of her thigh, behind which hid a Dirac stunstick. "We'll just give them what they want"—her hand jiggled the weapon—"and then we'll *go*."

"Tell you what," the woman said, "we'll just take everything."

Victor's gut sank into his seat, but he wore a mask of calm resolve. He turned toward the pair and whispered, "You can try."

The two extorters bent forward to hear him better. Victor snapped his seat back. Elena fired the stunstick, hitting the man in his face. Dirac forces played on his nerves as he growled, drooled, and jerked.

Victor slammed his hands on the steering disk and the car barreled forward, barely missing the woman. In the side mirror, Victor saw her dig in her pocket and launch what looked like a stone in the air after him.

He accelerated to maximum throttle.

A thunk hit the top of the car, denting the roof, and thunder exploded above them. Flames bloomed in every direction, followed by smoke, and suddenly Victor couldn't see anything.

He turned hard, leaving the cloud of smoke behind. They left the road, bouncing roughly downward through desert scrub and digging tracks into the dry, crumbly soil.

Victor looked at Elena, glad to see her conscious. She pointed toward a pair of giant cacti. He steered hard left, clipping them with his right mirror.

Back on the elevated road, one spider buggy turned to follow. Purple hair lady was climbing into the other. Victor sped faster. The vehicle bucked and rocked over the uneven desert floor. Ahead, a natural ramp rose to meet the road, and he accelerated toward it.

They reached the road with a gut-wrenching leap and violent touchdown. The spider buggies were behind them, closing the gap. "Great job," Elena said. "But now they've got us."

Cody Sisco

"Did you think I wouldn't come prepared?" he asked.

He reached down to the control panel the Springboard Café mechanics had installed and pressed all three buttons. In the rearview he saw thick sludge spread across the road. Tiny flashes of metal glittered in the car's wake, and haze spewed from the tailpipe. Victor accelerated the car to maximum.

One spider buggy broke through the cloud, speeding at an angle toward the side of the road. When it reached the shoulder, it dipped and wobbled, then flipped and spiraled end over end across the desert. They never saw the second vehicle emerge from the smoke.

Elena reached up to a fist-sized dent in the ceiling and ran her fingers across it. "Fire grenade," she said. "We're lucky the blast deflected upward. Are you okay?"

Victor realized he was hunched forward, straining every muscle. Checking the rearview and finding nothing, he restarted the autopilot and let the car take them forward. He started to feel the calming effects of fumewort.

"I guess that's where the saying comes from," Elena said.

"What?"

"No one leaves Vegas easy."

Victor scanned the horizon for the approaching Texas border.

PART THREE

32

I used to feel ignored, stepped on, and brushed aside. I'd give anything to return to those days. Now I feel an invisible force pushing me forward. Nothing I do or say can change its course. I'm not saying it's not my fault, but I couldn't have foreseen what would happen.

—Victor Eastmore's *Apology*

Republic of Texas
8 March 1991

When Victor and Elena arrived at the Lone Star Kennel, the sun had just disappeared below the horizon. As they pulled to the side of the road, light towers blinked on, lighting up the buildings, a parking lot, and a dry creek bed that cut across the sparsely vegetated plain outside Amarillo. Several black, insect-shaped vehicles were parked in front, and people clad in battle gear swarmed the building.

"My fa's in there." Elena covered her mouth. "Laws, I hope he's all right." She called her ma. "Mamá? Is Papá all right? What's going on at his work?"

"Elena? What's wrong?"

"Where's Papá?"

"He's here, with me, at home. Are you—"

"Oh, thank the Laws."

"Elena—"

"I'll call you back." Elena terminated the feed.

Victor nodded at the men and women flanking the kennel doors. "Who do you think they are?"

"Corps, no question," Elena said. "We'll never get in. Are you sure Ozie isn't trying to trap you?"

"He wouldn't do that."

"I hate to say it, Victor, but you're really not the best judge of character."

"Ozie wants to find the truth as badly as I do."

Elena gestured at the scene in front of them. "We're not getting in there without help. I count eight of them, and there could be more inside."

"Maybe your fa can tell us what's going on."

"I don't want to involve him."

"Ellie, he's already involved. I'm sure of it. Ozie's sure of it too. Let's just find out what he knows."

Elena took a breath. "Okay. But it's going to be awkward."

She leaned over and programmed an address into the steering disk. He noticed that her hair smelled of sweat. He was pretty ripe too.

The car turned around and headed back into town. They passed old ranch homes on large lots and entered a more compact subdivision.

They arrived in front of a house with a porch that wrapped around both sides. The car parked itself on the street. They got out. Victor shuffled behind Elena and followed her inside the Morales family's house.

As he passed through the front door, his shoulder caught on the frame, almost knocking him to the ground.

Elena grabbed his arm to steady him. "Are you okay?"

"Yeah. It's just . . . I'm rationing my fumewort, and I'm starving," he said, not surprised that his body was starting to twist away from his control.

"Me too," Elena said.

The scents of garlic, ginger, and other spices filled the humid house, which might have been built above a bubbling stew.

Elena's ma, Maria, bounced around the kitchen, preparing at least six dishes simultaneously. Her hair was tucked beneath a bright yellow knitted hat, and her face was heavily made up in bright streaks of color—reds, purples, and black—that reminded Victor of the canyon walls on the outskirts of Las Vegas.

"Mamá," Elena said, standing timidly in the doorway.

"*Dios mío!* Look who's back." Rather than doting on Elena, Maria coldly pointed at her daughter, "We need to talk, Elena Martina Morales. First, take this outside." She acknowledged Victor with a nod and sent them to the back porch with a pitcher of iced tea and glasses.

"How long have you been gone?" Victor whispered. "She's acting like it's only been a day."

"She's pretending," Elena whispered back. "She doesn't want to show how much she's missed me. I stole money from my parents when I was stimming. They're still mad, I bet. And ashamed."

Outside, beyond the porch, long shadows stretched across the dirt yard, spreading like purple inkblots between loops of lightstrips strung between the Morales residence and neighboring houses. There were no fences, just a large common area, some of which had been turned into a community garden.

The shadows thrown by the lightstrips appeared to move and curl like thick, dark tentacles. Victor rubbed his eyes and heard squeaking and rustling sounds. Great—he'd have to deal with Elena's family through a haze of synesthesia. He needed food, sleep, and a good dose of medicine, but with dwindling fumewort and bitter grass supplies, he would have to settle for two out of three.

Elena's fa, Hector, and her granma Julia were lounging on a wicker sofa. Hector had wild black hair as if he'd never met a comb and slow-shifting eyes that made him appear perpetually lost. Julia, on the other hand, had a hard stare and a quick tongue always ready to give a verbal lashing. Her gray hair was gathered in a tight ponytail. Victor imagined yanking it and almost giggled aloud.

Hector jumped up when he saw Elena and rushed over to her, wrapping his arms around her tightly. "Where have you been?"

"*Hola*, Papá."

Hector held Elena at arm's length. His gaze played over her face, inquiring. "We were worried."

"I'm fine. You remember Victor."

"Hello," Victor said. The sound of his voice alarmed him; it was hoarse and unsteady. The less he said, the better.

Hector shot an angry glance in Victor's direction. Victor felt as if he'd been punched in the gut. Julia, who was never a woman to waste words, even on politeness, nodded grimly to Victor. His skin chilled.

Victor started to lose his grip on the tray he was carrying. "Elena, the glasses," he said, panicking. She steadied the tray. Working together, they poured the iced tea and then sat on the wicker couch in the gloom. The tea tasted strongly of cinnamon and something he couldn't place. The lightstrips buzzed, and the tentacle-shadows writhed. Victor's thoughts moved on autopilot toward a dark and twisted place.

"The police broke the cease-fire today," Julia announced. "Two Puros dead. But I guess they deserved it."

Elena looked out at the yard. Victor imagined he heard her teeth grinding together, and then, glancing over, he realized that they actually were. Elena turned to Julia and said, "I'm sure they didn't."

"Good riddance," Julia said.

Hector and Elena both opened their mouths, shocked, but neither spoke.

Julia continued, "They are terrorists! No one feels safe anymore while they run about, doing as they please. They should be put down and—"

"Abuela!" Elena slammed her glass on the table.

Tea sloshed over the rim, and Victor felt weightless in his gut. The liquid splashed down on the tray with a crystalline tinkling that reminded him of wind chimes. It was almost beautiful enough to make Victor spill his own tea to hear the sound again.

Elena said, "They are not terrorists."

Julia snorted.

"It's a social justice movement, Abuela. They started farm collectives, joint savings banks, education funds, antinarcotics patrols. I mean, from what I've heard there wasn't much of a government in R.O.T. at the time, was there?"

"Still isn't one worth paying taxes to," Julia said. "I don't need a lecture from you about the past, Nieta. And you mind your manners. It's been months since you paid us a visit, and we know why. Don't make me regret allowing you back here."

"Mamá! That's enough," Hector pleaded.

Elena wiped her wet palm on her pants. "I'm just saying the Puros don't go looking for fights, so the police must be to blame. You don't see them arresting Corps, do you?" She sounded ready to snap. Victor put a hand on her shoulder. Both of them should eat and go to bed.

"They should get rid of all of them! Half your generation turn to drugs, thanks to the Corps, while the other half adopt that purity mumbo-jumbo. Kids should study, work, and start families like they used to. I assume that's why she dragged *you* here?" Julia looked at Victor, expecting a response.

Elena squeezed Victor's knee, which triggered a wave of nausea. He shook his head to himself. If only he could pick and choose his symptoms. *I'll take one portion paranoia and a double helping of spontaneous orgasms, please.*

He put down his glass and shied away from Elena. Of all the bad synesthetic effects he'd experienced, nausea was the least desirable. If he stayed perfectly still, the feeling might pass.

Hector cleared his throat. "I also overheard that the Puros found a new cause."

"What are you talking about?" Elena said, perhaps a bit too quickly.

He cocked his head. "The Human Life movement," Hector said.

Elena said, "That's ridiculous."

"What's ridiculous?" Maria came onto the porch and sat down in a nearby rocking chair. "Just a few more minutes until dinner," she added.

"What's the Human Life movement?" Victor asked, trying to ignore the ways his body was misbehaving. Information was good. Information was neutral. And it would distract him from the crone scowling at him.

"A bunch of sociopathic nutjobs," Julia seethed.

Elena turned to Victor, ignoring her granma's cursing. She looked surprised. "Seriously, you don't know?"

Victor shrugged his shoulders. Dizziness rose up and blotted out his vision. He said through his blindness, "No. Whatever it is, we don't have it in SeCa." His view of the porch returned, first in gray, then in color. Maybe he wouldn't pass out after all. *Hooray*.

Elena crossed her arms. "I guess it's only in R.O.T., or maybe it started here." She chose each word carefully. "It's a social movement. They believe human life is sacred and that we need to preserve our natural heritage."

"*Chiquitita*, what does that *really* mean?" Maria asked.

Elena sipped her tea. "They take the Puros philosophy to the extreme. It's on the papers they hand out in the plaza. Preserving humanity against technological corruption. Antiscience paranoia, most of it, but some of what they argue makes sense, especially about food. Without natural food, we can't be natural humans."

"See?" Hector said. "A bunch of horseshit. Enhanced food is more nutritious and affordable. They sound like they're a perfect match for the Puros. They can be insane together."

Julia pointed beyond the dusky yard. "The Puros used to be local boys fighting for independence from Washington-fascist Corps. Now they've all lost their way."

Elena tensed. Victor squeezed her knee, and she smoothed her hair, apparently rethinking the wisdom of getting involved in a discussion of Puro ideology with her family.

Hector turned to his ma. "What you say is not true," Hector said. "The Corps were trying to keep the States together."

Julia tut-tutted at her son. "That's what you were *taught*!" She wore a cruel smile. "They've got no representation in the government, and let's hope they never will. Enough lunatics live there already. They're trying to pass a bill to investigate the invasion of Miami."

Maria sighed, and her gaze wandered across the yard. "That again."

"That was decades ago," Victor said.

Julia said, "It's never too late to fight over the past." The scorn on her face hadn't gone away. Victor felt her derision like static electricity on his skin.

He could feel the family's annoyance with the old woman brimming over. His own volcanic anger wanted to escape. He needed to calm himself. He pictured covering his anger with an ocean, trapping the heat in his core with cool, firm pressure.

Julia clucked and continued. "They say the invasion was masterminded by President Kennedy before he was impeached."

"What?" Hector yelled. "That's crazy!"

Julia said, "A lot of people benefited from the invasion. Federal monies went to Florida and Cuba for rebuilding. The president doubled the defense budget overnight and got to look *so strong*. Venezuela established naval bases and won all sorts of trade concessions. I guess the only losers were the Miami people who died, but there are memorials for that sort of thing."

Hector said, "The death toll in Havana alone was many times worse than all of Florida."

Maria smiled at Julia. "That's a flawed theory. Kennedy definitely didn't want European troops on A.U. soil *again*."

"The law of unintended consequences," Julia said and then sipped her tea. "Or maybe he was secretly German."

Elena cackled. Maria and Hector were dumbfounded. "Okay," Elena said, "that's actually the funniest thing I've heard in weeks. Also the most insane."

Julia said, "It derailed the American Union's plans to enter the Sino-Nippon Conflict."

"Please, can we not talk about the Chinese Empire again?" Maria said.

Julia said, "We can't pretend there's no world beyond our borders. Millions of people were displaced."

Victor said, "I know. A lot of them came to SeCa."

Julia laughed, but it was closer to a bark. "And look what a mess that became. The Pacific Coast is going to slide into the ocean one day, and all those foreigners along with those fog-headed, sun-dazzled fruits and nuts are going to throw a party at the bottom of the ocean."

"Let me check on the food," Maria said, and went back inside.

Victor's head swam with hunger. He could make it a few more minutes, and then he worried he might literally lose his mind. He turned to Hector and said, "I want to ask you about the Corps and why there are so many at the Lone Star Kennel."

Hector froze.

Victor hesitated, puzzled. What could Hector have to hide?

After a moment of quiet, Hector turned and asked, "Victor, are you and Elena together again?"

"Papá!"

Victor reddened. The shadows under the porch probably helped conceal his reaction, but he couldn't think of a response.

Hector cocked his head, waiting.

"How much are you worth these days?" Julia asked with a mocking lilt in her voice.

What could Victor say? Truth, lies—they both dried up in his mouth, and he had nothing left. He took a sip of ice tea, which slipped into his lungs and set off a coughing fit. He doubled over, almost retching, feeling every drop of the tea burn in his throat as he coughed up a fine mist of saliva.

Elena patted him on the back.

"Excuse me," Victor said once he had recovered. "We haven't—"

"Are you an item or aren't you?" Julia asked.

"Abuela! That's not—"

Julia opened her mouth to speak.

"Drop it," Elena said with such ferocity that Julia rocked back in her seat.

Hector pointed at his daughter. "Elena, you shouldn't talk to your—"

"Enough!" Elena said. "We need to wash our hands before dinner. Come on, Victor."

Victor rose unsteadily and teetered past the table, following her inside.

Elena dragged him upstairs. Every step required focused effort. In her room, Elena hissed, "She always drags me into fights about nothing. Shocks, I wanted to smack her!"

Victor slumped against the bed. "Calm down. And don't let me fall asleep. If I don't eat . . ." He could taste the cooking smells in the air so strongly it was like chewing on garlic cloves and leaves of cilantro.

"I can't believe she said what she did. She knows just how to push my buttons. Laws!"

He asked, "How should I have responded?"

"You should have told her to stuff it."

They sat for a few minutes in silence.

"You know what?" Elena said. "I'll bet Abuela is secretly Catholic."

Victor's eyelids drooped. "Why?"

Elena said, "The way she hates on the Puros. You know they take credit for the Communion Crisis."

"I didn't know that."

Elena rummaged in her closet and brought out a set of square painted-metal plates. Victor examined them. Printed across the top, in bright orange letters, was "The Purity Caucus." The plates depicted scenes of protest outside cathedrals. The people wore fancy dress: elaborate hats, men in suits and ties, women in ankle-length dresses with bustles and corsets.

"These are from the late 1800s," Elena said, "before they named themselves the Puros. Anyway, they stopped taking communion and started documenting the withdrawal symptoms. When they published *A Microbial God* and petitioned the A.U. to start an investigation, the Communion Crisis began."

"Ah," Victor said, "that's starting to sound familiar. I didn't realize the Vatican's fall started here."

"Not *here* here. San Antonio, I think."

"Still."

"Yeah, I guess sometimes what happens in the middle of nowhere matters. But you see now why I joined the Puros? They've got *guts*. Abuela would drop dead if she knew. Not that I want my family to know, so make sure you don't say anything.

"Cross my heart," Victor said.

Elena laughed. "How do you say 'Cheers' in Latin? That's certain to set her off."

"I have no idea." Victor gave back the plates and rubbed his eyes. "Your fa didn't answer my question about the kennel," he said.

"We'll ask again at dinner," Elena said. She put the plates in the closet and started pacing. "I hate being back here. They shouldn't have asked you about us. It was rude."

The mattress beneath Victor's head was luxuriously soft. He wanted to crawl under the covers and sleep. He closed his eyes. For a brief delicious moment, he slipped into unconsciousness.

Elena's voice woke him up. "Why do you always trust everyone?"

Victor blinked, trying to stay awake. "Huh?"

"You could have come here without me."

"Do you think your fa would have helped me?"

"Is that all? Come on, Victor. Truly."

"I guess . . . I always assume that other people are more reliable than me. I'm so preoccupied with what's in my head, I figure everyone else has theirs screwed on better. I was disappointed that you screwed up. But you forgave me. You deserve my forgiveness too."

"Hmm . . . You've got a better grasp on things than most." She held out her hand and helped him to standing. "Come on, let's eat."

They took turns washing their hands in the upstairs bathroom and then went downstairs.

"Do you need help setting the table?" Elena asked her ma.

"Yes," Maria said, "but Victor can get started on that. I want to talk to you."

Victor collected plates, silverware, glasses, and napkins and began setting the table. He eavesdropped on Elena and Maria in the kitchen. They seemed to be discussing Elena's behavior over the past few months. Victor arranged all the place settings twice to keep his mind off the mismatch between his empty stomach and the piles of food just a few steps away. He wanted to eat spoonfuls directly from the simmering pot.

Each second oozed along at a snail's pace. Finally, after what felt like an hour, Maria called them to eat.

Cody Sisco

The Morales family jumped into action. Dishes were transported to the dining table, drinks retrieved from the second chiller in the basement, and seats pushed in and out so each family member could take their place. A complicated ballet of roast turkey parts unfolded. Many greens including kale, broccoli, and green beans moved across the table, along with potatoes and rice. All the dishes were generously spiced with dried *chili de arbol*, *epazote*, and cumin. Lime garnishes were squeezed and mashed onto plates and mole sauce sloshed freely over the servings. The diners moaned with pleasure. Maria beamed.

"So good," Elena moaned.

Victor controlled the urge to inhale the food all at once by methodically trying moderate bites of each dish individually and combining them to test the flavor combinations in his mouth. Meanwhile, his stomach had developed supercharged suction powers: he couldn't keep his mouth full; every bit was instantly sucked down his gullet.

Maria poured everyone a glass full of maroon liquid that at first Victor thought was wine, but when he sipped it, he discovered it was lightly carbonated and sweet, tasting like anise. He took another bite of food, and the flavors danced on his tongue, swirling and lingering. The drink accented the tastes of the food perfectly. He lifted his glass and chugged half of it down.

Julia pushed a few forkfuls around. She said, "It's good, but it's not truly Mexican."

"What did you do to this food, *mi corazón*?" Hector asked.

"My secret," Maria said, and rested her chin on the backs of her hands. "Mustard seed, curry powder, and cinnamon. Not too much. Some secret sauce. You like it?"

"Mamá, *delicioso*, super!" Elena said. "Mm-mmm." She had already inhaled most of her first helping, and paused for a drink of the wine-colored liquid.

"So Victor, how long will you stay in Amarillo?" Hector asked.

Victor took a bite of the green beans, tasting earth, chlorophyll, and umami. The browned parts added a smoky aftertaste. Crystals of curry powder and salt tingled on his tongue. The moment extended, the flavor developed and changed, becoming oily and bitter, the flesh of the green beans roiled in his mouth. He swallowed and closed his eyes. The tastes intensified, waves of soil and sprouts and spices—

"Victor!"

Elena was shaking him.

He opened his eyes. Everyone was staring at him. Elena looked concerned. Her parents, confused and embarrassed.

Julia reproached him with a disdainful look and said, "Such obscene sounds are not welcome in my house."

"What happened?" he asked. It had just been a moment. The food had tasted better than any in his life. Everything else had faded away.

Elena leaned over and whispered, "You were moaning for, like, twenty seconds."

"The flavors . . . It's because I haven't taken my . . ." This wasn't the right time to discuss it. Not in front of her parents.

Elena whispered, "No, I'm feeling it too. Like when I was on—like before. Supercharged senses."

"You did?" He took a drink. The aniseed splashed his tongue, and again he was on a roiling journey of sensation. "Maria, what is this?"

"It's Pump. You like it?" She smiled tentatively.

"But where did you get it?" he asked.

"The *mercado*. Everyone's drinking Pump now. 'Tastemaker. Pump makes dinner an occasion.' The ads are everywhere."

"This wasn't here when I was here," Elena said. She held up the glass, took a sniff, grimaced. She took a small sip while Victor watched. She nodded. "My tastebuds are *stim*ulated."

Stims. An amount so small no one drinking it would suspect. "This is sold legally?" he asked.

Maria said, "What do you mean 'legally'? Of course. Pump is everywhere. They've been giving out samples for free at the market for the past few weeks. Drives the Puros crazy."

"I wonder why," Victor deadpanned.

Julia gave him an angry look. She hadn't touched her drink at all. She moved it to one side.

Cody Sisco

"It's just a drink," Maria said. "It's not even alcoholic, so I don't know why they care. Too much sugar I guess." She sighed. "They don't want anyone to enjoy themselves."

Elena was silent, but Victor could tell she was having trouble staying quiet. Illegal stims like Aura were only the tip of the iceberg. The R.O.T. was being flooded with a product mimicking MRS physiology. Victor wondered what Ozie would have to say about it. He'd call him tomorrow after food and rest.

Victor helped himself to a few more slabs of turkey and turned to Elena's fa. "Hector, you worked with my granfa for a long time, right?"

"A dozen years. Maybe longer."

"We were so sorry to hear about Jefferson's passing," Maria said. "I wish we could have come to the funeral."

"And he helped you?" Victor asked Hector. "After the thing with the unions, he got you a job here in Amarillo?"

"That's right," Hector said, looking warily at Victor.

"He trusted you, so I'm going to trust you as well. I plan to visit the Lone Star Kennel in the morning. I need to know if it's safe."

Hector looked down and scraped together the few last remaining bits of food on his plate.

"Is it safe?" Victor repeated. "I saw a bunch of Corps out front."

Hector stiffened.

Victor concentrated on taking purposeful bites of his turkey. He let the remaining Pump in his glass go untouched.

"Papá?" Elena asked with a look of concern on her face.

Hector raised his head, and Victor saw fear swirling around his eyes like thick, black smoke. "They arrived today. I overheard—The kennel was always jointly held by Mason and Jefferson. When Jefferson died . . . I heard there was a lawsuit, but I didn't want to make it my business. The court ruled in favor of Mason yesterday. The Corps showed up today."

"So they're working for Mason?" Victor asked.

"Who knows? The Corps are in charge now. That's all that matters. And no, I don't think it's safe for you there. Or for anyone. You should stay away."

Victor slumped and put down his fork. How was he going to get past a flock of Corps to search the kennel for the XSCT compound?

Maria said, "There's no sense in wasting your trip out here. You should stay longer. It's so nice to see you." She watched her daughter's reaction.

Elena smiled, shyly, "We were hoping to stay here. At least for tonight."

"This isn't a hotel," Julia said. She was glaring at Victor. "You're trouble, and I want no part of it."

The other three Morales family members froze.

The spit in Victor's mouth dried up. What had he done to upset her?

Julia said, "We've had enough of you upstart Eastmores. You ought to go back to working the plantations where you belong."

Elena and Maria began speaking at once.

Victor cut them off. "I've been hated for a lot of things. This crosses the line. I'm not ashamed of my skin," he said, staring at Julia. The room fell silent. Not just the voices, but the clink of silverware and the sounds of chewing and gulping—all of them ceased.

Julia raised her eyebrows in mock surprise. This set Victor's blood boiling. He opened his mouth to yell, but Elena kicked him under the table.

She leaned over and whispered, "Deep breaths. Don't let her rattle you."

The anger faded, crowded out by a fondness and a connection to Elena that was deeper than family. He picked up a turkey drumstick, found a succulent bite, and ate, working hard at ignoring everything else around him. He said, "I thought all the racists had moved to Florida."

Elena put her hand on his forearm, a molten brand frying his skin. He jerked away and sent a glass tumbling off the table. It landed with a soft thump on the rug.

"Well done, young sir," Julia said mockingly.

Victor flinched. "All you've done since I got here is berate me. I've had enough."

Cody Sisco

Julia turned to her son and said coolly, "I won't be spoken to like this in my own house."

"Then treat me with respect!" Victor said.

The other family members were shocked, but Victor thought they all agreed with him, at least a bit. Julia, however, looked at him from underneath condescending eyelids; her mouth twisted in contempt. "I won't have you staying in my house."

"Mamá!" Hector complained.

"Please, Julia, don't be like that," Maria begged.

Elena lifted her hands above the table. "Everyone just calm down."

"No," Victor said. He was tired of people. All he wanted was to sleep. "I'd rather go."

"No!" Elena hissed. "You can't. It's not safe."

Hector and Maria looked at each other questioningly.

"I'll be fine," Victor said. Turning to Hector and Maria, he said, "Excuse me." He ignored Julia completely.

Elena followed him to the front door and said, "Victor, don't leave."

"I'll just set the car on autopilot to drive me around all night. That should be safe enough."

"If Lucky and Bandit are following us, what's to stop them from grabbing you on the road?"

"My cool head under pressure."

Elena's eyes bugged out. Then she laughed, but it soon turned into a groan. "If you go, I'm coming with you."

Victor sighed. His mind was shutting down. He leaned on the wall for support. "I can't stay awake any longer." He rested his head against the wall for a moment. His brain matter had collected at the bottom of his skull and solidified.

Elena bounced on her tiptoes. "I'll grab some blankets."

Victor dozed while he waited for her to return, aware that indistinct shapes lurked nearby, ready to come alive in his dreams.

She kissed him lightly on the cheek when she returned. "Let's go. Don't worry," Elena said. "In the morning we'll find the Puros, and they'll help us—you'll see."

33

We were wary of the twin dangers of imperialism and fascism. Our experiences in Asia and the spread of Teutonic ambitions in Europe highlighted the need to choose a different path. In a way, the South got its wish to destroy the Yankee's Union, a half century after the war ended, and by then racism, landed elites, and agrarian economies had been banished to history.

The Repartition reshaped every facet of American government. A mishmash of states and territories were reforged into nine strong nations accountable for the good of their people. The American Union represented a renewed promise of cooperation without coercion and with liberty for all.

It was a ridiculous dream, a farce from the beginning, and proof that unilateral disarmament, when faced with a superior foe, amounts to suicide. Strength, patience, and cunning win in the contest of nations.

—Robbie Eastmore's *Register of Resonant Earth Discrepancies*

Republic of Texas
9 March 1991

After driving throughout the night, rolling through darkened neighborhoods, and skirting the deserted downtown, the car took Victor and Elena to the outskirts of Amarillo, where, as the sun rose, they entered a residential neighborhood with closely packed houses. A sign read "Paradise Gardens," though there wasn't much idyllic about the run-down houses and unkempt yards. The car pulled up to a house destroyed by fire on a lot cluttered with debris.

Elena stared through the window. "That was it, where my Puro pod lived." She put a hand to her forehead and lowered her head.

Victor was pretty sure she was crying.

He looked at the abandoned, fire-gutted house. The blaze had consumed most of the roof and upper story. Charred black pits of ash dotted the dirt yard where flaming insulation and drywall must have rained down. The nearest building, a sprawling ranch-style home, appeared untouched.

Victor leaned back, feeling strangely numb. The scene should have upset him—the house's wreckage was far too similar to what he'd seen in Carmichael—but he felt something close to serenity. He should have been bothered that he couldn't search the kennel yesterday and that the promise of help from the Puros today wasn't panning out. Instead he felt empty. Perhaps he was becoming inured to setbacks. It no longer seemed strange when something didn't go his way. It seemed normal. The universe had a plan for him, and although the plan wasn't clear, it didn't appear to require his cooperation, and it sure as shocks didn't care what he wanted.

That didn't mean he would give up. He would keep fighting even if the spirit wasn't in him. So what if they couldn't find the Puros? He and Elena would figure out a way to get inside the kennel. At this point, he didn't care how dangerous it was. He only wanted to find the truth.

Elena turned toward Victor and said, "Can we go look? I want to see if there was anyone inside."

"Wouldn't the bodies have been taken away?"

"Maybe, maybe not. They're Puros. R.O.T. policy toward them falls somewhere between harassment and eradication." She banged the dashboard. "I'm sure those drug-pushing bastard Corps didn't think twice about burning this place down."

Victor had had enough of her wallowing. They should *do* something. "You don't know it was them."

She glared at him. "Call it a hunch. You're familiar with those."

"Do you know anywhere else the Puros might be? Assuming there's any left . . ." Victor stopped himself. There was no reason to paint a worst-case scenario for her.

Elena wiped her tears with her thumbs. "We can try the main square. They usually set up a produce market there. The police shut them down all the time, but they always go back."

Victor drank a fumewort tincture and followed it up with a bitter grass. The chemical heat burning his throat didn't bother him anymore. In fact, he welcomed it. "Let's go see. And if they're not there, we'll think of something else."

She programmed the destination into the car's system. It drove slowly, while Victor peered around, watching his mirrors to check if they were being followed. Cars passed them by. A few fretful pedestrians rushed across the wide streets, daring to cross mid-block, perhaps afraid to be seen waiting at intersections.

They passed warehouses and pinched their noses as a blood-and-shit reek invaded the car.

"Slaughterhouses," Elena explained.

Downtown, a few buildings reached as high as two stories, but most were as low rise as elsewhere. They parked in a half-empty lot, got out, and wandered past a few worn-down shops selling secondhand goods and cheap trinkets. Amarillo's central plaza lay ahead: a dusty, sunbaked slick of asphalt surrounded by a few restaurants, a post office, and a general store.

Elena pointed to the far side of the plaza, where catering tents shaded tables of produce from the harsh sun.

"The Puros will be there," she said. "But I need to talk to them alone. We didn't part on great terms."

She pointed Victor to a nearby café and insisted that he go there and wait, saying that Puros didn't like strangers, which seemed like flimsy reasoning to him. If he was going to ask for help investigating the kennel, he should get to know them and vice versa. More likely, Elena had some other rationale. She always seemed to have hidden motives, and—if Victor was being honest with himself—part of him must like that about her. Otherwise he wouldn't have welcomed her back into his life as easily as he did. It was a difficult irony that the things he liked in her—her unpredictability, her impulsiveness—were the things he couldn't afford to be himself.

As he walked across the plaza, Victor examined the town more closely and realized it wasn't as bleak as he'd first assumed. The architecture was surprisingly contemporary. A fountain tucked into one corner of the square provided limited relief from the steadily building heat. He'd assumed the town would be stuck in the Repartition era since, as a rule, only big cities thrived after the devolution of U.S. federal powers to the nations of the American Union. Although Amarillo didn't appear to be wealthy, neither was it falling down.

Tall-fluted elm trees lined a broad promenade stretching from the plaza to the main train station. He recognized the species. They had been genetically engineered to resist a fungi that had caused massive tree die-offs in the early twentieth century, a real-world application of science and a public demonstration of the benefits of biotechnology.

However, beneath the patina of civilization, something menacing lurked in Amarillo. People avoided eye contact, which he did all the time in SeCa, but here he felt it was the norm. They watched him when he wasn't looking, but when he turned his gaze to meet theirs, they looked away. Fine. He was as eager to slip past them and go about his business as they were.

Café Magyar, the place Elena suggested, had an outdoor area that wrapped around a mirror-faced building. A broad red-white-and-green-striped awning shaded the chairs and tables. Couples and a few loners lazed at various stages of eating, drinking, and taking in the best scenery Amarillo had to offer: the almost featureless plaza.

A fleet of young, fresh-faced staff in gaudy Hungarian-peasant-inspired suits and dresses navigated between tables. One of the young ladies came up to Victor and asked where he would like to sit. Her direct stare and flashing smile reminded him of a sweet bubbling drink, clear and sparkling in the sun. He could almost hear the server fizzing in front of him. Maybe the Pump he'd ingested was still in his system. He should probably double his dose of fumewort to get control over the sensations, but then he would run through his supplies too quickly, and besides, for the moment, it was a pleasant feeling.

The hostess tilted her head, waiting for a response.

Victor smiled, nodded to a seat, and then followed her, sat, and ordered a faux-café. There was no chance of finding real coffee in a town as small as Amarillo.

Victor rubbed the data egg in his pocket and wished it would open. He resisted the urge to bring it to his lips and speak whatever magic words might trigger it—although his voice print was more likely than semen to unlock it, he was certain of that at least.

Eventually Tosh would catch up to Victor, and he wouldn't be pleased by how he had been ditched. Victor would play it cool and call fleeing with Elena a spur-of-the-moment, tactically necessary decision. Of course he knew that Tosh would find him, he would say—he was counting on it. And Victor could use his help with breaking into the kennel.

The hostess returned with a steaming cup. He sipped the bitter drink and realized with a puzzled smile that he was actually in a pretty good mood. Maybe it was because he was on his own in a new place. Despite the setbacks he'd faced, and the feeling that worse things lurked just over the horizon, all the same, he was enjoying the drink, the solitude, and the novelty of his surroundings. For the moment, he was free, and it felt as good as a sun-break after rain.

Children played a catch-and-carry game in the plaza while their mas watched. The children's calls and hoots were aggressive, aggrieved. At any moment, the game seemed like it might dissolve into a fist fight.

Victor took out his Handy 1000, which told him, via squiggles, sigils, and letters, that Amarillo was blessed with fifteen Mesh towers, one of which he could see poking its silver-pronged crown above the multistory buildings by the train station. The computing capacity of the local node was negligible, especially compared to the bounty in Las Vegas. There couldn't be more than a couple hundred devices in total.

He wished Ozie had explained more of the features of his Handy 1000 before they left Springboard Café, but he'd been too busy manipulating Victor. The way Lucky and Bandit kept showing up meant they had some way of tracking him. The Handy 1000 might be able to disrupt it.

Playing with the analytics, Victor found a scatterplot showing the relative contribution of each device in the node. Aside from the towers themselves, the Handy 1000 topped the list. Ozie had clearly assembled powerful hardware. Victor was grateful for whatever tricks were masking his presence from the Mesh operators. If they saw the Handy 1000, they would surely want to get their hands on it.

A skull and crossbones icon near the bottom of the vidscreen caught his eye: alert settings. Victor reviewed the options and set an alert for any connection to a device that had "countermeasures"—whatever those were, they sounded problematic.

Elena emerged from the canopy of white tents on the other side of the plaza and half-jogged toward Victor. She was breathless when she sank into the seat across from him.

"They're not here. None of the big dogs. Just the farmers. Purely secular."

"When you say that—"

"I know it's not the right word." Elena rolled her eyes. "I mean the nonfighters, the ones who till the dirt. They're the moral center of the Puro movement. The guys I know, they were the enforcers, the protectors."

"The people who know how to handle a stunstick."

"Exactly. Stunsticks and more. They're not here."

"So what next?"

"Word will get out that I'm looking for them. We should make contact in an hour. Maybe two. We stay put."

"We can wait with drinks, I guess."

"You done with that coffee? Want a beer?" she asked.

"Yeah, a dark one."

Elena walked to the bar.

Victor turned again to his Handy 1000. There was another alert option: "Proximity." He activated it at the default ten-meter option. The alarm immediately sounded. Someone in Amarillo had been tagged. He tapped on the blinking icon. The details were unrevealing:

MeshID: 8428-94988-223585
Model: BioLoc.32 v2x03
Power: 32w
Distance: 8m

Victor reset the distance threshold for five meters, which would include only the people sitting in the outside patio.

"Doneghy's is all they had," Elena said, gently lowering a dark pint onto the table. She sat and took a sip from her own lighter brew, which had a full head of white-golden foam.

Victor took a sip. The alarm sounded again. He looked down. The distance now read *<1m*.

He looked up.

"What's wrong?" Elena asked.

A sinking feeling dragged on his bowels. "A BioLoc alarm went off. It means there's a flesh-compatible MeshID nearby." He took three full gulps of his beer before saying in a carefully level voice, "I think you have a chip in you."

Elena reared up as if he'd struck her. "No way. Why . . ."

He swiveled the Handy 1000's screen so that she could see. "That's you. No other explanation. It showed when you walked back just now."

Elena's eyes pleaded for him to say he was joking.

"You know what this means, right?" Victor said. "They're tracking you. That's how they found us in Vegas."

She pushed against the table and beer sloshed over. "I bet that fucking clinic chipped me! I went there to recover, not lose every shred of my privacy. Is chipping people without their consent legal in the Louisiana Territories? Does your ma knows about this?"

Victor smacked his hand onto the table top. "Forget that. We need to be practical. Maybe Ozie can figure out a way to deactivate your chip. Until then, we have to keep moving." Victor stood up. "I think I need to go to the kennel alone. Maybe I can talk my way inside."

Elena stood up too. "You're not thinking straight. Those Corps probably have the same orders as the ones who stopped us at the border. They're an *organization*. We need the Puros to—"

Revving engines interrupted her. Screams rose from the catering tents and market stalls, and people began to stream across the plaza.

"We should go," Victor warned.

Elena jumped up and started trotting past the café's tables and chairs, toward the commotion. "Let's see what it is," she said.

"Elena, wait!"

A crowd of young men wearing dark clothing and orange masks burst from the market and fled toward an alley. Three old roadsters pursued them. One sped around and cut off their escape, effectively corralling them.

"Laws!" Victor breathed. "What is this?"

People ran from the plaza, scooping up their children and hurrying to the alleyways. One man brushed past Victor, nearly knocking him over.

"Not good," Elena said. "When Corps meet Puros, people die." She took a few steps toward them.

Victor grabbed her arm. "Where are you going?"

Elena dragged Victor forward, stopping fifty meters away from the dickies. "We came here to find the Puros. There they are."

The Puros were on the defensive, penned in by the Corps' cars and menaced by additional members arriving on foot. The two groups circled, trying to slice each other with knives— machetes, stilettos, katanas, some so big they could have been cavalry swords. *There must be a thriving blade trade in Amarillo to supply the dickies with all these weapons*, Victor thought.

Victor tried to pull Elena away. The Corps might be too busy attacking to notice bystanders, but he didn't want to be there when their attention shifted. Except Elena wouldn't budge. She brought out her stunstick. The tip glowed red.

One Puro wearing a bright orange shirt backed away from the group. A purple-mohawked Corp who seemed to be the leader followed, flashing a foot-long knife. He hacked it down and up, lunging and cutting, grinning and laughing.

Victor had seen people like that in Oak Knoll, doped out of their minds, hallucinating voices and visitations from gods. Were all the Corps high?

The orange-shirted Puro, separated from his companions, glanced over his shoulder at the circling cars. The Corp must have sensed victory; he lunged forward. The Puro sidestepped, whirled, and jump-kicked the Corp in the back.

The Corp stumbled into the path of a black roadster. His hands flew up, knife abandoned, as he tried to lurch past the vehicle, but it was too late. The roadster was on him. His legs bent backward; then he disappeared under the car.

The Corp driver swerved, tires screeched, and the vehicle rolled, flinging two passengers to the ground. The other two roadsters slowed to a halt.

Victor felt tingling on his skin as he heard sirens. Two police vans barreled into the square. Officers jumped out and raised riot shields. Beyond the line of police, Victor spotted Lucky and Bandit scanning the plaza with viewfinders.

Victor hissed in Elena's ear, "They're here. Let's go before they spot us!"

An officer stepped forward with an air cannon strapped to his belly.

"Get down!" Victor yelled, pulling Elena to the ground.

A thunderclap erupted from the air cannon. A wave of shimmering light pushed forward, followed by a wall of dust. The confused dickies were blown to the ground.

The dust cloud blew across the plaza and swept over Victor and Elena like a hurricane. Windows from nearby buildings shattered, raining shrapnel.

Victor clutched Elena's hand. It was no use talking. His ears were ringing. They wouldn't be able to hear for minutes. Through the clearing dust, Victor saw gas canisters launch from the vans and begin spewing white fog across the plaza. Sleeping gas. Toxic at high concentrations. Nothing he wanted to inhale. But at least it masked him and Elena from Lucky and Bandit.

Victor pulled Elena to her feet and led her away from the plaza to an alley around the back of Café Magyar, scattering broken glass in their wakes. The gas wouldn't reach them in more than trace concentrations there. He patted Elena in a few places to signal he was concerned she might be hurt.

She did the same and made a fingerburst to say she was okay.

He patted his chest. "Me too," he mouthed.

Movement flickered in the corner of Victor's eye. The muscle-shirt Puro took a few lurching steps around the corner of the café. He doubled over and took one more slow, tottering step forward, then fell, rolling onto the ground on his side. The front of his shirt glistened with blood.

Elena approached him, leaving Victor yelling at her back. The Puro opened his eyes, locked them on Elena's, and silently said, "Help me."

Victor crossed the alley's stained and trash-strewn concrete with leaden feet. Orange-dyed scars decorated the young man's arms and legs. Danger stabbed Victor's nerves. He and Elena should leave before the Corps found them, before Lucky and Bandit found them, before the police found them. Maybe he could get inside the kennel *now*, while the Corps were distracted.

Victor ran to the corner and looked toward the plaza. A gust of wind thinned the sleeping gas. Police officers had subdued some of the fighters and placed them in restraints.

When Victor turned back, Elena was gone.

He sprinted to the back entrance of the café, avoiding the Puro who was mouthing the word "please" over and over and bleeding onto the concrete. The door was locked.

Where did she go? Why would she leave without him? He ran, panicking. The alley twisted around and met another alley, which led back to the plaza in one direction and a parking area in another.

A hand gripped his shoulder. Victor jumped and turned.

Elena mouthed, "Victor, come back." She led him to the bloody Puro.

Elena knelt and put her hand on the Puro's arm, which was wrapped around his wounded stomach. She gently pried it away and lifted his blood-soaked shirt, revealing a curving slice deep in his gut. The weapon might have nicked a vein—there was so much blood—and possibly his intestines.

A med kit sat next to her. She must have retrieved it from the café.

Victor saw her lips move and heard part of what she said. The only word he recognized was "artery."

Elena leaned over the young man and used pieces of gauze from the kit to wipe blood from his wound. Her fingers walked on his skin, examining the path the knife had taken and perhaps visualizing what vital subdermal pieces of the Puro the blade had encountered. Victor felt as if every one of his nerves were ready to fire at the same time, but she seemed calm, focused, her movements measured and confident.

"We need to get him to a hospital," she said, though her voice sounded far away. "Victor, call your car."

He started to respond with a disbelieving retort—*There's no way he's getting in my car!*—when the Puro grasped her arm and said, "No hospital. Please help me, Elena."

"You're hurt, dumbass." Elena tore a roll of gauze into strips. "You need a doctor."

The Puro was struggling to communicate. "Doctors fine. But hospital means police. Can't get caught. You can be my pretty doctor." The Puro's weak smile vanished when she applied more pressure to his wound. "Nice touch," he said through sharp and shallow breaths.

"How does he know your name?" Victor asked.

"We're acquainted," she said.

He saw in her expression evasiveness, stubbornness, and a purple hint of pride.

The Puro looked at Victor. "I have money. If you can keep me alive and away from the police, I'll give you thousands."

"That's not going to work on him," Elena said. She turned to Victor sharply. "Call your car!"

"You're not serious!"

"Trust me," she said without looking up from the Puro.

He summoned the car, but got no response. "There's no signal. I don't get it. There should be a signal. The tower is right over there."

"Forget it. Go to your car and bring it here. We'll load him in." She gave him her stunstick. "Watch out for Tosh."

He'd never held one before. They conjured up too many memories of Carmichael.

He said, "But—"

"Go! Run!"

Victor felt numb. It didn't matter that he wanted to leave. Elena was begging for his help, and he couldn't say no, despite her deception. He ran for his car.

34

"I'll pay you back for this," Chico said weakly. "Whatever you want. A million AUD."

Elena applied pressure to his wound. "Bribery is bad manners. And Xavi wouldn't approve."

Chico smiled at her through heavy lids. "You think I'm cute when I'm bleeding all over you."

"Shut up." The sight of blood didn't bother her, though it oozed in thick and heavy rivulets across his exposed stomach.

Chico's face, despite the sweat coming off it and his painful grimace, was nicely shaped. He had smooth skin and a surly mouth. She felt a sudden urge to kiss him. *Symptoms confirmed—I have a fetish for desperately helpless guys.*

"Do you like my scars?" he teased. "I got more that I can show you."

"Is that a bad circumcision joke? Stop kidding around, or I'll punch you in the knife hole."

"You wouldn't punch a dying man."

"Dying?" She laughed, intending to reassure him, but it sounded like a bark. "I don't think so."

She shifted and pulled Chico's torso onto her lap, keeping pressure on his wound.

Chico's eyes were a rich brown with dark, long lashes. As attractive as Victor, he was also street smart and emotionally normal, for a Texan dickie. Plus he understood the Puro life.

A good catch—for her. She couldn't expect much more from the world, and she deserved what she got.

A siren whooped. Paramedics were somewhere nearby. They wouldn't help Chico. The orange-tinted scars on his arms and belly were too noticeable. They'd turn him over to the police, and she would be charged with murdering Corps. That was the best-case scenario. More likely she could expect whichever policeman showed up to have a monster-sized grudge against the Puros. She'd heard of police killing dickies on sight and then covering up their crime.

Only Puros cared about other Puros. That was the first lesson they'd taught her when they'd pulled her from the path of an oncoming train.

Elena twisted her neck and watched the entrance to the alley. Before Victor had run off, she'd seen the resonance start to come back. Hopefully he hadn't blankly wandered into the dickie war zone.

Elena held her hands against Chico's wound. His eyes were closed; he'd passed out.

Five minutes passed. Was Victor coming back? she wondered. Maybe the Corps had found him.

Oh, shocks, the chip! She'd forgotten about it.

Gooseflesh rose on her arms. If Lucky and Bandit hadn't caught Victor yet, they would find her soon. That bitch Linda must have arranged to have her chipped. She would never set foot in an Eastmore-run hospital or clinic again.

Chico stirred in her arms. "Am I going to be okay?" he asked.

"You won't bleed out," she said, "but you'll still be dumb as a brick."

"Elena Morales, you can be a real *bruja*, you know that?" He found her arm and squeezed it. "Sorry. Thank you. Don't let me die, or I'll haunt you bad."

Her heart thudded. She should be taking action, not just sitting here. Chico's chances of survival were decreasing every minute. She couldn't let him die in her arms. She couldn't live with that memory.

Laws, she wanted stimsmoke to get her through this day.

It had been two days since her last puff, and more than a month clean before that. But it couldn't be helped. Call it the cost of minding Victor, which she'd screwed up royally. Now this mess. She would go on the smoke again next chance she got.

What was she doing with a Broken Mirror anyway?

Stop. He doesn't deserve to be called that.

Strivers, assholes, and meanmouths called him a Broken Mirror, but he was better than that. *She* was better than that. And she was the only person he could count on. That meant something. She had a responsibility to him. Just as he had one to her. So where the hell *was* he?

The lyrics of a Twisted Funburst song popped into her head. *For love or money, I'll stick with you like glue.* It repeated, just the chorus, again and again, droning in her brain.

Stop it. Do something useful.

Elena made a list of the steps she would take as soon as Victor arrived. Get Chico into the car. Find the Puros. Take a look at the wound. Treat it. Keep him alive.

And then?

As much as she wanted to help Victor get to the kennel safely, the Puros couldn't let an attack like this go unpunished. The carnage in the plaza—an attack in broad daylight—was on a scale beyond anything they'd experienced. This wasn't about harassing Puros—this was about destroying them. And if she was honest with herself, she knew it had something to do with Victor. Could Lucky and Bandit have teamed up with the Corps? Elena looked toward the end of the alley. How many Puros and Corps were out there, bleeding, dead, or captured? She'd seen four, maybe five. Whatever they thought was so damned important about Victor, it wasn't worth all of *this*.

The Puros would want to retaliate right away. They might even take her back if she helped them fight. But the Puros taking on the Corps was the equivalent of a fly swatting a human. They would be crushed. It would make a good distraction, though, and might give Victor an opening to get inside the kennel. Which was worth more? Her surrogate family or Victor's truth?

She heard the crackling of wheels and an engine's purr. Victor's car turned the corner, rolled forward, and stopped in front of her. He got out and paced, flicking his gaze between the entrance to the alley and Elena's patient. His face wavered between anger, fear, and the terrible blankness of a resonant episode.

"Grab his feet," Elena said. She tried not to think about the trouble ahead. "We'll put him in the back, and I'll hold him while you drive." She gently patted Chico's face. "Chico, wake up. You need to tell us where to go."

His eyes didn't open, and fear froze her lungs. Was he dead?

35

Although the Universal Small Arms Control Treaty laid a strong foundation, it was the failed attempt on President Kennedy's life, which eerily echoed the one on President Lincoln's a century earlier, that finally solidified public opinion in favor of gun restrictions in the American Union. Less than one month later, the A.U. Council of Representatives passed a unionwide ban on gun manufacturing, distribution, and ownership.

Modeled after similar efforts in Europe, the prohibition was phased in over several years and included significant economic incentives for gun owners to voluntarily give up their arms. The emergence of nonlethal and effective weapons for personal protection speeded the transition. The ban was challenged in the courts but eventually upheld, and it remains the law of the land.

—"Small Arms Control in the American Union"
(MeshKnows article)

Republic of Texas
9 March 1991

Victor picked up the unconscious but still alive Chico by the torso while Elena grappled with his legs. It was a hard-fought victory to load him in the car: his body sagging and swaying as they took small steps forward, the car door refusing to open itself on Victor's grunted command until the third try, Elena dropping Chico's legs and running around to the other side of the car so she could climb in and pull him through, and Victor lifting and shoving so Chico's head and shoulders finally rested on Elena's lap in the backseat. Blood streaked across the upholstery and Victor's shirt.

Victor got in, put the car in gear, and drove down the alley to the main road, keeping it in manual mode. "Where to?" he asked.

Elena coaxed Chico to consciousness and asked for the safe house address. His eyes fluttered as he said, "Fifteen Baldwin Street."

Elena directed Victor. "Left here. A couple kilometers."

"You've been there before?" Victor asked.

She said, "Never in my life."

Digging into his pocket, Victor took out a few leaves of fumewort and put them in his mouth. Sucking their sustenance was less effective than taking a tincture, but he didn't trust his coordination to single-handedly uncork a vial while driving. He mashed his jaws to get saliva flowing. The leaves began to soften and give up their pungent bitterness.

"Wait, stop!" Elena yelled. "Back there. That drugstore." She rattled off a list of necessities.

Victor parked in front. "You want me to go in there looking like this?" He held up his bloody hands.

"Yes. Just be quick."

Five minutes later, pulse racing from the awkward stare of the drugstore clerk, who had noticed the blood on Victor but hadn't mentioned it, he returned to the car with gauze, medical paste, and pills that might save the Puro's life.

They arrived at the house on Baldwin Street, a small two-story building with a driveway, shielded from its neighbors by tall hedges. Another car was parked in the carport, so Victor pulled up behind it.

Nothing from the outside would identify the house as a hideout for dangerous thugs. A wood-shingled roof. Slightly rusting rain gutters. Chipped white paint everywhere except for the dark red window frames. Victor heard chugging sounds from a few small chiller units dotting the exterior windows.

Victor and Elena got out of the car, and immediately three men with clean-shaven heads emerged from the house, followed by two women wearing odd, bell-shaped hats. The men approached and bookended Victor. When they recognized Elena and she told them about Chico, they helped ease the wounded Puro out of the car.

The leader—who issued orders to the others in a surprisingly melodious voice—was tall and broad-chested, with an orange scar running from his temple toward his ear. "What happened?" he asked.

Chico's eyes fluttered open as he was conveyed on the dickies' arms toward the front door. He said, "We were ambushed. The Corps. A lot of them."

The leader asked, "Where is everyone else?"

Chico shook his head and passed out.

Elena called, "Put Chico on the couch, tell him not to move, and get him some water."

"Tell me what's going on," the leader said as he drew Elena toward the corner of the yard.

Victor waited by his car, awkwardly avoiding the gazes of the two dickie women who remained on the porch whispering to each other. Elena and the leader argued, momentarily forgetting about Victor, which was fine with him. He tried to wipe Chico's blood from his arms, succeeding only in spreading it around.

The leader, Xavi, yelled at Elena, "You take care of Chico, and then you leave," and went inside.

Elena pulled Victor toward the front door, saying, "Come on."

Victor resisted. "We should get out of here. The longer we stay in one place . . ."

Elena grabbed his hand and said, "Look, Victor, this is one of those situations that you could very easily screw up. Play it cool, and Xavi might help us at the kennel."

Victor dug in his heels and stopped on the welcome mat. "We need to move on."

"We can't yet," she said. "Though maybe we should split up."

"What?"

"Lucky and Bandit are looking for you, but they're tracking me. If we split up . . ."

He saw the logic, but he couldn't help feeling that now that he'd brought her to her group, she was ready to get rid of him. "Where would I go?"

"Fine, stay here. We can talk after I help Chico." She turned to enter the house.

"Wait, I'm coming." Victor rushed to his car, grabbed his backpack, and hoisted it on his shoulders.

They went inside. The house looked as if every surface had been worn away, nicked, or cracked. Dirt caked the hallway.

The kitchen, by contrast, sparkled. Utensils were mounted on the wall, fitting cozily within their painted outlines. Pots and pans hung from the ceiling. The stove's gleaming chrome reflected a meticulous and obsessive cleanliness. Apparently, the Puros were brutes and slobs everywhere except in the kitchen.

Victor and Elena continued to a room with two couches, several overstuffed bookshelves sagging against the walls, and a sliding glass door that led to the backyard.

"I have bandages, antibiotics, and some surgical tools, just in case," Elena announced.

Xavi waved her to get to work. He stood next to Victor, towering over him. His silver-blue eyes were set in a round, powerful head. He probably weighed as much as Victor and Elena combined. Large masses of muscles prevented his arms from hanging straight.

Victor stood as tall as he could while not seeming to try too hard and said, "I'm Vic."

"She told me."

Chico reclined on one of the couches, which had been draped with a plastic tarp to protect it from blood, a dubious effort since Victor was sure he could spot at least three, maybe four dried stains on the filthy carpet. Might as well paint the whole room in blood.

Elena knelt beside Chico. He looked at her fearfully and said, "I don't think the bleeding stopped."

"I'm going to take a look, clean the cut, and seal it up," she said. "Then we'll get you some antibiotics and a sleeper pill—I

366   Cody Sisco

assume that's okay." She said, looking pointedly at Xavi. He nodded. Elena brushed the hair from Chico's forehead. "In a minute you can take the most luxurious nap you've had in a long time. Ready?"

Chico nodded, still scared, but less visibly anxious.

"This shirt is obviously not going to make it," she said cheerfully as she clipped it away with scissors. "Xavi, Victor, bring me some warm damp towels."

Victor followed Xavi to a closet to gather towels. They ran the warm water in the bathroom, wetted the towels, and returned them to the table next to Chico.

Elena cleaned around the wound with the towels. A trickle of blood oozed out, but the inside appeared to have mostly clotted. She pulled on a pair of gloves and opened a tin of antibiotic permapaste.

"This is going to hurt," she said. "I don't want you to twist or flex or do anything that's going to aggravate the wound." She smiled at Chico. "That's my job. Victor, take his hands. Not too hard, just to remind him not to move."

Victor took a few hesitant steps to the couch and clasped each of Chico's hands, applying pressure to pin them deep into the soft cushions.

Elena said, "Breathe calmly and concentrate on the feeling in your hands. Here we go."

She scooped a generous portion of the permapaste goop over her fingers, rubbing them with her thumb to spread it around. Then she inserted them into the open fissure, which provoked a gasp from Chico. He squeezed Victor's hands, and Victor squeezed back.

Elena brushed the permapaste inside the wound, leaving a generous coating. Blood began to pool in the crevasse. She'd disturbed a proto-clot. She seemed to realize what she'd done because she soaked the blood with a dry towel and grabbed an aerosol can of quick-clotting agent and sprayed the tissue.

Victor noticed a change coming across her features. The anxious scowl she usually wore lightened into concern and empathy. Her eyes brightened, her hands moved with competence, and her gaze flicked between Chico's wound, his face, and his body. Victor could tell she was watching every movement, every breath, every twitch of the man's face. Her hands—wiping away blood, dipping her fingers into the jar of ointment, spreading it in the wound—were swift and sure.

Elena was in her element, the way he felt when analyzing gene sequencing computations. Laying on hands and healing were the things that gave meaning to her life. The knowledge made Victor wince. She wanted to feel the same way by helping Victor, but his problems were too complex, too intangible, so she was never satisfied.

Words left his mouth before he knew he intended to speak. "Is that what I am to you?"

She didn't seem to hear him. Her focus never wavered from helping Chico.

Victor spoke louder. "Elena, what am I to you?"

She looked up, puzzled.

"Tell me," he demanded.

"Not now, Victor," she said, looking down again at Chico.

"Am I a health care project?" He couldn't stop himself. The words kept coming out, hurtful, rising from a pit of pain in his chest. "A salve to your bruised conscience? A way for you to keep going? What am I to you?"

"Who knows?" she answered cryptically. "This isn't really the time."

"Come on, man," Chico said, lifting his head. "Let her work."

Xavi raised an eyebrow, but he was mercifully silent.

Victor wondered how many people she'd patched up during her time with the Puros and why it hadn't been enough, why she'd returned to stims even at the risk of being thrown out, and why she'd decided on helping Victor for her next attempt at self-salvation. He let go of Chico's hands, stood, and turned away, looking through the glass door at the back of the house. The yard glowed under the midday sun.

Chico was breathing in slow, deep breaths, apparently doing his best to move beyond the pain.

Victor glanced back and saw Elena wipe around each edge of the cut with gauze. She stuffed another wad of it into the wound and taped it up. Her voice was carefully neutral as she

Cody Sisco

said, "The paste will slowly dissolve as the tissue starts to heal. We need to replace the gauze every day at first. It's going to make a great scar."

Chico said to Xavi, "Make sure you've got enough ink for my next scartoo."

Victor saw Elena smile. She fished more pills from the med kit and helped Chico lift his head to swallow them. She stood, placed all the bloody articles into a plastic bag, washed her hands in the bathroom, and strode to the front entrance, not once making eye contact with Victor. Both he and Xavi followed her, while the other Puros remained with Chico.

Elena told Xavi, "He'll be out for a few hours. He needs to take sedatives and antibiotics every few hours after that. It'll be a few weeks before he can get up and move like normal. You guys can handle finding a catheter and a bedpan?"

Xavi nodded.

"Okay, there's something I need to ask you." She pulled Xavi into the dining room.

The other Puro approached Victor, eyeballing him cautiously. "I'm Davinth."

"Victor."

Davinth's short grey hair pointed in every direction like dandelion fluff. Though he was skinny and much thinner than Xavi, muscles stood out on his forearms. He said, "Elena's not exactly someone who's welcome around here. She's trouble."

Victor stayed silent.

"The kind of trouble that can't stay sober."

"That's how you recruit people, isn't it, by finding addicts? You must expect them to relapse sometimes."

"Yeah, it don't always stick, but we try. They fall down enough, we tell 'em we're better off without 'em."

Victor said with iron certainty, "She's been clean for months. You'd be lucky to have her back."

The Puro nodded toward Chico. "If he lives, I'd say she's earned another shot. Not up to me. You want to put in a good word for her, go talk to Xavi."

Victor turned toward the front of the house, where Elena and Xavi were having a shouting match that seemed to be gaining in strength. The Handy 1000 vibrated in his pants. He took it out and looked at the display. It was a feed request from Ozie marked urgent. Victor walked to the glass door, slid it open, stepped into the heat, and sat down on the lip of a rickety unshaded deck. He opened the feed.

"Victor, I have news." Ozie's face flickered, but through the static Victor could tell he was smiling.

"What is it?" Victor asked.

"Pearl's here!"

"Hello, Victor," she said.

She was safe. Good. "Pearl, are you okay?"

"Fine. Fine. Not too badly bruised. And you? How are you feeling?"

"I'm running out of herbs," Victor said.

"We'll send some to you soon."

Relief washed over him.

Ozie said, "Vic, that's not all. The processing went off without a hitch. We have the mirror resonance syndrome gene sequence. There is a problem though."

"What?"

"The King of Las Vegas."

It was starting to sound as if Ozie blamed all his problems on a mythical ruler, a fiendish opponent responsible for the ills of the world—although Victor didn't mind hearing Ozie's theories, since it made him feel like the sane one of the pair.

Ozie continued, "He's sniffing me out. I found tracker worms in the dark grid. Every time I take one out, five more pop up. They're going to find us eventually. We're going to lay low. You might not hear from us for a while."

"Wait, I need to ask a favor," Victor said. "Elena is chipped. Is there any way to block people from tracking her?"

"I'll see what I can do." Ozie's face faded from the display.

The sun beat down from almost directly above. Victor's head felt full of steam, and his stomach flipped.

He was familiar enough with his symptoms to know they were rearing up again. It must be around noon or a bit later. He pulled a vial of the fumewort tincture from his pocket.

Thank the Laws, Pearl would send more soon. He would have to reserve a MeshLocker at the train station.

Tipping his head back, he poured the tincture down his throat. It was a game he played, trying to bypass his taste buds. Enough drops missed their mark, however, and the smoky, oily, and astringent taste flooded his mouth. The vapor stung his nose.

Victor's stomach flipped again, this time urgently. There was no food to cushion the arrival of the tincture against his soft muscles. He should eat. He got up and stumbled inside, carefully picking his way around the furniture and Chico.

In the hallway, Elena and Xavi were still discussing their plans. Elena looked at Victor quizzically. "What was all that about earlier? Are you okay?"

"Fine. Need food," Victor said, brushing past her. He opened the chiller door and almost cried out in delight. The cold box was filled with fresh vegetables and greenery. So much produce—a large bunch of carrots with their leafy tops, bags of lettuce, peppers, tomatoes, and plastic containers hiding more culinary delights. It was the last thing he had expected to find. He could make a satisfying and hearty salad. His eyes were also drawn to a dark, dense, and seedy bread on the bottom shelf. It looked eminently nourishing.

"We need to talk about what we're going to do," Elena said from the doorway.

"Do we?" Victor asked. A little voice inside his head told him not to listen to her, to forget the food, to leave right away, not to spend another minute in the Puros' stronghold.

"Victor, I think we should go," Elena said. "I don't want to lead them here."

"Oh, yeah? I mean, I agree, but I was going to make a salad. Do you—"

"Hold up there," Xavi said, pushing Victor away from the counter. "Lead who here? What's going on?"

"Hey, Xavi," Davinth called from upstairs. "There's a van parked outside. I think it's the Corps."

36

Davinth popped into the kitchen, yelling, "Those Corps fuckers found us, and I want to know how!"

"Show me," Xavi said. He and Davinth ran into the dining room and crouched by the windows. Elena was close behind.

Victor's gaze drifted to his hands, which held the salad precursors he so desperately wanted to assemble into a meal. He raised a carrot to his mouth, took a large bite, and followed the others. In the dining room, Elena stood while the Puros crouched at the window, their faces pressed close. Xavi's fingers pried the blinds apart.

"I can't see anyone," said Xavi.

"You can see them from upstairs," Davinth said. "They're watching the house. No doubt about it."

Victor paced behind the two Puros, straining to see outside, but it was useless. The two men were huge, immobile stones blocking his view. A bag of wet lettuce dripped from one hand. From his other hand dangled carrots by their leafy green tops. He took another big bite. If he remained calm, he told himself, nothing bad would come to pass.

"How long have they been there?" Xavi asked.

"Not more than ten minutes," Davinth answered.

The muscles on their necks flexed and tensed as they tried to get a better view outside. An artery that ran down the side of Xavi's face pulsed like something was trying to free itself from inside.

Victor's heart began to race—his own fault for not keeping his emotional distance. He lurched toward the back of the house.

"I have to go," he announced to the living room, empty except for Chico lying unconscious on the plastic-wrapped couch. The sunny yard beckoned to him through the sliding glass door.

He heard footsteps and turned. Elena stood close with her arms crossed. She gave him a hard look. "Victor, don't do anything stupid. You're safer in here than out there."

He leaned forward and, in a low voice, said, "It could be Lucky and Bandit."

"We're safe for now. Let's try to keep it that way. Running won't help. It could get you hurt."

He waved the carrots at Chico. "Yeah, but staying here could get me killed." He took a few breaths to calm himself. Maybe the Puros were overreacting. They didn't seem all that bright.

Xavi entered the room. His red eyes were surrounded by a black wispy halo of suspicion. Victor took a step sideways, searching for an escape route, but Xavi darted forward and wrenched him off his feet. Then his massive hands slammed Victor into the wall. Victor tried to squirm away, but Xavi pinned him in place.

Xavi said, "Did you lead them here? Who are they?"

Victor tried to shake himself free. "Who are who? I didn't see anything."

"I had a better view upstairs," Davinth said.

Elena tugged on Xavi's giant arm. "Let him go!"

He did. The floor slammed into Victor's legs. Xavi hauled him up by the shoulders and marched him upstairs. Victor stumbled into a room overlooking the front yard, and a massive paw, Xavi's, returned to his neck, pressing his face into the window.

"Who are they?" Xavi asked.

Outside a white van waited in front of the house, blocking Victor's car in the driveway. Several cars were parked farther away. A few R.O.T. flags flapped in front of neighboring homes.

Reflections off the windshield blocked his view of the van's interior, but Victor thought he could see movement inside.

There was no way to tell if it was Lucky and Bandit. "It's a van," Victor said. "A white van."

"Nobody knew about this house this morning, so how come they're here now?" Xavi said, spraying a cloud of moisture that came to rest on Victor's neck.

Victor shrugged. "I don't know."

Xavi spun Victor around and slammed him into the wall, his face pressed into Victor's. Pain screamed in Victor's wrist as Xavi squeezed the bones together.

"Stop it!" Elena yelled.

Xavi turned his head toward her. "Your friend here brought us some unwelcome visitors."

"No, it's not his fault! It was—"

Victor let out a cry of pain to interrupt her. He couldn't let Elena confess that the bad guys were following her. It wasn't her fault she'd been fitted with a BioLoc MeshID. As much as he disliked the Puros and their brutality, and as much as her actions had frayed his trust, he couldn't let her ruin her chances to reconcile with them. She needed them if she was ever going to quit stims.

"I didn't think they would follow me," he said.

Elena grimaced and shook her head.

Victor's chest heaved. "I stole something, and they're trying to get it back."

Xavi dropped Victor's wrist and started squeezing his neck.

"Xavi! Stop!" Elena wedged between them.

Xavi let Victor drop.

Victor steadied himself against the wall. Elena and Xavi faced each other, glowering.

A woman rushed onto the landing from a room down the hall. "Keep it down! Lila and I are doing the accounting." Another woman with glasses and frizzy red hair peeked out.

"Victor is rich, and he's got powerful friends," Elena said, pleading. "We need him."

"What's going on?" Lila asked.

Elena told her, "The Corps are worse than we thought. Did you know that Pump is spiked with stims? Who else would do that? If we don't fight back—Look, those two outside are

Corps." She turned to Xavi. "You want to get even with them, right? Us too. If we take care of the guys outside and help Victor search the kennel, you can name your price. Think about it. More weapons." She turned to Victor. "Right?"

He nodded. It might clean him out, money-wise, and he hated to owe these thugs anything, but he needed their help.

Xavi ran his hands over his bald head and stretched his shoulders and neck. He looked like a boxer about to enter the ring. Such stupid, muscle-bound confidence, Victor thought.

"Okay," Xavi said. "We need the bucks, no question."

Victor couldn't understand why Elena would associate herself with such an ape, but he kept his mouth shut.

Xavi turned to Elena. "Come on."

The two hurried down the hall into a bedroom, with the two women following. Victor stayed put and looked through the window again.

A cloud had moved in front of the sun, and now he could see through the van's windshield. Two people, a man and a woman: Bandit and Lucky.

They were leaning forward in their seats, peering up at the house, looking directly at him. Bandit still wore a silly pair of round-eyed sun-goggles that looked too stylish to be functional.

They could follow Elena, but they couldn't follow *him*, not if he was careful . . .

Victor backed away from the window and started down the stairs, treading quietly on each step. He tiptoed to the back of the house and looked through the glass door.

The yard had no fence. He could run that way, past a neighboring house, to the next street—but then where? They were on the outskirts of the city. He could try to call his car, but Lucky and Bandit could follow it to him.

He would have to run many kilometers to get anywhere useful. Still, if he could escape unnoticed, that might give him enough time to get to a taxi, a bus, or the train terminal. He'd have to give up his car, but that was fine. All he needed was his backpack.

He heard thuds upstairs and the sounds of large objects being shifted and dropped on the floor. Footsteps moved in circles.

Chico was still passed out on the couch. Davinth came into the room. His wiry frame and gray hair made him look about fifty years old, but he moved like a young person, fluid and quick. He watched Victor as he dug into his pocket and pulled out his last fumewort tincture. He popped the cap and drank it in one gulp.

"What was that?" Davinth asked. The lilt that came into his voice set Victor on edge and triggered his memories, his senses. Danger smelled like smoke in a forest.

"Herbs," Victor said. "To replace my medicine."

"Herbs," Davinth repeated. "Interesting. What did you steal from those guys outside? Drugs?"

The last thread of Victor's patience for his guardians frayed. "What is with the Puros and drugs?" Victor edged a few steps toward the glass door.

Davinth eyed him warily. "The Corps keep pushing them from Vegas. They control the border. The police are useless. No one to help us but ourselves."

"The drug the Corps are pushing. What is it?" asked Victor.

Davinth's face darkened. "Stimsmoke. Dream sauce. Some people call it Aura. Makes people see shit that isn't there. Gives them 'epic déjà vu,' as Elena would say. Makes addicts out of them. It's a stain on the purity of our homeland. To be truly pure is to know yourself, to know your weaknesses, to look to others to help you stand proud and free. How are you going to do that with a body full of poison?"

Victor heard engines outside. Davinth grabbed him and pulled him down the hall to the window by the front door. Three massive insect-like vehicles, similar to the ones Victor had outmaneuvered in the desert, had pulled up beside the van. Bandit got out of the van, spoke briefly to one of the vehicle drivers, and then approached the Puros' front door, stopping several meters away with his arms raised, palms open.

Elena and Xavi dragged several bags down the hall. Shapes made of metal and plastic peeked out of the bags. Weapons.

"More guys showed up," Davinth said. "This one outside looks like he wants to talk."

Elena put her hand on Victor's shoulder. "It's going to be okay."

Davinth jerked his head at Victor. "Let's give them what they want and be done with it."

"We're not going to do that," Elena said. "Right, Xavi?" Her eyes grew wider when he didn't answer.

"He's not a Puro," Davinth complained. "They outnumber us. Look at those tanks. Bet they've got better gear than us too. I say kick him out and cut our losses."

Elena took a step toward Xavi and lowered her voice. "We can call the police."

"And tell them what?" Davinth whined. "They'll be no help. They'll probably arrest us first."

Light thumps sounded at the door, too light for knocking. Xavi pushed past them and opened the door to look outside. He held a stunstick at his side. Victor followed with the others. Small stones littered the front steps.

Bandit stood on the walkway, smiling, but his eyes were hidden behind his creepy goggles. Keeping his arms raised, he pointed one finger at Victor. "All we want is him. Give him up, and we go away."

Elena ran back to the weapons. "Come get your gear," Elena called.

Victor turned, but before he could take a step, he was hurtling backward, through the open door, spinning from the force of Xavi's shove, and skidding across the grass. He landed on his butt as the door slammed shut. He could hear Elena shouting behind it.

He scrambled to his hands and knees. His bag lay a meter away in the grass. Hurting from scratches and soon-to-be bruises, Victor wished he could tear Xavi to shreds. But there was no time.

Bandit came at him.

Victor jumped to his feet and started to run, but there was nowhere to go. The yard's hedges penned him, and Bandit blocked his way.

Victor feinted left and broke right, trying to make it to the street. The man ignored Victor's gambit, approached in

Cody Sisco

three quick steps, and swung his arm directly at Victor's chest, hurtling him to the ground. Victor was dragged to his feet and flung over Bandit's shoulder.

Victor struggled, but Bandit managed to rush him into the van. Victor's head grazed the ceiling as he was flung inside and pinned there by Bandit's strong, wiry arms.

The woman, Lucky, sat next to Victor. "Got you," she said. "Victor, up close, you're such a doll." A hood descended over his face. She pressed something cool onto his bare wrist. The blackness of the hood grew darker, and his head lolled back. Unconsciousness overtook him.

37

Sometimes I wake up and wonder if this life is real or a dream. There's nothing that I don't question now. Even gravity seems mutable. I fear at any moment my ties to this Earth will snap and I'll go hurtling into space.

—Victor Eastmore's *Apology*

Victor woke up, seated on something hard. His head felt swollen, pounding as if about to burst. He opened his eyes and saw blackness.

When he tried to move, he discovered he was tied to a chair, restrained by something affixed to his chest, arms, and legs.

He called for help.

There was no reply.

Shapes shifted in the dark. He imagined coal-dusted ghosts clawing at his eyes. He held his breath. The shapes fell apart, and the darkness became placid. He breathed in, and the shapes returned, artifacts of his starved vision or synesthetic echoes of his hearing. Either way, he had no way of knowing, and they were an irrelevant distraction.

Victor twisted. His wrists, pinned behind his back, chafed against the restraint that bound them together. His ankles, thighs, waist, and chest were all tied to his seat.

Where was he?

A little voice in his head answered: *you're in SeCa, imprisoned in a Class One facility.*

His pulse spiked. Victor threw himself to one side, feeling a moment of weightlessness before the chair legs thumped back to the ground.

"My head hurts." Victor's voice crackled electric-blue in the dark.

He was in a small room judging by the echo. He smelled cheap plastic carpet, a subtle residue of paint, and the telltale odor of synthleather. Victor flexed against his bonds, and the synthleather scent grew stronger.

This wasn't the treatment standard for Class Ones. A doctor would have to look after him soon and set things right.

Or maybe not. Maybe no one cared about people with MRS once they were committed. Maybe he was doomed to whatever semicivilized tortures could be devised. He'd heard Class Ones could be shipped offshore, free from constitutional protections. Maybe they'd let the syndrome's effects eat away at his mind until only a husk remained.

A just punishment. Alik had been a husk for a long time, and he was only one example among many. For years, Victor had been a burden, a problem to be solved. Then, recently, a steady decline, his deteriorating behavior becoming more antisocial and aggressive. He'd horrified his family with his accusations of murder. He'd left Granfa Jeff's body out in the open air. He'd hurt the woman in the brothel by going blank. He might have killed the Corps who stopped him on the road from Las Vegas.

Shocks, the tally was bleak, wasn't it? There didn't seem a limit to how awful he could be.

Months ago he could have pictured himself living a seminormal life. Now he had to doubt that he was still sane. Egged on by Ozie's revelations, he'd come to believe in conspiracy. What if a manic fantasy had taken hold instead?

Granfa Jeff's murder, Victor's flight from SeCa, his pursuers, a mystery man named Tosh, Ozie's fantasy world—maybe it was all a delusion. Maybe his mind had finally fractured, and the darkness would never lift.

But if the last week of his life had never happened, where had his memories come from? Over the past few days, he'd met Pearl, Ozie, Tosh, the Corps and Puros, and Lucky and Bandit. They were real, weren't they?

Victor wasn't doing as well as he'd hoped if he was questioning whether the last week of his life had happened. At least he was aware of his potential insanity—the truly insane never questioned themselves, did they?

He couldn't have dreamed up a Puro safe house if he'd never been to one. He'd never seen Las Vegas or Amarillo, or taken in a view of Lake Tahoe and the Sierras. He held memories of those places in his mind as clear as day. These were the facts, they were his link to sanity, and darkness couldn't erase them.

Victor blinked his eyes, willing his vision to find light, and found a small yellow sliver of it beyond his right shoulder. A door, an exit, maybe? Proof that he wasn't imprisoned in his own imagination?

He inhaled. A Class One facility wouldn't smell so plain. It would reek of an institution: piss and bleach, and worse. Maybe this was a room somewhere on a ranch for Class Twos, where he would have nothing but time to read, study, and engage in productive work. Perhaps he could tutor the other residents. He had certainly gone further in his education than most Class Twos would have. There might be animals— horses to ride and care for, maybe goats and sheep. It could be fun.

He would be blessed with free time but not freedom.

Accept it, a part of him whispered. *No more struggling. No more fear.* The speaker, his doubt personified, was a glittering obsidian shape winking and sparkling in front of his sightless eyes, tempting him to give up and let his destiny unfold around him.

"No," Victor said.

A tiny flame burned in his chest. He wouldn't calmly accept his predicament. He wouldn't indulge delusions. He would never stop searching, never stop demanding the truth.

His body tensed against the restraints, testing the bonds. He flexed and relaxed his legs, earning a few millimeters of wiggle room. He flexed harder and heard a ripping sound. The straps must have been fastened with scratch loops. Not terribly secure. His feet jerked hard. A tearing sound. The straps ripped apart, and his feet and lower legs were freed.

"Hello? Is anybody there? I'm awake now."

No response.

Victor wriggled forward, moving his shoulders like a swimmer, back and forth, jerking upward, lifting the rear legs of the chair a few millimeters off the ground each time. The chest strap climbed his torso until it pulled painfully at his underarms. He leaned forward, lifting his shoulders and arms as high as possible behind him and pressing as hard as he could. The chest strap slipped free and slackened, falling to his waist.

Victor tugged his wrists, trying to raise them higher, but his back muscles cramped. He bent forward and pressed his forehead into his knees. He breathed, trying to direct oxygen to the spasming line of tissue, willing the muscles to relax. He would try again in a minute. Pressure on his bladder became toxic, but he ignored it.

Victor raised his arms again, took a gasping breath, and pulled them higher, leaning forward, straining and stretching muscles that screamed for him to stop. A high-pitched whine escaped his mouth. Then his hands jerked forward. His face smacked into his knees. It hurt, but he didn't care. His nose throbbed. His hands rested on the seat behind him, free from the chair but still bound together.

He twisted, feeling with his fingers around the left side of the chair behind him, where the strap circled his thighs. His middle fingertip found an edge of the strap and traced the seam where hooks and loops joined. He broke the bonds of one corner with his fingernail, running it back and forth until the edge of the strap pulled away. Twisting further, a back muscle strained. He ignored it, trying to make contact with more of his fingers.

It was too far. His breath rasped loudly in the lightless room.

He could almost pinch the edge of the strap with his fingers. Working his legs up and down, shifting the strap one millimeter at a time, he managed to grasp the free end. Finally, with a grunt, he peeled off the strap and released his legs.

Cody Sisco

Victor stood up quickly. Too quickly. The blood rushed out of his head. Losing his balance, he fell to one side, landing on the meaty part of his shoulder. He managed to keep his head from banging against the floor. Wriggling toward a wall, he hoisted himself to sitting.

One restraint remained binding his wrists. He slithered in the darkness. His shoulder bumped against the chair leg. He pushed it against the wall and used it to pry one end of the wrist strap away from the other. He repeated the motion, once, twice, three times, and the seal was broken, the strap flung to the side. He was unbound. Free.

Victor checked his pockets for his belongings, but they were empty. He crept in the darkness toward the strip of light under the door. People were talking outside. Holding his breath, he strained to listen. He could only pick out a few words: something about patience and money.

His hand hunted for the doorknob, and when he found it, he pulled himself up. A low hum filled his ears, and all his muscles clenched. A lightning storm of pain shot through him. He leapt back, electrocuted.

He howled, filling the small room with his cry. The pressure on his bladder seemed slightly relieved, and he felt a wet spot at his crotch. The doorknob had shocked the piss out of him. He slammed his elbow against the door.

A man's voice, Bandit's, said, "I wouldn't touch that again. I just doubled the power setting."

Bandit sounded amused and hostile. Had he been there the whole time? Listening to Victor struggle, refusing to answer his calls? Watching him, perhaps? There could be an infrared camera somewhere.

Victor resisted the urge to pound on the door and throw himself against it. Instead he asked Bandit, "Why did you bring me here?"

He put his ear against the door, avoiding the knob, and listened for any movement. Silence.

"Where am I?" he asked.

There was no answer.

"Did the Classification Commission hire you? You can't extradite me without a trial, you know. Your jurisdiction ends at the SeCa border."

Bandit chuckled softly. He sounded relaxed. "I couldn't care less about jurisdiction. Don't worry, we're taking you back to SeCa as soon as we get paid."

Paid by whom?

Victor's forehead rested against the door. He said, "I'll pay you to let me go. Please, if you give me my things I can make the transfer." As he spoke, his breath rebounded in his face, a sour stench smelling of acid and heat, metabolic byproducts of the sedative they'd given him.

"We've already got a buyer."

Victor slumped back against the door. A buyer? They must be ransoming him. Although, he had trouble believing any-one—even his family—would care enough to pay.

"What did you sedate me with?" he asked. "It feels like I was hit by a truck."

Victor waited for a response. None came.

"Hello? I really I need my medicine. I have a condition—I'm sure you know."

His hands searched the wall and found a touch panel. Light rained down from the ceiling.

Victor looked around. The box-like room was unfurnished. Thin beige carpeting covered the floor. There were no windows, only the single closed door. Plain and calming, the room looked like the one Dr. Tammet had designed to help him during blankouts. But Victor wasn't deceived. He had to get out.

The door looked solid, but there was no mechanism for locking the knob and no deadbolt. Those were promising signs. This was just another test to see if he could keep his cool and solve the puzzle.

Victor checked his pockets again. Still empty. He didn't have much to work with. The chair sat overturned in the middle of the room and the restraints lay nearby like shed snake skins.

Or insulators! The synthleather straps would let him grip the knob without getting zapped.

But Bandit was on the other side, and he was strong, probably steroid enhanced. Not the type that Victor could overpower. He would have to wait for a better opportunity.

Victor gathered up the straps. Minutes ticked by. Then shouting came from somewhere beyond the door.

"Hello?" Victor asked.

No answer, but he could hear strained voices.

It was now or never.

He stood and wrapped the restraints around both his hands. He tested making contact with the doorknob. A slight buzz tingled in his forearms, but it was nothing like the sharp zap he had received before.

He gripped the knob with both hands, but they slipped off. He pressed harder to create friction. His fabric-wrapped hands rotated uselessly. He tried again, felt the knob begin to turn, then accelerate on its own.

The door opened inward, and Victor stepped back.

An unfamiliar man dressed in black with glinting metal weapons strapped to each of his limbs stepped into the room. Definitely a Corp. He pointed a stunstick at Victor's heart.

Victor closed his eyes, cowering and bracing himself for a Dirac pulse that, at such close range, could leave him paralyzed for life. It didn't come.

He opened his eyes and caught a glimpse through the open door of a crowd of people dressed in battle gear.

Standing in the doorway, behind the man with the stunstick, as proud and authoritative as a military commander, with crossed arms and a wispy corona of hair, was his BioScan supervisor Karine.

"There you are, Victor," she said. "Don't worry. I brought some Personil. You'll be feeling fine soon enough."

38

I was living someone else's life. In his body, in his mind, viewing the world through a roiling inferno of rage and pain. I witnessed his every thought and movement.

He was running through some sort of medical facility. Visible through the windows was a lake. Low rolling hills stretched into the distance. It wasn't Oak Knoll. When I looked in the mirror, I saw the unknown man's bloody nakedness.

—Victor Eastmore's dreambook

Republic of Texas
9 March 1991

Victor staggered forward, covering the damp spot on his crotch with his hands. He followed Karine and her band of Corps into a large room packed with cubicle dividers, desks, and chairs. A thin layer of dust covered everything.

The sun was setting outside. Victor looked out a set of dirt-streaked windows at lightposts, asphalt, and tracks leading into Amarillo's train station. Low-lying neighborhoods, commercial strips, and farmlands stretched to the horizon, broken by the lighted line of the highway.

Someone cursed nearby. Victor turned. Lucky and Bandit were on the ground being tied up by the Corps and fuming. One of the Corps taped their mouths shut.

Karine whispered in another Corp's ear, then pulled Victor gently by the arm to a pair of office chairs. They sat facing each other.

Victor nodded to the people guarding Lucky and Bandit. "Who are they?"

"Corps, our security partners." She sounded genuine and even-keeled, yet queasiness churned his stomach. Until he sorted out who were his friends and who his enemies, he would suspect everyone. And none of it made sense yet. If Karine was working with the Corps, who were Lucky and Bandit working for?

Karine leaned forward, clasped her manicured hands in front of her mouth, grass green nails glinting, and watched him closely. After a moment, she said, "We're taking you home."

"What if I don't want to go?"

Karine looked at him, surprised. "You may not be thinking clearly. We found herbs among your possessions."

"Do you have the data egg too?"

She shook her head.

Victor lowered his head. He'd lost both the data egg and the Handy 1000. Not to mention his dreambook. Now Karine would drag him back to SeCa, where he'd spend the rest of his life in confinement.

"Listen, Victor," she said, "I don't expect you to be a fair judge of your recent behavior, but we're going to help you get past this. Circe has arranged a place for you in Carmichael."

His stomach flipped as he pictured a facility filled with vacant-eyed, piss-reeking invalids. But Carmichael was home to both a facility for Class Ones and a ranch for Class Twos. Which one would it be? He asked, "The ranch or the facility?"

"That's up to you," Karine said. "We need a full account of your activities over the past week so we can undo the damage you've caused. That includes the intrusion into our network. You can't possibly have accomplished that alone. If you tell us everything that happened and who helped you, then you'll go to a Class Two ranch. Otherwise, I'm afraid we'll have to take you to a Class One facility. It's your choice."

"You don't understand," Victor said. "There's a war over stims. They're flooding into the R.O.T., and they're part of it." He pointed at the Corps. "Stims are being added to drinks and sold in *supermarkets*. Everyone is becoming addicted. Wait!" Victor remembered sitting in Karine's office as she described how MRS and addiction were at the center of the project she wanted him to lead. "BioScan is going to benefit from this."

"It's time to get back on your medication."

Victor reared back in his chair. She wanted to silence him, didn't she? What did he really know about Karine LaTour?

An old friend of the family, she had worked with Circe in Madrid at the start of their careers. She was good at her job: fair, ruthless, and ambitious. She treated Victor as a project, a thing to be fixed and used, a resource. He'd always thought there was something more to her feelings than professional ties, a mysterious charge that filled the air when she looked at him, though he'd never known whether it was attraction or repulsion. Despite all that, he suspected she wouldn't hesitate to lock him away.

Karine blinked at him, and he was surprised to see a pink glow of compassion in her expression. Maybe he could persuade her to help.

Victor said, "They're not fantasies. Jefferson died of radiation poisoning. I found proof."

"I'm not going to validate your delusions by discussing them."

"My mind is not the problem. There's something wrong with the way people with MRS are treated in SeCa. In fact, as far as I can tell, there's nothing *right* about it. I know about plans to put ranches and facilities everywhere. Europe's next too, isn't it? You can't do that."

Karine crossed her arms. "We have a good system. A humane system. The rollout has been carefully planned."

"You don't even realize that what you're doing is wrong. How can you not see it? How can you go against what Jefferson Eastmore stood for? He didn't want the Classification System to expand. He was killed because of it. You have to see the logic in what I'm saying."

Karine sighed and reached inside her blazer pocket. She withdrew a pill case, which she opened, displaying two doses of Personil and three pills Victor didn't recognize. "You're making exactly the kind of illogical deductions that indicate mania." She was clinically cold, cruelly logical. She actually seemed to believe what she was saying. Laws, she was good at spinning the truth.

Except Victor knew that he was not the problem.

Karine held the pills out. "Last chance."

"I'm not taking those," he told her.

Karine signaled to one of the nearby Corps. Victor hadn't realized they were lurking so close. He started to turn, then felt a cool sensation on his neck. A medpatch. He reached to remove it, but the Corp clamped a hand on his neck to prevent him.

"That'll keep you docile for the ride to the airport," Karine said.

Normally, adrenaline would have flooded Victor's system at the mention of flying. The worst panic attack in his life had gripped him for hours during a flight from Oakland & Bay-shore to Oklahoma City. But the medication that moved from the patch into his skin dulled his emotions and made him feel as if he were wrapped in cotton and rocked by gentle waves.

Then, gradually, Victor moved outside himself, hovering, barely connected to consciousness.

"I won't force you onto Personil for now," Karine said, "but keep in mind that Class One facilities can do what they like, and Personil is a mild option compared to others. It's not too late to change your mind. Who helped you steal BioScan's data? Can you hear me?"

As she spoke, Victor felt himself drifting further away. He was only catching a word or two at a time. He focused his attention, trying to pull himself closer to her, but his body remained sitting upright, immune to his will. His mind wandered off.

Karine leaned toward him, cupping his face in her hands, which helped pull him back into his body for a moment. He heard her say, "I won't have to deal with you anymore."

Then, like a string had been cut, he floated up to the ceiling, hovering, watching the Corps lead Lucky and Bandit down the corridor while Karine gestured to Victor's body. Other Corps lifted him by the arms and led him docilely to the elevators.

It was a strange sensation to watch himself, to feel as if he were split in two—*two pieces!*—body below and mind above, separated. He didn't fight or struggle. It wouldn't make a difference if he did. Instead, he enjoyed floating, watching events unfold.

Karine, the Corps, and their three prisoners rode the elevator down to a subterranean parking garage. Two black vehicles awaited—*another two, always two, when would he know what two really meant?* Karine, a male Corp, and mindless Victor climbed into one, while the remaining Corps maneuvered Lucky and Bandit into the other.

Soon they were traveling through Amarillo at dusk and Victor felt as if he were trailing behind the vehicle, high above, buffeted by the wind, tethered to his body by the thinnest thread imaginable. Most strangely, there was no hint of blankness, and its absence felt like a piece of himself was missing.

From Victor's vantage point high above, he spotted two vehicles in the road ahead and saw with eagle-sharp vision that Tosh and Elena sat in each, blocking the way. Victor watched with growing alarm as two projectiles shot from one of the blocking cars—a violation of the global arms control regime.

A missile hit the vehicle carrying Victor. Flames bloomed underneath, and tires melted onto asphalt.

Rescue is here, he thought, as the tether connecting his mind and body snapped and his consciousness whirled into the infinite sky.

39

The most successful societies are those that hold themselves to ever-higher standards and evolve to meet the challenges of their day. For ancient humans, this required a constant battle with the environment and developing new tools to shape their world.

We have come a long way from our humble beginnings. Today our challenge is to master the accelerating technological innovation we've unlocked without becoming servants of that technology.

We need a new path forward for humanity that celebrates excellence and strives to transcend limitations. There are no fundamental restrictions, only passages to enlightenment.

—Circe Eastmore's *Race to the Top* (1991)

Republic of Texas
9 March 1991

Victor woke to find Elena leaning over him. He lay on a bed in a bleak room: dingy carpet, stains on the walls, sagging furniture.

"You're safe, Victor," Elena told him. "No panicking, okay?"

"I—Karine was here." He remembered being out of his body, but it was like a dream. He sat up, feeling aches and pains all over.

"She's next door, along with Lucky and Bandit. Tosh's got them tied up. We took you on the road. Do you remember?"

He nodded. "I wish I could make it through one day without being drugged, gassed, or knocked unconscious."

Elena said, "Understandable. I have good news and bad news. Good news, I'm a fantastic spy. I hid my MeshBit in Tosh's car earlier and got it back without him noticing. Bad news, it recorded a conversation between him and the King."

Haze interfered with his thoughts. Tosh was involved with the Corps? He shook his head and climbed out of bed. "He's like the boogeyman. You're as bad as Ozie, blaming some shadowy figure for everything."

Elena looked fearfully toward the door.

Victor said, "It doesn't make sense. Karine was working with the Corps. If Tosh was too . . . It's not possible, is it?"

She said, "The Corps aren't a tight-knit organization. They're dickies for hire. They fight each other as much as they cooperate. But they all serve the King. He has them all chipped." Victor opened his mouth to question this, but she held up a hand. "I don't pretend to understand how they work. Don't think of them as a single organization. They're more of a loose franchise of assholes."

Victor laughed.

"You know what this means," she said. "You can't trust Tosh."

Victor groaned. The shifting allegiances and rivalries made Victor's head ache. "You're sure it was the King of Las Vegas?"

Elena nodded. She said, "If you do ever get the egg open, whatever's inside, you can't let him have it."

Victor tried not to think about it. "I'll worry about that once I've got the data egg back. I want to talk to Lucky, Bandit, and Karine," he said. "This is my chance to sort out the truth."

They walked outside into twilight. Ten identical lodge rooms faced him across an empty parking lot.

Elena said, "The cars are around the back." She laughed bitterly. "Tosh brought weapons. No surprise there. The Corps are lying where we blasted them."

Elena led him to a door and keyed the code to unlock it. He stepped inside.

Someone lay on the floor—Bandit. He seemed to be breathing.

Tosh was tightening a set of ropes that bound Lucky, face-down, to one of two beds. Karine, unconscious, chin lolling on her chest, sat on a chair by the bathroom door, bound by

Cody Sisco

synthleather straps, much as Victor had been a few hours ago.

A slim desk and a chest of drawers shared the small space. Through a doorway, Victor could see a tiny bathroom. The unit clearly served only as a brief resting place for people on their way somewhere else.

Elena entered behind him and dead-bolted the door.

The lightstrips in the ceiling glowed dimly. Their biofuel reserves were running low.

Tosh saw Victor and calmly tucked away a loose end of a strap. Then he lunged at Victor across the small room and poked a stiff finger into his chest. "You run from me again, and I'll kill you."

"Guys, calm down," Elena said. "No harm, no foul."

Victor crossed the room and sat on the bed, running his hands across the bedspread's gaudy pattern of crammed-together luminescent Ws. "No, you won't," he said quietly. "You need me to open the data egg."

Tosh stared at him for a moment. Then he harrumphed.

"Speaking of the egg, where is it?" Victor asked.

"We looked but didn't find anything except this junk." Tosh waved at the bedside table, which held two sleep jabbers, a Dirac stunstick, and a pack of stimsmokes. There was no data egg and no Handy unit. His backpack and herbs weren't there either.

"You want your stuff?" Tosh asked.

Victor nodded.

"Let's ask this dickie," Tosh said and spit on the rug next to Bandit's face.

Victor helped Tosh lift Bandit onto the empty bed.

"One thing first," Victor said. He untied Bandit's shoes and wrestled them off. Reaching around the man's hips, he unfastened his pants and jerked them free as well. The most difficult step was slipping Bandit's floppy arms out of his shirt, which he accomplished as Tosh stood by and watched with a creepy leer. Soon only a pair of briefs clothed Bandit. Victor did the same with Lucky, stripping her down to her panties and bra.

"What's that all about?" Elena asked.

Victor tossed the clothing to the floor. "They'll be more eager to talk."

Tosh pulled coils of synthleather cords from a gear bag and twisted them around Bandit's body and limbs multiple times, trussing him.

Victor said, "Whatever happens, they brought this on themselves."

Tosh rummaged in his bag, then held up a cylinder and tossed it to Elena. "This'll do the trick."

She examined it. "Skinjection stimulant, wake-up juice."

"Do it," Victor said. "Him first."

Elena pressed the Skinjector into the soft skin behind Bandit's knee. Seconds later, his gasp echoed through the room, and he began to cough. "Ohh . . . Laws?"

"Where's my stuff?" Victor asked Bandit.

"Who?" Bandit strained against the synthleather and turned his head in Victor's direction. "Oh. Just the person I wanted to talk to. I have a question about Broken Mirrors. Why are they all such assholes?"

Tosh sat on the bed and leaned an elbow on Bandit's back. Bandit groaned under the bigger man's weight.

"Tell him." Tosh pressed down harder. "If you don't answer our questions, we'll start working on your companion. Where's the data egg?"

Bandit became still.

Victor asked Tosh, "Can you make him talk or can't you?"

Tosh pulled a cudgel from his black bag. "Most useful starting tool."

Victor looked into Tosh's eyes, and a pleasurable tingle suffused his lips.

Tosh traced the curve of Bandit's cheek with the cudgel's tip. Then he pressed more strongly, smooshing and lifting, tilting his head back at a sharp angle. Victor thought he heard Bandit's vertebrae grind against each other and couldn't be sure if it was his synesthesia or a real sound.

Tosh said, "I can shatter the bones around your eyes, break your nose, and knock out your teeth. I can leave bruises that won't heal for a month. I've beaten men so badly that they died from kidney failure, and I barely broke a sweat. Now, where is Victor's stuff? The egg, in particular, I'm interested in."

Cody Sisco

Tosh pressed the cudgel into the man's kidney.

Bandit's brow creased, and he let out a pained, angry moan.

Tosh said, "That was the easiest question I'll ask you. Might as well save your strength for the others."

"Forget him," Elena said. She turned to Lucky. "Let's see what she has to say."

Bandit strained against the straps. "Don't touch her!"

"Tell me where my medicine is," Victor commanded.

Bandit said with a sneer, "Or what? You'll cry?"

Victor jumped on the bed and snatched at Bandit's black, greasy hair, yanking as hard as he could. Bandit yelled incoherently.

Victor grabbed hold of his neck. "Tell me, or I'll squeeze until you pass out."

Tosh pulled Victor off of Bandit. "Let me handle this." He leaned over the female freelancer, found a suitable place on her neck, and jabbed her with a wake-up Skinjector.

"Don't!" Bandit yelled.

Tosh jerked a thumb at Bandit. "Stuff a sock in his mouth."

Victor found a sock. Bandit tried to move his head away. Victor pressed a finger against Bandit's eyelid. "Open up, or I'll blind you!"

Bandit said, "That's not ne—hehr—om." Victor scraped his fingers against Bandit's teeth as he shoved the sock in his mouth.

Victor backed away. The excitement churning in his belly wasn't to be trusted. He leaned against the wall, closed his eyes, and watched patterns form and evolve behind his eyelids: triangles, stars, fractals growing, moving, and decaying inside one another. The flows and turbulent colors were beautiful, but he would eat fistfuls of fumewort for a moment of inner quiet.

Victor felt a hand squeeze his shoulder. He opened his eyes. Elena looked at him with concern. Beyond her, Lucky's body writhed on the bed, her eyes fluttering. She opened them and saw Bandit tied up. She groaned.

Tosh sat on the edge of the bed next to Lucky. He stroked her back. "Morning, sunshine. Your friend didn't want to tell me where the data egg is. You're going to tell me now, or I'm going to beat him within an inch of his life."

She strained to look at Tosh. "You psychopath. Unless you let us go right now"—she jerked her head around—"What the hell is this? Did you *shibari* us to the bed?"

Tosh smiled. "Old habits die hard."

Questions tumbled from Victor's mouth. "Where is my stuff? Did you poison my granfa? Who hired you?"

Tosh clucked at him. "All in good time, Vic. It's important to establish a rapport."

Lucky tried to peek at her partner. "Bandit, you okay?"

Bandit's mouth was still gagged. His eyes widened, and his head alternately nodded and shook.

"Okay, I'm bored," Tosh said. "Where is the data egg? Now!"

Lucky was silent.

Tosh flicked open a knife. He held it up so both captives could see it. "One more chance."

"Don't be insane," Lucky said.

Tosh walked to the end of the bed and sat heavily on Bandit's left foot. He gripped the right foot, pulled it upward against the restraints, and clamped it underneath his arm. Then he carved a slit across the arch of Bandit's foot. Bandit's screams leaked out of his gagged mouth. Victor watched, feeling hot, wet tingling in his own foot.

"Stop it!" Lucky screamed.

Elena grimaced and crossed her arms, but said nothing.

Tosh cut Bandit again. As the blade traveled, he pressed the point in deeply while twisting. Blood streamed onto the bed covers.

The room flooded with shame that smelled like muddy riverbanks.

Victor moved to the window and peeked out between a gap in the curtains. A hobo trudged along the dirt sidewalk across the street. Trash blew by. A scratchy place at the back of his throat wouldn't go away despite his attempts to clear it. He wasn't responsible for Tosh's actions. The shame that surrounded Victor was illusory: it wasn't his; it wasn't what he deserved.

Tosh seemed to be forgetting that the point of the torture was to get answers to questions. Victor walked to Lucky and slapped her face. "Where are my things? Tell me before he does something worse."

"Bastards," Lucky groaned. "We were going to sell it. It's in our van. Secret compartment to the left of the passenger's feet."

"The van's out back," Elena said.

Victor bolted outside, running to the rear parking lot and the van. He tore open the door, jumped in, and found the hidden compartment. He took out his data egg and the Handy 1000, whooping and smiling, feeling complete again.

Victor breathed on the data egg, licked it, tried rubbing it between his hands. The device stared back at him like an ominous black eyeball, uselessly foreboding. He shoved it into his pocket.

The Handy 1000 blinked, indicating received messages. He quickly unfurled it. One message from his parents questioned where he was and why he hadn't called them. His aunt asked the same questions. Another from Ozie read: "More bad news: Systems hacked. Café raided by the King. We're on the run."

There was nothing Victor could do about that. He fished into the recesses of the secret compartment, searching for his medicine. There was no sign of the bitter grass and fumewort sachets. The empty vials and alcohol for making tinctures weren't there either.

His bowels squirmed. Without the herbs, what would he do? He was barely holding himself together.

He searched the van, checking the glove compartment and the cargo bay. He came up empty. He looked under the seats. Nothing. Lucky and Bandit must have put the sachets somewhere else, maybe back at their office hideout. He would have to ask them. Perhaps ungently.

Victor climbed out of the van and went back in the lodge, holding the objects above his head in each hand. Faster than he could react, Tosh snatched the data egg, putting it in a pocket and zipping it shut. Victor opened his mouth to protest, but Tosh pointed the knife at him and shook his head in warning.

Victor asked, "Why do you care so much about the egg?"

Tosh said, "Jeff gave it to me, but at the last minute he changed his mind. Said he should be the one to do it. He seemed particularly worried about what might happen to you. And, man, let me tell you, he was right. You're a magnet for trouble."

"What else do you know?" Victor asked. "Now is the time to tell me, Tosh. Before you torture them any more, we should compare notes."

"Jeff didn't tell me anything. That was the way he operated, but this time . . . I keep kicking myself for not forcing the truth out of him. Not that I could have. Stubborn goat. But—I mean, he wasn't . . . All he said was to look after you."

That's not an answer. "What are you going to do when it opens? Are you going to run to the King?"

Tosh stiffened but didn't say anything.

There it is, the truth, finally, Victor thought. *Tosh is working for the King.*

Victor would deal with Tosh later. He walked to Lucky. "I couldn't find my medicine. Where is it?"

"What are you—"

"The herbs! Little glass vials!" Victor turned to Bandit. "Do you have them? Are they in that office building?" He removed the gag.

Bandit shook his head. "I don't know what you're talking about."

"The herbs. My medicine. We'll cut you again if you don't tell us."

Lucky groaned. "Oh, Laws! They're gone, okay? She got rid of them."

"Who did?" Victor asked.

"She said they were junk."

"Who?" Victor asked. He felt as if he was finally getting to the bottom of why these two had been following him.

"Karine, you dumbshit! Ever since you went to that herbalist, she's been complaining about your herbs. She told her Corps to flush them. "

"*She's* been complaining? You knew her before Amarillo, before kidnapping me?"

Lucky laughed bitterly. "Who do you think hired us? You twit."

40

Over and over in my dreams I see a beautiful woman's face, and, for no discernible reason, it makes me incredibly sad. How can I have such strong emotional reactions when the cause is unknown and, perhaps, unknowable?

—Victor Eastmore's dreambook

Republic of Texas
9 March 1991

Victor sat down on the bed, speechless. The world jolted—he'd slipped to the floor. The ceiling loomed above him, precariously held aloft by the lodge's flimsy construction, an ineffective barrier to the force that threatened to rip him apart and hurl his pieces into space.

What did he know about Karine?

She had access to the genetic sequence linked to mirror resonance syndrome. She could have used that knowledge to manufacture stims.

As a business leader in SeCa, she could have obtained polonium from one of her many contacts overseas. She had close enough ties to the Eastmore family to administer the poison. After Jefferson Eastmore died, Karine had maneuvered her way onto the Health Board, where she helped shape SeCa's policy on mirror resonance syndrome. She was perfectly placed to pull all the strings. And when Victor had started snooping around, she'd hired Lucky and Bandit.

Shocks, it was obvious now. Karine had killed Granfa Jeff.

He looked at her, tied to the chair, unconscious. The sight of her made his stomach heave.

Victor crawled to the bathroom, arms shaking underneath him. He closed the door behind him and started the tap in the tub. He doused his head and sputtered and swallowed the sulfur-tasting liquid.

"Victor?" Elena called from the other side of the door.

"Leave me alone!"

"Why were you following him?" Victor heard Tosh say over the sound of the running water.

Victor slumped against the tub and shuddered, breathing hard. His heart raced. His mind was caught in the resonance again. Fear spiking. Losing control.

Blankness loomed over him. Compared to his anger, the blankness was soothing, but he didn't want to go blank. He stood and gripped the sink with both hands.

Bandit's scream, muffled through his gag, surged through the closed door.

"Tell me everything Karine told you," Elena said from the other room.

Karine's wrongdoing could be bigger than murder. She might be responsible for all the addiction and conflict ravaging the Republic of Texas. She could have killed his granfa, organized a drug cartel, and tracked him to this wasteland.

He pictured his hands closing around her neck and the look on her face as he crushed her windpipe. He had to confront her, but he needed a fail-safe, in case he couldn't control himself.

Water dripped along the curve of his scalp and down his face. Shivering, he focused on the sensation of the drops crawling on his skin. He had to remain calm, coherent, and sane, but he didn't have the bitter grass and fumewort to help him. Fine. It would be difficult, but he could do it.

Bandit was whining in the other room. Bile rose in Victor's throat and his mouth watered. He tried not to picture Bandit lying down, restrained, at Tosh's mercy. How far would Tosh go to get answers? Maybe Victor should try to stop him. But he wanted answers as much as Tosh did. Maybe more.

Cody Sisco

Tosh asked Lucky, "Did she order you to kidnap Victor?"

Lucky gasped, "What are you doing? Stop it!"

"Answer the question."

Lucky said, "We did it to protect him. To keep him safe from the dickies."

Tosh laughed cruelly, a sickening sound from someone holding a knife.

No use letting Tosh have all the fun. I could carve up Lucky and Bandit and do the same to Karine.

It was a terrible thought. He couldn't let himself walk that dark path. He needed a distraction.

The wise owl listens before he asks, "Who?"

Victor pulled out the Handy 1000, pressing the first name he saw: Circe Eastmore.

The call connected right away.

"Auntie?"

"Victor! Are you all right? Karine said she was going to bring you home."

"No, I'm . . . I'm in Amarillo. I—I think I know . . ." Victor had trouble forming words. He took a breath. He had to tell her, to warn her about Karine.

"Amarillo? I'm not sure where that is. Did Elena drag you there? Oh Victor, I'm sorry we ever got her involved."

Victor blanched. "*You* got Elena involved? I thought Ma found her."

"I thought you might need a friend with all that you were going through, so I suggested it to your mother."

A hot flash of indignation seized Victor. He terminated the feed and threw the Handy 1000 to the floor. Everyone in his life was pulling his strings, lying to him, compounding his problems.

In the other room Tosh asked, "Why did you kidnap him? Think carefully. This knife is getting cold."

Lucky answered, "I told you! We were working for Karine. He stole data from BioScan, and we were supposed to get it back."

"Uh huh," Tosh said, "and how long have you been follow-ing him?"

Victor's curiosity pulled at him. He opened the door and peeked out. Tosh was holding Bandit's ankle and waving his foot back and forth. Blood trickled down his leg. Karine hadn't moved, was still unconscious.

"Victor, are you all right?" Elena asked. "Do we need to get out of here?"

"How long?" Tosh asked.

Lucky craned her neck to see what Tosh was doing. "As soon as the data went missing—"

"Wrong answer," Tosh sneered. "I was there at the grave-yard, and so were you, *before* he stole BioScan's data. This is going to hurt, buddy." He cut into Bandit's foot, a deep slice that ran from the ball all the way to the heel. Bandit's entire body vibrated and jerked as he screamed in his gag.

Victor tasted metal in his mouth, probably from the water. He wiped his lips with the back of his hand, which came away streaked with blood. He pursed his lips and felt pain. He'd bitten them.

Tosh said, "You were following Victor for weeks before he left SeCa, way before he took the data."

Lucky said, "Okay! Okay! Stop it, you sicko. We started following him back in December."

"Why?" Tosh asked.

"We were watching him for Karine."

"Why?"

"Ask her!"

Tosh grinned. "I will, but I'm not done with you two yet." He put down the knife and took the cudgel in hand, adjusted his grip, stood, and pinned Bandit's ankle against the bed with his boot. He swung the cudgel hard against the bottom of Bandit's foot. It landed with a wet smacking sound that turned Victor's stomach. Blood splattered the sheets and carpet. Bandit screamed and moaned into his gag.

"Tosh! Enough!" Elena yelled. "Let's wake Karine."

Tosh pointed at the captives. "I'm not done. These two stimheads need a lesson. Maybe you should step outside. In fact, take Victor with you."

Elena looked at the half-naked bodies strapped to the bed.

Cody Sisco

Victor said, "I'm not going anywhere." He walked to Bandit and removed his gag. "You recorded everything I did for weeks, didn't you?"

Bandit said, "We saved your butt in Little Asia."

"And kidnapping me? You have an excuse for that too?"

"You got mixed up with the Puros. It was for your own safety."

"For my own safety." Victor wanted to rip Bandit's head off and toss it like a bowling ball.

Elena walked to Bandit and let a drop of saliva splat against his cheek. "You messed with the wrong people, *idiota*."

Bandit growled.

"Bandit!" Lucky yelled. "Stop antagonizing them."

Bandit whipped his head toward his partner. "I told you! This was a bad job from the start." He turned to look at Victor. "Karine wouldn't say. My guess is she wanted you reclassified."

Victor's vision filled with light. He didn't dare move, afraid he'd trip and fall. Could she hate him that much? Blankness threatened to return.

"I need to think," Victor said.

"Are you okay?" Elena asked.

Tosh watched him closely. Elena stared at him, eyes wide with concern. Victor didn't care. Only Karine held his attention. She sat in the chair, unconscious, and he felt a tide of hate surge within, threatening to carry him into blankness.

"Did you poison Jeff Eastmore?" Tosh asked Bandit, sitting on his back, suffocating him. He let up on the pressure, and Bandit took a gasping breath.

Bandit said, "That's *his* crazy fantasy."

"Turns out Victor was right about Jeff being murdered," Tosh said. "Did you poison him?"

"No!"

Victor said, "We need to wake Karine. Now."

Tosh nodded, and he and Elena moved over to Karine.

While they had their backs turned, Victor snuck over to Tosh's black duffel bag, pulled out a small fist-sized metallic sphere—a gas bomb—and shoved it in his pocket. He took out a gas mask and hid it under the bed.

Elena said, "We'll need to turn the screws hard to get answers. Agreed?"

"Don't worry about it, princess," Tosh said. "I can take care of this."

Elena took a menacing step toward Tosh. "If you're saying I don't need to get my hands dirty because I'm a woman, you're going to see them soaked in *your* blood."

Tosh chuckled and raised his hands in surrender. "All right, you convinced me. You've got the biggest balls in the room."

Elena tested the straps around Karine, the way someone might handle fruits at the market to test their ripeness. She gave Karine the wake-up shot.

Karine raised her head, blinked, and looked around. When she saw Victor, she rolled her eyes, saying, "I hope you haven't completely lost your mind."

41

Victor felt his eyes boiling in their sockets as he looked at Karine. He tried to speak, but words failed him. He held out his hand for the cudgel, which Tosh supplied.

Karine's fiery hair-frizz quivered when she laughed. "I was too lenient. You should have been locked up long before now." Her confidence almost convinced Victor that she still had the upper hand. But she didn't know how desperate he'd become.

"You murdered my granfa," Victor said.

"You've really gone over the edge," Karine said.

Elena added, "She's a cold-blooded maniac."

Karine stared blankly at Victor, ignoring Elena. Disdain hovered around her eyes, irrepressible, butting up against a sliver of black fear. She covered the truth well, though. He admired her composure.

Karine said, "It's my fault, in a way. I shouldn't have hired amateurs. They were young and cheap, and I liked them. Well, her anyway." Karine glanced at Lucky's mostly naked body. "Victor, you can still come back, you know."

Elena leaned close to Karine. "You are one fat cunt."

Karine spit in Elena's face. Elena wiped it, then threw a punch that whipped Karine's head around. Victor heard something crack. He didn't know if it was Elena's hand or Karine's cheekbone. Karine sobbed and moaned, then stopped. She looked at Victor, her face the color of naked embers. Her rage flowed into him and met its twin.

Victor wanted to kill her.

A tickling sensation danced on the back of his neck, and it was a moment before he realized Bandit was calling his name. "Victor! She's not going anywhere. How about you cut us free so we can put our pants back on?"

"No," Victor growled.

"I never meant for them to hurt you," Karine said. "They were only supposed to watch you."

Victor felt himself twitching, rage crackling just under the surface of his skin. "Is that supposed to make me feel better? That they were only *watching* me?"

Karine's tongue flicked against her lips. "To make sure you didn't slip up. Circe was adamant."

Breath caught in Victor's throat. Auntie Circe had known?

Karine seemed to read his mind. "Of course she knew. She wanted you followed—for your own protection. Then you hacked our network and disappeared."

"Why are you here?" Elena asked.

"These two called me when they saved you from the Puros," Karine said.

"I wouldn't call it 'saving,'" Victor said.

Ignoring him, she shot a withering look at Lucky and Bandit. "Unfortunately, they got it in their heads to ask for a ransom. Rather than pay it, I hired the Corps to get you back."

"Are those your Corps at the kennel?" Victor asked.

"Yes. Mason Charter filed a lawsuit, claiming it belonged to him rather than your family. The Corps are a hedge against the lawsuit's outcome. Possession is nine-tenths of the law, after all. Why are you so interested in it?"

Bandit pleaded, "Look, this is all just a big misunderstanding."

"You were going to *sell* me," Victor said, swinging the cudgel into Bandit's thigh. Bandit's yell sounded more surprised than pained. Victor reached down, found the sock, and stuffed it in his mouth again.

"I know you're upset." Karine spoke in soft and measured tones.

Victor felt her voice burrowing into his skin like a tick. "Be quiet!" he snapped. He paced the room, watching Karine. He was going to smack the truth out of her one blow at a time.

Lucky said, "We got greedy. Just let us go, and we'll disappear. We've got nothing against you."

Victor's ears were buzzing. It was too loud to think. Perhaps the universe had dark plans for him after all.

"Not one mistake," he mumbled aloud. "A lifetime of them." He put a hand on Karine's shoulder and looked into her eyes, light blue like a clear SeCa sky. "You hired them to watch me?"

Karine nodded vigorously. "That's the truth."

"For what it's worth, Victor," Tosh said, "people only say that when they're lying."

"You can still get out of this," Karine said. She looked at Victor intently. Her lips curved slightly, as if she enjoyed this stupid circus. She was certainly clever enough to poison his grandfather and get away with it.

"You were playing with my life!" Victor smacked her in the face. She was still. He paced in the small space between the beds, not sure what he would do next. Whom could he trust? Everyone seemed to have their own version of the truth. His uncertainty was tearing him apart. He fingered the Handy 1000 in his pocket, then gripped the gas bomb.

Karine said, "Untie me, and let them go. We'll forget this happened. A little slip-up. Completely understandable, but if I have to press charges, they'll put you in a Class One facility."

She was threatening *him*?

"Or I could kill you," Victor said. The calm, measured tone of his own words surprised him.

Karine laughed. "You'd never do that," she said.

Victor pulled Karine's hair—hard—jerking her head back. "You don't know what I'm capable of."

Karine laugh, a rusty, coughing cackle. "Are you trying to scare me? Look at you, playing at a rampage. You can't kill us. You wouldn't put your family through that."

Victor looked at the two freelancers bound and gagged on the bed, at Karine sitting in the chair, trussed like a turkey. It wouldn't take much. A blow or two to the head for each of them. They could drive the bodies to some remote piece of land and drop them off. It would be easy.

Elena stepped forward and said to Karine, "It'll look like you got caught in a turf war. Victims of dickie violence in the R.O.T., simple as that. An investigation could take years."

Elena shoved Karine's head down. Her hair had lost its lift; red strands hung in her face like copper wire.

Victor remembered the incident in the juice shop. His hands had wanted to transform into claws and rip out that young woman's heart. It was the same feeling he had now: a pounding thunderous anger. And why not feel that way? He had a right.

But he'd been wrong about the woman in the juice shop, hadn't he? Ric had wondered if she had MRS too. Maybe she did. She could have just wanted to talk to Victor. Everyone had a different truth.

Lucky's sobs grew louder. Bandit tried to say something through his gag.

"Victor?" Elena put her hand on his shoulder. "I think we have to get rid of them."

"Agreed," Tosh said, "Nothing personal, of course."

"Everybody shut up!" Victor yelled. He felt his heart racing. In a lower voice directed at Tosh and Elena, he said, "I'm going to decide what's next. No one else."

Karine's voice pierced the dim room. "Victor, don't."

Elena whispered in Victor's ear. "She was going to lock you up and throw away the key! I'll do it, so you don't have to." Elena nodded toward Tosh. "We'll do it for you."

Victor looked at the bodies writhing on the bed, at Karine's hard, desperate face. They deserved to be punished. Tosh cocked his head to the side. He wore a know-it-all smirk under scheming eyes. Elena stood tall.

"Not yet," Victor said. "I need to know if she murdered my—if she assassinated Jefferson Eastmore."

"That fantasy again," Karine said. "I don't know anything about that."

Victor peered at her face. "You knew him. You poisoned him. You took his place on the Health Board. You got your fingers in his company."

She said, "You have a disturbing ability to ignore the facts when it suits you."

Victor said, "Radiation killed him. That's a fact. Tosh saw the evidence."

Tosh nodded.

Karine pursed her lips. "That's why the body was exhumed, wasn't it? What makes you think it wasn't an accident? Or suicide!"

Victor said, "He didn't want to see any of this happen—what's happened to people with MRS. Stims showing up everywhere—he would have hated that."

"More conspiracy nonsense."

"It's not nonsense. Stims mimic my condition."

"Of course they do. That's an open secret. You know about stims? Hooray for you. Pretty much anyone paying attention to the epidemic knows that. Why do you think we've been adjusting the diagnostic protocols?"

Elena sucked in her breath. "You want to treat addicts the same way you treat people with MRS?"

"Why not? The Classification System is comprehensive, humane. If Jefferson hadn't closed Oak Knoll, we'd have better treatments by now." She pulsed against her restraints. "The bigger problem is that we're constantly being hacked. That's what started this whole mess."

Victor leaned forward and smelled her perfume: lavender and sandalwood, hints of the ocean. He heard waves on the shore and tasted salt spray. "What do you mean?"

"Apparently, stims are based on a first-generation XSCT compound that was stolen from the Holistic Healing Network. Mind you, I was told all this secondhand after the merger." Karine's voice took on the monotone she used when dispensing updates at company meetings. "It wasn't just your family's company that got hit. Last year, there was an intrusion at Gene-Us, too. The accessed data included the MRS gene sequence. Clearly, someone used the stolen information to design and manufacture stims."

XSCT was the compound that had been shipped to the Lone Star Kennel. Victor had to find a way around the Corps guarding it. Maybe Karine wasn't completely useless.

Victor said, "But even my hacker buddy couldn't decrypt the sequence."

"Maybe your buddy is lying. Maybe *he's* the thief," Karine said.

Victor narrowed his eyes.

Karine continued, "We assumed that the person who stole the sequence had a decryption key. There aren't many, but every member of the Health Board has one. Victor, are you sure Jefferson wasn't . . ."

"Wasn't what?" he asked.

"Now, don't get upset. But what if he was responsible for the stim epidemic? Maybe he meant for it to be an unsanctioned clinical trial. He could have manufactured the drugs at Oak Knoll and then hidden everything."

"That's . . . He wouldn't . . ."

Karine said, "Perhaps Jefferson couldn't live with what he'd done. You said he died of radiation poisoning? He certainly had the means to obtain polonium."

Tosh stepped forward. His hands were balled into fists at his sides. "Jeff Eastmore was a great man. He would never kill himself. Never."

Karine said, "I always thought so too, but how else do you explain this? The other Health Board members are all policy wonks. They don't have the skills to pull this off."

"How do we know it's not you?" Elena asked.

Karine turned to Victor. Her eyes were large, open, hard. "I didn't poison him. I hired these flackies to protect you and to protect your family's company. Ask your aunt. Things didn't go as planned, but it wasn't my fault. If you're looking for a culprit, you have to look further. Who benefits from stims?" Karine nodded at Elena. "Addicts get their fix. Drug pushers profit. The underworld wins. Not me."

Victor looked from Karine to Elena and back again. "You know about her?"

"I arranged things with the clinic in New Venice, yes. As a favor to Circe. We were trying to help you."

Elena squared her shoulders. "Your clinics profit off treating addicts."

Karine said, "If I could wish away your addiction, I would. We tried to help you."

Elena said, "They chipped me!"

"A precaution. Which paid off, I might add." Karine smiled.

Elena got in Victor's face. "Let me kill her. If you let her go, she'll make sure you're locked up. Victor, it's the only option."

Victor closed his eyes and pictured a solitary island. Waves crashing on a shore. Wind shaking palm trees. Sand shifting in the dunes. Chaotic sounds and motion, blissfully meaningless. Soothing.

He'd come all this way for nothing. He had only a rough idea of what was really behind the stim market. He had no proof that Karine killed Jefferson. He barely knew who he was or what he was capable of anymore.

Victor opened his eyes. They were all looking at him.

Elena crossed her arms. Victor felt numb. The one person he cared about more than himself wanted to turn him into a murderer, a monster.

"I need to think," he said. The room buzzed and hissed.

Karine was either innocent or a crafty killer. Which was it?

Victor fingered the gas bomb in his pocket again.

Tosh strode to the bathroom door, saying, "Let's talk in here. Fewer ears."

"It's okay," Victor said. "Elena, will you—can I talk to you outside?"

Elena nodded, moved past Karine, and stepped around Victor. She opened the front door, cleared the threshold, and looked at him expectantly.

Victor slammed the door and flipped the dead bolt.

"Hey!" she yelled from the other side.

In a fluid motion, Victor triggered the gas bomb and threw it at Tosh's feet. White smoke jetted into the room, billowing across the floor. Victor dove to the bed's edge, grabbed the gas mask, and pulled it over his head. He curled into a ball, blocking the front door.

Tosh tried to pull him away to get outside. Victor tensed, his arms pinning the mask to his face. Tosh tried to pry it off, but his body was wracked by coughs. Victor squirmed, twisted, and kicked his foot up. It connected with Tosh's belly, and the man sucked in a breath.

Smoke filled the room to the ceiling. The freelancers coughed. Karine screamed, perhaps not realizing it hastened her unconsciousness. She quieted, and her head drooped.

The two figures on the bed writhed. Then they, too, succumbed to the gas.

Tosh dropped to his knees. His hands latched onto Victor's gas mask. He coughed and pulled more lungfuls of smoke through his mouth. Victor held onto the mask. Tosh cursed, slumped down, and passed out.

The room was quiet. Victor was on his own. It was time for murder. Or perhaps something else.

42

From the depths of my future, a dark breath returned and collapsed the lives I hadn't yet lived into a single path.

Choices that weren't mine propelled me forward.

Even now that I know the truth, no decision turns in the direction I expect.

—Victor Eastmore's *Apology*

Republic of Texas
9 March 1991

Fog-white sleeping-gas particles filled the room's air like Mesh static. The filter on Victor's gas mask made it difficult to breathe. Like trying to suck a juicebulb through a too-thin straw.

Victor wondered how long he could hide in this room. Elena was banging on the door. He couldn't just sit there indefinitely. He tried to open a vidfeed to Ozie and was surprised when the feed request was approved.

Ozie asked, "Laws, Victor, what is on your face?"

"A gas mask. Long story. Did you—"

"Look, can't talk long. I don't trust my programs to secure the feed. The King of Las Vegas didn't like me messing with his MeshSats, and he traced me back to the café. Pearl and I are on the move."

"Ozie, did you steal the MRS gene sequence from Gene-Us last year?"

Ozie laughed. It sounded genuine to Victor. "Of course not," Ozie said. "If I had it already, why would I have had you steal it from BioScan?"

Victor said, "Someone broke into Gene-Us. Someone also stole an early version of the XSCT formula from Oak Knoll. That's what Karine told me, at least."

"And you believe her?" Ozie asked.

"I don't know what to think."

Ozie stroked his chin. "If she didn't do it, I'll give you one guess who else might be involved."

"The King?" Victor said.

Ozie said, "Correct. We'll get to the bottom of it. Meanwhile, Pearl and I going to set up somewhere quiet. Private. What are you going to do?"

"Search the kennel. "

"Let me know what you find. And let us know where you'll be. Pearl's got some herbs for you." Ozie terminated the feed.

Victor sat watching the sleeping-gas eddies curl gently in the lodge room's still air. He had to find out what had happened to the XSCT compound, and the kennel was the key. Without Karine's help, though, it would be tough to get past the Corps.

Victor got up, leaned over Tosh's unconscious body, unzipped his pocket, and took back the data egg. Then he opened the door and stepped outside, leaving it open a crack. He removed the bulky mask from his face and threw it on the ground.

Elena tried to peek inside, but Victor blocked her view. "What the shocks did you do?" she asked.

Victor brushed his sleeves and wondered how much of the sleeping substance had accumulated there. "I bought us some time. I couldn't think with everyone yelling at me."

She grabbed his arm. "Did you—"

"No." Victor shrugged her off. "If I didn't shut them up, though, I might have killed them."

Elena looked relieved.

"They'll be fine," he said.

She nodded, biting back whatever she really wanted to say. Her eyes were sickly green; even in the fading light, he could see how hard a day it had been for her. He could blame stimsmoke's effects for running her down or her own bad judgment. He probably looked awful, too. His gaze flicked toward the motel window, but he turned away quickly. He didn't want to see his reflection.

Victor paced the parking lot and then stopped and looked up at the stars. Only a few dozen peeked through the evening's dusty veil: Sirius, Betelgeuse, and the more prominent nodes of familiar constellations. Mars and Jupiter bracketed the moon, deceptively equidistant from each other in the sky, but so far apart. Time and distance obscured the rest of the universe.

He turned to Elena. "You wanted me to kill them."

She flinched as if he'd slapped her. "I didn't—"

"How could you even suggest it? Ever since I was little, people who hate what I am have attacked me, treated me like I'm a bomb about to explode. You tried to light the fuse."

She shook her head and backed away. Only a car width separated them, but it could have been a wall of radiation. "I can't imagine what that's like. I know you're a good person, I do," she said, "but sometimes we have to do a wrong thing for the right reason."

Victor hung his head. He couldn't believe what she was saying. "What happened to you?" he asked. "When you joined the Puros, it's like you gave up the good part of yourself."

Tears streaked down her cheeks like meteors, catching the lightpole's glare and sparkling. Her voice was ragged. "I lost that a long time ago." She wiped her cheeks with her sleeve. "They saved me. I . . . They gave me a reason to keep going."

Could the Puros and their cause have replaced him in her heart? They were something for her to take care of, a reason to put her needs and problems second.

He saw her clearly now, and kept his mouth shut. There were so many things he might say. He loved her, but they weren't good for each other. She had to feel complete without him. She had to be happy by herself.

Victor peered in the lodge room. They would probably be unconscious for hours. He nudged the door open to allow the remaining gas to escape. A breeze kicked up, and the air chilled his skin.

"I have to let them go," Victor said.

Elena said, "But that means they *win*."

He sighed. He hated that she argued when his choice had been made. "No, if I kill them, that's when I lose. There's no other option."

"She killed him!"

"She very well could have. But nothing I can do will bring him back, Elena. I refuse to become a killer."

"I don't think I could be so forgiving."

"I'm not forgiving. I'm going to find out the truth and if she did kill him I'm going to make her life a living hell. Or who knows?" Victor raised a hand in priest-like benevolence and met Elena's gaze. "Someday I may pardon her sins."

One sole laugh escaped Elena's lips. Then she wrapped her arms around her chest, looking young, like her life clock had wound backward.

He hugged her.

She pulled away and looked at him with narrowed eyes. "You're not thinking about going back to SeCa, are you?"

Every minute of his life in SeCa had been contingent on the mercy of people who didn't understand him. His family had formed an oasis of support, beyond which only suspicion, hostility, and contempt existed. And then they'd hired thugs to keep him under surveillance. No, he would never go back to SeCa, even if he wasn't reclassified. Life for him there would always be circumscribed by the radius of his family's wealth, power, and ability to carve out a safe place for him, which would be another kind of prison.

"No. I need to go someplace safe and civilized. SeCa's off limits, and it's too dangerous here." He smiled at her. "I've been thinking about moving to an island in the Mediterranean."

She gaped, then laughed. "Stop joking around."

Insects began singing all around them. They might have been buzzing the whole time. A slight breeze rustled his hair. Trajectories of dirt painted the pavement, eroding the boundary between city and desert.

Elena said, "Stay here. Please. You'd never have to worry about the Carmichael stuff again." She looked as if she wanted to reach out and touch him, only she wasn't sure of herself.

Winds buffeted Victor and Elena with dust and shards of gravel. What to do? The few clothes and supplies he had brought with him could all fit in a small sack. He hadn't prepared for a journey longer than a week or so. He'd have to find a new source of herbs, a new regime for managing his condition. It would be like starting over again.

That doesn't sound so bad, he realized.

Amarillo wouldn't be his final destination. He was sure of that. For a brief time, though, it wouldn't hurt as a stopover, while he sorted out where to go next.

Elena cocked her head. "Why the goofy smile?"

"It's nothing. I just—I'll stay. For a little while, at least."

Inside the room, the haze had dissipated. Victor untied Karine and gently slipped her body down to the floor. Elena brandished Tosh's bloody knife and cut the ropes that tied Bandit and Lucky to the bed. Searching around the room, she and Victor found the freelancers' clothes and confiscated belongings and placed them on the beds.

Elena pulled out a wad of cash and placed it next to Bandit.

"What's that for?" Victor asked.

"He needs to get his foot sewn up."

"Keep the cash. It's not enough." Victor transferred ten thousand AUD to Bandit's paystick with a note: "For your troubles. Let's hope this is the last time we meet." He did the same for Lucky.

"Now for Tosh." Victor started the Handy 1000's sonorecorder. "Tosh, no hard feelings, I hope. When the data egg opens, I'm willing to make a trade. Information for Jeff's tongue. That seems fair to me."

He sent the message to Tosh's feed queue.

"What about her?" Elena nodded to Karine.

"Now I make a devil's bargain. Any more wake-up juice in Tosh's bag?" Victor asked.

43

Victor paced along a paved riverside promenade, aware that he was dreaming and expecting to wake at any moment. Usually his dreams could not continue for long once he became aware of them—especially without a bitter grass supplement—but somehow this dream went on.

A fog rose, encasing him in a cool, gray void. The suspicion that he had forgotten a vital clue to his grandfather's murder crept over him. He needed to act, but he couldn't remember what he was supposed to do.

Waves lapped nearby, invisible in the mist, lulling him into a trance. This was a peaceful place. Victor sank to his knees, sitting on his heels, content. He pressed his hands on the promenade's smooth, cool stones, and a little joy sparked in his chest.

Wind played in his hair, and the mist receded, its tatters blown into thin filaments. The sky cleared. The waterfront was bright as day, though the sun still hid behind a rocky hill covered in elm trees.

On the other side of the water, marshes and low hills extended to the horizon, and an earthen levee upstream walled off his view. The locale seemed familiar but altered. He couldn't place it at first, but then he knew. *This is New Venice.* In the distance, he spotted the town's tightly clustered buildings, aligned to the stone-lined canals.

A figure scrambled onto a boulder at the promenade's edge. Shadows cloaked its form, light draining from its surroundings.

The figure bounded toward him like an enraged bear, moving impossibly fast and flickering.

Closer now, the figure resolved into a naked man-monster with bloodshot eyes. He leapt on top of Victor, pressing him against the promenade. Jagged teeth descended and pierced Victor's neck, tearing flesh and tendons. The creature's fists slammed down, caving Victor's chest. He opened his mouth to scream, but his lungs no longer worked—they oozed through the beast's upheld fingers.

The monster-man's fists smashed down again, crushing Victor's nose and blinding him. Wet warmth flowed across his face. A final slam shattered his skull, the pieces rammed into his brain, and he died, his spirit propelled out of the world into the void.

Victor jerked awake. His heart thumped in his chest, yet his limbs were cold and almost numb. The world was bathed in violet predawn light.

He must have fallen asleep in his car outside the kennel.

Negotiations with Karine had taken a few hours. Eventually, she'd agreed to his terms. She ordered the Corps guarding the kennel to allow him inside. She provided him with classified research on MRS, which he'd been reading when he fell asleep. And she'd agreed to intercede on his behalf with the Health Board and try to keep him a Class Three. In exchange, he'd untied her and agreed to her demands: to give up his "fantasy" that Jefferson Eastmore had been murdered and to tell her who was supplying him with tech. He planned to double-cross her, of course. For now, though, his path was fixed. Nothing save a meteor strike could keep him from searching the kennel.

A tap on the window made Victor jump. Hector rapped on the glass again.

Victor opened the car door, swung his legs around, and hoisted himself out. Hector held out a steaming mug. Victor accepted it silently, trying not to shake. His neck ached where the dream monster had torn into it.

Cody Sisco

Hector took another cup from its temporary perch on the car's roof. They stood a few steps apart, taking tentative sips. Faux-café, and not a very convincing brand. A few Corps stood guard in front of the kennel.

"I could have convinced Mamá to let you sleep at our house," Hector said.

"I was fine," he said. The words sounded hoarse in his mouth.

Hector took another sip. "I won't have time to show you around today."

"That's okay. I just need to speak with the logistics manager. If you introduce me—"

"We don't have one of those."

Victor's gaze followed Hector's as it shifted to the stubby bushes fronting the kennel. They looked dead, but then, so did most of the vegetation Texans had imported to the semi-arid desert. In parts of SeCa, people adapted to the changing climate with succulents and other drought-resistant plants. Here they tried and failed to nurture the iconic garden varieties of the East.

Victor waved his cup toward Hector to get his attention. "Someone in charge of the records then."

Hector rubbed his nose and sniffled. "Maybe Leroy, our sort-of accountant. Usually he's the one who unloads the trucks and oversees the warehouse. But what are you looking for?"

Victor said, "It's something my grandfather asked me to take care of a while ago." He felt Hector's scrutiny as a tingling on his face. He had to get more fumewort. It had been about eighteen hours since his last dose. Hopefully, Pearl could send some soon.

"Do you know why he came here in September?"

Hector flinched and took another sip from his chipped cup.

"What's wrong?" Victor asked.

"Nothing. Hot coffee," Hector said, but it was a lie, an obvious one. His look askance, quavering voice, and a false boldness in his stature gave him away. "I didn't work that day."

"Please, Hector, it's important to me."

Hector looked at him for a long moment. Then he shrugged. "Better get going."

As they walked to the entrance, Hector summarized the layout of the kennel complex for Victor: cotton fields on one side and a golf course on the other. An administrative building welcomed new arrivals. Nearby, another large building housed the animals. A service road led beyond an automated gate around the back of the complex to a set of smaller buildings, where supplies were stored and the on-staff veterinarian worked.

"Is the vet here today?" Victor asked.

"No, she isn't."

Hector led Victor past the guards and inside the administrative building, a low-ceilinged, flimsy, unimpressive aluminum shell not much more solid than a trailer. A conference room was tucked into one corner. A polished wooden bar ran at waist level below the front windows. A sign said, "Hitch Your Puppies Here," in loopy, hand-painted letters.

Drab brown curtains separated the entrance area from the remainder of the building. A female receptionist greeted them with a thick and happy drawl. Hector made introductions. The minutes stretched. She apparently didn't know the complicated legal history of the kennel's ownership—"I was wondering why those rough guys were hanging around," she said—requiring Hector to provide explanation about Jefferson Eastmore, Mason Charter, and the Eastmore family foundation.

Victor's feet itched, but he forced himself to stand still.

Hector excused himself to clock into his shift.

"It might be a minute," the receptionist said, happily oblivious to Victor's stomach flipping and twisting.

A smile remained frozen on his face. He would say nothing to jeopardize his search.

"You can wait in the conference room. We have a Mesh-Line." Her eyes lit up with pride.

Victor went into the conference room and sat down, running his hands along the surface of a table to calm himself. The vidscreen on the wall pinged that it had a live MeshLink.

Victor entered his MeshID to access his message queue and entered his parents' IDs into the recipients field.

"Arrived in Amarillo day before yesterday," he said—had it really only been that long? "I'm safe. I'll be in touch soon." The words displayed on the vidscreen as he spoke them. His parents would want to speak with him directly, and he wanted to hear their voices, but that could wait until later. He paused for a moment to appreciate the deep well of patience that had filled him recently.

Victor found a new message from Karine. *You've been reclassified in absentia. Class Two. We'll work on the appeal.*

She was backing out on that part of their agreement. Fine. He'd never really expected her to follow through, and he wasn't going back to SeCa anyway.

He looked at the previous message, which she'd sent him last night. *The studies are not part of the official record. DON'T SHARE THEM!*

Residual sleepiness and the lack of juices and tinctures clouded his thoughts. How much had he read before he fell asleep? The prospect of digging into the research was like hitting a mother lode of endorphins and oxytocin at the same time. His brain revved up. The memory of the man-beast chewing his neck bones sent a shiver up his spine. He ignored the sensation and focused on the Health Board's research.

He skimmed the first paper's abstract. Two years after Carmichael, a genetic study had identified a mutation in the Lee-Lambda chromosome pair. The mutation was a single nucleotide polymorphism, meaning it was one small difference in the sequence of nucleic acids that coded for a neurologically important protein. Complex conditions were usually the result of many genes' interactions with the environment, but mirror resonance syndrome didn't appear to follow that pattern, even though the symptoms were extremely varied.

Fine. They'd found a genetic fingerprint for mirror resonance syndrome. But *how* they found it was odd. They had made brain scans of study participants and compared them to a single unnamed reference case. The study's subjects were "volunteers" from the unions in SeCa, some of whom were subsequently found to have MRS. This had been a sore point between Jefferson Eastmore and the unions for years. Why focus on that specific pattern of brain waves? What was the reference case?

It must have been a neural excitation wave from someone unequivocally diagnosed with mirror resonance syndrome.

Who?

Oh, of course!

Samuel Miller. It had to be.

The Health Board had studied Samuel: his genes, his brain. Through him, they'd found the first clues into mirror resonance syndrome.

Victor cursed. Everything seemed to trace back to Samuel Miller. He'd ruined so many people's lives! It wasn't just the Carmichael dead and their surviving loved ones. His crimes had also led to a draconian response: the Classification Commission. Samuel Miller was responsible for every misery suffered by every person with MRS. If Victor ever met the man, somehow he would avenge the life he *should* have been living.

Victor turned to the next document. Researchers had studied neural networks grown from stem cell cultures. The mirror resonance gene changed the way electrical impulses traveled through the brain, making the neurons easier to excite and harder to suppress—in effect, relaxing the brain's natural brakes.

Okay, fine, so in the second study researchers found a link between genetics and MRS people's neurological function. Good for them. As Victor had always thought, and as the SeCa Health Board maintained, mirror resonance syndrome was a real, serious condition, with a genetic basis.

There was one more study to review, but a visual hallucination of sparks erupting in time with dogs barking blocked Victor's view of the vidscreen. He repeated the owl mantra ten times, which caused the tiny fireworks to fade.

He pulled up the third document, a longitudinal study of the disease's progression. The conclusions in the abstract were all he needed to read. The mirror resonance gene created an unmodulated cognitive resonance, which manifested as symptoms of blankness, susceptibility to suggestion and heightened flight or fight response, among others. However, the syndrome's effects were not deterministic vis-à-vis mania, aggression, and delusional thinking, and deterioration wasn't assured. In other words, the paper explained, not everyone with mirror resonance syndrome was doomed to psychosis, violence, and catatonia.

People with MRS weren't inherently dangerous.

Breath caught in Victor's throat, choking him. The SeCa Health Board had exaggerated the threat. Perhaps they'd even *increased* the likelihood of MRS people becoming violent by treating them as dangerous.

It was a monstrous injustice. Thousands of people had their lives cut short, sequestered, diminished. Of course people with MRS ended up catatonic. When everything is taken away, what does a person have left?

Sparks flared all around Victor. The world turned white, burning. His entire life had veered off track long ago, and he was just now realizing how bad it had become.

The receptionist knocked on the glass conference room wall. Victor jumped in his chair.

"Sorry to spook you, hon!"

The blankness ebbed and left Victor numb. He terminated his connection to the Mesh and followed the receptionist to an area cluttered with desks. They navigated through the disarray and arrived at a desk where a young man sat.

He had slick hair, polished to a midnight black and pasted to his skull. All his clothes were black or near-black: jeans, a collared shirt, and a slim-fit jacket. He even wore a black pair of thick, square-rimmed glasses. Only his face, hands, and glinting silver jewelry hanging from his wrists, neck, and ears offset his dark clothing. The young man continued tapping, swiping, and clicking on various input devices while Victor and the receptionist hovered nearby.

Eventually, the woman interrupted gently. "Leroy, this is Victor Eastmore. He's the grandson—"

"I know. Give me a minute, okay? I'm lost in something," he said, continuing his frantic movements. "Victor, sit down.

Chair's back there. Thanks. One second. Okay. Done!" Leroy wiped a hand down his cheek and shivered. "What brings you here, Victor? Do you want a coffee? I've got a stash of the real stuff."

Without waiting for an answer, he got up and headed deeper into the building. Victor followed a few steps behind and watched as Leroy pulled cups and an unlabeled canister from a cabinet in the kitchen, placing them in the maw of an autobrew machine. While Leroy waited for the cups to fill, his fist hammered a rhythm on the top of the machine. Victor watched him, unamused. Caffeine was a mild drug compared to whatever else Leroy was taking, judging by his motions. Stims probably.

"Sorry to hear about your grandfather," Leroy said. "What brings you here?"

"I'm looking after a few of his investments." Victor struggled to keep any sense of urgency out of his voice. If he showed too much interest, Leroy might get defensive.

Leroy nodded and then led Victor toward the back door, holding both cups in his hands, maneuvering the door open, and continuing into the yard.

Outside, a large fenced area with lush grass, trees, and manicured bushes extended to fill most of the property. A group of dogs were running and nipping at each other. Leroy chose a bench outside the fence and sat down with Victor. Only then did he relinquish Victor's cup.

"Do you like dogs?" Leroy asked.

The thought of chitchat wore through Victor's last nerve, but he tried to sound nonchalant. "Yes, of course."

"Hey, no need for the heavy sarcasm. I'm not much of a fan either."

Victor gulped the too-hot coffee and choked it down.

Leroy raised an eyebrow and then turned his attention to the three dogs running around the yard. "I used to like them. But now I *hear* them all the time—yapping, hysterical monsters. My tolerance for them is gone, gone, gone."

After Victor coughed and got his voice back, he said, "Jefferson arranged a shipment in September last year. Supplies in cold storage from a hospital in Oakland & Bayshore. Can you help me find them?"

Leroy sipped his coffee. His gaze bounced quickly between the snarling animals. He hiccupped and then tapped his chest the same way he had tapped the coffee machine. "Excuse me."

"Can you help me track down what happened to them?"

"We can look through the records, but if you know the category or a shipment date or the name of the sender, it will help."

"I know the name of the compound. XSCT-19900032."

"Let's give it a shot."

Leroy led Victor back to his desk and pulled up the warehouse records, quickly finding a log noting the supplies in question. He showed it to Victor. "See? Easy. The shipment arrived on the twenty-fifth of September last year. Nothing here to indicate what was done with it." He tapped a few commands, and pages rose and sank in response. "Huh, that's strange. It's not tied to any other records. Usually we would have a receiving bill or something like that. No reference in the Mesh either. Chances are we put whatever it was in our chiller. Do you want to go see if it's still there?"

Victor wanted to scream, "*Of course!*" Instead, he merely choked out a quiet, "Yes."

Leroy took Victor past the kennel cells. Clouds of aerosolized dog dander, urine, and feces wafted through the space, despite the loud rumbling and churning of an air chiller and filtration system hanging from the ceiling. Shiny ductwork snaked out the windows. Vibrations in the room were visible to Victor as a shimmer in the air.

The dogs ate and slept on two floors of rooms lining the sides of the long and narrow building. Their barks and whines followed Victor and jangled his nerves so much that his legs grew wobbly. Even Leroy picked up his pace. The dogs sounded murderous.

"I hate when they get like that," Leroy yelled over the noise. "It's like they want to rip us apart. 'Man's best friend,' right?"

"Maybe they don't like being locked up," Victor yelled back.

They exited the opposite end of the building. Victor breathed fresh air and listened with relief to the muffled cacophony of the kennel.

They took a footpath to a nearby warehouse. Inside, Leroy showed Victor two rooms holding chilled supplies, one freezing and one a few degrees colder than room temperature. They donned spare jackets and gloves when they entered the freezing one.

Leroy explained the contents, his breath emerging in frosted puffs. Specialty foods in large plastic tubs filled most of the shelves. These were for the high-end doggy guests with specific dietary requirements. Veterinary supplies sat in a chiller cube.

Victor picked up each bottle or package in turn, scanned the label, and moved on to the next, shifting them so he could reach the back of shelves, forming piles on the floor when necessary. He touched and examined every article in the room. His breath puffed out in clouds of frozen vapor.

He looked everywhere. Leroy followed his lead and reported finding nothing. Victor double-checked everything Leroy did anyway. They didn't find anything labeled HHN, Oak Knoll, or XSCT.

In the other chilled room, Victor searched just as thoroughly, examining each vial and container and a small self-contained chiller, but he didn't find anything labeled for humans.

"I guess it's not here," Leroy said.

"We keep looking. Everywhere."

Leroy helped him search the rest of the warehouse. They looked through the records in the small warehouse management area. They looked inside boxes and plastic containers.

One question repeated over and over in Victor's mind. *Where's my cure?*

They examined all the labels. Could the labels have been switched? It would take Victor days to check.

They found nothing. Nothing to indicate anything. A dead end.

Victor couldn't move, couldn't think. There was nothing to do. He had failed.

"I'm sorry, Victor," Leroy said. "We clean out supplies every three months, so if we weren't sure what it was, it would have been disposed of. I can ask the other employees if they

Cody Sisco

remember anything, but it will take some time. I can contact you if I find anything."

Victor looked carefully at Leroy's face. There was no sign of the compound, nor what Jefferson Eastmore had done with it while he was here. But one thing was certain: Leroy was lying. He was keeping a secret and was nervous that Victor would discover it.

"Vic, you okay?" Leroy asked.

Thickly, through a congealing morass of anger, Victor gave Leroy his MeshID, and they walked to the administration building. Whatever was hidden in the kennel was hidden deep, and he'd need to return to uncover it. Victor was resolved but weary: with each step, his knees threatened to collapse and send him reeling to the ground.

Softly, as if through tightly packed cotton earplugs, Victor heard noises from the dog pen growing louder and more alarming. They rounded a corner and saw a worker frantically attempting to drag two dogs apart—*why two?*—a boxer and a black lab. Vicious growling and barks pierced Victor's eardrums. The dogs lunged and strained against their collars, trying to tear each other to pieces.

"Oh, Laws," Leroy said. He ran inside the building and returned immediately. Yelling at the man beyond the fence to get his attention, Leroy passed a sleep jabber to him. The dogs bared their fangs. They fought, a whirling ball of growls, teeth, and injured yelps. Within seconds, one had gone limp. The other continued to attack. Blood covered its snout.

The man inside the fence hesitated, afraid to get too close. He had already been scratched on his hands and arms.

Victor's heart raced. The last time he'd seen dogs acting like this was when the terriers attacked Granma Cynthia. She'd said they'd been acting strangely for months—the trouble must have started around the time Oak Knoll was shut. Around the same time the compound XSCT made its way to Texas and Jefferson had visited the kennel.

Hector had lied to him. Leroy was lying now. Jefferson had been here with the compound.

Did it have something to do with the dogs?

Victor looked at the dogs again. There were two here in the yard and dozens within the kennel. A good sample size for an experiment.

Perhaps the compound was still here, only it was hidden within the animals, waiting for someone to extract it.

Victor shook. A growl leapt from his throat. He couldn't take any more lies and secrets. If Jefferson had trusted Victor, he would have told him about this months ago. He wouldn't have hidden the cure. Victor was a big mess that everyone tried to work around. No one trusted him.

He fled through the administrative building. The office furniture flowed around him, and then he was standing in the front parking lot, staring at his reflection in the glass wall. Shell-shocked eyes. Sagging skin. Wild hair. He looked haunted.

He stumbled away, crossed the parking lot into a weedy meadow. The blankness invaded. All he had to do was surrender. Like dust and gas hurtling around a protostar on the verge of fusion ignition, soon he would be either trapped in a scorching orbit or swept away to the cold loneliness of space. And there was nothing he could do. Might as well try to break the laws of physics. He was on a path from which he couldn't escape.

His grandfather's words returned. *Never surrender*. The Eastmore motto. No matter how bad it got. *Never surrender*. He imagined he could hear his voice, "You have a value and strength, a decent core at the heart of your brokenness." He remembered Jefferson giving him the data egg. "Listen. Hear my words. Never surrender." Despite the challenges, knowing his life would be cut short, Jefferson had urged Victor to keep going, no matter how bleak his future appeared.

The blankness converged. Unlike hundreds of times during his life when he was on the brink of a blankout and he had succumbed, this time he faced it and fought back. Nebulous blurs at the edge of his vision expanded; then everything went white, as if thick, puffy clouds had descended. Forms swirled in the mist. He felt a presence, a sense of place.

Victor steeled himself, refusing to be moved, and watched the blankness evolve into something full and dynamic, fractal patterns and kaleidoscopic colors. He couldn't make sense of what he was seeing, but he couldn't deny an overwhelming feeling of fullness. Blank space wasn't blank at all—it was a full world calling to him, demanding that he cross over. He moved toward it.

The data egg buzzed in his pocket. At first Victor thought he was imagining the sensation. The data egg buzzed again. He snapped back, heard grass rustling, saw clouds high above, motionless. He stood completely still, and again the data egg buzzed, vibrating against his thigh. With one hand he removed the egg and cupped it in his palm. A red circle ran around its circumference. The egg was hatching.

A hologram appeared and hovered in the air. Jefferson Eastmore—only his head, but big as life—stared at Victor. He sat down. He reached out, his fingers grazing the face, casting shadows amid the dry grass. The dead man gazed above Victor's head and began to speak.

"Victor, I made this recording because there are things that must be said and I'm afraid that time is not on our side."

Victor watched and listened, mouth open, scared to make a sound and interrupt the voice he'd loved hearing, the voice that had always made him feel safe and worthy.

Jefferson continued, "The data egg opened now because you've gained control over your episodes, as I knew you would. I'm very proud of you. Also, by now, you've passed at least one reclassification with a little help from this data egg. It's a remarkable piece of technology, and I hope it continues to serve you well."

So that's what had opened the data egg—Victor's new-found ability to stave off the blankness.

"There's no delicate way to say this, and I wish I could save you from the shock, but I had best just come out with it: if you're seeing me, I've been murdered. I've been exposed to small doses of radioactive polonium over the course of a year, which have collected in my tissues and are killing me. It took me far too long to figure out what was happening, and now it's too late."

Victor clenched his jaw. He'd been right all along. Jefferson had known about the poison. Why hadn't he said anything?

"I know my murderer, and I know why I was poisoned. I can't tell you who it is yet. I'm sorry. The truth is far more dangerous than ignorance."

"No, no, Granfa, you have to tell me!" Victor felt sick to his stomach. He reached out to the hologram, and his fingers sliced through it uselessly.

"There are competing views about the future for people with MRS: some believe they can be cured, some believe they are gateways to other planes of existence, and some believe they can be fashioned into weapons. I believed you could be cured. I still believe that, you must believe that, and you must fight against anyone who doesn't agree with my vision."

Victor asked, "Who did it? Why tell me all this and not who killed you?"

Jefferson's recording said, "A cure is possible. But the compound we were working on had unpredictable effects. I couldn't allow it to be used to turn others into mindless, ruthless soldiers or crazed cultist sycophants. I could not let that happen. I may be dead, but I am not defeated. Through you, I still hope to change how people with MRS are treated."

Victor's eyes shone. Granfa Jeff hadn't gone quietly to the grave. He'd died as he'd lived with big dreams and the capacity to take on the world. "Tell me, Grandfather. What do I need to do?"

"My top priority is to keep you safe. Just as it wouldn't have been responsible to announce the true cause of my death publicly, it wouldn't be responsible of me to tell you who killed me before you're ready, before what I've set in motion bears fruit. In some ways my murderer is more deeply disturbed than even Samuel Miller."

The name sent shock waves through Victor: his skin prickled, and hairs stood up.

"I need to warn you," Jefferson continued. "People may try to tell you there are spirits and demons in congress with humanity, that you are chosen to be a bridge between worlds, to lead an army. These are all devious dreams and deluded fantasies. The only solution, the solution you must pioneer, is to change the political climate. To gain acceptance and integrate people with MRS into society. This is your responsibility, your future. To be a leader. To change the world."

Victor felt his gut chill. *No, no, what are you thinking? No one will listen to a Broken Mirror. I'm an untouchable.*

"You can't do it alone. You'll be contacted by people I trust: Ming Pearl; Ozie, your friend from school; and a close associate of mine named Tosh. When the time comes, they'll reach out to you. Listen to their advice. Learn how they are making progress happen. But remember, the only person you can truly trust is yourself."

When the time comes, they'll reach out to you. But that's not what happened. Victor had found them: in Little Asia, beneath Oak Knoll, in the O.W.S. wilderness. He'd gone in search of them *before* they'd come to him, and he might have ruined Granfa Jeff's plans in the process.

Jefferson said, "I want you to return to Carmichael"—Victor cringed at the thought—"and work as a member of the staff at the Class Two ranch there. I've hired them myself; they're open-minded and believe in my vision. Spend time with Samuel Miller. The data egg will help him too. You must prove that alternative treatments are effective."

Victor swallowed thickly. Go back to Carmichael? Hang out with Samuel Miller? That was Granfa Jeff's plan? Of course, he probably thought that Victor would never leave SeCa, but still. It was lunacy.

Jefferson seemed to hesitate. He looked away, and his next words were tentative and haltingly spoken.

He said, "Victor, don't tell anyone what I've told you. Nobody. Not your parents. Not Circe. Not even Cynthia. No one. You have to do this on your own. The data egg will open again; there's much more I have to say when you're ready. I love you. Good-bye."

The hologram ended abruptly and disappeared. The egg returned to its solid black color, except for a thin slice of red ringing it.

44

Dry grass crunched behind Victor. He turned to find Hector approaching. In the distance, Corps standing in front of the kennel watched them across a field of waving, brittle grass.

"What are you doing, Victor?"

His mind was reeling. Granfa Jeff had said a lot yet left so much unsaid. "I got a message from my grandfather."

Hector frowned and narrowed his eyes. "Are you sure? I know about your delusions."

"A real message. I—" How much should he say? "Trust only yourself," Granfa Jeff had told him. But Hector knew something. "I know he came here. What aren't you telling me?"

"You must be imagining—"

"Stop. I've had enough. I can tell when someone is lying. Is it the dogs?" Victor asked.

Hector wiped his brow with a handkerchief. "You're supposed to tell me what to do. But Jefferson said you'd be here a year from now." He tugged on his ear. "You don't know, do you? Not the whole story."

Victor's face heated up. "What are you hiding?"

Hector glanced back at the Corps. "Those guys let you wander around today, but they've got no loyalty. They weren't part of the deal. They're *new*. I've got to work with them watching me everyday. I have to look out for my family, for their safety. Don't come back until you can guarantee that."

Hector stalked away, leaving Victor alone in the waving grass.

Victor stared at the data egg in his hand. The truth was never a revelation. It was a sliver lodged in his skin, evading his efforts to pluck it out.

No matter, he'd keep searching.

Victor's Handy 1000 blinked with a vidfeed request from Auntie Circe. He opened it as a sonofeed.

"What's going on? Victor, are you all right?" Circe asked.

"Yes, I'm fine. You got my message about Karine?"

"Yes, I spoke with her. Thank the Laws she found you."

His auntie seemed to actually believe the story he and Karine had made up: he'd gone hundreds of kilometers on a joyride with Elena, got caught up in gang warfare, and Karine had swooped in to save the day. It was astonishing how much his auntie trusted Karine.

Circe said, "You realize your parents, all of us, are still worried sick about you."

"Yeah, I do. Sick enough to have me watched by Elena and two thugs."

"Why do you call them thugs? Karine assures me—"

"I'm not going to get into it with you. I'm just trying to find somewhere I can breathe. There's no such thing as a Broken Mirror here."

Auntie Circe clucked. "I hate that term. It's a horrible misnomer. You're not broken, Victor. You hold up a mirror to the people around you. If we see you as broken, it's because we don't like what we see in ourselves. Still, I think you'll be better cared for by us. The Class Two ranch in Carmichael is a model community. Not like the others."

"I'm not coming back."

"Victor, don't you—"

"Do you believe people with MRS are dangerous?"

It was a moment before Auntie Circe spoke. "Maybe not all of them. Maybe they weren't before, but the situation now is clear. Some may be dangerous, but all of them are in danger. Without the Classification System to reassure the public, there would have been riots and lynchings. You see that, surely. For their own protection, they must be separated."

"You really believe that?"

"Of course! I may just be Auntie Circe to you, Victor, but I'm the chief of BioScan. I've seen the world beyond SeCa, beyond Europe—there are thousands of different cultures. I've learned from them. And one lesson is clear above all."

Her voice was growing strangely harmonic, as if every word she spoke carried multiple meanings.

"Every culture yearns for the good old days. They want to go back to their roots, to find the good in them that has somehow dissipated with the passage of time. But they cannot go back. As much as my views differed from Father's, we agreed on that point. The wheel of progress, he said, pushes us all forward. Now, he was thinking too mechanically when he needed to think biologically, but the principle is correct. Cultures evolve. Organisms evolve. Our minds evolve. We develop new traits, new abilities, new norms, and one thing is certain: we cannot go back."

Victor gulped down a hint of sour bile, and he wondered at his strange reaction to her words. He said, "He said something like that to me at Oak Knoll the day it closed."

"You've been tested," she said. "That's how I see it. You know . . ."

"What?"

"Well, if you don't want to return to SeCa, and if we really want to jump-start the research again, New Venice would be the perfect location. The Louisiana Territories are booming. The authorities are desperate to attract business. We could expand the clinic and create a full-fledged research center. Would you like that?"

"I—I'd have to think about it. Maybe," he said. He couldn't tell her that he'd just dreamed about New Venice. "But what about Europe? I could work from the office in Cologne."

"Maybe," she said. "You better brush up on your German first. Let's talk about it again in a few months. But what about New Venice, hmm? It's quiet, sophisticated. I'm sure your grand-granma Florence would let you stay with her."

He hadn't seen Florence in years. "She must be ninety years old," he said.

"Exactly. I'll tell you, Victor, family connections grow more important with age. I'm sure she'd love to see you. Let me know soon, and I'll start the paperwork for Samuel's transfer."

Flames and smoke danced around the edge of Victor's vision. "What?"

"I know how you must feel about him. But he is essential to the project. We can limit your contact with him."

Victor remembered his grandfather's message urging him to study Samuel. A queasy feeling turned his stomach. Had everything in his life been predetermined? He had trouble forming words. "I never said—I can't stand the thought of being near him, but the chance to study him might . . . I think . . . maybe help us study the connection between mirror resonance syndrome and dreams."

"Dreams," she said in a quavering voice.

He asked, "What's wrong?"

"Nothing. We'll need to discuss this later. We'll have a nice long chat about your treatment and our plans for the clinic. I've got to go. Take care, Victor."

She terminated the feed.

Victor walked to his car. The blankness had been *full*. What did that mean?

A single phrase from his grandfather's message repeated in Victor's head. It was the one he'd been warned to disbelieve: "Chosen to be a bridge between worlds." That was the psychosis that had broken Samuel Miller.

The blankness was gone for now, but it would surely return. One day Victor feared he would dare to invite it in and cross over.

(This page intentionally left blank.)

EPILOGUE

45

I didn't know at the time that moving to New Venice would expose me to people with such twisted minds. I thought Samuel Miller would be the worst. But it was bound to happen—I am an Eastmore. We attract them like gravity.

—Victor Eastmore's *Apology*

Republic of Texas
15 April 1991

Some wicked parasitic vine had sent its tendrils into Elena's skull. Nothing else could explain the pain and pressure in her head. It might crack at any moment.

The agony pushed out all words, and Elena waited, willing the tide to recede, but as minutes passed, she remained submerged, silent, and suffering. She couldn't wait. She needed relief. Flinging the covers off, she opened her eyes.

The clock on the nightstand blared its message: seven a.m. Sunlight coming through the glass doors to the balcony seared the room. More drapes. They needed more drapes. The word repeated in her head. *Drapes, drapes, drapes.* Next item on the list, next step in the cohabitation process. Always something to add to their nest.

The throbbing in her head threatened to blossom into a full-blown migraine unless she did something. The solution was obvious. Stimsmoke. Unfortunately, it would also worsen the problem. Just a single puff. She could inhale the precise amount needed. Just a puff.

Her first waking thought was about getting normal—*Yep! Congratulations, you're still addicted!* She hadn't taken Aura yesterday, opting for the cheap stuff instead. Big mistake. Half the high and twice the hangover. Never again.

Elena rolled over and pulled an arm across her face, covering her eyes, temporarily masking the headache. She needed relief. It was a stark choice. She could either start her day with a pick-me-up or suffer through withdrawal for hours, likely days. Even the best pharmaceutical pain relievers were pretty much ineffective.

She had brought this on herself. No one else to blame.

Except maybe Victor.

He ingested a different substance every night, now that Pearl was shipping him herbs. There were no rules for self-medication, he'd said. Whatever worked. Anyone could do it.

His side of the bed was neatly tucked in. Had he slept in it at all? She thought she remembered him snoring next to her, but that could be a memory from anytime over the past few weeks. Usually he was a loud-growling, dream-tortured sleep-monster. But last night she'd been pretty much dead to the world, stim-crashed beyond the ability to form any memories. He could have had sex with her, and she wouldn't have noticed. Not that he would do that. But he could've.

So why couldn't she smoke stims? Living with a person with MRS should be classified as a medical condition meriting the strongest prescription available. His moods, the whiplash of being emotionally tuned to someone on the edge—that's what had pushed her to stims again.

The covers exploded away from her thrusting arm. She rolled to the edge of the bed and sat up. Her headache spiked. She pulled on a clean pair of pants, wrapped herself in a silk button-up, and stepped into a pair of dull gray flats. She was slimming down again, fast. Too much stimsmoke. If she didn't stop the upward trajectory of her usage, she would be emaciated and knock-down sick within a week or so. Typical see-saw. Healthy sick, sick sick, healthy sick, sick sick. Never normal once you've been addicted. *You can never go back to who you were.*

"Victor?" she called out.

The house sounded empty. That didn't mean anything. He wouldn't be able to hear her from his hideout downstairs, and vice versa. If he had gone somewhere, she could step out onto the balcony and take care of her problem. A quick puff and be done. Her luck, though, being what it was, meant that if she ever let her guard down and took the easy route, he would catch her in the act, which was definitely against the rules: his rules, the Puros' rules, and her own, until recently.

She had become skilled at breaking the rules in secret. That meant no smoking indoors, or on the balcony when he was home, and no smoking outside in public places—it was too likely one of her fellow Puros would spot her. They would punish her brutally; it puckered the skin on her arms to think about getting caught. He'd seemed more perceptive lately, but her denials thus far had kept him in check.

She would only smoke when she was absolutely certain no one could spot her. Lockable one-person restrooms in sparsely trafficked establishments were the best. Or in a car at night far away from any streetlights was another good option. It would be so much easier to be a Corp, to relax with your mates, do whatever drugs you wanted, and never have to worry about it.

Maybe she could get away with a quick puff on the balcony. Just this once.

Elena hunted around the bedroom for her purse. It wasn't on the dresser, by the bed, or hanging from the doorknob—all her usual places. The headache surged as she moved faster, but she powered through, looking high and low, determined to put an end to it as quickly as possible.

There was nothing, no bag in the bedroom. Had she left it downstairs? She must have. Elena pulled a scarf from the peg in the closet. It was never warm enough now that she'd shed so much weight.

She trudged downstairs and hunted in the living room and the dining room, but still couldn't find her purse. A ragged growl escaped from her throat. Her bag must be in her car.

A muffled shuffling sound came from Victor's hideout. So he was home. She would just pop by his cave to say a quick good-bye.

When she pulled back the curtain, she found him hunched over his Handy 1000.

"Morning," she said, half expecting him to ignore her, which he did at first, and then he raised his head and met her eyes. She patted his shoulder. "I'm going to the store."

He blinked at her but said nothing.

"Do you need anything?" she asked.

Victor didn't respond. His lips were pressed together, almost covered by his mustache experiment. He hadn't shaved his upper lip in two weeks, and she could barely stand it, but this wasn't the time to pick a fight.

Elena said, "As soon as I find my purse, I'm out of here."

Victor reached behind his chair and pulled up her bag. He held it at arm's length toward her, bunching its synthleather material in his hand. His eyes narrowed.

"Give that to me," she said. "What do you think—"

"I found your stims," he said.

His voice grated on her ears. Elena snatched her purse and plunged her hands into it, digging underneath cosmetics, tissues, keys—she found it. The tension drained out of her when her hands closed over the small cartridge of doses and the fireglobe.

"You need to stop," he said.

"Hush," she commanded.

Victor scratched his cheek rhythmically. "It's changing you."

She wanted to pull and tear at his face.

"Elena—"

"I know. I'm trying. It's just a little bit." Her hands vibrated, eager to begin the ritual.

He looked down at her feet as he spoke: "I have to go."

Elena maneuvered the bag's strap onto her shoulder and tucked her paraphernalia carefully inside. She couldn't do it with him watching. "No, it's fine. I'll go to the store. Tell me what you need."

He looked up and cocked his head. "No, I mean: I have to leave Amarillo."

"What are you talking about?"

"Listen. It's time. I know what I need to do."

"Vic, I've got a bad headache this morning."

"They're moving Samuel Miller to the clinic at New Venice. I'm going to start working on a cure there."

"What does he have to do with a cure?"

"I don't know, but I have to find out."

"No. No, you don't." He shouldn't put his life, his stability, at risk again. "Please say you're kidding," Elena said.

He shook his head slowly.

Hot tears started to swell her eyelids. She wanted to punch his face, to shake the stupid notion out of him.

He watched her, his eyes cold, his mouth firm.

Her words finally found their freedom in a whisper. "I'll stop using stims. I'm done. Starting now."

"Elena—"

"I promise. From now on." She threw the bag off her shoulder, and it landed on the ground with a thump.

His pressed his hands together and lifted them to his lips. "I'm going to do this. I have to. And you're coming with me."

She ran a hand through her hair. It snagged, and she yanked free more than a few strands. She looked away, toward the home they'd not yet finished making. "No way."

"The clinic there—"

"This is crazy."

"I might find some answers, and you might finally beat your addiction."

She screamed at him. It felt good, like pieces of her lungs were ejecting from her mouth and splattering him with her anger. Who was he to speak to her so sanctimoniously? She wanted to get clean—of course she did. Yet here she was screaming at him, willing to do anything to take another puff.

He got up and hugged her. "I've been in touch with Ozie and Pearl. They're going to help you. They've got more brain-fixing tricks than any doctor in the world. Between them and the clinic staff, we'll make you better."

Shock him. Shock them. Shock everyone to hell. She had wasted months on him, fantasizing that they could be friends again, and now that she had him, she'd ruined it. But she still had her Puros. She would get by without him.

Victor placed his bags in the trunk and pushed the lid closed. It clicked pleasantly. He felt the urge to open it, just so he could close it again and hear the sound again.

Elena stood by, watching him sleepily. Her fight for sobriety used every bit of her strength. He wished it were easier for her. They'd fought for an hour before he finally convinced her to come with him.

"I know what it's like," he'd said, "and the best thing is to start some place new."

Now, standing by the car, he said, "We're ready?"

"Is that everything?" she asked. "Did you pack all my clothes too?"

"I think so," he said. He smiled at her. "Are you sure you're ready for the Louisiana Territories? Can you manage to live somewhere stunsticks are illegal?"

A smile flickered on her face but left a moment later. "I'm going to be fine."

"The Louisiana Territories are civilized, especially New Venice," Victor said. "We'll be safer there than here, that's for sure."

"Tosh is going to find you eventually," Elena said.

Victor had used the Handy 1000 to disable the tracking device Tosh had put on Victor's car. "I know. But he's got Granfa Jeff's tongue. I'll have to deal with him some day."

Victor opened the car door, glanced at her, and nodded. She climbed in. He started the car and they drove away.

Low, dust-caked houses of Amarillo spread across the plain. The car rumbled across a set of train tracks and crossed a bridge over a dry arroyo. At the edge of town the street came to a T. Left would take him to the O.W.S. and SeCa, and to the right was New Venice in the Louisiana Territories. He turned right.

They passed a turn off that would have taken them through a subdivision and to the kennel.

Good riddance, Victor thought.

Two minutes later, without thinking, he turned the car around, bumping across the dirt median, and took the turnoff. Soon the façade of the Lone Star Kennel appeared, and he pulled into the parking lot.

"Why are we stopping?" Elena asked.

Victor said, "Give me a minute."

He got out of the car. There were no other vehicles in the lot, only pavement, grass, and sky, covered by high clouds—big, remote, and unhelpful. The wind brought an acrid, stinking tang of animal waste. He tapped the car with his fingertips, in three-second intervals.

If Jefferson had done something to the dogs, getting proof wasn't going to be easy—he'd need a laboratory. Victor could be patient but not endlessly so. He'd be back soon.

Grasses rustled in the breeze. A flock of birds flew in from the north, alighting on scrubby trees at the edge of the parking lot, and twittering loudly to each other. Victor imagined the dogs in the kennel rolling over in their sleep, twitching.

Circe's words came back to him: he was a mirror to others. He was the world's reflection. What is a person, if not a consciousness that makes meaning by relating to others? Why not be happy with that?

His mind wasn't the problem; it was his surroundings. What might he become, if he was away from negative influence, free to make his own way? Independent? Stable? Like a noble gas in the atmosphere—present but nonreactive?

He wanted to lead a life of his own choosing. He wanted to trust the people around him. He wanted Jefferson Eastmore to be avenged. He wanted to stop wanting everything so fiercely.

Most of all he wanted to *not* want a cure so badly.

If he could accept himself now, he wouldn't need a cure. A cure would change how he saw the world, how it smelled and felt to him. His neural currents would trace new courses through his brain. A cure would be a mental reboot, a reprogramming, an overdue arrival of an as-designed and as-intended normal-functioning mind that should have been his from birth. He'd be someone new.

Yet, strangely, for the first time, he didn't want to become a different person.

Birds chirped, oblivious to his musings. It wasn't just flight that gave them freedom. They never had to ask themselves why they sang.

Victor strode to the wire-mesh fence surrounding the kennel and looked over at the automated gate. It didn't open for him, of course. He paced on a small strip of landscaped grass, back and forth, straining to hear sounds from within the kennel, instead hearing only the rush of wind and the chirruping of excitable birds.

He returned to his car and leaned against it, feeling the sun's warmth. Despite being low in the sky, the heating force carried by its fusion-born photons felt like warm rain on his skin, marvelous.

Victor climbed back in the car, squeezed Elena's shoulder, then sat back and stared out at the dry plains and a big, gray, hazy sky.

New Venice or bust.

TO BE CONTINUED

Cody Sisco

(This page intentionally left blank.)

Afterword

Thank you for reading *Broken Mirror*. I'd love to hear what you thought of the book. Head on over to Goodreads or the retailer's page online to leave a review.

When I began writing this story in 2012, I envisioned a series of books that would follow Victor Eastmore's adventures on Resonant Earth. However, the scope of the tale I wanted to tell was far grander and the world much more sophisticated than my story telling skills. I finished the first draft in 2013 and realized that I'd written an opening trilogy to a series that would have at least six and possibly more installments.

As I write these words, ending the first book of many, I'm looking forward to taking up the rough drafts of the second and third books in the series, which are mostly complete yet still in need of restructuring and editing—and good titles.

I mention all this because I know how it feels to read "To Be Continued" and not be able to immediately move on to the next installment. As a teenager, back when the Internet was new and giant chain bookstores were ubiquitous, I would routinely browse the science fiction section, head to the *R* authors, and check to see if Kim Stanley Robinson's Mars sequels had been published. It was a long wait, but well worth it.

All that said, I promise to be diligent, to be open, and to be focused. I promise the sequels to *Broken Mirror* are coming soon.

About the Author

Cody Sisco is the author of speculative fiction that straddles the divide between plausible and extraordinary. *Broken Mirror* is his first novel, and the first in a series that focuses on Victor Eastmore's journeys on Resonant Earth and beyond. An avid reader of Frank Herbert, Haruki Murakami, and Kim Stanley Robinson, Sisco strives to create worlds that sit in the "uncanny valley"—discomfortingly odd yet familiar, where morality is not clear-cut, technology bestows blessings and curses, and outsiders struggle to find their niche. He currently lives in Los Angeles.

Acknowledgements

This section could also be titled, "A Litany of Thanking."

I am deeply grateful to my family, friends, colleagues, and strangers who encouraged, critiqued, supported, and spurred me on during the three years it took to write, edit, and publish *Broken Mirror*.

The editors who helped shaped this novel also deserve thanks. They are are very talented professionals without whom my novel would, frankly, suck. My thanks to Lindsey Alexander, Stephanie Mitchell, Justin Taylor, and Beth Wright. I'm also deeply in debt to my Beta Readers. They have seen this novel evolve and improve thanks to their insightful feedback. Thank you to Cynthia Cason, Derek Jentzsch, Jessica Barnett, Jason Groves, Luke Klipp, Stuart Kochmer, Jeffrey Lais, Kristin Larson, Holly McHugh, Richard Merrill, Cecile Oger, Jack Small, and Katie Vigil. A special shout out and thanks to three other members of a "group of four" who diligently shared their writing and insightful critiques over the past year: Nick Duretta, Cristina Stuart, and Suki Yamashita. And my thanks to the members of the Northeast Los Angeles Writers Group, especially Margaret Mayo McGlynn, Stephen Brown, Mike Radice, Gabi Lorino, Peggy Gregerson, and Jodi Lampert.

Dan "Thomas" Small: thank you for years of friendship and mind-shattering discussions, and for all your help making this story live up to your standards and mine.

Most of all, I want to thank my husband Jay Fennelly for believing in my dream, loving and supporting me, and being there for me throughout cycles of confidence and doubt, satisfaction and despair, and the mundane day-to-day process of getting the words out.

Finally, "thanks" doesn't do justice to the impact my family has had on my writing—thank you all. Grandma Lois, your signed copy is on its way. Tom and Sue, thank you for raising me amidst books, libraries, and stories, and always encouraging me to try new things and rise to any occasion. And to Jess, Abi, Marcel, and Luca: you mean so much to me—I'm so grateful to be part of your lives.

Connect

Check out the *Broken Mirror* website for deleted scenes, alternate history timelines, and more:

http://www.brokenmirrorbook.com

Sign up for the newsletter:

http://www.codysisco.com/about-the-author/newsletter-sign-up/

Website:

http://www.codysisco.com

Twitter:

https://twitter.com/codysisco

Facebook:

https://www.facebook.com/codybriansisco

G+:

https://plus.google.com/+CodySisco_Author/posts

Made in the USA
San Bernardino, CA
17 February 2016